CITY
OF
SALVATION

MARIE MARAVILLA

Cover by TRC Design
Editing by Between Chapters Creative Co.
Proofreading Como La Flor
Art: Rosie Fables

Sorry, no "good girls" here.
This book is for those who'd rather be told what a good job they're doing as someone spits in their mouth.
Xoxo Marie

TRIGGER & CONTENT WARNINGS

City of Salvation is book three in the Toxic Paradise Series. While you could read the books as standalones, it is highly encouraged that you read them in order to fully grasp the over-arching plot and avoid spoilers.

This book revolves around criminal organizations, and due to the nature of that, this story is on the darker side of romance. It is for those 18+ as it contains explicit sex/language, violence, and death.

<u>Trigger warnings:</u>

Graphic torture/death, murder, sex trafficking (this does not occur to the main characters. No graphic details are given), use of weapons, physical assault, emotional manipulation, including from a family member, grief, mentions of death of a family member, brief mentions of depressed thoughts, brief mentions of suicidal thoughts, misogyny, and emotional abuse (it's referenced from the FMCs past).

ONE
NIKKI

WHY FILE FOR DIVORCE WHEN YOU CAN PUT A HIT ON YOUR HUSBAND?

THREE YEARS EARLIER

"...UNTIL DEATH DO YOU PART."

Here's to fucking hoping.

As if my husband-to-be could hear my thoughts, onyx eyes met mine. Cruelty shone from within their inky depths as his gaze dragged down my body. It didn't matter that we were in the Lord's house or that a priest stood not two feet away, performing our wedding ceremony. Yuri was still blatantly undressing me with his thoughts.

It took all I had not to bolt back down the aisle.

He knew what lay under the layers of lace and tulle that swathed my body, having already *checked out the goods*. Sick fuck had made me strip down naked in front of my own father a few weeks ago, telling him he wouldn't accept the offer if I wasn't up to his standards. I'd been poked and prodded like a piece of meat at the market. It was a pretty accurate comparison.

Shame—that was Yuri's favorite control tactic.

I'd seen it clear as day as he'd made me stand there in front of his men, their dicks hardening behind crisp suit pants, fingers furling and unfurling as they held themselves back from reaching out. They were accustomed to being able to touch the women Yuri *acquired*, but none of the other girls had been engaged to him.

Bile gathered at the back of my throat. The memory had me fighting the urge to throw up all over the Bratva leader's leather dress shoes, but instead, I stood there—the picture of a good Bratva wife. For now.

If control was what Yuri wanted, he'd chosen the wrong woman. He wouldn't use my body against me—I wouldn't allow it.

My freedom might've been sold, but my obedience and submission weren't for fucking sale.

Movement drew my attention back to my betrothed, the corners of Yuri's lips curling up in a taunting sneer. On anyone else, the expression might've come across as suggestive, but on Yuri—it was pure evil. I stood straighter, jutting my chin. He narrowed his eyes at the small act of defiance, the look promising punishment later.

Yuri looked like the type of man who broke his toys for pleasure, and I was his latest procurement. I had to clench my teeth to keep them from chattering as adrenaline pumped through my veins, every cell in my body screaming at me to take flight.

I must not have done as good of a job as I'd thought at hiding my fear because the glare dropped away, replaced by the smile that had women willingly running to his bed. It pissed me off that he was actually handsome. His thick black hair was pushed back and neatly styled, complementing the trimmed beard along a strong jaw. A hint of his Bratva tattoo peeked just above the collar of his dress shirt.

The random bridesmaids they'd stuck by my side—not that I had any actual friends that I would have asked to be at my wedding—had sneered at me as I'd cried while they dressed me, telling me I was lucky to be marrying someone who would be nice to look at while he fucked me.

How did they miss how fucked up that statement was?

I hadn't been crying over the wedding. I was mourning the loss of the life I never got to live, the dreams I would never get to accomplish because a man felt he had the power to dictate my decisions—my worth.

In the end, my father had decided I was nothing more than a pretty face and cunt for someone to fuck. I'd been *gifted* to Yuri Sokolov, the leader of the St. Petersburg Bratva, as well as the Circle.

The monster who managed to hold even the most powerful of men by the balls.

At least, that was what my father's loose lips had divulged when he'd been drinking. He'd assumed, since I was a woman, I wouldn't pay attention. My role was to sit in the corner, to be seen and not heard. Arrogant of him to assume I'd remain obedient—loyal—when he'd made the choice to give me away.

Yuri may have been ten years my senior, but thirty-five was practically infantile in the Bratva—yet his ruthlessness and black soul had propelled him to the top of the food chain.

"Tasha, you are bringing this family honor."

My father dared to feed me that line of bullshit. I wasn't bringing honor. I was bringing him wealth at the expense of my freedom.

My body.

My sanity.

A cacophony of emotions pooled low in my stomach, thoughts shuffling through my mind, none of them sticking for long. The oxygen in the air began to thicken, making it difficult for me to swallow down the panic clawing at my throat. The murmur of the audience and the droning on of the priest faded away, replaced by the whooshing of blood in my ears.

The irony. This is how I die, a heart attack in my twenties, standing in front of a cathedral in an atrocious wedding gown I didn't choose.

My panic was pushed aside by the pain radiating from my ring finger as Yuri shoved an offending piece of jewelry on me at the priest's direction. Asshole had probably made it too small on purpose so I'd never be able to take it off.

At the end of a trail of angry red skin sat a diamond-encrusted band that glinted under the sunlight, peeking through the church's stained-glass windows. How appropriate that I was being wed before the depiction of the crucifixion.

Death was always destined to be a part of this bastardly union.

Icy fingers slid across my cheek, directing my attention away from my hand and into the eyes of my enemy.

"My bride, you'd better give our guests a show of a proper kiss, or you will *not* enjoy your wedding night," he taunted, his stifling breath sweeping across my face, stealing the air I needed in order to breathe. Disgust rolled through me as he plastered his mouth against mine, biting and sucking the plump flesh of my lower lip while I stood there unmoving, fists clenched.

The disgust was followed quickly by an anger that ran so hot I was sure his hands would burn where they gripped my biceps. He pulled away, his face smug, and I nearly broke my teeth, biting back my snarl.

Resist spitting in his face. Wait for the signal.

I sent up a silent prayer that god would smite this man where he stood. Hell, I'd take a vow of celibacy and serve only the church if he would open up the ground to swallow Yuri.

But, of course, my pleas went unanswered. For my sake, I was glad I'd learned to do what was needed to survive—otherwise, my evening would be spent consummating a marriage with the devil.

"I present you, Mr. And Mrs. Sokolov," the officiant declared, causing the church to break out in applause as Yuri swung me around, presenting me like some sort of prize. Most of the people in attendance didn't give a fuck about the wedding, much less me. They just didn't want to be on Yuri's bad side. Unrest had broken out in St. Petersburg, and the Bratva was quietly splintering, factions rising up in secret.

My wedding was about to be the catalyst for the streets running red with blood.

My new *husband* just didn't know it yet.

I glanced at the confession booth to my left, searching the blackened spaces between the latticework for proof that Viktor was in place. Worry crept up my spine as the seconds ticked on, sweat dripping from my brow.

Why hadn't I insisted on being here when he hid so I knew they would hold up their end of the deal?

Then, from one breath to the next, chaos erupted.

An ear-piercing shriek rang out, sprays of bullets bursting from the confessional booth and the other hiding spots of the Ruska Roma's men. Maxim, Yuri's right-hand man, jumped in front of my husband, using his body to shield his boss from the shrapnel raining down over the wedding party.

The iron grip on my arm disappeared as Yuri dropped to the floor and hurried to find cover. For a split second, I thought about what an awful fucking husband he was—he didn't even consider my well-being during a goddamn ambush—but then I remembered I'd been banking on it.

Another round of gunfire popped off, this time from Maxim and Yuri, and I knew I needed to move while their attention was elsewhere. I scrambled to my feet, unsheathing the blade I had hidden under the excessive tulle.

Yuri's and Maxim's backs were to me as they hid behind the wooden altar, sending off retaliation rounds. People were pushing and shoving to make it out the back doors unscathed. The sounds of sobbing women were drowned out by gunfire and glass shattering.

All the calamity faded away, leaving nothing but the pounding in my ears, my feet carrying me forward. The shake in my hand was so bad I had to grip the hilt with both of them, but my determination and hatred overshadowed my fear.

"What do you think you are doing, girl?" My father's voice cut through the muffled bubble my mind had created.

"You need to get out of here. Yuri will have my head if his bride dies," he said.

Any hope that the concern in my father's tone was for my safety leeched from my soul.

"That's what you're concerned about? How *he* will react if I get hurt? How *you* will be punished? Not what *I* will have to live through as his wife?" I yelled, distraught.

Blood meant nothing to him.

I meant nothing to him.

The flash of his anger told me he'd heard me despite the chaos, and my own anger and hurt fueled my moves, with no room left to think of the consequences.

He opened his mouth, but all that came out was a gurgled cry as I sank the blade intended for my husband into my father's gut. Rage morphed into shock and horror as blood swallowed up the white of his dress shirt.

The sight was morbidly mesmerizing.

I might have grown up in the Bratva, but I'd always been shielded from the violence. The best spot to stab a person had never crossed my mind. Andrei had drilled into my mind and body where to aim at Yuri's back, but he'd never gone over where to slide a blade if a man was facing me, or what it would look like once the blade was in someone's flesh.

Survival instincts finally kicked in, and I pushed past my stunned father. "Death before betrayal," I spat, running for my life.

Fucked up. I'd fucked up.

I'd wasted the one opportunity I had for killing Yuri on my father. Now, I had to hope that Viktor, Andrei, and their men could finish the job. I didn't give a shit who won this battle. All I cared about was getting the fuck out of this city.

This country.

I pushed my way through the mass of guests, ignoring the shouts of my name coming from the altar. I couldn't tell if it was Maxim or Yuri calling out after me, but the calls faded into the background as I surged through the double doors, making a sharp turn to rush down an abandoned hallway, and slammed into a hard body.

"Fuck, are you okay?" a deep voice rumbled in English as he steadied me.

I peered up, blanching at whose hands held me.

I knew the face in front of me.

Nikolay Volkov, second son to Dmitri Volkov, the head of the Bratva faction in New York, and an ally of my new husband.

My body refused to budge, no matter how loudly my mind yelled at my limbs to move. His oceanic eyes drilled into mine, and I was struck by how young he was. Probably close to my age, maybe a few years older, but those eyes held a jaded edge to them—something I was very familiar with.

Was that what I looked like now?

Rumor was his father beat him for the simple fact that he hadn't been born in Russia.

"Are you running from him?" he asked, his firm voice carrying over the noise spilling out of the sanctuary.

My heartbeat kicked up in my chest, fluttering like a bird attempting to flee its cage. My throat felt rough, unable to form words. All I could do was nod my head, before dropping my gaze to the floor, fear flooding my body of what the spare heir would do.

Would I ever be given another opportunity to run from Yuri? He'd have me under a fucking microscope, locked up in my ivory tower. I was probably destined for a cell when he discovered it was me who'd helped plan the ambush. Or a grave.

"Go."

My head snapped up at the gruff command, the heat from his hold disappearing. I didn't understand—turning me in would mean a raise in his station, and as a hated second son, that must've been enticing.

Nikolay's brows furrowed, sneering at me when I didn't move. "Do you speak English? I said, fucking go." He jerked his head toward the abandoned hall. "Leave while you still have the chance. Yuri and my father's men are winning. You won't have much longer before he sends someone to find his bride. I'll tell them I saw you being shoved into a car. That should buy you some time." He ran a tattooed hand over his head, mumbling to himself about learning Russian.

I was stunned, not stupid.

I turned and sprinted, having no clue if Nikolay Volkov would keep his word or not. And I wasn't about to fucking stand around and find out. My hand shook with adrenaline and fear, slipping off the smooth brass doorknob.

"Fuck," I called out as I tried to open the door again.

The word felt clunky in my mouth, but there was something so satisfying about saying it with every ounce of frustration flowing through my body. I'd been bilingual from a young age, but over the last few months, I'd pushed myself to refine the language. If I made it through today alive, English would be the only language I'd speak from now on.

A loud bang rang out as I fell into the supply closet, my knees slamming into the old cobblestones. The layers of tulle did little to absorb the blow. I scrambled across the floor, not even bothering to stand as bile pooled in my mouth. The distant shouts grew louder. Time seemed to slow as I attempted to rip off my dress, not caring that I was taking chunks of skin with it in my haste.

I barely registered the chill in the room as I stood there stark naked, staring at the virginal white lace set that lay in tatters on the ground. The first thing I was doing when I made it to the States was getting laid. This stupid, arbitrary idea of being valuable because of my *innocence* was going out the damn window.

I wasn't innocent.

They may have dressed me in white, but my hands were now stained in blood. These men had expected me to just lie on my back obediently? Fuck obedience.

The rough fabric of the men's hoodie scraped against my skin as I yanked it over my head, pulling some blonde strands free from my updo. Thankfully, they hadn't chosen something with a zipper because I was too shaken for that kind of precision. I dug into the black backpack that had been hidden in a darkened corner, holding my breath as I searched for the forged documents that were supposed to be in it. My shoulders sagged in relief when my fingertips met the hard ridge of the fake passport.

No more than five minutes had passed since the chaos had broken out, but I knew my window was closing quickly. I threw the bag over my shoulders and climbed over the precariously-stacked furniture. I'd picked this closet because there was a window that faced away from any of the main exits.

I clambered out, cool air kissing my flushed skin as, steeling myself for the small drop. Air whooshed from my lungs, my feet sinking into the damp earth. I turned, searching for a familiar figure, smiling when I spotted a man crouched. His lithe body pressed against the stone of the building as he peered around the corner, reminding me of a jungle cat.

Sleek. Precise. Deadly.

As if sensing my thoughts, he turned his head to face me. The sharp lines of his handsome face seemed harsher than usual, his blue eyes cold.

"Andrei." My voice cracked with tamped-down emotion. I stepped toward him, but my movements faltered at the tick in his jaw as he looked me up and down.

"You didn't kill him, Tasha," he said, the words as icy as his glare.

This was the tone he used with others, never with me.

That was part of the agreement with the Ruska Roma. I get them access to my wedding, and then I kill Yuri while they mow down as many others as possible.

But surely, they'd understand—Andrei, at least, would understand.

"Andrei." I raised a hand as if to touch him, but there was still so much distance between us. "We can try again, no? Once you and I are in America. We will make a new plan when we get to New York." I let my arm drop when he looked away, gnawing on his bottom lip. The scar that cut through his eyebrow glinted in the setting sun.

Anxiousness prickled over my skin.

There was something he wasn't telling me.

Hope drained from my body as he glanced back to me, his handsome face set in a harsh scowl. "There is no *we*, Tasha. Now go, keep the plan. I will see you in a few weeks."

The words hit like a slap. He'd been so nice to, made me feel included, like I had a say in my future.

He was playing with me.

"I said, fucking go. This little *crush* you have needs to stop." He spat out the words like they were bitter on his tongue. "Leave. Katya will house you when you arrive." He turned his head, dismissing me.

I ran, my world shattering in my wake.

I would never trust another to hold my heart.

I'd walked miles away from the cathedral before getting in a cab and taking it to the airport. My body was starting to manifest signs of my distress physically, and I had to pull my sleeves over my hands to hide the tremor. Freshly box-dyed brunette locks fell into my face, but I didn't bother pushing them out of the way, letting them act as another layer of defense between my identity and those looking for me.

"Miss. Miss?"

My head popped up when I realized the lady behind the counter was speaking to me. I moved to the ticketing window, and the cheerful smile she'd started with fell at the sight of my battered state. The men's sweatshirt I wore was covered in filth, and I knew my eyes were rimmed with dark circles.

"I need to buy a plane ticket," I muttered, peering around to see if anyone was watching me too closely.

Her thin lips opened and closed, making her look like a gaping fish.

"Can you help me buy a ticket or not?" I bit out, gripping the wad of cash and the fake ID tucked in my pocket. The irritation in my tone snapped her out of her trance. She pulled her eyes away, a tinge of pink crawling up her wrinkled neck. She shook her head as if that movement alone could clear the awkwardness of my presence.

"Yes, of course. Where is it you want to go?" She asked, the clacking of keys filling the uncomfortable silence stretching between us.

"New York. A one-way ticket." I turned my back slightly to the person standing at the window to my right, making sure to keep my voice low.

The Bratva had ears everywhere in this damn city, and I didn't want to take a chance of someone overhearing. It was already a risk talking to someone, but there was no way around that. I'd waited in this elderly woman's line for a reason—she was the least likely candidate for being on Yuri's payroll. Of course, the paranoia had been screaming at me for the past fifteen minutes that maybe that's what made her the perfect spy.

But there was no going back now.

Her head bobbed once in acknowledgment of my request. "And the name on the ticket?" she asked, clearly avoiding looking at me.

"Nat...Nikki. My name is Nikki Adams," I breathed out, panic clawing at my throat as my new name fell from my tongue.

Natasha was dead. Burned to ashes.

And Nikki was the woman who'd risen.

TWO
NIKKI

LIAR, LIAR, DISH TOWEL ON FIRE

"SHIT, SHIT, SHIT." The acrid scent of a burning dish towel filled the kitchen. "Where the fuck do I set this?" I yelled, to absolutely no one. Steam intertwined with smoke as I doused the polyester fireball in what was supposed to be my boiling pasta.

A sound that was somewhere between a growl and a scream escaped from my lips, and I stamped my feet like a toddler, blonde locks slipping free from my claw clip as I hung my head. Dammit, how could I not even make fucking spaghetti?

"This is why Ryan and I always ordered out. Neither of us can cook for shit," I muttered, pouring the ruined dinner down the sink. An unexpected knock at the door had me jumping. Apprehension crawled along my skin, leaving a wake of raised hairs. I'd been on edge ever since the shit eight weeks before.

Mario might be dead, but he'd never been my Boogeyman, so it did little to ease my nerves.

I inched along the wall to peek into the lookout, relief rushing out of my lungs when it was Ryan on the other side.

"How did you know where I live?" I asked, pulling the door open.

She let out a huff of disbelief, shouldering past me. "Oh,

please, Nikki. You think I couldn't find your ass?" She looked over her shoulder at me, cocky grin on her face. "I looked for the trail of fuckboys walking out of an apartment close to La Victorias. Why didn't you give me your address, by the way?" she asked, wrinkling her nose at the smoky scent.

Or maybe the face was in response to the fact that I hadn't told her where I lived. I hadn't told *anyone* where I lived now.

"Damn. I'm really that predictable?" I asked, skipping the last question and joining Ryan on the couch. "Well, I'll have you know that not a single dick has been in my apartment."

Ryan gave me a look of shock, her eyebrows up in her hairline. "Are you unwell? Joined a convent? Your waxer on vacation? Like, your pussy has just got to be confused," she sassed, her hand resting on her heart as if she were scandalized by my lack of fucking.

I swatted at her. "Stop making that face. You're going to give yourself wrinkles, and listen, Mrs. *I've-got-my-man-groveling-on-his-fucking-hands-and-knees-with-this-tongue-buried-in-my-pussy*, not all of us have a man at the ready." Ryan choked, her mouth falling open.

"Yeah, that's exactly how Gunner likes you to look at him." She flipped me off, not fighting her smile.

"Oh, please. You've never wanted a man at the ready."

I pushed away the thought about how, at one time, that was exactly what I'd wanted—before I'd learned what a weakness it was to let people in. A risk I wasn't willing to take, which was why I was pulling away from Ryan.

"I call it like I see it. And I'm doing just fine in the dick department," I said, smiling as I stood to grab us drinks, needing to move away from her before she caught something in my face that told her I was holding back.

The woman was like a damn lie detector when she was in her interrogator mode. Which wasn't usually a problem for me, but it seemed she was changing our status quo.

i.e. Me.

I *was* doing fine in the dick department. As in, I was fine not getting any dick lately. There was no way I was bringing a random ass man to my new place. It was one thing when I lived with Ryan, who was in the cartel and would literally threaten them with a gun when it was time for them to leave. But now it was just me, and I couldn't afford to let someone I didn't know into my space.

And I only slept with men I didn't know.

No attachments or commitments. That was the deal—always.

"What are you doing here?" I asked as she reached for the canned margarita I'd brought her.

She reached into a bag I'd missed her holding, pulling out a stack of envelopes and boxes. "Bringing you your mail and shit. You know you and I can still live together?" she said, frowning.

"Please, you and your man wanna bang on every surface and at any time. You don't want me there," I said, noting how the room had that undercurrent of tension again. Like a splinter under the skin, small but uncomfortable.

Threatening to lodge in deeper.

I swallowed down the heartache. After telling Ryan the shit I had about my past, I knew I needed to pull away from her, put some distance between us. Letting us get close was a mistake. A mistake I was aware I was making, though I hadn't cared enough about the consequences at the time.

Now I need to re-establish my boundaries. It was better for her, too, because I had no clue what Yuri's next move was. My gut had been turning for weeks, and I wasn't going to be able to pretend my past wasn't catching up to me much longer.

Denial was my best friend, but I was going to have to part ways with that bitch soon. I'd already started to feel as if someone was watching me. Maybe it was paranoia, but I knew Yuri was bound to rear his ugly head soon. The worst part was that I didn't know how or when.

Smiling, I took a large drink, hoping it would help ease the chaos swirling in my brain. "And listen, I'm a down bitch, but I don't really wanna watch your man's sweaty balls bounce off your cheeks," I added, keeping my voice cheery and light.

"Nikki, I fucking swear." She threw a pillow at my face, and we both burst into laughter.

Silence settled over us, neither knowing what to say next. Life had changed so much recently. *I* had changed so much.

"Haven't seen you much outside of Lotí, Niks. There a reason for that?" Ryan asked, her tone shifting to the one she commanded her men with.

It took all my effort not to flinch at her observation, forcing my body to remain relaxed as I responded. "No, you haven't. You've been busy lately."

"So, my schedule is what's causing you to avoid me? *¿Es todo?*" She arched a brow. Her bullshit radar was sounding off, and if there was one thing about Ryan, she was going to get her answers. "It's got nothing to do with the shit you told me about having a husband out there somewhere, maybe looking for you? Or the fact that you haven't said a damn thing about that shit since?"

Dance had taught me a lot of things, but by far the most useful skill was how to perform under pressure. I knew how to plaster on a smile even if my feet were bloody and beaten from hours on end practicing pointe as Katya yelled critiques on my Relevé. Turns out, that skill also translated into faking being unfazed in front of your only friend, even when it hurt.

"I'm pretty sure it's bad luck to discuss someone's dying words," I shot back, smiling at her eye-roll. She hated it when I brushed things aside with my humor, but it was how I survived the heaviness of feeling.

"You didn't die, Nikki."

"Eh, I think it was close enough that we can extend the protection. You know?" I quipped.

Ryan let out a string of curse words in both English and Spanish as she moved toward my door to leave, pointing a manicured finger up in my face. I might be taller, but she was more intimidating. Especially if you knew she always carried at least one type of weapon.

"Listen, I'm not going to push this *now*, Niks. But I'm having Scar set this place up with security, okay?"

"She doesn't have time for that. That bitch is busy being *well* taken care of. I'm bummed I didn't catch a peek at the hotties," I said, wiggling my brows. "They were gone by the time I finished my set, and I couldn't get a good look through the damn house lights."

Ryan shook her head as she walked down the sidewalk leading to my place, doing a shit job at hiding her laugh. "Yeah, well, when she sets it up, you can ask her to send you a picture of them."

I waved a hand in dismissal, not bothering to mention that I might not be here very long anyway. "Tell your boo thang to be careful because you're notorious for leaving a single square on the toilet paper roll to avoid changing it," I yelled after her, smiling even wider when she raised both middle fingers over her shoulder before getting in her car and pulling away.

Something behind her SUV caught my attention. A guy leaning up on a motorcycle glared at my apartment. A chill ripped through me, my breath stalling in my lungs as I tucked myself back inside. I'd noticed more and more bikers lately, and couldn't tell if it was a coincidence, paranoia, or exceptional observational skills, but there was no questioning *this* man was staring my way. Or he had been, before he'd turned and straddled his ride, giving me a clear view of his rocker as he pulled out of the apartment parking lot turning the same direction as Ryan.

Fuck. Reapers MC.

I ran to grab my cell from the kitchen, being sure to first lock the door behind me.

Those fucking assholes were always causing problems. Ryan had banned them from the club, so I didn't have much personal experience with them other than when they'd shown up a few months ago. I didn't know all that much about the inner workings of the cartel or the MCs. Certain aspects were similar to the Bratva or the Rusko, like the hierarchy setup, but other than that, I didn't know shit about how things worked here.

It rang twice before she finally answered. "You miss me already?"

"A Reaper MC member pulled out right after you. He tailing you?"

There was nothing but silence on the other end of the line after a whispered, *"Shit."*

"It looks like I'm all clear. You sure that's what you saw?" she asked.

Without a doubt, but if he wasn't following Ryan, why was he outside my apartment?

"Nikki?"

"Sorry, yeah, I'm sure it was a Reaper," I said, moving toward one of the windows that faced the street he'd pulled out onto. There wasn't the sound of an engine, but I had this overwhelming need to confirm he was gone.

"I'm sending someone over to keep an eye on you."

"What?" I screeched, pulling my face away from the blinds. Nothing was out there, but it didn't help my unease. "No, Ryan, I don't need anyone here. Besides, I'll be at work in just a few hours anyway."

"At least let Beto pick you up. It'll make me feel better," she said, using what I referred to as her 'mom voice.'

A groan left my lips—she wasn't asking. She was telling me he was coming to pick me up.

"Fine, but tell him I want La Vics when he comes," I grumbled, making my way to the bathroom to shave my legs.

THREE
NIKKI

ENTITLED SNOTS DESERVE A STILETTO TO
THE FACE

THE HUM of the music caressed my skin like a lover's touch—a sensuous exchange between my body and the vibrations of the rhythm. Dancing was always bittersweet for me. Part of me wanted to abandon it forever, but what else would I do for a job?

A chill seeped into my hand as I wrapped my fingers around the pole of the main stage, my calf muscle straining as I went up onto the ball of my foot as best I could. These were the wrong fucking shoes for this move, but what was a girl to do? Daddy didn't raise a quitter. A humorless laugh slipped out as I kicked up the other leg into a graceful tilt, my arm flowing out toward my side.

He did create a survivor with enough daddy issues to keep a therapist busy for a lifetime.

The crowd let out hoots and hollers as I brought my leg down and looped it around my static dance partner, leaning back as far as I could, letting my hair splay down my back. That particular combination always gained me applause and extra tips.

It was ironic, really. I'd hoped and dreamed of being on stage. That my talent would be enough to forge a future of my own. And I'd done it. This just was not the stage or the dancing I'd imagined, or the name I thought I'd see up on a sign.

I smiled as bills started collecting on the black lacquered floor. Amber lights bathed the club in warm light, mixing well with the red underlighting of the stage. Everything about Lotería was meant to feel sexy. My body was on autopilot, performing the moves I knew so well while lost in thought.

I'd spotted Ryan perched on Gunner's lap earlier tonight, their heads tucked together as they whispered things back and forth. She'd looked at ease, and disgustingly in love. I was happy for her—the last couple of months had been a shit show, with her recovering and all the construction that was needed to repair the club. Apparently, shit had also been going down over in New York with Scar at the same time. I hadn't even realized that Scar was part of the criminal life.

She did all of our security, so I'd assumed she was like a hot tech chick. Vaguely, I was aware that her uncle had some connection with the Italian mafia, but I hadn't realized he was the fucking bastard in charge.

Scar and I had only met a handful of times when she was out here setting up security, and those nights had been filled with laughter, shots, and teaching the two of them how to work a pole like a pro.

Skills that she had used two weeks ago on her *three* men.

Damn, how do I get that to happen? Not that I want any fucking man to stay around longer than one fuck.

My heart twinged at the same lie I'd been telling myself for years. Being a runaway bride to a man you were gifted to by your father really fucked up your views on love and men.

I gave my head a shake, sending my hair flying. The patrons loved it when I whipped my hair around. They'd never guess this was my attempt at clearing out all the shitty thoughts clouding my mind lately. Ironically, the kidnapping wasn't the part that fucked me up. It was knowing that my ex knew I was alive and not knowing what he had planned.

It'd been two months since the incident, and I hadn't heard anything more from him. I'd almost convinced myself that it had all been Mario bluffing to get me to come back so he could snatch me up and use me as bait for Ryan. It was just a note on a door, after all.

And them flat out saying, "Hey, bitch, we're sending you back to your deranged ex-husband in Russia."

There was this sinking feeling in my gut, a bone-deep belief that something was lurking on the horizon, and it had me worried. For the millionth time since I was forced to tell Ryan a little bit about my past, I wondered why the fuck I was still here.

I willed my body to relax as I sashayed to the front of the stage.

"Hey, bitch," someone said, followed by the sting of a hand slapping my ass. Blonde locks slapped me in the face with how fast I whipped my head around. My eyes narrowed in on the asshole who wore a grin a mile wide.

He was young, probably in his early twenties, based on his baby face. Robert was probably already making his way to the main stage, but I wanted an opportunity to give this asshole a piece of my mind.

It's always the entitled little snots who think everything is theirs.

The heel of my stiletto met the tender flesh of his shoulder, and he flashed his too-white veneers at his friends, thinking he'd won the lottery, and I was about to fall on his dick. He probably thought I'd profess my love for him in hopes he'd take me home and train me to be a *good little obedient wife.* That's always how these types of guys treated me.

The poor, lowly stripper who was waiting on a nice man to come save me from my wicked ways.

I scoffed, digging my heel in deeper until his smirk turned into a wince. Hands that felt like he'd never worked a day in his life wrapped around my ankle, attempting to ease the pressure, but I only pushed harder.

"Hey, bitch, you're hurting me. Ease up," he shouted over the music.

"Oh look, you also don't like being touched without

permission," I responded. My hands hit my hips slightly above the lace of the crimson set I wore.

The wince was now an angry look of entitlement smeared across his face. He was probably about to tell me who his father was. Or ask to speak with the manager.

"I pay to be here. That means I can do whatever the fuck I want."

Wrong fucking answer.

I yanked my leg out of his grasp, kicking his face as I pulled it back onto the stage.

"Oops," I said, dropping down into a crouch in front of him.

"Fucking bitch," he yelled, clutching his nose as blood leaked out. Pathetic. I hadn't even hit him that hard.

FOUR
DEX

HER IRE MADE MY DICK HARD

"*PA'arriba, pa' abajo, pa' centro, pa' dentro.*"

I let out a groan as tequila slid down my throat in a delicious burn. Fuck, I needed this damn drink. I needed this damn night, period. I'd spent the last two days tracking down a Reaper piece of shit and then spending some *quality time* with him.

It'd been happening more and more lately.

"Heard *la jefa* is letting you use her playground." Robert's voice was low so the other patrons at the bar didn't overhear him. The club was all legit on this side of the walls, and Ryan wouldn't appreciate it if we scared them off with talk of hacking off body parts. "I'd have thought y'all would have one," he said, glancing over my way.

All I gave him was a grunt as I tried to track down where the bartender had run off to. "We do. Problem is, we are toeing the fucking line with starting a war with those fuckers. Don't want anyone to find a Reaper in our...*playground.*"

"*Claro.*" Rob nodded in understanding. "Since they aren't welcome around here, there's no real chance of them showing up looking for their man," he said, connecting the dots as to why I was torturing someone on cartel soil.

If the Reapers started sniffing around the dude's disappearance, we could claim he'd trespassed on Los Muertos's turf, and La Brujita doled out his punishment. She'd already marked her line in the sand a few months back when she'd dropped off another Reaper body at their clubhouse gates after they'd showed up at Lotería.

Which was a fucking boss ass move on her part.

Pres figured we'd be in the clear with this cover, but fuck, shit had been wild over the last few months, and we still hadn't recovered.

"Can we get two more doubles," I called out, shoving our shot glasses toward the pretty brunette who'd been eyeing me all night. She giggled at the wink I sent her. When she walked away, I dragged my hand down my face like I could wipe away all the shit of my past.

There was this danger zone with alcohol, where I'd had too much and couldn't keep the memories locked away, but not enough to feel oblivion. I always tried my damnedest to get through as quickly as possible.

That's what we were going for tonight, the sweet embrace of oblivion.

A flirtatious voice had me moving my hands away and reaching out to grab our refills. "Thanks, doll," I said, giving her the charming smile I'd perfected years ago—the one I used to ease people's concerns about how I was really doing.

I pushed one of the glasses toward my newest friend. His tanned hand snapped out to catch it.

"*¿Otro?* I'm supposed to be working tonight," Robert responded with a growl of annoyance. Throwing the shot back, I rolled my eyes at his weakass attempt at getting out of being completely sloshed tonight. The smokiness lingered on my tongue and a cough escaped.

She hadn't skimped on the tequila, pouring it to the tip of the rim. I didn't know if that was because I was with her boss's right-hand man or because she wanted a ride on the *güerito*.

"Beto, there's, like, a fuck ton of criminal bikers here tonight. What's going to happen?" I threw my arm out behind us toward the area of the club that housed the main stage, which was where all my brothers were hanging around. "Plus, Ryan's here. She's a menace on her own. Fuckin' told my whole club she'd cut their balls off and shove them down their throats if any of them touched the girls without consent. Which I would have done, regardless of her feelings on it," I said, blowing a kiss to the bartender when she dropped off a whole bottle of mezcal, noting the number scrawled on the napkin below it.

Yeah, it's definitely because she wants to fuck.

"*Pendejo*," he mumbled.

I could feel him glaring at me as I watched the woman walk toward the end of the bar, a little extra sway in her hips.

"Close your mouth. You're drooling all over the marble. It's gross, especially because Isabella is like a sister."

"Well, your *sister* has a nice ass." I turned my body back toward Robert. "*Salud*. Here's to drinking till we fucking forget." I took a pull from the bottle, pocketing the napkin. "You know, the real answer to why we are only using ten percent of our brain is because the other ninety percent is made up of all the trauma threatening to take over."

Robert eyed me, blinking a few times before his face morphed into a look of concern. Shaking his head, he peered into his glass. "Damn, man, not even Vicks will fix you." There was a slight pause, like he was trying to decide if he should say aloud what was running through his mind. "Also, it really scares me that you said that with a smile. *Salud*." He threw the clear liquid back.

Robert's response had me grinning wider. He had no clue.

We might've been from completely different cultural backgrounds, not to mention criminal organizations, but I knew he was a cool fucking guy from the moment he spouted off that brilliant shit about needing to stand behind Ryan or kneel in front of her. Of course, those words had been for Gunner. It'd been clear to anyone around that they'd end up together.

Eh, well, some moments I'd thought maybe they'd kill each other—pretty sure it was foreplay for them.

I reached down and swiveled Robert's barstool so we were facing the stage.

"Oh, *now* you want to watch the show."

"There's half-naked women dancing…of course I want to watch the show, Beto." I was lying to myself and him that the move had nothing to do with the fact that I knew *exactly* which dancer was coming up next. The house lights changed, bathing the club in crimson. The crowd cheered with anticipation.

"Sure, and it has nothing to do with the fact that your *bestie* is up next," he taunted, throwing up air quotes around *bestie*.

"Never shoulda told you dick about that whole thing. Nikki and I aren't besties, but our friends are fucking, so we hang out now." I paused before tacking on, "As a group."

He chuckled from beside me. "God, it's hilarious to watch you two. I don't know who wants to bend who over more."

Disappointment left a bitter taste on my tongue.

"Well, it's not her. She made that *abundantly* clear."

Dickwad burst out in laughter at my expense. Memories of Nikki chucking a shoe at my head and telling me we would *never* fuck replayed in my mind every single time I was around the woman. I slept around a lot, and every one of those hookups knew the score.

No relationships.

No emotions.

Definitely no Old Lady offers.

I knew how to fuck a woman and then walk away. So, I didn't understand what Nikki's hang-up was. Especially since she was the vagina version of me. Maybe it was the fact that she wouldn't sleep with me that had me feeling all funny when I saw her?

I wanted to let out a pained groan when a stunning blonde strutted out onto the stage. Her legs went on for miles in her clear stilettos. I didn't know if I loved or hated the lacy crimson set she wore. The sensual rhythm of "Mimosa" by LATENIGHTJIGGY bled into the room and Nikki's body movements matched it perfectly. Something about the way she moved was elegant—beautiful.

I flicked my chin toward the stage. "I've seen a lot of strippers, but I've never seen anyone move like her," I said, reaching back and grabbing the bottle. I was going to need it to make it through this performance.

From the corner of my eye, I caught Robert nodding his head. "You should've seen her when I taught her how to dance some Latin styles. She was a natural. It's how she ended up headlining. No one else picked it up the way she did."

Nikki chose that moment to kick her leg up, lifting it so high that her legs practically made a straight line. "Damn. That's some flexibility," I said, taking a large swig and shifting in my seat, my jeans suddenly a little too tight in the crotch. Nikki was *firmly* in the off-limits zone, and I was not helping myself by staring while her lace-clad body moved into positions I'd only seen in my dreams.

Robert snickered beside me. "The guys fight over who gets to help her stretch out her splits."

My head whipped to the side so fast I was surprised I didn't give myself whiplash. "Stretch her out how?" He shrugged his shoulders, not seeming to notice the way the tone of my voice had changed.

"Depends on what she needs. One guy she asked had to sit behind her and hold her legs open as she leaned forward and laid her upper body flat on the floor. Pretty sure she just wanted to fuck him, though."

I fought to keep my voice neutral and uncaring because that was *exactly* how I was supposed to feel about Nikki. We'd agreed after a few little *incidences* that we couldn't be anything other than friends—and that was a generous term— since our best friends were now both fucking and in love.

"He still work here?" I asked.

"Nah. I don't know what happened to him." His eyes followed a group of girls walking by. "Nikki probably crushed his ego and he couldn't handle it. Dudes always seem to think they will be the ones to break her "no attach-ments" rule," he said, clearly no longer into the conversation.

This was why I was the perfect fuck for her. I was the captain of team "no attachments".

I shoved Robert's shoulder, pushing him off the stool and laughing as he fought to catch his balance. Fucking light-weight. "Go. Go get your dick sucked or whatever," I said, pointing to the girl who kept looking toward Robert.

His eyes bounced back and forth between the stage and the girl, indecision clear on his face.

"Go," I insisted. "I'll make sure nothing happens while you're away. Besides, there's no way you'll last more than two minutes."

He smirked, flipping me off. "Fuck you. I can last at least five." With that, he ran off toward the group, scooping up the one he'd been eye-fucking.

Any trace of a buzz I was feeling from the tequila disap-peared the moment my attention went back to Nikki. She'd moved toward the front of the stage, a look of rage painted on her face. My body moved toward her, weaving through the crowd before my brain processed our actions.

I got there just in time to hear the douchebag in the front row spout off some shit about him paying to be there, and that meant he could do whatever he wanted. She had the heel of her stiletto shoved into his shoulder, but as soon as I was standing beside the little prick, she yanked her foot up, catching him in the face.

"Oops," she said in a mocking tone. Nikki was a fucking spitfire. There wasn't an ounce of remorse in her voice and it had me grinning from ear to ear.

That was until he opened his mouth.

The club and all its patrons faded away. My fingers dug into tender flesh, and I yanked the kid toward me by the throat, relishing how his Adam's apple bobbed against my hand. "Silly me. I thought I heard you call her a fucking bitch. But that can't be right, can it?" His tongue swiped across his bottom lip, sweat starting to bead on his nose as he frantically searched for his two buddies.

No loyalty amongst the rich and entitled because they'd run off the second I'd walked up.

I leaned closer to whisper in his ear, not wanting anyone to hear my threats. "Because if you did call her a bitch, I'd have to cut out your tongue and feed it to my dog," I said, pulling away to give him a wide sneer.

I didn't have a dog, but he didn't need to know that. The threat to cut his tongue out still stood.

Angry eyes met mine.

I chuckled at the vitriol on his face. I'd give him props. Most men couldn't glare at me the way he was, but my guess was that he could do it because he was dumbass, not because he was brave.

"Do you know who my father is?" he spat out.

A burst of laughter came from beside me. Nikki was no longer on the stage. Instead, she was close enough that I could smell the coconut scent of her hair. I wanted to lean over and bury my nose in it.

"Called it. I knew you would say some shit about your *powerful* daddy." She stepped between us, her back brushing my chest. I wanted to rip the little fucker's eyes out when they dipped to her breasts. I did the next best thing, forcing his head up with the hand still wrapped around his throat.

Nikki reached back and patted my thigh, and I felt like a fucking proud peacock at the gesture of praise. I was so wrapped up that I almost missed what she said to the punk. "Please, tell us who he is. I guarantee he's dirty. Taking bribes and orders from the real people who run this city." She leaned in close, lips turned up in a sneer. "Bet I could get him to crawl on his knees and beg at my feet like the dog he is." Her ire made my dick hard.

God. I love an angry woman. I'd crawl to her...fucking bark too.

She signaled toward me with her thumb. "This is my friend Dex. He's the enforcer for the Skeletons of Society MC." The kid began to pale when he spotted the rocker on my cut, confirming her claim. "And the owner you were probably going to demand to see, she—"

My free hand shot out and covered her mouth when I realized where she was going with that sentence. Her muffled insults vibrated against my skin as I pulled her back to my chest. She was *pissed* I was manhandling her, but I'd prevented her from spouting off that a Los Muertos cartel's female kingpin owned the club. I doubted that Ryan wanted that fun little fact to go around Tucson.

Plus, I knew Nikki would regret it the moment the words slipped out because, normally, she wouldn't share that shit.

I cut in. "The owner would tell you that she's calling the cops on your ass for assault, and your daddy wouldn't like that shit stain smear on his reputation, I'm sure."

The way he flinched confirmed my suspicion. Pops was the real Boogeyman in his life. I let him go, but to my surprise, he didn't run off the first chance he got. He looked at Nikki, needing to get in the final word. "I didn't want to watch you dance anyway. I was sent in to give you this." He shoved a white envelope toward her. Painted nails plucked the stationery from his hands.

I pushed him away, worried he might try to take a swing at her. "Get the fuck out of here, kid, and don't come back."

I released the hold I had on Nikki as soon as he was far enough away, surprised she hadn't fought harder to get out. When I looked down, all I caught was her blonde hair flying behind her. She practically ran toward the private rooms.

"What the hell, woman," I mumbled under my breath, heading off after her.

Natasha Petrov.

THAT WAS ALL that was scrawled on the stationary the asshole had shoved into my hand. There went my hope that Yuri was looking for me elsewhere, because my name alone was a threat. No one here knew that name.

Not even Ryan.

I slipped into one of the vacant private dance rooms, my heart hammering in my chest as if I'd run for miles and not just down a hall. The rooms were about the size of a walk-in closet. Intimate, with a deep tufted bench that ran along three sides of the room and a pole smack dab in the middle. For safety reasons, there wasn't an actual door. Instead, a heavy velvet curtain hung from the ceiling and pooled on the floor, looking like spilled blood under the red lighting.

The normally comforting environment felt stifling.

I was so lost in thought about what I'd need to do next that I forgot Dex was following me.

He pulled the fabric closed behind us. For a big fucker, he was silent when he moved. I folded the note, stuffing it into my bra while trying to block out the memory of the last time he and I were in one of these rooms. He'd returned to the club the night after the meeting with Ryan and Sergio. Somehow, we'd drank an entire bottle of alcohol which led to getting to know each other more intimately than planned.

My mind was a bitch, flashing images of me spread out on the back bench. Dex's head buried between my legs, his sinful tongue and fingers giving a *performance*.

Dex's fingertips dragged down my rib cage, leaving a trail of goosebumps. He kneeled between my thighs, caressing my lace-covered core. The rough pads of his fingers played with the edges of my underwear. A moan slipped out when he yanked them to the side, exposing all of me to his greedy gaze.

"Fuck. Look at this pretty pussy just waiting for me. Begging to be taken care of." The intensity of his attention was unnerving. He teased me with his touch, knuckles brushing lightly everywhere but where I wanted. "I'm going to fucking devour you, Nikki. Coat my fucking face with your desire." He ended the sentence with open mouth kisses on my inner thigh, shoving my legs farther apart with his broad shoulders.

"I'm going to have to sneak away to find you before every gun run."

His words had been like ice water, but I was too fucking weak to push his head from between my thighs. Seeing a man after we fucked was hard no for me. That night, I'd let him give me the best orgasm of my life with his mouth. Then I'd run, like a total bitch, leaving him with blue balls in the very room we now stood. I'd thought about sending one of the other girls in to help him out that night, but fuck, something selfish in me couldn't do it.

I gave my head a quick shake, trying to focus.

Of course, now my nipples were hard despite the fact I was *not* supposed to be turned on. Not when I had another note from a psychopath singeing my skin where it lay hidden in my bra cup.

Dex's deep voice cut through the silence, causing me to jump. "Wanna tell me why you looked like you'd seen a ghost?" His toned arms crossed over his chest, the white fabric straining against his muscles. Confusion washed over me at his question.

How had he noticed that?

I thought I'd hidden my reaction well.

Before I could answer, he swatted at my hand, catching me by surprise. "Quit chewing on them. Didn't your mom teach you it's a bad habit?"

My back stiffened, frozen like a deer in headlights.

This was why I didn't get close to people. Even the most innocent of questions about myself required giving away secrets. How was I supposed to answer him?

Nope, my mom didn't teach me shit. My dad took me away from her as soon as she pushed me out. Put me in the care of nannies and tutors whose sole purpose was teaching me to be the perfect Bratva wife. Oh, and the husband I ran from is sending me threatening notes, one of which is in my bra.

But I didn't say any of that.

"Yeah, of course," I lied, fisting my hands at my side to avoid chewing on my nail beds.

I'd forgotten what it felt like to fabricate a past for people. Ryan never demanded answers about who I used to be. She just accepted me for who I was and ignored all the inconsistencies and awkward subject changes. Not once did she demand my secrets…because I never demanded hers.

Then Mario had ruined that. Or, more likely, this fabricated bubble was always destined to pop.

I'd moved out of our shared apartment while she was hospitalized. Told her it was because I figured she'd want more privacy with Gunner. We both knew it was bullshit.

She knew too much about me, and I felt too much for her.

I'd made her swear on my life that she wouldn't tell a soul about what I'd shared when we were in Mario's custody. His lackeys had been killed, so Ryan was the only one who knew I was running from my criminal ex-husband. Current husband? Fuck, I didn't even know if we counted as being married.

None of that mattered to Yuri. In his eyes, I was his property, and he was damned determined to get me back.

So, I'd started rebuilding those barrier walls, preparing myself for when I'd need to leave if my ghosts got too close. Tonight was a perfect example of why that'd been the right move, and why I couldn't let Dex know *anything* about me.

"Answer the question, Nikki," Dex growled, his body much closer than before I'd spaced out.

My jaw ached as I clenched. "Holy fuck, Dex. I'm not allowed to be pissed and emotional?" I used my anger to steer the conversation into safer waters. To distract him from the fact that I was dancing around his questions. "That guy slapped my ass without permission. So sue me if I'm not acting happy. What are you going to say next? I should smile more?"

I knew I was laying it on real thick, but I was feeling frayed.

His hazel eyes narrowed. They were more like inky pools in the crimson light. The only sign of his anger was how his nostrils flared, bringing my attention to the hoop piercing. He was the only biker I knew who had one, and it somehow worked on a muscled, tatted dude. Dex wasn't quite like any of his club brothers, with his shoulder-length hair that he wore up in a bun and trimmed facial hair. I'd never seen him in anything other than black Dickies, Air Force Ones, and some sort of graphic or white T-shirt. He was devastatingly good-looking, and it pissed me off that this bossy attitude only made him hotter.

When he spoke, his voice was calm and controlled.

"Nikki, drop the bullshit. That look of fear wasn't from a slap on your ass. You don't need me to handle a handsy man. You've got that covered on your own."

My hands hit my hips at his call out. The sensation of my fingertips on my bare skin reminded me that I wasn't wearing any clothes. "I didn't ask you to come handle shit to begin with, Dex. You showed up at the front of the stage on your own." I went to move past him, but he sidestepped in front of me. Blocking my exit.

Our bodies were so close I felt the heat radiating off him. Even in my shoes, we weren't eye level. My head hit right under his chin, and when he spoke, it felt like a caress across my face. That was until his words registered—they were more like a slap.

"No, Nikki, you didn't ask. I went up there, and then you looked like you saw a ghost and bolted. My dumbass followed you because I forgot…that's your M.O., isn't it?"

I glared at him through my lashes, my shoulders tensing at the blow he'd delivered with his words.

What the fuck could I say to the truth?

Turned out I didn't need to say shit because Dex filled the tension-fueled silence.

"Don't worry, Nikki. I won't ever step in again unless asked." He turned and flung open the curtain. The room filled with the noises from the club, but I still managed to hear what Dex called out over his shoulder. "Thanks for the reminder that I fuckin' hate playing white knight. I'll stick to what I'm good at, having a good time." His voice was bitter with a clear tinge of hurt.

He disappeared from the room, leaving me standing there all alone with a pit in my stomach I hadn't felt in years. The one I used to get when I disappointed my father.

"Fuck," I shouted, like a proper fucking lady, rubbing my face and focusing on the beat of the music in an effort to blank my mind. You don't have to address your problems if you shove them into a deep, dark hole and hope you die before they rear their ugly heads again.

And how had that strategy worked for you so far, bitch? You barely made it three years, and shit is already coming back to haunt you.

There was no time for a goddamn pity party. I needed to get out of there before I had a run-in with anyone else.

"Hey. You okay?"

Ryan's voice sent my heart into overdrive, the pit growing

wider as I let out a started yelp. She quirked a brow at my reaction.

"Aren't you supposed to be banging your boyfriend on your desk or something?" I asked, plastering on a smile in an attempt to throw off her suspicion, but she was too observant.

Caring for people was her blind spot, though.

It's why she'd missed that the ones she loved the most were lying to her through their teeth. I couldn't help but feel like she looked at me differently after she'd learned what she had about my past when Mario had trapped us in that room.

Her gaze ran up and down my body. There was suspicion in her tone. "Yeah, I should be, but then I saw some punk ass kid running out of my club with a bloody nose claiming that, *'The blonde slut broke it.'*"

I rolled my eyes at his dramatics. "Pussy. It wasn't broken."

She ignored my commentary. "Then I looked over and you're running off with Dex." Her shoulder hit the frame of the opening, making it clear we would be here until she got the answers she wanted, which pissed me off. I didn't need or want a keeper. If I needed her help, I would've gone and found her.

"There a question in there, Ryan?" I bit the words out, feeling cagier the longer I stayed in the club.

This was how it'd been between us lately. Strained.

"*'What happened?'* feels like the obvious one."

The tone, the stance, the air of authority. I hated everything about this exchange. I hated fighting with her, but I was unraveling—quickly. There was no putting the attitude back in the bottle, so if I was going to have a shitty night, I might as well commit. I'd kiss and make up with her later. Right now, I needed this release.

"Yeah, Ryan. While you were busy sitting in Gunner's lap or whatever the fuck you were doing, one of your *patrons* slapped my ass. Maybe you should do a little more managing when you're in your club."

I knew what saying those words would do.

Shove one more brick in the wall I was building between us.

Shock flashed across her face, quickly morphing into the emotionless mask I'd seen her wear countless times. The one she used to give me back when I was *just* an employee. My heart ached at the change, but I shut the emotion down.

Good. This is what you need. Distance.

Her tone was icy when she spoke. "Thanks for the information. I'll be sure and figure out where the fuck Beto was when this happened," she said, spinning on her heel and strutting off toward her office, shoulder-checking the man who'd come up and tried to speak with her.

My lids fluttered closed. I needed a moment to collect myself. Would I ever know what peace felt like? To fucking rest and not be thinking about survival?

You thought you had that here…

Fuck.

I hadn't meant to get Robert into trouble, I'd just wanted to get her off my fucking back. I wanted everyone off my fucking back. Why couldn't people see I was like a livewire?

I stomped off to change so I could get home, drink an entire bottle of wine and melatonin, and let Keith Morrison's dulcet tone lull me to sleep.

"Hey, Nikki," one of the newer dancers called out as I entered the dressing room.

Poor girl had shit timing. "Do I have a sign that says *'talk to me'* on my forehead or what? Can't people see I'm on the verge of a mental breakdown that might lead to a murder spree?" I yelled, throwing my hands up in the air and letting out a frustrated sigh when the poor girl scampered off, looking at me like I was unhinged.

Which…accurate.

WHO KNEW HOLDING YOUR ARMS IN FIRST POSITION HELPED WITH HOLDING A GUN...

IT'D BEEN a long time since I'd felt like more of a passenger in my life rather than the driver, but that was the way I felt lately.

Yuri and I were playing a game of cat and mouse. I'd already pushed my luck by staying, playing some dumbfuck version of reverse psychology with myself, and justifying it with the idea that Yuri would assume I'd fled Tucson and begin searching somewhere else.

But the note from last night left me with no choice. I needed to do *something*. Starting with finding out some information. Normally, that would mean asking Ryan, but I didn't want to drag her into my bullshit. She had too much on her plate already, and after the way I'd treated her at the club?

I was a smart, capable woman. I could do this...probably.

A car alarm went off, and on instinct, I ducked behind a beat-up delivery truck, peeking out to look for danger. My confidence was boosted a little bit by my own quick reaction.

See, you've got survival instincts. Maybe not the final girl in a horror movie, but I'd last 'til mid-movie.

I wasn't sure if my realistic outlook on my skill level was a pro or con.

When it was clear it was nothing more than some kids attempting to mess around, I kept moving. Fuck. That was how vigilant I should've been this entire time I'd been in Tucson. The air seemed to vibrate with anticipation—or maybe it was all in my head. Either way, I checked that my hair was still tucked under my ball cap as unease settled in my stomach.

I looked like some punk teenage boy ditching out on school, with my too-baggy pants and ill-fitting hoodie pulled over my head. Anything to help hide the fact that I was a woman.

The mini-mart came into view, and I turned my head as I passed the camera hanging in the corner. Unlike most places on this side of town, Val actually had her surveillance hooked up and running. But the threat of her turning over evidence to the police wasn't why no one messed with her place. She'd never turn that shit over. She had her way of doling out justice, and it came in the form of a shotgun tucked by the register. There were countless tales of her running after assholes who'd tested if she'd really use it.

"Hood off."

The gravelly voice boomed through the liquor store, overpowering the chime of the bell over the door. Val never struggled with people hearing her, that was for sure.

"That's a new rule since last time," I said, halting before the counter. Cleaner and stale cigarettes tickled my nose. I'd been around Los Muertos long enough to recognize Vicente Fernández playing from the ancient speakers. The garbled sound quality somehow added to his music rather than taking away.

The older woman's face lit up when she recognized me. "Well, if it's not my troublemaker of a stray finally coming to say hello." Her gnarled hands hit her hips, the corner of her thin lips tipping up in a smirk.

When I first got to Tucson, I'd tried stealing from Val, and the tough broad threw a shoe at the back of my head. Told me I was lucky she was feeling nice because she could have shot me instead. I was *almost* positive she'd never actually shot anyone. But truthfully, even though I liked her, I was fucking scared of her. Which was the reason for the shake in my hands that I'd tucked into my front pockets.

"Please, Val. I come see your old ass all the time," I teased, ducking when she raised her hand.

"Stop moving so I can hit you. Fucking disrespectful brat."

I barely caught the last part over my laughter.

"Ernesto, get your ass out here and watch the front. I've got a meeting," she called out, moving toward the small office tucked in the back corner of her shop. I swore she had a sixth sense because I hadn't even told her I needed her help, yet she somehow knew this wasn't a social call.

We passed the rows of liquor bottles, all locked behind white caged doors. Val sold all sorts of things, including items you wouldn't find on shelves. Those sales happened back here.

"What brings you in here, *mija*?" she asked, sitting in an office chair held together by duct tape and prayers. I'd tried to get her a new one, but she'd swatted me away, saying my generation was addicted to buying shit. She had accepted the new shoes I'd gifted her after she'd complained about her back for the millionth time.

The click of the door behind me felt like an omen.

I'd gotten comfortable here. Too comfortable. When I'd landed in the States, I'd planned to move every few months and stay out of the major cities—especially New York. I'd stuck to that until I met Ryan. Told myself that being in cartel territory would protect me, but the truth was, I'd looked for any excuse to stay after clicking with her. I'd seen some of myself in her and her fucked up relationship with Mario. I couldn't leave until I knew his hold on her was broken. Now, it was.

"Can you get me a burner phone?" I asked with a heavy sigh, finally pushing off my hood. The stifling heat of her office wasn't helping my already frayed nerves. She leaned back in her chair. I waited for it to collapse under her weight, but the thing held.

"Stop giving my chair those dirty looks and explain why

you're coming to *me* to get a burner when I know damn well you *personally* know La Brujita."

I knew she'd ask that. It was the obvious question. I'd hoped my rapport with her would've earned me a *no questions* deal, but Val was too smart for that. Information was the real bargaining chip in the underbelly of the streets.

Pushing off the old door, I slid into the metal chair in front of the folding table turned desk. Stacks of paperwork and God only knew what else teetered on the edges. Val didn't have any ties with the cartel, but she had her own little world she was in charge of. Los Muertos didn't give a second thought to the smaller organizations that operated in Tucson. They could do whatever they liked as long as they never crossed Los Muertos's boundary lines or took any of their business.

My elbows dug into my knees as I leaned closer to the old woman, careful to keep my voice low. The walls in here were paper-thin, and someone was always listening.

"Alright, I'll cut to the chase here. My feet hurt, I'm hungry, and my life is slightly fucked. So, pretty please, will you tell me what the fuck you've heard lately?" I asked, ignoring her questions, hoping my pouting bottom lip would earn me some sympathy.

It was doubtful though.

She steepled her aged fingers while her shrewd gaze picked me apart. Behind the wrinkled skin and graying hair, Val was a predator watching for the weak spot to strike. When stripping, a mile wide smile that was borderline painful was my go-to mask, but that wouldn't work with Val. The pout clearly wasn't doing it. I blanked my face, keeping my body relaxed. Then I leaned back, kicking a leg over the other like I was at a fucking Sunday brunch.

She might be fond of me, but there was still a price for her intel. If she sensed how desperate I was for what she knew, that price would take a steep turn upward.

Finally, she broke the silence. "You're not very good at this, *mija*. You want any ol' information I have or you wanna know something specific?" She didn't give me a chance to answer. "I assume you mean what I've heard about you? Consider this a warning to get the fuck out of town. Because someone wants that cute white ass of yours."

My heart kicked up in my chest. It wasn't anything I didn't know, but the confirmation from some else moved it firmly from the category of *you're paranoid* to *you're fucked.*

She opened the top drawer of her filing cabinet and sent a phone skittering across the top. "Few months ago, some anonymous person started asking about dancers at Lotería. Specifically, this one." Vic paused to pull something else out of the metal drawer. This time, it was a pack of cigarettes and a piece of printer paper with a grainy image, an image I knew far too well. I stiffened in my seat.

Fuck. I shouldn't have come.

She lit up a cigarette, taking a long drag and quirking an eyebrow at me as if to say, *"Who the fuck did you piss off?"* But I kept quiet and didn't make a move for either of the things she'd pushed across the desk toward me.

It was a lesson I'd learned as a child. Nothing was ever a gift unless you were expressly told, and I didn't want to be indebted to anyone without knowing the price. The corner of Val's mouth inched up ever so slightly around the dangling cigarette. The lines on my face had apparently revealed my thoughts.

Tension built as smoke wafted between us, creating a hazy filter as we stared at one another.

"Picture is shit, but I'd recognize that determined look anywhere," she said, the crepey skin around her eyes wrinkling further as she narrowed them.

The tiny room felt like it was growing smaller by the second. The weight of my past threatened to crush me, yet I didn't let any of my fears surface, keeping them tucked down deep. I shoved my hands under my thighs, preventing myself from gnawing on my cuticles. A bad habit my ballet professor, Katya, never managed to break me of.

"You give them a name?" I asked, shifting my weight to my toes in case I needed to dash for the door behind me.

She ashed the white stick on the plastic top, filling the room with the foul scent. "I'm not a fucking disloyal narc." Her words were harsh—offended. "Though, I should've given you up if that's what you think of me." Her tone was hurt, and I gave her a sheepish, apologetic look.

"Sorry. I had someone come into Lotería with a note for me and I am trying to figure out who sent the messenger." I pulled my gaze away to study the aged newspaper clippings that adorned her walls. Yellowed and curling at the corners, a collage of Tucson's history, and her own, no doubt. I already knew who'd sent him, but there was a small delusional part of me that was hoping it could be someone else. Someone like Katya or a person from my past that wondered what happened to me when I never showed up in New York as planned.

But I knew that wouldn't be the case.

"You've been burned before." It wasn't a question, yet I knew she was looking for confirmation. She sighed when I didn't respond, continuing to study the black-and-white text until she continued on. "No. I didn't say shit."

Something in the way she said it told me it was the truth.

"Anything else you can tell me?" I asked.

A flash of black peeking up from just below the tabletop caught my attention. In the next moment I had a gun in my hand and trained on Val. Her laugh echoed off the cinderblock. She didn't look the least bit concerned that she was staring down a barrel as she set down her firearm. Her hands raised in mock surrender.

I may not have been as comfortable as Ryan with a weapon, but desperate times called for desperate measures. The last time I'd shot had been in the hallway at Lotería. One shot, dead center to the head. Surprised the fuck out of Ryan with that.

The hard grip felt familiar. The weight of the piece in my

palm was like an old friend, and my trigger finger rested right above. Ready to move if needed.

Please don't make me shoot you. I don't know shit about cleaning up those types of bodily fluids.

Val's voice cut through my inner musings. "You might survive this still, *mija*. Now put the fucking gun away."

"I think I'll keep it out if it's all the same to you," I responded, tracking her hands.

Thank fuck for all the hours I'd spent holding my arms out in position while Katya came around and checked to see if we were shaking, because aiming a gun at someone for an extended period of time was surprisingly heavy.

She did nothing but stare at me for a few agonizing minutes. "You need to see a man named Jardani. He's the one who was asking around, but I doubt he's the actual backer—just the mouthpiece. Pretty sure he's *Russian*," she said, her smile looking anything but friendly.

Cunning old bitch somehow knew I had ties to the Russians. The gleam in her chocolate eyes as she said the words was all the confirmation I needed. "Last I heard, he'd been spotted at the Pretty Pink Pussy Cat. That Reaper strip club sure does attract *quite* the crowd."

Fucking, Jardani. That ass-kisser probably loved that he was sent to drag me back home.

I'd only met him once, and that was more than enough. I remembered the way he'd whispered in my ear that he was going to ask Yuri for a *taste* of me as his promotion prize. Sick bastard would probably have allowed it.

A chill seeped into my bones. What would Yuri allow if he captured me?

"You're a gem, Val. Sorry for the whole pulling a gun on you. I'm trying to think like the final girl, you know?"

She looked at me as if I were an idiot. "Actually, no. I have no fucking clue what you mean. Young people, I swear."

We all needed therapy—who had casual conversations while weapons were drawn? "Like the final girl in a horror movie…"

Her face didn't change, so I decided to cut my losses with the explanation. "Those a gift? Or do they come with a price?" I asked, nodding toward the items on the desk with my chin, still keeping the Sig aimed at her, despite the playful banter.

She let out a boisterous laugh, her graying bun swaying as she threw her head back. "Nikki, I don't know where the fuck you came from, but you know more about this way of life than you let on, huh?" A crooked finger was pointed in my direction. "Oh, the secrets you must keep. Bet not even a young cartel kingpin knows them. That's why you needed the burner from me." She nudged the photo and phone forward. "Take them. A gift. That and the information, but I'm keeping my gun. Clearly, you don't need it."

I tucked the phone and paper in the pocket of my baggy jeans. The cold metal door handle met my fingertips as I reached behind me.

"Nice seeing you again, Val," I said in a cheery voice, turning the knob and stepping out of the office.

She called out after me. "Oh, Nikki, if you ever pull a gun on me again, you'd better pull the fucking trigger too, because I'll be pulling mine."

Then, like the deranged person I was, I smiled and blew a kiss in response.

NIKKI

NOW I'D NEED TO GARGLE BLEACH.

THANKFULLY, pulling a gun on Val only made her like me more. I wasn't sure if she'd answer me when I texted later to ask if she could find out if Jardani would be at the Reaper's club tonight, but she was more than happy to share—for a price. Threw in a new office chair with the stack of hundreds I had to send her way.

The information was worth the money. Ryan was out of town, and the last thing I'd have wanted to do was to ask her, anyway.

Or be forced to use my last resort.

Flicking the mirror open, I inspected the wig, ensuring no blonde was sticking out from the inky black waves. A pair of plain brown eyes stared back at me from beneath blunted bangs. It was a risk showing up at the Reaper's strip club tonight. I wasn't totally sure the disguise would prevent Jardani from recognizing me. Truthfully, it was really fucking reckless, but I didn't have a ton of options at this point.

My body jolted, colliding with the car door. It was like the driver was aiming for potholes.

"Sorry about that."

His tone didn't match his words. He'd quit trying to make conversation five minutes ago when it was clear I wasn't in the chatting mood. Since then, it was as if he was determined to give me whiplash.

God, I wished I knew how to drive.

Another fun control tactic of my father's. Back when I was younger, I thought nothing of it. Why would I, while I sat in the back of an armored vehicle with a driver who took me to and from events? Now, as I sat in the back of a rideshare vehicle with a man suggesting I could use *other forms of payment,* I was really regretting not learning.

Dust kicked up as he pulled into the dirt lot they used for parking. I turned my nose up at the windowless rectangular building. The neon light displaying the name only worked on a portion of the sign.

"Pussy. Nice. Sure that wasn't intentional or anything," I muttered to myself as I gathered my bag.

"So, um, did you give any thought to my proposal?" the shifty man in the front seat asked, his hands no longer on the wheel of his Ford Focus, but tucked down in his lap.

Why wasn't there an option to select a female driver if you were a female passenger?

"Yeah, I'm good with paying you cash," I said, sliding over more than the asshole deserved. He should pay *me* for dealing with his shitty driving and misogynistic views on women.

He turned in his seat. The greasy hair he'd combed over did nothing to hide his balding, but that wasn't what made him unattractive. It was the way he peered at me like I was property. *That* showed what a disgusting piece of shit he was.

"Listen, bitch. Your money isn't good here." He pointed a grimy finger my way, a slight tremor in his hand, matching the one in his voice. "You're about to go in there and whore yourself out anyway. I want a private show." The clicking of the door lock was deafening.

What the hell was wrong with men that they thought they could treat women like this?

Without warning, I launched myself forward, biting his finger, hard. Teeth were a great weapon, until the question came up of where the thing you'd put in your mouth had been. His howls filled the small car. It hurt like a bitch when he yanked the digit back out. A coppery tang coated my tongue, and I spit the bits of flesh at him.

Now I'd need to gargle bleach.

"Fucking, bitch." He moved to hit me but stopped mid-slap when he registered the sharp tip digging into the soft underside of his chin. The asshole wasn't smart enough to realize it wasn't a knife I held to his throat. Really, I should've kept the gun on me, but I'd been nervous that the club might dig through my bag. No one would bat an eye at some hair-cutting shears.

I need to rethink my stance on carrying weapons.

"Now listen here, you spineless waste of fucking flesh. You're going to unlock my fucking door right now." His body shook like a leaf, either in fear or in anger, but he reached behind him and did as he was told. "Good, now turn off the car and hand over your keys and wallet," I demanded. Confusion flooded his face, but he didn't argue.

Muggy night air wrapped around me when I pushed the door open. I'd never been so happy to feel Arizona's heat. The noise from the engine cut out, leaving nothing but the faint thump of music from the club a short distance away. I snatched the keys, tossing them toward the farthest corner from him. I didn't want him to try hitting me with his car when I got out. This would at least buy me a few moments to reach the bouncer.

My adrenaline was waning, but I kept my mask of confidence on.

"Johnathan Carter. 1456 Quincy Rd." I looked up from his driver's license, flashing him a cruel smile. "I'm going to get out of this car now, Johnny, and you are going to drive your-self home. Delete your rideshare app, and be on your best fucking behavior, because I *will* be sending someone to check in on you."

I dug the tip of the scissors in deeper when he scoffed, whispering menacingly. "La Brujita doesn't take kindly to men assaulting women in her city." All color drained from his face. Most predators knew her name. She was their Boogeyman, after all. "Good boy," I said, shoving the wallet in my bag. I practically leaped out of the car. His hiss told me I'd nicked him when I pulled away.

There were a handful of other cars and an entire line of bikes. I practically ran to the large bouncer at the front, his barrel stomach sticking out so far I couldn't see part of his waistband. He looked me up and down before glancing behind me.

"You good?" he asked.

"Yeah, just creeps, ya know." I cleared my throat, internally sighing with relief when his attention didn't hold any real suspicion. "I'm hoping I can go up tonight. Just passing through and want to make a little extra money," I said, hiking my bag up higher on my shoulder, glancing to see if Johnny had left.

The doorman grunted, pulling the solid door open and ushering me inside. "Go to the bar. Ask for Bianca."

I tipped my head in thanks before scurrying inside. It was as if I'd been transported back to the seventies—faux wood paneling covered every surface, including the bar front. Neon beer signs hung on every available free space. The place was already pretty packed even though it was only nine.

"Is Bianca here?" I asked when I reached the bar tucked along the back.

The bartender gave me an irritated look before tilting her head toward the other end, where a woman with black braided pigtails was popping the tops off drinks.

Not bothering to mutter a thanks, I moved.

"You Bianca?"

The woman cocked an eyebrow, looking me up and down, taking in my fishnets, shorts, and the velour jacket I had zipped up to my chin. "Who's asking?" She propped a hand on her hip.

I smirked. "Dumbass question. Clearly, I'm asking."

She smiled at the response, giving a sardonic laugh. "Well,

you've got the look and the bitch attitude of a seasoned dancer." She pulled out a rag from her back pocket and began wiping down the counter. "You want up tonight, I'm guessing?" All I gave her was a quick nod. "You can go up—your job to work it out with the girls where you fit in the lineup. The house gets twenty percent before you leave tonight." She looked me over again. "This is a biker-owned club, girl, so don't even think about stiffing them. Otherwise, they will take other forms of payment you may not be willing to give," she said, her voice much lower than it had been.

Yeah, that's not fucking ominous.

"Got it. Where's the dancers' room?" I asked, looking around and clocking all the exits and doors in case I needed to make use of any of them.

She gestured. "Over to the left of the stage. You do laps or privates?" she asked, pouring three shots and placing them on a tray.

Private dances here were probably *very* different than what I'd become used to since working at Lotería, but they would allow me an opportunity to get closer to some of these guys. I was good at getting men to let their guard down and talk to me.

"Yeah, I do that. But I wanna pick the ones I do," I said, staring her down to make sure she knew I meant business.

"How long you been dancing?"

"Long enough." She didn't seem offended when I didn't offer up any more information on myself—probably used to it. From what I'd heard of this club, no one stayed too long, and most were running from something. Or someone. I quirked an eyebrow as she shoved the tray of whiskey toward me.

"I'm guessing those aren't all for me," I said.

The club manager smirked. "Look at that, pretty and smart. They're gonna hate you."

"The men or the women?" I shot back. The question caused her to break out into a full-blown smile.

"Both. Now, do me a favor and take that to the table over

there." She pointed to a rounded booth, set away in the left corner. "That's the boss's table, Diesel. If he doesn't kick you out right there, then you're welcome to stay and dance…" She let her statement trail off, waiting for me to supply her with a name.

"Sugar Tits," I said sarcastically, grabbing the drinks and balancing the tray on my palm with ease. Thank god I'd done this enough times at Lotería.

Bianca snorted, rolling her eyes. "Smartass. Okay, *Sugar Tits*, take it to them before I get chewed out."

Weaving through the crowded club was easy since my heels were still tucked inside my bag. I was accosted with catcalls and far too many slaps to my ass. If I weren't trying to lay low, I'd have tased more than one man already.

Several bikers were at the front of the stage, harassing the young girl performing. Blue-collar men who were either coming after work or before milled about with an occasional woman sprinkled in the mix.

A flash of someone in a suit drew my attention. Tucked into a corner was a man who looked more like he should be in a boardroom than a rundown biker strip club. Next to him were two men who *did* fit right in. I didn't need to see the back of their cuts to know they said Reaper across the rocker. That, and they were in the booth Bianca had pointed me to.

Their heads were all tucked together. One was flinging his arms around animatedly. Slipping around the corner of the hallway, I pulled off my sweatshirt, stashing it in my bag. My boobs were practically in my throat in the bra I'd worn, hoping Jardani would stare at them rather than my face. The lining was close enough to my skin color that I looked bare underneath. I bit down on my bottom lip, willing my nerves to settle so I wouldn't spill any of their liquor. That would be just what I needed, fucking up their drinks.

Whatever they'd been talking about came to a halt the moment I approached their table.

"I haven't seen you around here, girl," The one with the VP patch said, spreading his arms across the back of the booth. There was an edge to his tone that told me I'd better have a damn good reason to be at their table.

"Nope." I let the p pop. "It's my first night. Bianca said I was supposed to come over and introduce myself." I pulled a shot off the tray, setting it in front of the prick.

"That so." Suspicion was thick in his tone, but I ignored him, swinging my attention to the man to my left. Jardani, in the flesh. Panic threatened to hijack my nervous system.

Why the fuck hadn't I taken a shot before this? Hell, ten shots.

He was clearly trying to make eye contact, but I looked away, shielding my face with the curtain of black hair.

Knuckles peppered with Cyrillic letters wrapped around the shot glass I pushed toward him. The men resumed their chatter, sticking to inconsequential things as they waited for me to hurry the fuck up and leave. Sweat rolled down my spine, my tongue swiping across my suddenly dry lips. If I didn't find a fucking way to make an impression now, this night might be a bust. Because Jardani hadn't even *glanced* at the topless woman on stage, meaning this was all business tonight, unless I convinced him otherwise. The final whiskey felt like a gavel, and it was time to plead my case before sentencing. I took a leap of faith, hoping the change of hair and eye color would be enough for him not to suspect I was the woman he was after.

His eyebrows shot up, lips parting slightly, when, in Russian, I asked him what brought him to this area. After so many years of not using it, my mother tongue felt clunky in my mouth. I didn't meet his gaze, hoping my avoidance read as bashful and not, *"I'm fucking guilty."*

He started to respond when the president cut him off.

"Hey, hey, hey. Let's keep this to fucking English, yeah?" He glared at both Jardani and me. "This bitch with you or something, *Jardi*?"

I winced, hugging the tray to my chest, deciding to abandon the idea—too much testosterone at the table. I'd have to find another way. Before I could walk away, Jardani reached out a hand and pulled me down into his lap. Thank god I was still in a pair of biker shorts. They offered a little more protection against the tough fingers biting into my thigh. At least with this arrangement, Jardani didn't have the opportunity to study my face.

"You're staying here, new girl," he said in my ear before continuing the conversation with the two men. "Tell me again why you aren't delivering your portion of the bargain? When are you going to have the girl?"

Clearly, these three were not getting along well.

The conversation continued as if I weren't there, which was pretty par for the course with my job. Most men assumed we weren't anything more than something pretty to press against.

"We're working on it," the VP, Snake, from the looks of his cut, said between clenched teeth. "But we won't be able to do jack shit until you and your boss hold up your end."

Against my back, I felt Jardani sigh. His heavily accented voice rumbled against me. "That was not what we planned. You go in and take the girl, quietly, and then we help you."

Snake folded his hands on top of the table, squeezing them so tightly it was a wonder his fingers weren't broken. "Well change the damn plan then."

I studied the chipping MDF table, curling my shoulders in and trying to make myself as invisible and forgettable as possible. The plan was to get Jardani alone so I could do what I needed, not get stuck on the lap of my enemy while he spoke to two other gems of humans.

"And why is it that Yuri would send men to help you with your little…" Jardani paused, rubbing up and down on the top of my thigh. The intensity of his stare was overwhelming, exactly what I'd been avoiding. "What is the word?" he whispered his question and the Russian term in my ear.

"Turf war," I said, clearing my throat when it cracked. "It's called turf war in English."

Two rough squeezes. His stamp of approval on a job well done. Meanwhile, my lunch was threatening to make a reappearance at the party. What the actual fuck had I gotten myself into?

"Exactly." He gestured toward them with his hand. "Why should we help with your *turf war*?"

The President spoke this time. He was young, probably only around his early thirties, with cruel eyes. Leaning forward, he folded his arms on top of the table, staring right past me at Jardani. "Because if we are in charge of the area, your boss gets to run skin through here. And this close to the border, you and I know why that would be appealing. He was already looking to stake a presence down here with Mario, but now that deal is fucked, so we're proposing a new one." His glacial eyes cut to me, narrowing before darting away.

Shit. Shit. Shit. Shit. *Shit.*

This was *too* detailed to share around someone you didn't know. I watched enough *20/20* to know you only spoke this openly about the damning details if the person listening wouldn't be around all that long. As in dead, or gotten rid of…and they'd said skin trade.

My mind worked at a million miles a second, trying to come up with how the hell I would get out of becoming the next missing person's case.

I only had one option in this situation, and it was the man I'd just bitched to about coming to my aid when I hadn't asked. His words echoed in my mind, causing that same tinge of regret I'd felt when I'd lashed out.

"Don't worry, Nikki. I won't ever step in again unless asked. Thanks for the reminder that I fuckin' hate playing white knight."

I *knew* he was not going to let me live this shit down.

LAUGHTER FILLED THE CLUBHOUSE, mixing with the music blasting from the overhead speakers. The place was packed, brothers spread all over. It seemed like there was an ass in every leather barstool or couch.

The place had been built to party, or at least the first floor had been. Only members had access to the second level—well, members and whichever fuck-of-the-day they wanted. Whiskey coated my tongue as I took a pull from the bottle I'd jacked from the bar. Nearly caused the prospect manning it to piss himself when I told him to fuck off after he tried to tell me I couldn't take it. He was for sure not getting a rocker. A flash of skin lightened my sour mood, but only slightly.

Johnny Boy had his dancers here tonight. He ran the MC's strip club on the outskirts of town and, by the looks of it, he'd gotten some new meat recently.

Or maybe it hadn't been recent.

I'd stopped going after Lotería—that damn *Latin burlesque* club—fucked me up. Now, I was a high-class strip joint kinda man.

No, you're a blonde-who-doesn't-want-your-dick kinda man.

My pissy mood was back in full force, but I forced my body to appear relaxed, a lazy grin painted on my face. If there was one thing I was good at, it was faking happiness for the sake of the masses.

These ladies were here tonight to put on a show on the poles peppered around for all the brothers. Some of them even wanted to put on something more *intimate*, and who was I to deny the wishes of a lady?

"Now, take it off slowly, Jazzy. You know I like my cock teased," I said in a lazy drawl as I spread my arms across the back of the couch, widening the position of my thighs so she could step between them. Actually, I didn't know if she knew that or not. Couldn't be sure if I'd fucked this chick before. She'd walked up as if she knew me, and I'd rolled with it.

Her red hair appeared even more unnatural under the LED lights.

I'd have remembered that color, right?

It wouldn't have been *my* first hair color of choice, but what the hell did I know? Truly, I didn't give a fuck what color her hair was—as long as it wasn't blonde.

I winced at the thought of the blonde bombshell who had made me swear them all off. My irritation must have shown on my face because Jazzy ramped up the sway of her hips as she danced between my legs. I tried my damnedest to refocus on the practically naked woman in front of me, but there was no use.

Nikki is not going to be the cause of my blue balls again.

With renewed determination, the pad of my finger brushed along the string of the chick's thong, pulling it back before letting it snap her skin. I opened my mouth to say one of the usual pickup lines when the front pocket of my jeans vibrated.

Once.

Twice.

Three times.

"Hold on, baby," I said, reaching in to pull out my phone. "This is probably Gunner."

Everyone else who'd need me was at this damn clubhouse, and they all knew if they wanted to talk they could walk their asses over here. Pretty sure every brother and prospect had seen my cock being sucked. It was basically a rite of passage at this point.

My brows furrowed in confusion at the name that popped up. Without a second thought, my thumb swiped across the screen. A foreign fluttering feeling entered my chest, but quickly plummeted when I read the texts.

> NIKKI (BOMBSHELL WITH THE TASTY PUSSY AND KILLER THROW):
>
> Hey. I need you ASAP. Think someone is trying to take me.
>
> NIKKI (BOMBSHELL WITH THE TASTY PUSSY AND KILLER THROW):
>
> I would've texted Ryan, but she's not here, and you're my only choice.
>
> NIKKI (BOMBSHELL WITH THE TASTY PUSSY AND KILLER THROW):
>
> Warning. You won't like where I am…

Everything in me went rigid at the last message. The noises all faded into the distance. Only the blood pounding in my ears was audible. Subconsciously, I knew Jazzy was saying something. Her plump lips were clearly moving, but I was laser-focused on the screen. My body seemed to reboot in seconds, and I practically leapt out of the leather bench, plowing over the woman between my legs. Normally, I'd have apologized and promised to make it up to her, but not when I was in this mode.

> ME:
>
> Nikki. WHAT. THE. FUCK. DOES. THAT. MEAN.

Three little dots appeared and disappeared several times before her message finally came through.

> **NIKKI (BOMBSHELL WITH THE TASTY PUSSY AND KILLER THROW):**
>
> I'm at the Pretty Pussy or whatever the fuck the Reaper strip club is called. I need a ride, like, now.

A million questions swirled in my mind as I shot off another text, shoving anyone who didn't move out of my way fast enough.

> **ME:**
>
> I'm on my way. Can you get out into the parking lot? Who's trying to take you? Like, kidnap you?

The damn dots played with my emotions again, but all the color drained from my face when her text popped up.

> **NIKKI (BOMBSHELL WITH THE TASTY PUSSY AND KILLER THROW):**
>
> Ugh. Probably not. I'm kind of stuck in a private dance room with an asshole...
>
> **NIKKI (BOMBSHELL WITH THE TASTY PUSSY AND KILLER THROW):**
>
> Bring zip ties, maybe.

It took all of my willpower not to crush the small device in my hand, but I knew I needed it to communicate with her. Why the hell would I need zip ties? I was killing the motherfucker.

I made it outside in what felt like a blink of an eye. I wasn't even sure if anyone had tried speaking to me, but when I looked beside me, Torque was standing at the door of the bulletproof SUV. Usually, that would've been Gunner, but he was down in Mexico with Ryan.

"You lead and I'll follow, brother," he said, opening the passenger door and climbing in.

I'd taken a liking to the kid over the last year, and it seemed he'd done the same. The engine roared to life followed by the tires kicking up gravel as we tore off through the clubhouse parking lot, rounding the corner faster than I normally would. Thank god there'd been a party tonight and we'd left the main gate open. Otherwise, I might have taken the fucker out in my haste to get to Nikki.

The city zoomed by in a blur of lights and shadows. The gas pedal was practically glued to the floor of the SUV.

"What's the plan, brother?"

I respected the fact that the kid didn't ask too many questions. We were alike in that way. You wanted me to know something? Then you'd better fuckin' tell me, otherwise I figured it wasn't any of my damn business. Gunner said that kind of detachment was why women didn't like me—some shit about the fact that they *wanted* me to ask questions about them.

"Nikki sent me a text. Said she needed a ride." I paused, turning my head to look at him. "From the Reaper's strip club." Torque's brows hit his hairline.

"Oh, shit. That's Ryan's friend, right? Why the fuck is she at a Reaper club?" There was a hint of suspicion in his tone. He cleared his throat, shifting in his seat uncomfortably. "You think she's setting us up?"

His question hit like a punch to the gut. I hadn't even considered that. My heart rebelled against the accusation, but my mind couldn't produce a single defense for Nikki other than her being friends with Ryan. I chewed on the inside of my cheek before shaking my head.

"No. Not Nikki. If she texted me, it's because she really needs the help."

"Okay," Torque responded, with no sign of doubt.

Neon pink shone in the distance. "Just like that?" I asked, pulling into the dirt lot, and kicking up a sandstorm.

"You say your girl's good people, then that's enough for me."

Agitation at how much time had passed bubbled inside, and I threw the car into park. A lot could happen in ten minutes, but we'd gotten here as fast as possible. I just h oped it was fast enough.

I'd taken a spot in the back. We were about to run in there with our fucking dicks out we were so unprepared, but I was hoping we'd be able to sneak in and out through the janky metal door.

Rein it in, Dex. In for four, out for four.

My breathing slowed as I repeated the mantra in my head, my heart rate dropping with each four-count. *This* was why I was good at my job, because I shut everything down. There was no room for emotion when I was at work.

Precision and ruthlessness.

"Here's the plan. We walk up like we're supposed to be there, all casual. I'd rather not have shit pop off there if we can avoid it. Gunner's not in the FBI anymore, so if we get in trouble with the five-O, we're fucked," I said, stripping off my cut. There was a *very* short list of acceptable reasons to take off my cut: fucking and avoiding bringing heat to the club. Torque copied me, pulling his off and stashing it in the back seat. He checked his Glock before shoving it back into his waistband and giving me a stern nod.

I broke into a crouched jog, Torque right on my heels, ducking behind a dumpster a handful of feet away. I listened for any signs of trouble. Nothing but shitty music made its way through the cinderblock. My phone screen lit up as I typed out a message to Nikki, praying to every deity I could think of that she was okay.

ME:

We're here. Your room close to the back door? Any intel would be helpful, spitfire.

The heaviness in my chest eased slightly when her reply came in almost immediately.

NIKKI (BOMBSHELL WITH THE TASTY PUSSY AND KILLER THROW):

Hold on. I'll be right there.

"She'll be right here?" read Torque over my shoulder. "I thought she was in danger or some shit."

Before I could respond, the metal door popped open, and a woman with black hair popped their head out. We stiffened as she scanned the area. Shit. Did someone have Nikki's phone?

"Dex," she whispered harshly.

"Nikki?"

Her head whipped to where we were hiding. "Of course it's me, who else would it be?"

The attitude and hands on her hips were all the confirmation I needed that the black-haired beauty was, in fact, the same person as the blonde who haunted my fantasies. Her pulse thudded underneath my fingertips as I wrapped them around her wrist, pulling her toward the car. The *rescue* was turning out to be easier than I'd thought it'd be.

That was, until she resisted.

"Wait, wait." Her normally blue eyes were gone, replaced by a dull brown, but still, I could read the emotion in them. She was nervous. "Um, think we can get an unconscious body out of here? Hypothetically speaking, that is…"

My chest brushed hers as I invaded her space. Of course, the woman wasn't fazed. Instead, she straightened her spine, standing tall under my glare. "Nikki, what the fuck is your middle name?"

Her look of determination slipped at the question. "Huh?"

"Middle. Name," I bit out, pinching the bridge of my nose and counting down from twenty, all too aware that we were standing out in the open—our window of going undetected closing by the second.

When she answered, her tone was thick with suspicion. "Why do you need that?"

Right. She doesn't share shit about her past.

"Because," I opened my eyes, moving closer and caging her between me and the exterior wall with my arms, "I'm about to tear you a fucking new one for being at an enemy club and apparently needing help disposing of a body." Her throat bobbed, tempting me to run my tongue along the delicate skin. Even while pissed off at her, I wanted her. "Yelling *'Nikki'* doesn't have the desired effect."

The brat had the nerve to laugh instead of feeling ashamed.

I cupped her face, needing to feel her soft skin. "At least act like you're sorry for giving me fucking gray hairs." My heart was convinced we should always touch her like this, but my brain was screaming we needed to stay away. Luckily, our moment was interrupted before I could do something stupid. Like kiss her.

"This is cute and all, but can we get the fuck out of here?" Torque asked.

Nikki pulled away, opening back up the metal door, kicking away the rock she'd used to prop it open. "Come on. I'll show you where he is."

Of course, the body question wasn't hypothetical. That would have been too easy.

All I saw was red when I followed her into the private room. There was a man slumped in a chair, his suit pants down around his ankles. My knife was in my hand before I could register it.

"Shit. Don't kill the asshole, Dex." Her hands gripped onto my forearm and yanked away from his gut. "You really were going to kill him," she said incredulously when I faced her.

My mouth literally fell open at her statement. "Well, no shit, sweetheart. What did you think I would do when you told me someone was trying to *take you*? Which, fucking Christ, woman. It's abnormal to be kidnapped once, and you're at what? Fucking three?" I asked, throwing my arms up in the air. Why did I like the ones who were determined to give me ulcers?

The guy in the suit chose that moment to come back to, moaning and shifting around in his seat. A shiny flash sailed through the air before connecting with the side of his head.

Thwack, thwack, thwack echoed through the room. I stared in disbelief at the downed man, blood seeping from his head.

The trance was broken when Torque doubled over in laughter.

"Holy shit, girl. You knocked him out with your fuck-me shoe?" He wheezed, clutching at his side. "We need to teach you some actual technique because fuck, you've got the balls to be a fighter."

"We are *not* teaching her how to fight," I grumbled, taking the bloody object from her hand, and pulling her away.

"Why the hell not?" she asked from where I was cradling her.

I glanced down. The faux bangs had parted, giving a full view of the crease between her brows. Her irritation made me smile. So fierce for something so beautiful and soft. Her small hand came up and whacked me on the chest when I didn't answer right away.

"Because you're dangerous enough with a shoe. I would know."

She rolled her eyes in mock annoyance. "You deserved it. Who tells a woman to let the men handle it? And for your information, *Dex,* it hasn't been three times. So don't be fucking dramatic. It was once. This was just an attempted kidnapping—"

I snorted at her ridiculous reasoning before realizing something about the man in the chair. "Is his tie being used as a noose?"

"How else was I supposed to choke him unconscious?"

NINE

NIKKI

CLEANING UP HOSTAGE DRAG MARKS HELPS WITH PANIC ATTACKS

I NEEDED to get some normal friends. Or better yet, some therapy. I hadn't been even slightly fazed when Dex pulled out a knife, ready to stab the ugly fucker. Instead of the normal reaction—fear, tears, hell, a damn scream—my heart beat faster with the idea that he was protective over me. Some sick part wanted to see Dex wild, bordered on out of control. If I didn't need more answers from Jardani, I'd have let Dex gut him.

There was a not-so-silent voice telling me the reaction was caused by the sheer reality that I wasn't used to being a man's choice.

At least not in a way that wasn't solely sexual.

"I'm sorry, I must have had a stroke or a sudden loss of brain function because I thought you said you choked him out with his *tie*." The vein in Dex's forehead popped with every word he bit out. If we didn't need to be quiet on the whole account of needing to sneak out, I was positive he would've yelled. "Have you done that before? For the fucking *love* of god, please tell me you've done it before and knew what you were doing before you tried to strangle a man twice your size."

Sure, when he laid it out like that, it wasn't the smartest idea I'd ever had. But honestly, most of my ideas weren't all that much better—didn't have the luxury when you were trying to survive.

"Yeah. Do it all the time," I said to get him off my back before shoving all of my and Jardani's shit into my arms so we wouldn't leave anything behind. "Now, can we stop fucking around and get him out of here? He was meeting with the president and VP of the Reapers tonight. I don't know how long it will be before they come looking."

Torque let a low whistle from where he stood guarding the door.

Dex ran a hand down his face, clearly stressed. "Damn it, Nikki. We gotta leave him then." He reached out a muscled arm, his hand latching onto my upper bicep. "If we get caught here…let's just say I want you to run and not look back. They aren't going to take kindly to Torque and me being here."

Unease prickled over my skin, the comfort I'd felt seeing Dex in the parking lot waning. Their plain white shirts were like a neon sign of how much they were risking coming here tonight. They'd had to stash their cuts somewhere so they could rescue me from enemy territory. And now, I was going to ask them to help carry out the body of a high ranking Russian Bratva member.

I shut down that line of thinking.

There wasn't room for guilt when trying to survive.

"No, we can't do that." The words were quiet, almost weak, the reality of the mess I'd dragged them into settling on my shoulders.

Dex's arm shot out, pointing to the slumped man. "What the hell do you mean? He's unconscious. You're in a fucking disguise, which, don't think you're off the hook for those questions either, but he doesn't even know who you are."

In any other situation, the exasperation in his voice would have been funny. But not while we were hiding out in a room with shag carpet that the CDC should investigate. Thinking about the bodily fluids hidden within the fibers made me want to gag. Thank fuck I'd beaten Jardani with the shoe from my bag—at least my feet were still safe from infection.

He's not going to like this next part…

"That's kind of the whole problem," I said sheepishly, tucking a strand from the wig behind my ear. "He *does* know who I am, and that is a very, *very* bad thing for me…"

Dex's attention beat down on me, making me feel two feet tall. "Torque, help me get his jacket back on. We'll carry him out between us like he's had too much to drink."

The two of them draped Jardani's limp arms over their shoulders, propping him between them. I reached out and pulled his tie forward. My palms were still sore from when I'd pulled with all my might on the silky fabric from behind. I'd gotten lucky that the chair had a solid back, the perfect surface to brace my feet against.

Leverage was a girl's best friend.

The two boys discussed how to carry him while I made sure the coast was clear. Lighting was non-existent, the only source at the mouth of the hall. Didn't take a genius to figure out dancer safety and comfort wasn't a top priority here, but the dark would help hide our exit. Giggles came from the room to the left, but otherwise, all of the commotion was still out in the main part of the club. I motioned the boys forward, dashing to push the exit open for them.

My shoulders cramped with how rigid I held myself. Closing the exterior door as quietly as possible felt like diffusing a bomb. Our fate depended on not drawing attention—we were so fucking close to being out of this mess.

Your mess.

Dex and Torque moved with impressive stealth—this was clearly not their first time playing in this kind of fire.

"There doesn't seem to be any cameras on the backside of the building," Torque said quietly.

I scanned the squat building. The entire back was one long windowless wall, nothing back here besides the singular dumpster and the door we'd come from. Still, I kept the wig and contacts on. Jardani may know who I was, but if a Reaper came out, I didn't want them to realize their mark was basically in their grasp.

I looked around, unable to wait patiently by the car, needing my body and mind occupied so I wouldn't fall into a panic attack. I'd managed to hold it back this long—I wasn't going to fall apart at the end. The tips of Jardani's shoes left a trail from where they dragged along the dirt, and I busied myself concealing the lines while Torque muscled our hostage into the back row with him. It was quiet, other than the sound of the tightening plastic teeth of zip ties.

Dex's deep rumbled in my ear, his proximity causing my breath to hitch as he slid a hand across my waist, pulling me into him. "Nikki, I need you to follow directions now and get your perky ass into the car so I can get us out of here." He gripped my chin between his thumb and forefinger, turning my head so our eyes met. "Think you can do that, spitfire?"

And damn if I didn't listen to him.

Dex peeled out, taking off out of the parking lot like a bat out of hell. My ass had barely hit the supple leather seat, and we were already down the isolated road.

For the first time that night, I was able to breathe normally. That was until I remembered the pile of shit I was still in, including having a large, tatted biker mad at me.

I'd only seen him this focused once before—the night I'd run out of Lotería, straight into his arms, screaming at him to go and save Ryan. Moonlight hit his handsome face, dampened slightly by the tint from the windshield. The tick in his jaw was a neon sign about his mood.

The man was pissed.

Torque's head popped between the two of us, his leather cut back on. "So, how did you get him to be quiet?" he asked, clearly unable to tamp down his curiosity any longer.

"Dex?" I asked, turning in my seat.

Torque scoffed. "Naw. He's quiet because he wants to wring your pretty little neck." Dex let out an honest-to-god growl, but the younger man didn't bat an eye. "I meant sleeping beauty back here." He pointed over his shoulder with his thumb as if I wouldn't get who he was referring to.

I peeked around the seat to look at Jardani. "I shoved a pair of panties in his mouth."

Torque fell back in a fit of laughter. Even Dex let out a snort of a laugh, which he quickly covered up with a cough. Turning back around, I kicked off my shoes, tucking my legs up under one another criss-cross style and replaying the night's events in my mind, deciding how much to tell them.

The Reapers president and VP had argued they needed Russian firearms and support immediately. I could still feel the lingering press of Jardani's fingertips gripping my skin whenever the Reapers had said something that irritated him. Which had seemed to be the whole conversation.

They really thought they'd be able to throw their weight around and get Yuri to fall in line with their plans. The Reapers should have done more research—offering to expand his skin trade wasn't going to appeal to the Bratva leader. Not when what he really wanted was me.

Yuri was a ruthless bastard with a mean streak a mile wide. It was his way, or a coffin for you and your family.

My father had spoken about it on more than one occasion. Yuri didn't garner the respect of billionaires through diplomacy, but through tyranny. He became the leader of the Circle by butchering the family of his predecessor—and not only the immediate family. Yuri hung a family tree and ticked them off one by one.

Well, *he* didn't. Fucker wasn't hands on, but he was damn good at getting people to follow orders.

"When I got there, the club manager said I had to serve their table and see if they'd let me work tonight." The heat from Dex's attention licked up the side of my face, but I refused to face him. "Homeboy back there pulled me into his lap and said I was to stay by his side, but then they started talking club business." I finally turned to face Dex. "They were talking about expanding the skin trade in the area. Then he took me back to a private room, and the ass thought he was about to have the night of his life. I went with him because I figured I'd have a better chance of getting away."

"Did they threaten you?" Dex's voice was devoid of any emotion, making it all the more chilling. His grip was so tight on the steering wheel, there were bound to be indents when he peeled them away.

"No. No one threatened me, but I'm not dumb enough to think they'd let me go after openly talking about selling women. To them, I was a nobody who'd shuffled in looking to work one night…"

"An easy mark. How did you get him unconscious?" Torque asked. He'd popped his head between the two front seats again, resting his arms on the center console.

I couldn't stop the proud smile. "Took his jacket halfway off and hooked it onto the chair to trap his arms. Gave him some bullshit line about how it was so he'd be a good boy and not touch me while I gave him a lap dance. Then I shoved a thong in his mouth, did a few moves, and bam. Choked him with his tie," I said, recounting the event.

There were a few details I left out.

Like how after I'd trapped his arms, I *did* give him a lap dance, trying to entice him to share why he was in town. I'd hoped I could loosen his tongue enough to tell me something useful without blowing my cover. But that failed epically. Making him pass out was never part of the plan, but the moment his eyes had widened and he'd whispered my *real* name, I'd known there wasn't another choice. And now I needed to figure out what the fuck to do with him…and with Dex.

"So," I started, "hypothetically speaking, if I were to ask you to drop him and me off at my place wh—"

A loud squealing noise pierced my ears, my body shooting forward. My already damaged hands collided with the dash, barely preventing my face from hitting the plastic. Torque yelled out at the same time I did.

"What the fuck, Dex!" I yelled, sending him a scathing glare.

His thick finger nearly poked me in the nose. "You listen here, Nicole Marie Whatever-the-fuck-your-full-name-is, under *no* circumstances am I going to let you be alone with a man you felt you needed to *choke unconscious*." He tapped against my head, rather hard, if I was being honest. "Now I know you're smart, so that means the only reason you'd ask me such a stupid fucking question is because you're hiding something."

We were at a standstill.

Both of our chests rose and fell faster than normal. Every fiber of my being wanted to fight with him. To tell him to fuck right off with his suspicion. Problem was, he was spot-on with his assessment.

The other issue was that I was turned on by how much he clearly wanted to protect me—because that was what I heard in his voice when he growled out that I was going home with him tonight and continued driving. Instead of fighting and telling him to take me to my own home right that moment, I sat back and went along for the ride, pushing away all the warning bells about why this was a bad idea.

NIKKI

ALRIGHT, WE'LL GO THE CHICKS BEFORE DICKS ROUTE HERE

I DON'T KNOW why I was surprised to find a full-blown rager happening at the one-percenter motorcycle club, but I was. The thumping sounds of bass could be heard from outside.

"It's like two in the morning."

"Yup," Dex responded, popping the *p*. "Torque, take him to the Shed."

"You got it," he answered, jumping out of the SUV and dragging the unconscious man out by his feet, not caring that his head was bouncing off the ground like a ball.

My fingers wrapped around the door handle, but it was ripped from my grip when Dex flung it open. He slid his arm underneath the crook of my legs, pulling me out of the car bridal style.

"Dex, I can fucking walk." I wrapped my arms around his neck to avoid falling to the ground.

"Yeah, which means you can run, too. You've gotten into enough trouble tonight," he grunted.

"So what, you're going to carry me wherever we're going?"

"That's the plan."

He held me closing, crossing the club grounds as if I weighed nothing, his hard chest warm against my side. I was so focused on not nuzzling my nose into his shirt that I forgot to keep my mouth in check. "You'd be a great partner."

Embarrassment didn't come easily to someone who danced nearly naked for a living. Half of Tucson had seen my ass cheeks and I'd never batted an eye over it, but this…

I didn't need a mirror to know my face was bright red as I stumbled over my words to clarify. "Like you're strong."

Now, he looked at me like I'd grown a third head, sincere concern swirling in his hazel eyes.

"Did you get a concussion and not tell me? Because you're spouting out some weird shit." He leaned down and pressed his cheek to my forehead, lips brushing against my skin.

"What are you doing?" I squeaked, unsettled by his lips so close to mine.

"Checking to see if you have a fever," he said matter-of-factly. "That's a sign of a concussion, right?"

"How the hell would I know?" I gnawed on my nail, willing myself to think through my words *before* they left my lips this time. "I don't have a concussion, Dex. What I mean is that you're strong, and you'd make a good dance partner. Like for performing lifts." Without a doubt, my neck and cheeks were bright red.

"You do lifts and shit in pole dancing?" His tone seemed genuinely curious.

"Um." I looked away. I never spoke of this particular subject, but pretty soon, he was likely to learn a whole fucking lot more about me now that I'd gotten him into this shit. "Well, you can do partner work with a pole, like duo-pole routines. I've only ever done it a few times and always with another female dancer. But I meant it more, like, with classical dance styles."

When he didn't say anything in response, I glanced up, startled to see that his full attention was on me, and not where he was walking. The shadows playing across his face from the bonfires and floodlights made his stare even more intimidating. I averted my eyes the moment they met his, afraid they would give away all my carefully kept secrets, because I *knew* that was what he was searching for in that moment.

Dex's talent was getting people to underestimate him and his intelligence. He was goofy, loud, and impulsive. Not to mention he said stupid shit all the time. Sure, that was a part of him, but it was also a tactic to get people to pay attention somewhere else while he was busy dissecting you, finding the flaws he could exploit.

How did I know this?

Because like recognizes like. The only difference was I used my body to manipulate people and get what I wanted. Like I'd tried to do tonight.

"So," I said, changing the subject as we entered the metal building. He set me down, the place too packed with people to continue to carry me. He didn't let me move from his side, though, draping a heavy arm over my shoulders and tucking me in close.

"Is this what you were doing when I texted you? Partying?" I asked, looking around the metal warehouse-type building.

Smoke engulfed the space, creating a hazy red effect under the LED lights. Voices and laughter melted into the rock pouring from the speakers—"Porn Star Dancing", a stripper staple. I'd recognize the opening notes on my deathbed. My hips involuntarily started moving to the rhythm with each step I took. I knew my walk now looked more like a strut. It happened anytime music was on, and there wasn't a damn thing I could do about it.

Music and dance were in my blood, the only remnants of a past I hadn't completely severed. I couldn't. I'd rather have died that day all those years ago. Movement in my peripheral drew my attention to the woman up on the stage. She wasn't bad, but definitely new. Men were scattered throughout the compound, the majority in the same black leather vest Dex and Gunner wore, but some in regular clothes.

The whole scene was grungy and sexy in the way only an MC clubhouse could pull off—people everywhere all in various stages of intoxication. I felt *painfully* sober for this introduction to the biker lifestyle.

Dex drew closer the farther into the clubhouse we moved, his arm brushing against mine, sending unwanted tingles down my spine. "I was actually getting a lap dance when you texted me," he said nonchalantly, his deep voice easily cutting through the noise.

Suddenly, I had no coordination, and my face was headed straight for the floor. Strong, calloused fingers closed around my biceps, hauling me back to an upright position. A deep chuckle rumbled against my back.

What the hell was I supposed to say to that? Sorry?

Part of me wanted to say I'd make it up to him, to make him feel as unsteady as I did at that moment, but those were dangerous fucking waters. I was painfully aware of how much I liked the guy, and not only on a physical level. That was the whole fucking problem—I didn't *do* men I liked more than on the physical level.

It turned out no response was needed because a woman with fire hydrant red hair chose that moment to storm on over. She was zeroed in on Dex, and the pinch of her eyebrows told me she was not happy. It took me all of two seconds to figure out *she* was the one who'd been giving the dance I'd interrupted.

"Dex, you fucking asshole," she spat, her lips twisted up. "You literally knocked me over and didn't say shit. Just ran out of here while I was dancing for you." Her attention cut over to me, nostrils flaring as she flung an arm in my direction. Clearly, I was about to be brought into this shit. "Oh, and then you come back with another bi—"

"Hey," Dex barked out so loud it caused her to jump, stopping her mid-rant. He'd been silent while she'd berated him. Even sheepishly rubbed the back of his neck when she'd mentioned knocking her over, but now a pissed-off scowl replaced his bashful demeanor. "Finish that sentence, Jazzy, and your ass will be out of here. Got it? Nikki's had a shit night, and she doesn't need to become your damn verbal punching bag because you're pissed at me."

Her mouth fell open at the scolding. Clearly, she hadn't anticipated being the one in trouble.

Everyone was looking over because the two were practically shouting at one another while I awkwardly stood there wringing my hands. It's not that I wasn't good with confrontation. Quite the opposite, I was very good with confrontation. But technically I *was* the reason he'd left, so tearing into her didn't feel right.

Alright, we'll go the chicks before dicks route here.

I flashed the room a smile, the one I used on stage all the time when I was trying to get the crowd to loosen up. "Nothing to see here, folks. Just Dex's dick game leaving women disappointed."

The guy next to me, who looked too old to even get on a motorcycle, laughed so hard I was concerned he'd keel over.

"Ha. Ha. Ha," Dex bellowed, his cheeky grin back in place. "So funny. Now everyone, get back to whatever the fuck you were doing and stay out of my shit."

Within a matter of seconds, the whole clubhouse acted like nothing had happened. Jazzy had dipped out at some point. My guess was she decided it wasn't looking good for her to make it into Dex's bed tonight.

Warm breath caressed the shell of my ear. "She was only disappointed because she never got my dick. If she had, she would've come over here begging for another ride." In an instant, Dex was back standing, pressing a hand to my lower back, propelling me toward a metal staircase. "Come on, Nikki, we're going up to my room. I think you've had enough excitement for tonight."

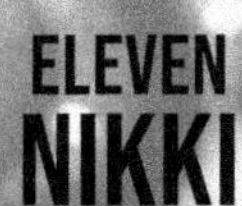

HIS ROOM WASN'T anything like I'd been expecting.

I'd pictured chaos. Maybe a keg in the corner, definitely a navy comforter with no bed frame. Oh, and women's panties hanging from every possible surface. That's what I'd anticipated from what I'd witnessed tonight. Women watched his every move with looks of longing on their faces before the looks morphed into something closer to jealousy or rage when they spotted me.

But instead of a shrine to his conquests, it was neat and tidy. Sparse, almost.

"How long have you been here?" I asked, taking in the lack of anything personal as he pushed past me toward the wooden dresser tucked into a corner.

"Um. I've been with the club for like four years now."

I trailed my fingertips over the stark white bedding, noting the way the corners were folded under with precision. The sight triggered a memory of Ryan mentioning that Gunner was in the Marines. Gingerly, I rested my butt on the edge of the bed, keeping the majority of my weight off so I didn't mess it up.

"And you've lived here the whole time?"

Dex glanced over his shoulder. His brows pulled together slightly. "Yeah. Why?"

For some reason, his response made me sad. He didn't even realize how depressing his room was.

"Here." He shoved a shirt my way. "There's a shower and toilet in there. Extra toothbrushes are under the sink. I don't have any girly wash shit, so you'll have to settle for smelling like Old Spice." He rubbed the back of his head, shifting from side to side like he was nervous.

The reaction was weirdly endearing, but I swallowed those emotions down. "Dex." I waited for him to make eye contact again. "I know I'm not the first woman you've had in your room, so stop acting weird about it," I teased, clutching his shirt to my chest, trying my damnedest to resist sniffing it to see if it smelled like him.

A hint of a smile tugged at the corners of his lips, but there was still a touch of uncertainty in his expression. "You're the first woman who's going to be *sleeping* in my bed. I dunno what the proper etiquette for that shit is."

I laughed when I realized I didn't know what the etiquette for that was either. "Fuck, I don't know. I normally kick them out after fucking," I responded truthfully, noting the way he seemed to flinch slightly at the confession. I quickly changed the subject to something safer.

Like torture.

"But we aren't going to sleep right now anyway. Don't we need to question that asshole?" I went to stand, but Dex's large hand landed on my shoulder, pushing me back down onto the mattress.

His tone was resolute as he spoke, tinged with authority. "*We* aren't going anywhere. I'm going to go help Torque get the fucker into our back shed, and you're going to go shower and scrub the blood off your chest."

He was right. I could feel the dried specks pulling at the tiny hairs on my skin.

But anger boiled in my gut, and I raised my voice in frustration. "Fuck that, Dex. I want to question him," I said, trying in vain to pry his fingers from my shoulder.

Even the fucker's fingers are heavy.

"And I wanted a blow job tonight. We don't always get what we want, Nikki."

"Those are *not* even remotely comparable, and you know it." I glared at him, my eyes darting toward the door that was slightly ajar, trying to decide if I could get to it before he did.

Maybe if I kicked him in the balls…

Suddenly, I was no longer sitting. I was cradled in two powerful tattooed arms.

Dex's voice rumbled against my side. "Since it looks like you aren't going to follow directions, I'll have to teach you a lesson."

My eyes widened as I protested, "What?" I flailed in his grasp, desperate to free myself from his hold.

Dex, however, was unyielding. He whispered in my ear, his warm breath sending shivers down my spine, "Yell all you want, Nikki. They're used to hearing those sounds coming from my room." With that, he dropped me onto the plush mattress. My body bounced, disorienting me, and before I could even attempt to make a run for it, he covered me with his body, pinning both of my wrists above my head.

His powerful thighs bracketed my hip, and there was an unmistakable hard pressure against my center. Desire surged through me, but it was quickly replaced by a jolt of reality when soft restraints tightened around my wrists.

"Normally, whoever I put these on is naked." He looked down at me, a cocky smirk on his face. "If you want to continue to misbehave, I can cut your clothes off, too."

Heat flooded my center at the image of us naked, but I hid my reaction with a hiss. "You wouldn't dare." I narrowed my eyes, giving him my most threatening tone. Bastard only threw his head back and laughed so hard strands fell out of his bun.

The move caused him to rock against me. A low, involuntary moan escaped my lips as I felt the weight of his body pressed against mine. All humor bled from his face. I was positive my cheeks were beet red in that moment. I hadn't meant to make that noise, but now he knew *exactly* how I felt about his body on top of mine. Hazel eyes homed in on my lips, his cock twitching against my center. It was always like this with us.

The sexual tension so taut, waiting for one of us to snap.

Maybe that's the key to freedom.

I pushed up against him again, my breath hitching as his jean-clad bulge rubbed my clit. Fireworks were going off behind my lids. When I opened them again, I caught Dex looking like he was in a trance. Unable to stop myself, I rocked against his cock again, debating taking him up on his earlier offer. Our labored breathing played like a soundtrack.

Holy shit. Why didn't I dry hump more often?

I was supposed to be seducing *him*, yet here I was with my eyes fluttering closed, my nipples pebbling, and soaked leggings.

"Fuck. I haven't dry-humped a chick since I was like twenty." His tone was husky. I wanted to laugh at how similar our line of thinking was.

My lips parted. "If you untie me, I'll let you do more than dry-hump me, Dex."

The next moment his weight was gone, and I was left feeling…empty. My eyes flew open, trying to see where he'd gone. Fucker wasn't getting naked like I'd hoped. He was over by his bedroom door, a blank look that was a complete one-eighty from how he'd just looked at me.

"Nice try, Nikki. But I get plenty of pussy on my own. I'm not interested in filling yours if you're only looking to use me," he said with a wicked look as he walked back, bending over and sucking on one of my nipples through my bra, drawing an involuntary gasp from me before he bit down.

Hard.

Warm breath tickled the side of my face. "Just wanted to make sure you weren't faking being turned on. Bet your pussy is fucking weeping for me like last time. Now, tell me who he is," he demanded, swirling a painted black nail around the nipple he'd bitten.

A snarl that sounded more like an animal had made it came out of my mouth. "Fuck you."

"You just tried that. How about we do something else instead?" he asked, opening his bedside drawer. Inside was a literal *row* of vibrators, dildos, and I swore I saw multiple butt plugs, but it was hard to tell with my arm obstructing my view.

"Why the fuck do you have those?" I asked, my voice coming out huskier than normal.

"Why? Have you seen these sausage fingers? Great for filling a pussy. Not great for stimulating a clit gently. So, I provide a plethora of options for that." He smiled, proudly waving a hand across the selection, but my brain fixated on the whole *fingers filling a pussy* portion of his explanation. I was suddenly far too aware of how empty I was.

"Now, Nikki, why don't you tell me who that man is," he demanded, his voice dropping an octave, becoming deliciously deep.

A buzzing noise cut through my haze. I moaned in pleasure when vibrations hit my clit. Asshole was going to try and torture information out of me with orgasms.

"Who said I was going to let you orgasm?" He asked, making me realize my thoughts hadn't stayed in my mind like I'd intended.

"Fuck. You. Dex."

Each word was a struggle to get out. Moaning was the noise my mouth wanted to produce. I clamped my lips shut, not wanting to give Dex the satisfaction of my answers or the evidence of my pleasure.

His hazel eyes danced with anticipation. "Spitfire, I know you want my cock driving into this soaking pussy," he taunted, pressing two fingers against my core and pushing the damp spandex up inside me just slightly. A low, involuntary moan escaped my lips.

Fuck.

"But that's not what this playtime is about. I'm going to rip out every single one of his nail beds for the answers I want. So, why don't you give me his name and I'll let you tell me what questions you want answers to. Because he's going to be dead come sunrise," he finished.

Playtime. Fuck, why was it so hot when he said that. Focus, Nikki, he told you he'd kill Jardani.

There were things that I wanted to know, but I wanted to be the one there to ask them, and this fucker was going to keep me from that.

"Jardani," I breathed out. "His name is Jardani."

The pressure increased, rocketing me closer to the edge. I caught the shadow that rolled through his hooded eyes as he dipped his mouth next to my ear.

"I'll let you come if you tell me what your connection to him is."

My mind was foggy with lust, the need to find release messing with my resolve. I was up a fucking creek. I wanted to spill every secret, if only so he would run his hands up and down my body.

"Nikki," Dex growled when I still hadn't answered. "Normally, this would be the part of my *interview* where I'd cut off an appendage. But you'll need your fingers to fuck yourself later." He dragged his nose up the side of my throat, trailing up until he stopped by my ear. "So, let's try this instead."

The vibrations clicked up to a speed that bordered on painful. His fresh scent enveloped me, adding to the stimulation. I was seconds away from release when he pulled away.

"Bastard," I spat, earning me a full-fledged smile. He was enjoying this.

Without my permission, my eyes dipped to his crotch. He was *really* enjoying this. A finger lifted my chin, bringing my gaze to his face.

"Answers, spitfire."

I signed, knowing there was no getting out of answering. "I have some people who are after me." I looked him in the eyes.

All of Dex's teasing ceased, the room growing quiet other than the muffled sounds from downstairs. A deep crease appeared between his brows, and what looked like worry painted his face.

"Mario promised me to some people, and they are coming back to collect." The half-truth rolled off my tongue with ease. "I wanted to find out if they knew I was still in Tucson. I...I thought maybe they'd moved on, but then I got a note the other night. The night with the kid. *That* was the real reason I was shaken up. He was there to deliver a note," I said, chewing on my bottom lip.

Dex's face blanked and, without another word, he stormed toward the door.

"Wait," I called out, silk digging into my wrist as I tried to sit up to see him. Dex's hand stilled on the door, his body already halfway into the hall. "I think the Reapers are planning something. Jardani was meeting with the president and VP, saying something about a turf war..." I didn't want his club to end up ambushed. He gave a curt nod, raking down my body with a look I couldn't quite read before slamming the door behind him.

Leaving me tied to his bed.

"I fucking hate men," I yelled out after him, hearing the deep chuckle from the hall even through the closed door.

TWELVE
DEX

MY SKIN ITCHED, the rage bubbling beneath the surface like a physical demon trying to claw its way out of my solar plexus. If Mario wasn't already dead, I'd kill the fucker slowly and painfully. How *dare* he try and sell a woman, period—but to sell Nikki…

Chunks of cinder block scattered across the hall as I slammed the heavy metal door into the wall. Torque quirked a brow at the outburst, but otherwise remained silent. He knew better than to provoke me further. Smart man.

"He give you any trouble?" I asked as I entered the shed.

Calling it a shed was actually pretty deceiving. It was a concrete bunker big enough to fit all the brothers and their Old Ladies if needed. But there was one special wing where I did some of my best work.

The harsh, fluorescent lights bounced off white tiles that covered most surfaces, save for the special addition I'd wanted. Three-quarters of one wall consisted of a one-way mirror, allowing Pres to observe the interviews. But for the assholes who found themselves in my domain, it served a more macabre purpose. Who wouldn't want to look over and see the bloody fucking mess I'd made of them? It was my way of reminding them they had entered the darkest depths of hell.

The prick we'd taken from the Reapers' club was suspended from the hook in the ceiling. Jardani, according to Nikki. His shoulders were up by his ears, and the leather loafers he wore dangled a few inches above the floor. This was not going to be pleasant for him, especially if he was in the business of selling skin.

A small pool of blood had formed beneath him, the crimson liquid running down the side of his bare body. The image of Nikki using her stiletto to knock the man unconscious brought a smile to my face. There was no denying that she was a fierce and cunning woman, a deadly combination that made her a force to be reckoned with.

Upstairs, I knew the change in her demeanor wasn't because she wanted me. At least, that wasn't the sole motivation. Still, I'd allowed for a few blissful moments of her body against mine.

Torque's voice shook me out of my thoughts. "Naw. Nikki put him out cold. He woke up when I poured some cheap vodka over the gash, but the pain knocked him back out. She say anything about how she knew he was after her?"

I pinched the bridge of my nose, trying to piece together the puzzle. "Yeah, she said that some people Mario promised her to are after her."

"How did she know that? And how did she even find this guy?"

Both of those were good fucking questions. Ones I hadn't thought to ask, too busy being distracted by her perfect tits and how her nipples nearly popped out from the top of the cups. I sighed, realizing there were still many unanswered questions.

"I don't know," I bit out. "But Nikki's a resourceful woman. She must have her ways. We need to get more out of her when the time's right. Until then, let's focus on this asshole."

If Torque judged me for the misstep, he didn't let it show. He moved beside me, his eyes not moving from the unconscious body. Not everyone could handle torturing another human. It didn't make someone weak because they couldn't stomach the idea of blocking out the screams or the pleas for mercy. Honestly, Torque's reaction was a sign that he was more mentally stable than I was.

"You don't need to be in here, Torque," I said, moving toward the metal cabinet in the corner by the mirror. I'd left my cut back in the room. Blood managed to spray out in patterns and distances you weren't expecting. Spent a fucking fortune replacing clothes that got ruined in here. I reached back and gripped the collar of my shirt, pulling it off with one quick yank, revealing the tattooed canvas underneath.

"I need you to show me how to do that shit. Women love that trick." Torque's comment had me smirking. "And I've got to get used to this shit at some point, right?" He didn't sound overly confident about it.

The worn leather of my boots was soft against my callouses as I pulled them off before shucking off my jeans and placing everything on their designated shelf.

Torque let out a choked laugh. "Crocs? Seriously, Dex? And how the fuck did you find one of those dumbass sticker things in the shape of a bloody knife?"

I shot him a deadpan look. "First of all, they are called Jibbitz, you uncultured swine, and I ordered them special. Duh." In my peripherals, I caught the way Torque shook his head. Whether it was in approval or not, I didn't know, but it didn't matter because no one could tell me shit about my choice of footwear. "If these bad boys are good enough for doctors, then they sure as fuck are good enough for me."

A pained groan interrupted the conversation. Our guest was starting to stir.

"I've got a speaker for them coming too," I tacked on, winking at my brother as I moved toward my workbench. I kept this space neat and organized, like my room. The chaos in my brain and life was more than enough—I didn't need it reflected in other areas.

"Whatever you say." Torque's shoulder brushed against

mine. His face seemed a few shades paler than normal, and we hadn't even started yet.

"You sure you wanna be here for this?" I asked, concern in my voice.

A curt nod was all I received as a response. I wasn't the kid's mom, so if he wanted to stick around and risk blowing chunks all over, I wasn't going to stop him. I winced a little at the thought of the nightmares he was likely to have. The first one I'd watched still haunted my dreams.

Before I could slip into the memories of that desert hovel, I turned toward my subject, blanking my mind. When I was in this room, I was methodical and precise. The jokester everyone knew was shoved aside for the cold and calculated man who always lurked right under the surface.

"Find anything helpful on him?" I asked, noting the inky black art peppering his body. We had stripped him of his suit and tie, leaving him with nothing more than a pair of briefs. Some of the writing looked suspiciously like Cyrillic. The wolf tattooed on his neck triggered a distant memory just out of my reach. Under the unforgiving glare of the fluorescent lights, it became clear that he was likely in his thirties.

"He had a wallet. The name was different than the one Nikki gave you, so either it's fake, or he lied to her," Torque reported, crossing his arms as he joined me. I nodded in acknowledgment, circling around the man and noting several scars that looked suspiciously like knife wounds.

"No, she knows him. I don't know what the connection is, but I could tell from her expressions that there's a pile of shit she's not saying," I replied, my unease matching Torque's.

"And you wanna be a part of that?" Torque's question held no judgment, but it was clear he was uncomfortable with the situation.

I joined him again and sighed. "Don't think we have much of a choice," I said, looking him in the eye. "Nikki said the Reapers want this guy and whoever he's associated with to help them win a turf war."

Torque cursed under his breath. We both knew we were

getting pulled into this shit regardless of how Nikki worked into the mix.

I grabbed the smelling salts, shoving them under the brim of his nose. "Wakey, wakey, sunshine," I taunted as his eyes shot open.

"What the fuck," he yelled, his voice carrying a heavy accent. Eastern European of some sort—my money was on Russian.

Eyes frantically searched the room. I clocked the exact moment he realized he was in deep shit. The whimper he released when his attention dropped to his body was satisfying. He did seem momentarily relieved that all his limbs were still intact. For now.

"Glad you're awake." Angry red lines erupted where I dragged the edge of a serrated blade down his chest. "We've got much to talk about, you and I."

"I'm not telling you shit." Spittle flew from his mouth, hitting the painter's jumpsuit I'd put on.

They never wanted to share information right away. Without any preamble, I threw a right hook into his gut. The metal restraints clanked when he doubled over in pain.

"Fuck you," he coughed out, pulling against where his wrists were attached to a meat hook.

"No, thanks, you're not really my type."

Torque's laughter echoed from the corner he'd positioned himself in to enjoy the show.

"Huh. This whole time I thought you slept with anything that breathed," Torque quipped.

I flipped him off, ignoring his chuckles at my expense because we both knew *exactly* what my type was. She was currently strapped to my bed in silk restraints. Even at a time like this, she managed to make my dick stir to life with a single thought.

Jardani thrashed about like an idiot. All he would manage to do was tear some ligaments in his shoulders if he kept it up. He practically foamed at the mouth, like a rabid dog waiting to bite anyone who neared him, yelling out obscenities in multiple languages.

"They will kill you. Hunt you down like animals," he snarled, another wad of spit hitting my jumpsuit.

I give him five minutes before he pisses himself.

"First question, Jardani." Bushy eyebrows hit his hairline at the use of his name. "Why were you trying to grab the girl?" I asked, being sure I sounded as indifferent as possible. I didn't want him to know she meant anything to me—otherwise, he'd make it a point to keep that shit to himself.

If he was angry before, he now looked downright murderous. "Where is the fucking bitch?" he demanded, his voice dripping with venom.

Another pained groan fell from his lips as my fist met his flesh in the same spot as the first. His suffering sent a thrilling shiver up my spine. Fucking and fighting. For a while, those were the only two things that made me feel alive. Then I'd tried my hand at getting a man to spill all of his sworn secrets, and *that* took the cake.

I tutted my tongue at the comment, my fingers gripping his jaw hard enough to bruise. "Watch yourself, Jardani. I am not a patient man, and I've perfected getting the answers I need. What are the Reapers planning?" I asked, switching my line of questioning.

He squirmed, craning his neck, trying to track me as I moved to his blind spot. The tips of his shoes desperately tried to find traction, but they were a hair's breadth away from reaching the silver drain below.

"Answer the question," I said. Another punch collided with his flesh—this time, it landed by his liver. But his reaction wasn't what I'd anticipated. He laughed, his head falling forward.

My fingers slid through his greasy locks, gripping the shit-brown strands and wrenching his head back so he was forced to look at the bloodthirst swirling in my eyes. I wanted him terrified of me and what I'd do if he didn't tell me every fucking detail.

There was no terror, though. Instead, he wore a gloating smirk.

"You give me the girl, and I can ensure you and your club win this little skirmish. Because your rivals are working a deal to have you all exterminated with the aid of the Bratva." He turned his head to face the mirrored wall, yelling his next sentence. "You hear that, Mr. President. That's who's watching behind the glass, no? All we want is the girl. We have no loyalty to the Reapers. We're happy to be on your side."

Asshole looked me dead in the eyes and winked. He thought making a plea to my president would get him what he wanted. Problem was, he was fucking right. Worry made me tense up. Nikki wasn't my Old Lady. Fuck, she wasn't *anything* to me, period. If it came to a choice between her and the club, Pres wouldn't bat an eye. Her only saving grace in this moment was that Pres was still inside the clubhouse, but I was going to have to tell him about this shit eventually.

Without thought of the repercussions, I jammed the serrated blade into his hip. His scream was ear-piercing—the kind I loved to hear when in this room. Blood welled up around the hilt, running down and soaking the gra y fabric of his underwear.

Coppery tang lingered with the rancid scent of piss.

"There's something particularly brutal about a serrated blade being yanked out of the body. Now, why do you want her, and what do the Reapers have planned?" I leaned in close. His sweat and BO were almost unbearable as I whispered the next part. "Tell me what I want to know, and I'll kill you quickly. Otherwise, I'm going to make this so *incredibly* painful for you for a *long* time."

He fell silent, hanging his head so his chin rested against his heaving chest. Another ear-piercing shriek, loud enough to shatter glass, echoed as I yanked out the blade.

The shouts morphed into sobs. Neither of which were helpful to me.

"I'm going to start sawing off your ball sack, Jardani."

Another sob as the metal tip brushed his family jewels. "One. Two. Thr—"

"Because the Bratva always collects what is ours," he rushed out, contorting his body to move his balls away from my blade. "I don't know what the Reapers have planned. We didn't give a shit. They were supposed to collect the girl, and then we would provide them with firearms and bodies." He whimpered, his head lolling to one side. "They want Los Muertos gone too."

"Why?" Torque was now beside me, glaring down as he asked the question I'd been about to ask.

The Russian shook his head, sending snot flying everywhere. "I don't fucking know why. Only want the girl," he breathed out.

Jardani's response earned a menacing growl from me. "Wrong response."

Metal met soft flesh and I sliced into the sensitive skin. Mother Nature had real jokes, putting all our shit on the outside, leaving it vulnerable. He shouted in protest, thrashing about from the meat hook he was suspended by. He'd been reduced to a blubbering mess.

My next move was interrupted by the insistent vibrating of my phone against the metal shelf where I'd placed it. I wanted to ignore it, but it continued to vibrate over and over again.

"For fuck's sake," I muttered, storming over to the cabinet. I checked my phone and saw three missed calls, all from Gunner. Before I could call him back, it vibrated in my hand, this time with a different name: La Brujita.

"What the fuck, Ryan?" I began, but she cut me off.

"What the hell did you do to Nikki? Why is she calling me saying you're not letting her out of your room? That you locked her in there?"

I was caught off guard. "How the fuck did she get out of her restraints?" I muttered without thinking.

Ryan's yell was so loud that I had to pull the phone away from my ear before she blew out my eardrum. "Her what?!"

DEX

"YOU CAN'T BE PISSED at me. I tried to warn you, dude. Called three fucking times," Gunner said.

I stuck my tongue out at him from where I sat in one of Ryan's velvet office chairs.

"Oh, real mature, Dex."

"Oh, real mature, Dex," I mimicked, not giving a shit that I was being a child. "My balls are no longer my own. A scary short Latina now holds them," I mocked, crossing my arms over my chest. "You let her fuck you too? Okay, that one I get, who doesn't like a little ass play."

Gunner glared at me from where he leaned behind Ryan's desk.

Fuck, shit had changed from the last time we were in here together. If memory served me right, and it did, Ryan was the one leaning there and glaring at us. Now, I sat on this side of the desk, alone, and it was my own brother staring me down.

The door behind me opened, a secondary conversation floating through the space.

"You didn't mention anything about someone trying to *kidnap* you, Nikki." There was a fierce edge to Ryan's voice. A tone I'd heard her use before, but never on Nikki. Then again, when the four of us had been around each other, it was all drinking and partying. None of us had been really getting to *know* each other. Well, except Ryan and Gunner, that was.

Angry footfalls grew closer. "I didn't think it was important," Nikki bit out, plopping into the emerald chair beside me. Bare legs curled up, tucking underneath her. It pleased me way more than it should have that she was wearing my shirt. My eyes dipped to her nipples, wondering if the fabric would still show evidence of where I'd sucked on them.

"Narc," I whispered her way when she caught me staring. I savored how her blue eyes cut over to me, irritation flaring.

"You've said that already, Dex. About a hundred times on the way over here. Find something new to say." She flipped me off, facing forward once again.

When Ryan had called, they were only about thirty minutes outside of Tucson, and she'd ordered me to meet her at Lotería for this little chit-chat. I liked her, but I wasn't fucking her, so I sure as shit didn't take orders from her. Only reason I was here was to share what I'd learned. I had some questions for Nikki, too.

Jardani's words played over in my mind. Everything was about to go to shit, and Nikki had managed to get herself smack dab in the middle. I rubbed my chest. There was a twinge every time I thought about something happening to her. But she'd made it *crystal clear* she didn't want my help.

Ryan lowered into the chair behind the desk. Dark circles rimmed her coffee-colored eyes, and her inky hair was piled up on top of her head. It looked like she'd been raking her hands through it. Truthfully, she looked fucking exhausted, making me wonder what went down during her time in Sinaloa.

"You look like shit, Ryan." My comment gained me a scolding look from Gunner and a middle finger from her.

"Yeah, well, fuck you too," she said. Her head popped up, looking between Nikki and me, pointing a long nail at us. I wondered how she gave Gunner handjobs with those claws.

"We fuck, Dex. If he wants a hand, he can use his own," she responded to my apparently not-so-silent question.

I shrugged a shoulder at the glare still coming my way from Gunner. He should have been used to the shit that came from my mouth by now. I didn't know why he was looking at me like I'd pissed in his beer.

"Okay. Someone fucking explain to me what the fuck happened tonight," Ryan commanded. The hair on the back of my neck stood on end, but not because I was intimidated. Authority Issues was my honorary middle name, and she was running dangerously close to setting me off.

In my peripherals, I caught Nikki pursing her lips. Silence grew between the four of us.

Trouble in paradise for the best friends?

Interesting. I'd thought those two told each other everything from their favorite foods to their shit schedules. I cleared my throat, the heavy silence unsettling, knowing that we needed to address the situation sooner or later.

"Nikki sent out the distress signal tonight." I turned in my chair to face the woman of the hour. "Which, by the way... How did you know that he would be at the Reaper club? And did you know he wanted to take you beforehand?"

Ryan stood so quickly that I thought we were under attack, but she was just royally pissed.

"Where the fuck *were* you? And what the hell do you mean someone wanted to *take* her?" she asked, her eyes landing on me.

Nikki quirked an eyebrow at Ryan, but her anxiety was evident as her pink tongue darted out, tracing her full bottom lip before nervously tugging it between her teeth. "Sorry, *Mom,* I didn't realize I needed to tell you my every move," Nikki said pointedly. "And Ryan's not the only one who's got connections." Their eyes met, and a million unspoken words flowed between them.

Yeah. There's more to this shit than they're letting on.

I felt marginally better when Gunner's face was screwed up in suspicion too. At least I wasn't the only one in the dark here. I kicked a booted foot up on Ryan's desk, ignoring her bitching about getting dirt on it. I was tired as fuck, and were rolling into the early hours of the morning.

Clapping my hands to gain everyone's attention, I launched straight into the shitstorm we were about to find ourselves in. "Okay, I don't have time for this. Here's what I know: the Russians want Nikki…badly."

Her blonde bun careened to the side as she whipped her head toward me. She didn't need to speak for me to know she wanted to skewer my balls. I had to cover my laughter with a cough. Her anger was adorable, but if I told her that, she'd find one of Ryan's stashed knives and stab me.

"How do you know that?" she demanded, folding her toned arms under her breasts. The move accentuated the fact that she wasn't wearing a bra, and like a fucking teenager who'd never seen boobs before, my dick jumped at the thought of her nipples touching my shirt.

I can never wash that now. I'm gonna fuckin' use it as a pillowcase.

I smirked, loving her ire and needing a distraction from the shitstorm we were all in. "Jardani clued me in. Reapers are supposed to trade you. In exchange, the Russians will help take Los Muertos and us out." Nikki blanched at the statement. "Wanna share with the class why they want you so badly?" I asked, an edge in my tone.

Nikki could keep her childhood secrets, but if anything in her past put my club in danger, I needed to know that shit. I had a duty as club enforcer to protect us from threats, even if the threat came from a five-six blonde spitfire who clobbered men with her heels.

"What are you saying, Dex?" Gunner asked, now resting his hands on the top of the desk. He'd moved closer to Ryan, shielding her with his body. Ryan's eyes hadn't left Nikki until now—now, they were staring me down.

"They want the territory," Ryan whispered.

I nodded, confirming her suspicion with my own, noting she'd yet to demand Nikki answer my question about why the Russians might want her. Nikki was gorgeous—stop you in your tracks gorgeous—but offering to send weapons and bodies in exchange for one woman? Yeah, that wasn't your run-of-the-mill skin trade agreement.

Nikki was worth a lot to them for some reason.

The woman in question looked like she was mentally a million miles away. Her thumbnail found her mouth, and she started gnawing on it. Irritation started crawling up my spine. There was something else going on here, and it didn't look like the girls were going to fill us in—or not me, at least.

Clearly, I was not part of the group.

Which was fucking fine with me. I could go back to my bed and fuck my hand till I fell asleep. Tonight, I'd tell Pres what I'd learned, and we'd decide what action the club would take. I wasn't part of Los Muertos anyway, so they could do whatever the fuck they wanted, and they didn't have to tell me jack shit about it.

But I wasn't going to stay and feel like an outcast.

I pushed myself up out of the chair, ignoring the three sets of eyes on me as I turned to leave. "Alright, this has been fun. Try not to get kidnapped again, Nikki, and we've got church tonight, Gunner. Try and act like you wanna be a part of the club."

As I reached for the doorknob, I heard some commotion behind me. "Wait, Dex," Ryan called out.

I glanced back over my shoulder, my hand hovering over the door handle. "What is it, Ryan?"

She was standing, her arms crossed, a look of irritation on her face. "You can't just leave," she said.

Now I was pissed. I could do whatever the hell I wanted. I sure as fuck knew I didn't *want* to sit in here and be left in the dark. I might play the part of a golden retriever, but I was no one's fucking dog. They weren't going to get me to lie at their fucking feet and wait for scraps of information. A familiar pang of betrayal hit me in the chest when Gunner remained silent. The fact that *he* wasn't demanding that they fill me in hurt, opening up an old wound between us.

I refused to look at him.

Let him feel the cold shoulder from me.

"And why the fuck not, Ryan? Because, clearly, the two of you don't want to share what the fuck is going on. I can see you both know more about why they want her, but you're not saying shit. I just happened to be the convenient person standing by to come to the rescue. I'm not going beg for y'all to fucking fill me in."

"She doesn't know the details," Nikki piped up, her blue eyes lit with fire. "Listen, them wanting me is less of the problem here, right? So, some Russian guy wants to collect on a bad deal from Mario. The focus should be on taking down the Reapers." Nikki spoke confidently, her chin raised high as she locked eyes with Ryan, but there was a stiffness in her body that told another story.

She was worried. I just wasn't sure about what.

"They clearly want you badly, Niks." Ryan shifted her attention back to me. "Which is why I need you to stay. I need you to be Nikki's bodyguard."

A humorless laugh left Nikki's pouty lips. "Excuse me? I'm not Princess Diana. Rest in peace." I chuckled despite myself when she traced the symbol of a cross over her chest before continuing on. "I don't need a bodyguard. I need a massage and a bottle of wine."

Another silent conversation flowed between the two friends.

The damn pull I felt for Nikki kept me rooted in place to hear out Ryan's proposal.

"Your boy toy would probably give you a better rate," I said, crossing my arms over my chest to keep from flipping him off.

Ryan grimaced, peeking over at Nikki, and I swore she braced her body like she was preparing for a blow. "Yeah, well, I need someone to stay *with* Nikki, twenty-four-seven."

"Should he wipe my ass too? Come on, Ryan, this is ridiculous," Nikki protested, throwing her arms in the air.

"Nikki, the Reapers don't know we have Jardani, so they are going to continue with their plan. They're going to come after you." Ryan stared her down—the expression on her face said she was daring Nikki to protest the facts she'd just laid out.

I covered my face with a hand to hide my smirk when Nikki pouted and gave a small, "Fine." It was a talent to lace that much attitude into a single syllable, but she'd managed it.

The two BFF s were clearly going through a rocky spot. It was something that Nikki and I had in common at the moment.

Love and relationships? Fuck them. This situation only reaffirmed my belief that they were nothing but trouble. I hadn't realized how bad it was for friendships too.

I was never getting involved with a woman other than in the sheets.

FOURTEEN
NIKKI

I SANK down into the chair, irritated that I was here having this conversation and not snuggled up in bed pretending my life was all sunshine and roses. "Nikki, you can be pissed at me all you want, but we both know there's been a *lot* of shit that's gone down lately," Ryan said.

Dex's hands clasped onto the back of my chair, his fingers lightly brushing along my shoulders. It sent a thrill up my spine, a reaction I tried to suppress, even as I found myself leaning into him ever so slightly.

"What's the plan?" Dex's usual cheerful tone had vanished, replaced by a seriousness that felt cold and detached. "Are we all just going to sit around with our thumbs up our asses playing house? The guy was pretty clear: the Reapers want blood and territory. Nikki, here, is their bargaining chip. The bastard even offered me help if we handed her over. We need to take these guys down and then deal with the Russians, apparently." He slammed his hand on the chair, making me flinch, and muttering, "Dammit."

My palms were screaming for me to stop digging my nails into them, more with every word Dex spoke.

"Dex," Gunner growled out.

"No, don't you fucking 'Dex' me, Gunner. Just because you don't take the club seriously doesn't mean I don't," Dex said, pointing at his MC brother. The corners of Gunner's mustache pulled down into a frown.

"That's not fa—" Gunner tried to protest.

Dex cut him off, his voice growing louder. "Not fair? Listen, I'm grateful you stepped in when you did for me, but let's not fucking act like you *wanted* to live like an outlaw." Dex's muscled arm brushed by my ear as he gestured to Ryan. "It wasn't until her that you even committed to it."

The tension in the room ratcheted up even higher. It felt as if we were a powder keg waiting for the spark that would send us all into a fiery blaze. I peeked up at Dex, careful not to draw too much attention to my observation of him. My angle only allowed me to see his arms, but the straining tendons of his forearms and the whitening of his knuckles painted a pretty clear picture: there was a lot of baggage between these two.

When he spoke again, his voice had dropped to a growl, carrying a menacing undertone that sent a chill down my spine. Even Ryan appeared concerned, uncertain if this heated confrontation would escalate into a full-blown brawl.

Gunner's words were laced with threat. "Be *very* fucking careful with what you wanna say next. Do you really want to air our dirty laundry? Maybe talk about your history with the Russians?" A flash of regret crossed Gunner's face the second the words slipped out. He broke eye contact, looking away in shame. "I'm sorry, Dex. That was a low blow."

The warmth from Dex's body disappeared, and when I turned to find where he'd gone, he was all the way to the door leading back into Lotería. "No hard feelings," he said. The words were the complete opposite of his tone.

That sounds like a lot of hard fucking feelings to me…

"Nikki." I jumped at Dex's bark. "Let's go. Your ass is now my problem, apparently. Ryan, I'll send you my price. You can fuckin' wire it to me."

The door slam was like a gunshot in the quiet room. No one moved for several seconds.

"Fuck," Gunner called out, slapping his hands on the

desk. I was surprised when the wooden top didn't splinter under the impact.

"I've gotta go after him," he said, already moving toward the door.

Ryan released a deep sigh, her head falling into her hands. My stomach turned at her reaction. She was always collected, never letting anyone see the chinks in her armor—no one other than Gunner, that is . Even when we'd been attempting to escape Mario, she'd been strong.

But now, sitting her, she looked…worn.

I wet my lips, racking my mind for what to say. All the emotions from earlier were still turning in my gut, but watching her look so close to falling apart had me tucking them away to focus on her.

Another sign that you need to get the fuck out of here. You're too close. You c are too much.

Ignoring the warning bells, I scooched closer to the desk, reaching a comforting hand her way. "Hey, maybe we all take a breather, yeah?" I said, giving a squeeze.

Ryan's head popped up, and dark brown eyes searched mine. "He shouldn't have said that."

"Said what?" I prodded. I didn't have a clue which man she was talking about. The verbal brawl between the two felt evenly matched, with both saying some pretty coded shit to one another.

She pulled away, turning her head toward the wall of glass, but clearly not really *seeing* anything on the other side. "This is your ex who's after you, huh?" she asked, changing the subject.

My body stiffened. Damn, I almost wished I was drunk for this chat, but then I'd probably let too much slip. "Yeah. I wanted to find out how Mario even found out about my past. Turns out they were looking for information on me," I said as she studied my face. "But when I asked my contact about it, the timeline matched up with when all that shit went down with Mario. Kinda figured it was old news," I shrugged a shoulder, pulling at the stray threads on Dex's shirt.

"But?" Ryan asked, knowing I was leaving out key information.

I looked up, locking eyes with the woman who'd become as close as family. I worked on memorizing her features, because I didn't plan on sticking around much longer, especially now.

"But then someone showed up at Lotería with a note for me. It had my name." Panic welled up inside me at the memory, causing my throat to constrict.

Ryan's voice, tinged with confusion, cut through my distress. "I don't understa—"

"My *birth name*, Ryan," I muttered a curse when she continued to look puzzled. I'd forgotten that she didn't know. "Nikki isn't my name. At least not the name that I was given. *No one* here knows that name. It—"

"Was sent as a message," she cut in. "He knows you're still here. But why not grab you then?"

"One, he's not an idiot—he knows it's a cartel club. And two, he's playing with me. He's got the Reapers doing his dirty work, so he's never directly involved or linked," I answered.

"Then why the fuck would you fight me on having Dex watch over you?" she demanded, her frustration evident.

This was where she and I were different. Ryan didn't know what it felt like to be caged, to have decisions made *for* her. Even when she was under Mario's thumb, it was a choice. She'd chosen not to rock the boat of her life, dealing with that narcissistic asshole until he'd threatened the ones she loved.

She didn't understand what this meant for me.

"Because I don't want to be someone's burden, Ryan," I said, my voice laced with irritation. "I want to handle my own shit."

Ryan leaned in closer, her tone sincere. "Nikki, it's not about you being a burden. It's about having people watching your back. That isn't a sign of weakness."

I looked away, still feeling a sense of frustration. "I get

that, but it feels like I'm losing my independence, my free-dom. I've already had that shit happen once, Ryan. I'm not being placed back in a box."

She offered a small smile, coming to stand in front of her desk. "Nikki, there's *no one* who would be able to place you in a box, girl. You are fierce, intelligent, and frankly, downright scary when you want to be. We're a family, and families look out for each other. I care, and I'm here to support you—not control you."

Too bad family was who'd locked me away last time, too...

But maybe family had nothing to do with the blood that ran through our veins. Maybe Ryan was right and family really did look after one another.

I nodded, exhaustion taking a toll on me. I was ready to be done with this conversation.

Hell, this day.

Maybe she knew better. Maybe letting people in wasn't a weakness. Or maybe I was making a huge mistake by staying even a little while longer.

"I'll try to remember that," I said, slapping on a soft smile.

FIFTEEN
DEX

A DASH OF EMOTIONAL AVOIDANCE, PER USUAL

"DEX. Dex! Fuck, I'm sorry, man," Gunner called out from behind as I took the stairs two at a time.

I spun on my heel when I hit the bottom step, driving my finger into his chest. "I would, and have, taken a bullet for you, Gunner. Don't fuckin' leave me in the dark now. I thought we were past this shit when you joined the Skeletons."

He looked off to the side, sucking in air through his teeth before blowing it out and facing me. "It was a low blow. I'm sorry. I just thought you'd want to be in on this since the Russians are involved."

I scoffed. "Not every Russian is responsible fo—"

"But this one is," he cut in. His green eyes pinned me in place, the words hitting like a punch to the gut.

"How do you know?" I asked, unable to hide the shake in my voice.

Gunner studied my face, searching for something. It was the same look he'd given me the night he'd picked me up from the jail cell in Huachuca City. Without answering, he pushed past me, heading straight for the empty bar and grabbing two lowball glasses, offering one to me as I followed behind.

"I thought I found him three years ago, too, Gunner, and

look where that got us. Where it got you," I said pointedly, throwing back the finger's worth of whiskey.

The burning of the alcohol mixed with the burning of guilt in my gut. I was the reason Gunner wasn't off being Captain America for the FBI. Sure, my fuck up was the reason he'd met Ryan, and his eyes were open now to how much good the Skeletons did, but there was always this nag at the back of my mind, wondering if I'd failed him too, by dragging him down into the mud.

Guilt over nearly killing a man had never kept me up at night.

Failing the people I loved was the demon that did.

A firm hand landed on my shoulder, pulling me back. "Don't you go there, Dex. That night, the bastard got what he deserved. More justice than Uncle Sam would have handed out, and I would make the choice to come for you over and over again until I died. Because that's what brothers do, and that's what you'd do for me. Hell, you fucking ran into a club riddled with cartel members to save the woman I wasn't supposed to fall in love with."

I didn't know what to do with all this. Emotions made me uncomfortable, and my fallback was always humor, but in this moment...part of me didn't want to push the feelings away. Seconds ticked by as we just stood there staring at one another before I finally gave a curt nod.

"Alright, let's cut the sappy shit now. You know it makes me wanna puke," I said, smiling when Gunner barked out a laugh. "Now, how do you know this asshole after Nikki is the same one?"

Gunner sobered at the question, folding his arms across his chest and shifting into professional mode. "Scar looked into Mario's phone records after all the shit went down. Ryan needed to know what else he had cooking, and who the potential enemies were. One number stood out because it was the same number as the man Scarletta killed back in New York: Maxim. Guess he was the right-hand man of the *leader* of the St. Petersburg Bratva."

"Fuck," I yelled out, rubbing my hands through my hair to avoid throwing the glass across the room. All the aggression I'd worked out in the shed was back.

After Gunner had bailed me out of jail for beating a man within an inch of his life, he'd used his connections to help find me some answers when it came to Kell. Turned out he'd been looking for them, too, even when I thought he'd abandoned me. It was slow going—all we knew was that the Russians were heavily involved with the skin trade, and up at the tip of the pyramid was the St. Petersburg faction.

And now, we found ourselves entrenched with these assholes. Maybe god *was* real, because I'd given up on ever exacting revenge on the top assholes running the trafficking ring.

"Gets better. Turns out, the same man runs the Circle…"

"You're telling me the Bratva and the Circle are the same thing?" I asked, trying to wrap my head around all this shit.

Gunner poured us both another shot and threw it back. "Yes and no. The head asshole runs both organizations. Buddy back at the FBI did me a solid, probably the last one I'll get. The Bratva used to be under the Circle's thumb, too." His eyes cut over to me. "Until there was a hostile take-over."

"Dammit. That's who's after Nikki?" I asked, rubbing my forehead in frustration. "Why the fuck does he want her?"

"No clue, but fuckers like that have their own set of rules. He might just be pissed that Mario promised him women and then never delivered."

Or she has a tie to them somehow?

Jardani's words echoed in my mind. "Where's Nikki from?" I asked.

Gunner shook his head, shrugging his shoulders. "Fuck if I know. I always assumed she was from here."

I'd met Nikki the first night we'd shown up to Lotería, when we'd shoved our feet so far down our throats they were coming out our assholes. She was downright beautiful, with her golden hair haloed around a heart-shaped face, and lips that taunted me every time she spoke. It was her eyes, though, that had caught my attention. Those cornflower blue eyes held so much attitude and confidence it made my dick hard, but lingering in the background was a vulnerability she tried her damnedest to hide, and from the moment she smiled up at me, I had the strangest urge to convince her to let me in.

Instead, she'd only pushed me away.

"Why he wants her doesn't really matter. What matters is the fact that he does, and we have to fucking deal with the Reapers," Gunner said when I'd been quiet for too long.

"Going at them will start a war," I said, my mind running through all the potential outcomes. Every single one of them was bloody.

"A war is what they want anyway. We might as well be the first to strike."

My fists hit the marble top. "And how the fuck does that solve the situation with the Russians and Nikki?"

Gunner swirled the last little bit of his drink, staring into it as if it would provide him with answers. "Listen, I think we have to solve this in sections. First, we deal with the Reapers—seems that's who the Russians hired anyway, so we take out that threat." His face turned toward me. "Then we deal with the Russians. Hell, I'm hoping they decide collecting the women they were promised isn't worth it, and Nikki will be left alone."

My instincts were screaming at me that there was more going on with Nikki and the Russians. I just didn't know what that was.

But I would find out.

Whether she wanted me to or not.

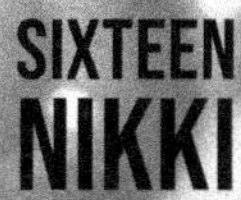

EAT ME OUT AND FUCK ME GOOD— THAT'S ALL I CARED ABOUT

"WHAT THE HELL did you put in here?" Dex asked, his voice strained as he carried one of my boxes up the stairs of a nondescript apartment complex.

I rolled my eyes, pressing my thumb to a discrete pad on an otherwise normal-looking door. "Don't be a pussy. It's not even that heavy." It had been a little more than twenty-four hours since I was given my sentence of round-the-clock babysitting. Ryan and I'd had an epic argument ending in three rounds of rock-paper-scissors to determine *when* I had to enter Dex's custody.

I won.

Mainly because I'd cheated—Ryan had a clear tell every time she was about to throw out paper. Bought myself a few hours of freedom. Kind of. Ryan only conceded because I'd agreed to stay at Lotería and sleep on an air mattress in the office, and then I'd worked as normal that night. But now here I was, moving into some random apartment with a giant tatted biker who continued to grumble behind me.

The door swung open, revealing a sparse apartment. The entryway was about two feet of linoleum, barely big enough for Dex's big ass feet. The flooring transitioned right into carpet and the living room kitchen combo. I moved farther into the space, peeking around the breakfast bar that at least gave a little bit of separation, and let out a sigh of relief when I saw they'd put linoleum in the kitchen, because I'd been seriously worried that the beige shag continued in there.

"Dammit." Dex's outburst had me turning around, looking for danger or…something. He looked like someone kicked his puppy, with slumped shoulders and honest-to-god pout. "That wall isn't big enough for an eighty-inch television."

It took my brain a moment to come back online because, surely, he wasn't throwing a tantrum, as a grown-ass man, over a television.

"What the hell could you possibly need to see on eighty inches." I regretted my question as soon as I saw his frown transform into a smirk. "Nope. Nope. I do *not* want to hear what your answer is for that. I've heard too many of your freaky sex stories. I can imagine what you want to watch on that size of a TV," I said, crossing my arms in the air, hoping the giant 'X' would ward off his freak-tales.

He scoffed, dropping my box on the sofa so he could put his hands on his hips. "What freaky sex stories have you heard?"

"Oh, I don't know," I said, moving down the singular hallway that I assumed led to the bedrooms and bathrooms. "The one that, like, cosplayed as an Australian bird or some shit?"

The bark of laughter from behind me was contagious, and I fought cracking up with him.

"She wasn't pretending to be a bird. She told me to attack her pussy like a magpie."

"What the fuck does that even mean?" I called back, coming to the first of three doors.

"Didn't ask. Didn't care."

I shook my head at his logic, but I couldn't say shit because, honestly, I took the same approach when fucking someone. We weren't together to get to know each other.

Eat me out and fuck me good—that's all I cared about.

Dex's voice bounced off the walls of the sparse apartment.

"Also, you're one to talk. Didn't you fuck a guy because you needed a bank account?" I winced at the accusation. He had no clue how close he was to the truth. I hadn't done that *yet*, but only because I wasn't interested in storing my money in any of the traditional places.

I walked through the first door. "Not a banker. He was some finance asshole, and I needed help with my stocks." Another round of Dex's laughter sounded from the living room.

"What's his name? I may need his help," Dex teased.

I flicked on the light switch, taking in the bathroom. It looked like it had been renovated at some point. The vanity was on the smaller side, but that didn't matter. What I cared about was the giant glass shower that looked to have two showerheads and body spray.

"He was shit in bed," I called out loud enough to be heard over the opening and closing of kitchen cabinets. "Plus, Ryan ran him off with a gun while looking like an extra from a horror movie."

"He couldn't find your clit?"

The corners of my lips pulled up in a smirk. This conversation was a mirror image to the one I'd had with Ryan the night said encounter happened.

"Not even if I shoved his face where I wanted him," I said, moving on from the bathroom to find the bedrooms, hoping to snag the better one before Dex finished whatever the fuck he was doing. We'd been pretending that everything was normal since the meeting. Neither of us mentioned the elephant in the room. The most either of us had spoken about it was when I asked why we weren't staying at the clubhouse. Dex had grumbled about not wanting to fight off a pack of rabid animals every time I wanted into a room. My apartment was out, too. We'd gone with the assumption that the Reapers knew where I lived, and if they didn't, they'd be working on it.

So here we were, in some random safe house that Los Muertos owned.

I knew the questions were coming though. Dex would eventually tire of waiting on me to tell him why the Russians wanted me and demand answers. I just wasn't sure I'd still be around to answer him.

The first room was pretty basic: a single window that looked out over the parking lot, its faded curtains drawn back to allow the natural light to filter in. A queen bed with neatly-tucked sheets took up the center, flanked by cheap night-stands sporting aged table lamps. As much as I wanted the shower, it looked like the hall bathroom was for this bedroom. I hoped the main bedroom's ensuite was renovated too, because I could definitely put the detachable head to use. The last door was across the way, which wasn't ideal. I'd have rather been on the other side of the apartment from my unwanted roommate, but I really didn't have a say.

"What the fuck?"

Loud footfalls come barreling down the hall. "What happened, Nikki?"

"That's what fucking happened," I shouted at him, pointing at the door I'd just swung open, noting the fact that he had his gun drawn. The scent of leather and cologne hit me as he stepped closer, peering into the open door. He smelled so good I had to resist leaning in and rubbing my nose along the collar of his white T -shirt. Maybe I could convince him to do my laundry— my whites never looked that crisp.

"You don't like the hall closet?" he asked, clearly confused as he searched for what it was that could have caused my outburst.

"No. I don't like the hall closet that should be another bedroom," I said, crossing my arms and stomping my foot like a child. The irony wasn't lost on me that I had just been commenting about Dex throwing a fit. But my complaint was *much* more serious.

"What do you..." He crossed the hall, disappearing into the bedroom. The *only* bedroom. Before popping back out and barging into the bathroom. All while I stayed rooted.

"There's only one fucking bathroom, too." His shout echoed off the tiles, and then there was a muffled conversation. "Am I supposed to stay in the apartment next to her?" I overheard him say.

Please, god, let that be the case.

Maybe Ryan had forgotten to mention that we were going to be neighbors, not roommates. I mean, that could work. He would be right next door, and I could shout for help if something went down. Hell, I'd even let them put one of those puppy cam things if it meant I got some breathing room. Tension in my neck caused me to close my eyes and roll my head from side to side as I dug into the tissue with my fingertips, trying to work out the knots that riddled that area.

I needed to sit.

I looked one more time, as if the closet would magically transform into a bedroom, before making my way into the living room. It might not have been the furniture I'd have selected, but the couch was pretty damn comfortable.

Dancing was tough on the body, and all the extra stress from the last few months wasn't helping. My sleep was shit, my eating was shit, and I desperately needed a massage. A soft moan slipped out when I hit a particularly tender spot, but the relief was short-lived when I heard the clearing of a throat close by.

When I opened my eyes again, Dex was staring me down with an expression I couldn't quite read, which quickly morphed into one I knew well. He was pissed.

"Well, spitfire, turns out we're sharing a one-bedroom, one-bath." All I could do was gawk at him as he plopped beside me. Surely, he was fucking with me. "What's your shitting schedule? Because that could be a real problem if we take our morning shits at the same time," he said.

I pinched the bridge of my nose. Everyone who said *calming breaths* helped was a damn liar because they weren't doing shit to help me avoid a breakdown. "That's what you're concerned about? What about the whole where the fuck are we both going to sleep?" I waved my hand between us to emphasize the fact that there were two people here with only one bed, as Dex didn't seem to understand that part.

His face scrunched in confusion. "What do you mean? It's not like the bed is a twin. Both of us will fit in it," he said, leaning back and propping his feet up on the worn coffee table. You'd think the cartel could afford to have some nicer fucking apartments, but beggars couldn't be choosers, and in all fairness, I'd stayed in a lot worse since my fall from grace.

The first night I'd slept on a park bench and woke up to someone digging through my backpack. Luckily, they'd only taken the few dollars I had left and didn't find my forged identification. I'd never had to think about hiding or watching after my things before. My father was a formidable figure in the Bratva. No one would dream about stealing any of his things- or his daughter's.

"Earth to Nikki. Come in, Nikki," Dex called out, waving a hand in front of my face. I'd zoned out and hadn't even noticed Dex move in closer. He sat facing me, his arm stretched across the back of the couch, our bodies inches from touching. "Listen, don't worry about the bed thing. I'll sleep out here on the couch, okay?"

My heart clenched at the genuine expression on his face. "Are you sure?" I asked, eyeing him and the sofa, trying to determine if it was even long enough for him to fit on it.

"Yeah, don't worry about it," he said, pushing my hand away from my neck and replacing it with his. "Here, turn that way. You're not going to find any relief doing that yourself."

Of course, my brain instantly turned his words sexual, thinking of all the *other* ways he could help me find relief. We'd already made some unspoken pact that we wouldn't cross that line.

But we can get close, right?

Thank god my back was to Dex, so he couldn't see my eyes rolling back when he gripped my hips and pulled me closer, but there was no stopping the groan when his strong fingers worked their magic on the knots in my neck. I struggled to resist the urge to lean into his touch.

His dark chuckle wrapped around me, shooting straight to my clit. "You like that?" he asked, his breath brushing my ear. "Tell me what you want, spitfire. Harder? Deeper? Faster?"

He was fucking with me, but I didn't even care because the sensation of his skilled hands kneading my tense muscles sent shivers down my spine— soothing and electrifying. I tried to maintain my composure, but every stroke made it increasingly difficult to resist melting into his body.

"Holy fuck," I breathed out, my nipples pebbling when he wove a hand into my hair. The combination of the pads of fingers digging into my scalp and the slight pull of the strands was—orgasmic. I desperately tried to bring up my mental list of all the reasons it was a bad idea to hop on his dick, but was coming up blank.

Then, as suddenly as it'd started, it stopped.

"Now, let's go get the rest of your shit," he said, patting my leg before standing and heading out of the apartment. His long fingers had brushed the inside of my thigh since the shorts I wore covered next to nothing. The contact was like a brand on my skin.

My hair slapped me in the face as I attempted to shake off the horniness thrumming through me, and then Dex ruined all of my efforts when he walked back in with a stack of boxes and a bare chest.

"Want me to put these in your room?" he asked, completely ignorant to the fact that I was seconds away from climbing him like a tree. Thankfully, the boxes were hiding the majority of his muscled body.

All I could do was nod.

I groaned when he turned and walked down the hall. Why did he have to have a sexy back? A sexy, tattooed back. I peeked between the fingers covering my face, cursing that decision the moment I noticed how well his jeans hugged his ass. God, this was going to be awful.

I needed to fuck someone before I ended up fucking my roommate.

DEX

FUCK. WE WERE BOTH FUCKED UP, WEREN'T WE?

"NIKKI, what the fuck is taking you so long?" I yelled loud enough for her to hear down the hall and through her closed door.

I opened the cabinet above the fridge, hoping to score.

Would it be frowned upon if I drank my weight in tequila tonight? I let out a humorless chuckle. Ryan would beat my ass if I was drunk on my new *job*, and Nikki…she'd run away. The look of determination in her beautiful blue eyes told me everything I needed to know. That woman was biding her time, but she wasn't going to be locked down. I had to be just as worried about her *leaving* as someone taking her.

"Dammit," I muttered when there was nothing but dust in the cabinet.

There was no going back on this shit, either. After the meeting with Ryan and all of them, I had to go deliver all the news to Pres at church. The vote was unanimous for me to take the security detail, and they didn't vote that way because they were concerned for Nikki. Well, maybe Gunner's and Torque's votes were for that reason, but everyone else? No, they wanted someone from our club close to Nikki since she seemed to be the coveted prize.

My fist curled thinking about the look on Boe's face when I'd mentioned what Jardani had said about partnering with us instead if we gave her over. The wheels were fucking turning in that slimy bastard's mind. The whole point of an MC brotherhood was unwavering trust, but that fucker made my gut turn.

"Nikki," I yelled again. I felt…confined, and needed out of this damn shitty apartment.

It'd been a few hours since we moved our shit in. I'd brought a few things over, mainly clothes, thankfully, since the only place I had to store my stuff was a hall closet.

A closet that was supposed to be another bedroom.

Fucking chewed Gunner's ass for that little oversight. How did the cartel not have a safe house with two bedrooms? In their defense, the point of a safe house was to lay low. You weren't supposed to stay in one place for too long, because if someone was watching you, constantly moving was the move.

Or killing the fuckers.

Which was the problem, in Nikki's case. We were barely tiptoeing around an all-out war with the Reapers, so I couldn't just take all those fuckers out for Nikki.

I rubbed at my chest, scowling at the fact that, once again, I had the urge to do just that, despite the fact that it would put my brothers in deep shit. I'd chucked up the reaction to wanting to protect a woman since I wasn't able to save—

"Fuck." I slammed my palms down on the chipped formica, rattling the overmount sink riddled with watermarks. The sting helped distract me from where my thoughts were headed. I didn't think about Kelly anymore.

I couldn't.

Not unless I wanted to slip back into that twenty-something *kid* who sat drunk out of his mind under the freezing stream of the shower, hoping it was enough water to drown him. Only reason I was still here was Gunner.

I was fucking babysat every minute of every day for weeks after I got the phone call from Kelly. He'd made sure I didn't have access to a firearm, either. It was touch and go there in the beginning. Her disappearance weighed on me like a fucking pile of bricks. The self-loathing took a pretty quick turn into rage and hatred for authority figures once it became clear the fuckers weren't going to do a goddamn thing to try and save her.

When Greyson had joined the Feds after our contracts were up it'd felt like a slap in the face. He'd said he wanted in so he could make a real difference. So others wouldn't experience what I had.

I'd given him a black eye.

Told him he was fucking delusional to think they were anything but rats. And then we didn't speak. He'd run off to be a white knight, and I went and became the thing he'd hated: a criminal. Then, one night I'd had to call him from a fucking cell in the middle of nowhere while a trigger-happy deputy loomed over me. Told him I needed his help, or I'd go away for attempted murder. The law didn't fucking care that the man I'd beaten was the fucker who'd sold Kell to the Russians.

"Dex?" A soft voice cut through the chaos swirling in my mind. I blinked a few times as I looked up at her, clearing the remaining dredges of the memories. Blonde curls framed a heart-shaped fresh face. Her blue eyes were fixed on me, and I swore she looked concerned. I wanted fucking badly to be the one sucking on her berry-colored bottom lip.

Something about the way she stood there in an oversized shirt that read, "I'm late because I don't want to be here," felt like a ray of sunshine breaking through the clouds threatening to close in.

"You…You okay?" she asked, looking around like she might spot what was bothering me.

I forced a smile, a skill I'd mastered over time. "Yeah, girl. Just worried about you being late for work," I said, glancing over my shoulder at the microwave's neon numbers that read nine.

"What are you talking about?" Her nose scrunched up in the most adorable way. It was disgustingly cute, if I was being honest.

"It's nine p.m., and you work tonight, right?" I asked, not seeing what she was confused about.

"Yeah, at like ten, that's an hour away."

Her response had me frowning. "And you haven't eaten yet. When were you going to do that, huh?" I frowned when she burst into laughter, which grew louder every time she looked at me. At one point, she was full-on bent over at the waist, laughing so hard there were tears in her eyes.

"I'm sorry," she said, seeming anything but. "You just looked so much like a mother hen right there. No one's ever asked me if I've eaten before." Her humor died out in those last few words.

Fuck. We were both fucked up, weren't we? I wasn't ready to unpack either of our traumas tonight.

I cleared my throat, changing the subject before it got too awkward. "Well, I'm fucking starving. Get your ass dressed so we can go get food." Something didn't sit right with me about her going to work on an empty stomach, so I wasn't going to give her a choice.

"Dex, do you think I travel to work with my ass and tits out? I am ready. I only take my clothes off for money," she said, smirking.

She had to mention her ass and tits, didn't she?

Now I was shifting uncomfortably, forcing myself to think about grandma tits and taxes so my dick could chill. It was already going to be a bitch riding with her on the back of my bike all the time and not pulling over to take her on the side of the road. She rode like a damn pro, gluing herself to me and leaning at all the appropriate times. Even fuckin' knew to tap my leg if she wanted me to turn a certain way.

"Alright then. Well, um, I guess we should go?" I said, rubbing the back of my head with my hand when I realized I'd been standing there checking her out.

When the hell did I start having trouble talking to a woman? We stood there in awkward silence for a few seconds before she moved, breaking the spell.

"I should probably grab some different shoes," she said,

shuffling toward her room before pausing and facing me once more.

"You're not going to have a bottom lip if you keep chewing on it, Nikki. Spit out whatever you're worried about." The flash of annoyance and anger brought a smile to my face.

"How are we supposed to explain why we're always together all of a sudden?" she asked.

The question took me by surprise. I hadn't thought about it.

"I've never had to address that during a protection detail, so I'd say we don't have to worry about it." I shrugged, stepping around the counter. "What we need to be worried about is the fact that you haven't had any food, and you're about to go do some strenuous shit."

I couldn't quite read the look she gave me, but after a few seconds, she nodded and disappeared down the hall.

EIGHTEEN

DEX

IF YOUR BURRITO ISN'T WRAPPED IN FOIL, IT DOESN'T FUCKING COUNT. THAT'S NOT EVEN A SEXUAL EUPHEMISM...WELL, UNTIL NOW

WE RODE my Harley through the warm Tucson night, the engine's purr resonating in my ears, the hot desert air rushing past us. My hands gripped the handlebars, forcing me to focus. Nikki's body was pressed close against mine, her hands clinging low on my waist, a few mere inches from where I'd like her to touch. The city lights blurred into a streak of colors as we weaved through the sparse traffic on the way to Lotería.

The white walls of Lotería's building came into view, standing stark against the dark night. We'd made it with fifteen minutes to spare. I cut the engine, and the muffled sound of the crowd waiting to get in over by the main entrance carried through the night, laughter blending with the warm breeze.

I threw my leg over my bike before lifting Nikki off. She could get off herself with no problem, but I used any reason I could find to get my hands on her—like I'd done on the sofa earlier. Nikki pulled the helmet off and the dim streetlight cast a soft glow on her, accentuating the golden highlights in her tousled blonde hair. The flush of adrenaline from the ride gave her cheeks a pink hue, her eyes sparkling with excitement.

"God, I love being on the back of your bike."

Pride swelled in my chest at how she'd specified *my* bike. Who knew if she even meant it that way, but I sure as fuck was going to take it as such. The evening air carried her coconut scent on it, and I had to shove my free hand in my pocket as we walked toward the side entrance to resist the ridiculous urge to hold her hand.

"Beto!" I yelled as we got closer.

"Dammit, Dex." Nikki's manicured hand whacked me in the chest. "Do you *have* to yell? Just go look for him."

I scoffed at her suggestion. "First of all, ow. And second, I already got him a damn burrito. Now I gotta go find him to deliver it?" The delicious scent of some bomb-ass al pastor taunted me. If he didn't come get his food soon, I was going to inhale this one, too.

"Don't you dare eat Robert's burrito," she hissed.

My head snapped to her. "Did I say that shit out loud too?" If I had, this was getting out of hand because I'd sworn I kept that one inside.

The left side of her mouth pulled upward, revealing a dimple. The sight had me thinking all sorts of wild shit, like the fact that I'd like to kiss the cute little indent.

"No, you didn't say it out loud. The look on your face was enough to tell me you're considering devouring it before it ever makes it to Beto." She chuckled, walking away.

I pulled on her arm, yanking her toward me without thinking it through. She let out an *oomph* as her back hit my chest. Her scent invaded my senses and I leaned to whisper in her ear. "Tell me, Nikki, did I have the same look on my face before I devoured your soaking pussy? Because I'm just trying to figure out how you correctly guessed what I was thinking."

I wanted so badly to run my tongue up her neck, following the trail of crimson that was currently creeping up it with every dirty word I whispered. But she was so still that I paused, thinking maybe I'd pushed too far. Misread what I could say without making her feel awkward or uncomfortable.

Shit.

Nothing pissed me off more than when men made unwelcome sexual advances on women, and here I was, doing exactly that. Her hair hit me as I spun her around, needing her to see my face when I apologized. When I caught her blue eyes, I dropped my hands to my side, not wanting to make the situation worse.

"Sorry, Nikki. I shouldn't say that shit to you. You've made it clear you just wanna be friends, and there I go crossing a line."

The nervous *tap tap tap* of my fingers on my jeans seemed deafening, a reminder of her silence as she stared at me like I'd grown a third head. It was making my skin feel too tight, and I needed to fill the space. "Do you want me to find someone else to watch over you? Or, like, stand ten steps behind you?" I asked.

Still, there was nothing from her, though her lips were now tightly pursed. It seemed as though she was battling to contain her thoughts while I continued to blurt out words in my desperate attempt to fix my fuck up. What puzzled me was how badly I needed her to tell me she forgave me.

"You wanna slap me? Would that help? I mean, violence tends to help me. Okay, now I'm rambling. Dammit, woman, say something," I called out desperately, pacing in a circle. It wouldn't have surprised me if Ryan's employees thought I was high on something, given the way I was fidgeting.

Nikki burst into laughter so loud that it made me jump. Tears streamed down from the corners of her eyes, and she wiped them away with her knuckles before sobering. Something about the way she looked at me felt as if I was completely exposed.

She cleared her throat. "I've never had anyone apologize for something they've said to me." She stepped in closer, and the proximity had me fisting my hands to avoid reaching out and touching her. But then she wrapped her arms around my middle, pressing her cheek into my chest, and I went as stiff as a board.

"You can hug me back, Dex," she said into my chest with a chuckle.

I placed my arms around her, holding her to me. I wasn't sure I'd ever let her go. "I can't even remember the last time I hugged someone," I admitted, relishing how perfectly she fit against me. The crown of her head rested just below my chin, and an inexplicable desire to kiss the top of it washed over me. All my usual physical contact was either of a sexual nature or non-existent.

Nothing soft and innocent like this…not since Kelly.

The thought choked me up, the grief taking me by surprise. Like it always did.

Grief was a selfish bitch who infected every emotion you possessed. It infiltrated each moment and memory, poisoning them with the knowledge that things will never be the same.

"I don't ever hug anyone either," Nikki said, mimicking my thoughts, but all I could give her was a grunt of agreement, too overrun with thoughts of the past. A soft smile greeted me when she looked up, but it quickly morphed into a frown, and she pushed away. "Now I'm the one being an ass. I should have asked if I could hug you."

I reached out, freeing her bottom lip from between her teeth, unable to resist running the pad of my thumb along the plump flesh. "You can hug me whenever you want, Nikki. I'm pretty sure friends do that shit all the time." We stared at one another until I cleared my throat, breaking the strange moment we'd shared. "Alright. Let's go find Beto and get him his burrito, because I seriously do want to eat it."

My stomach rumbled right on cue, and Nikki was quick to roll her eyes at me, tossing playful insults in my direction. We went in through the warehouse door on the side of the building. Nikki had mumbled back at the taco truck something about not being able to handle all the horniness if we walked in through the dancer's entrance.

My eyebrows basically hit my hairline when we passed into the heart of the Los Muertos operation space.

"Damn, it doesn't even look like there was a full-on

gunfight in here." Without meaning to, my gaze drifted to where I knew Ryan had killed Mario.

They'd done a good job of cleaning, but there was still an area of the concrete that was slightly darker than the rest. There was a reason we covered our interrogation rooms in tile —porous surfaces soaked up too much blood, and it was impossible to get out. Ryan hadn't known that I was perched up on top of one of the bays, zeroed in on Mario. Ready to take him out.

But that wasn't how it all went down.

She'd taken the motherfucker out herself, getting herself stabbed in the process. In all my years with Gunner, I'd never seen him go ghost-white like he had in that moment.

I stared at the dark spot.

"Fuck!" Gunner screamed, sliding down the wall of the hospital. They wouldn't let us into the surgery room, and I'd had to physically hold Gunner back from attempting to force his way in. Only thing that had made him calm the fuck down was when I pointed out the tremor in the surgeon's hand.

"You want him sewing up your girl while his hand shakes like a fuckin' leaf? Because that's what's going to happen if you don't get your shit together right now, Gunner."

Only then did he stop thrashing in my arms.

"Is this what it was like?" he asked me. Devastation poured from him. I didn't have to ask him what he was talking about. I knew.

To lose someone you love was a cruel form of punishment.

I kneeled before him, clamping a hand on his slumped shoulder. "Naw, brother. The real pain comes when you put them in the ground. And everyone shows up to pay their respects, and you know they get to go about their fucking lives right after like nothing happened. The moment is nothing but a small blimp on their week. Meanwhile, every fuckin' day, you're taunted with the fact that you'd somehow fucking made it, and the person you love didn't."

He blinked at me, his mouth falling open, but what the hell did you say to a trauma dump like that?

"But you aren't going to feel that despair, because your girl is

gonna make it," I said with confidence as I stood, walking away and calling out that I was going to grab us some food.

I couldn't stay around to see the pity in his eyes as he processed what I'd just unloaded onto him.

Nikki's gentle voice caught me off guard. "You saw her do it, huh?" I blinked a few times, snapping back to reality after my brief mental escape. I hadn't even noticed that she'd paused alongside me. Her petite hand lay on my forearm, and the urge to hold it came roaring back. I just wanted to see how it looked intertwined with my own.

"Killing someone you loved, especially when they've betrayed you, is…" her voice trailed off.

Nikki looked like she too was somewhere far away rather than right next to me as she stared at the spot on the ground. The grip on my forearm tightened, her contemplative expression growing increasingly tense—angry.

"That a secret wish? Or…" I asked tentatively, keeping my volume low so all the guys milling around wouldn't hear our conversation. Something told me she wouldn't want anyone else to know what we were talking about. Hell, I wasn't certain she wanted me to know the details.

Her shoulders tensed, making her already good posture near perfect. There was something in her tone when she spoke that had my gut telling me it wasn't theoretical.

So, who was it that betrayed her? Was that why the Russians wanted her? Did she kill someone she wasn't supposed to?

"I wa—" Whatever she was about to say, or not say, was cut off.

Robert came barreling between us, shattering the little bubble of intimacy we'd been sharing. The vulnerability in her blue eyes vanished, replaced by a playful smile and a cheery tone—a tactic I could spot from a mile away.

As the saying goes, *like recognizes like.*

"Hey, fucker. Where's my burrito?"

The paper bag got snatched from my hand, and Robert wasted no time unwrapping the foil. He took a bite, moaning obnoxiously loud around the mouthful. Annoying fucker. I couldn't blame him—I'd done the same thing earlier. Nikki had teased me about how vocal I was, so, naturally, I told her she should hear me in bed.

Which fucking backfired on me because the way she eyed my lips while licking hers caused my dick to stir to life. Tonight was going to be a total bitch. I *had* to watch her dance because it was my literal job now, which meant blue balls were an inevitable part of my life for the foreseeable future.

My hand was going to be busy as hell.

I shoulder-checked Robert, hoping to distract myself from thoughts of having to see Nikki's body in lace and somehow act professionally. "Listen, asshole, go somewhere else while you eat that thing because I'm hungry as fuck," I bitched.

Nikki stopped mid-sentence, putting a pause on the conversation she and Beto were having about tonight's show. "You literally just devoured a burrito and three tacos. How can you still be hungry?" she asked, giving me a shocked look.

"Tacos don't count," Robert and I said in perfect unison, bumping fists at how in sync we were.

"In fact," Robert said with a mouthful. "Some *tacos* don't even have calories. They're just deliciously juicy." He jammed his elbow into my ribs as if I needed the hint.

I smirked at him. "Robert, don't act like you eat pussy. Who's letting you near them when you eat like that?" I asked, pointing to how he was making an absolute mess of his burrito. "No fucking finesse." My teasing earned me a middle finger.

I *almost* slipped up and told him he could ask Nikki how good *I* was with my tongue, but I'd just gotten myself out of hot water from talking about eating her out. Which, in retrospect, I wasn't entirely positive she'd gone completely still because she disliked what I'd said.

"Y'all are weird," she said, throwing her hands up in the air like an actress in one of those Spanish soap operas Beto played in the background when I'd chill at his place. I never had any idea what they were saying, but clearly whatever was happening was juicy as fuck based solely on the amount of times people slapped each other.

At that moment, Nikki looked like she was ready to do the same to us, or maybe knock our heads together.

She left us, yelling over her shoulder. "Go find something to do. I'll see you both later. And don't you *dare* get any private dances tonight, Dex."

Her tone was downright scary, but I swore there was a tinge of jealousy in it, and it did something to my insides. I loathed when women got territorial on me—meant they were getting too attached. So why the fuck was I willing to let Nikki put a fucking leash on me if she wanted to?

Robert shot me a glance as he chewed the last of his burrito. "Why the fuck can't you get a dance?"

I shrugged a shoulder, fighting to hide the smirk.

But I was thinking it might be time to change my views on girlfriends.

NINETEEN

NIKKI

IF YOU'RE A CUNT, I'M A CUNT RIGHT BACK

EVEN LOTERÍA'S slow nights were fucking busy.

Back when I'd first started, I was just another dancer in and out of clubs. Not all, but most who got in this line of work had some shit they were running from. Either our past, present, or future. If you were extra special, like me, it was all fucking three.

Dancing was all I had.

Daddy dearest had shelled out for the finest classical training money could buy. I'd been naive enough to believe it was a sign of his confidence in my talent, that he thought I had what it took to become a professional ballerina. Little did I know, it was all just a way for him to keep me in check and under constant surveillance.

"Shit."

I sucked off the bead of blood that welled up where I'd managed to cut myself with the tiny scissors I was using to trim my false lashes. Crystal let out a chuckle from beside me.

"Girl, you've been out of it for a few days now. What's got your G -string so far up your ass?" she asked, eyeing me from the vanity mirror. We'd been vanity neighbors for a year now, and I'd always liked her. She kept to herself and was cordial to everyone, but never asked too many questions. Naturally, she had to pick tonight of all nights to break that pattern. I blew on the glue, buying myself a few seconds to figure out an answer that didn't sound like a total lie.

"Ehh." I made a noncommittal grunt, shrugging a shoulder. "Tired is all. Ryan's been in and out a lot. Adds some extra shit to my plate, you know?"

The best lies are versions of the truth. Dear ol' dad taught me that, too.

"Of course, I think you will do great things."

He'd left out one important part of that sentence.

"Like make me a very important man when I trade your freedom for power."

Crystal's toffee-colored eyes stared me down for a few seconds before she gave a slow nod and went back to applying her own strip set.

The dancers' room was lively, and normally, I loved that about our space. Tonight, it was grating on my nerves. Concha had "16 Shots" blasting so loud I was surprised Ricky hadn't walked back here already, yelling at us to turn it down. And two of the new girls were fighting over who would go up first. It was usually the shitty spot. Most patrons didn't show up until closer to ten, so I didn't get why they were at each other's throats over it. It wasn't like it was the only dance they'd get tonight.

"Hey," I hollered, swinging around in my chair to face the two of them, still locked in their showdown. "Cut that shit out. This is *not* how this club works." I stalked over toward where they were standing. They stared at me like two deer in headlights. "If you can't act like professionals, find a new club, got it? This is *not* how my dancers behave."

On any other night, I would've pulled them aside separately and been more diplomatic about this. But tonight— tonight, I was itching for someone to fucking try me. I secretly hoped someone slapped my ass out on the floor so I could claw their eyes out like I'd lost my damn mind. Then, at least, I could blame my need to act out on the situation instead of admitting to the truth.

That there was this swirl of emotions turning in my gut and making me feel restless.

One of the girls sneered. "What do you mean, *your* dancers?"

A sigh came from behind me. I guessed it belonged to Crystal, but didn't turn around to confirm that theory. Instead, I stepped closer to the bottle blonde who'd been mouthing off for weeks —Sapphire or some shit.

Ballsy bitch. I might have liked her if she wasn't a cunt to everyone.

"What part of that do you need help understanding? Want me to pull up the dictionary definition?" I canted my head to the side, laying on the condescending tone *thick*. She stepped up, and her courage brought a smirk to my face. Mainly because she probably thought I'd back down.

"What part did *you* not understand, bitch? " Spit landed on my chest, which was unfortunate because I'd already dosed myself in the devil's dust—which wasn't a drug, it was glitter. I couldn't even wipe off her disgusting DNA.

Crystal appeared next to me, her hands raised between us placatingly. "Alright, let's all calm down. Maybe take a shot? Fucking hug it out?"

Sapphire, or Emerald, or whatever the hell her name was, slapped Crystal's arm away. It was the proverbial straw that broke the camel's back.

I wasn't a girl's girl.

If you were a cunt. I was a cunt right back.

"Listen here, you fucking twat-waffle," I yelled, launching myself at her with the intention of punching her in her stupid face, with her drawn-on freckles and blush that was so intense she might as well use pink face paint. She shrieked as my fist flew toward her, thumb untucked like Ryan had taught me so I didn't break anything in my hand again.

But it never connected.

A steel band wrapped around my midsection, and suddenly, my back was pressed against something warm and hard. Something that smelled like leather and cedarwood.

Something vibrating with a deep voice that made my insides flutter.

"Woah, woah, woah. What the fuck is going on in here on this day?" Dex asked, clearly amused if the shaking of his chest with silent laughter was anything to go by.

"She tried to attack me," the bitch sobbed, laying the tears on thick enough she could flood the place.

Oh, please. Your ass deserved it.

Or maybe she didn't deserve the black eye I was planning for her, and I was being over dramatic…but I never claimed to make the best choices in life.

"Spitfire?" I looked up, meeting Dex's hazel eyes, noticing that there was more green than brown in them that night. "What happened that you decided to go all WWE on her?"

"It was more UFC," I mumbled. The sarcastic answer earned me a genuine laugh from him, and as much as I wanted to stay pissed off, the belly laugh brought a smile to my face. I had two realizations in that moment.

One, I liked making Dex laugh.

And two, even though he said the most outlandish shit that had everyone else laughing, he didn't laugh often.

Now I was staring at him, racking my brain for memories of him laughing. My musings were cut short when the newbie was dumb enough to open her mouth again.

"Aren't you going to do anything about her?" she asked, her eyes wild. "She tried to *punch* me. Crazy bitch."

Dex's laughter came to a dead stop. "What did you call her?" His tone was cold. "Get the fuck out. Pack your shit and find somewhere else to dance."

The girl's mouth opened, probably to argue, but Dex cut it off before it began. "You're not too bright, are you? Get the fuck out before I let Nikki go. I'm already regretting saving your face the first time. I only stopped her because I didn't want her hurting herself. I don't care if she fucks you up. She probably has a good reason."

Now the girl was shaking like a leaf. I almost felt bad.

"You got a robe or some shit?" Dex said in my ear. He was

so close I could smell the alcohol and mint on his breath, and I had the urge to turn my head and see what that combination would taste like on my tongue. "Nikki?" he prodded when I still hadn't answered.

"I'm sorry. What?" I asked.

Dex chuckled and repeated his question. "Do. You. Have. A. Robe?" He punctuated each word as if that would help my comprehension.

I rolled my eyes at his antics. "I didn't hear you, asshole. And what do I need a robe for?"

He released the arm he had around my middle. My bare skin instantly pebbled up with the loss of his heat.

How had I not even realized he was still holding me?

"Because," he moved around to where we were facing one another, "you can't walk out there dressed in a thong and a sheer bra."

I snorted. "That's, like, the whole point of what I do, Dex."

Crystal walked over to Dex, holding out a silky piece of fabric with plumes of feathers along the bottom and at the sleeves. He took it, making her blush as he thanked her and winked. *That* was why I didn't want him walking through the dancers' entrance. He was far too fucking charming.

It has absolutely nothing to do with me not liking him showing other women attention. Nothing.

Because that would suggest I wanted Dex's attention.

And I most certainly did not…

He held the thing open, staring at me expectantly. "Put it on, Nikki. You're not dancing tonight."

"Like hell, I'm not," I said with a chuff. "What? Are you going to pay me for tonight?" I instantly regretted the words when I saw the glint of challenge in his eyes. He prowled toward me—it was the only way to describe his movements— sending a thrill of anticipation through me.

What the hell was *wrong* with me?

Dex moved behind me once more, assisting me in putting on the silky garment. I was used to having men help me out of clothes—I had never experienced how intimate it was to have someone dress me. A shiver of excitement ran through me as the fabric caressed my skin. I was so entranced by the whole moment that I didn't even bother resisting, lying to myself that I would just take the robe off after he was done.

The coarse hair of his beard rubbed against my cheek as he leaned into me, reaching for the two open sides from behind. His fingers brushed the skin right above my hips, a featherlight touch that had my head swimming.

"Ask me nicely," he purred into my ear, grabbing the two strings of the robe and securing them in a knot at my front. The thin material was the only barrier between his hand and my stomach, and I had to bite back a moan at the contact.

"What?" The word escaped me as little more than a breath.

A warmth brushed across the side of my face. "Ask me nicely to pay you for tonight, spitfire, because I will. I'll cover whatever you would have made. Hell, I'll even double it," he whispered, his voice low and seductive.

His strong arms dropped away, leaving me feeling bare even though I now wore more clothing than a moment before. I noted how turned on I was, when he'd barely touched me— nothing beyond that initial contact when he'd held me back. But we were so close that if I leaned back just a bit, our bodies would practically meld together.

I turned to face him, neither of us moving back. We were almost eye height when I was in my shoes, but he still had a few inches on me. His attention was intense. I wanted to look away, but he had me pinned in place.

"You need to release some of that built-up tension, Nikki."

Yeah. In bed. With a hot biker, one that's not you…maybe.

Dex continued to talk, unaware of the internal debate I was having with myself about the pros and cons of us sleeping together. "And if you go up on stage, you'll end up in a damn fight. So, instead, ask me nicely to help you let loose," he said, smirking when the entire room erupted in a symphony of encouragement, with the other girls eagerly urging me to go for it.

I blinked, looking around at them. Some of them were borderline salivating as they watched us.

"Aren't all of you hoes supposed to be getting ready? " I called out with faux irritation. Truthfully, I'd forgotten we were surrounded by people. That seemed to happen a lot with Dex—we fell into our own little bubble, and everything else faded away.

"What's it going to be, Nikki?" he asked.

The whole room went quiet, awaiting my response. Concha had even changed the music to something sappy and romantic. Which was completely *not* what this was. Hell, Dex even admitted this was all so I didn't end up with an assault charge. There was nothing at all panty-melting about the fact that he offered to pay for my time while he helped me release some steam…

"Fine," I finally said, though I wasn't sure if my words were audible over the cheers from the other girls. I added, "But you're paying for my drinks," poking his chest. I had no intention of letting him pay for my time, but I was more than happy to let him pick up the tab for my alcohol.

Dex hit me with a blinding smile that sent a shiver down my spine. I couldn't help but wonder why I liked seeing that smile so much.

"I'm sorry, I can't hear you," he taunted, holding his hand up to his ear. "My ears don't work with attitude."

I mumbled *smartass* under my breath before stepping even closer, our chests touching, relishing the way his throat bobbed. "Dex, baby," I said in a sickly-sweet tone, walking my fingers up his leather cut. "Will you, *please*, entertain me tonight?" Despite the ungodly amount of sarcasm in my voice, Dex's eyes heated when I said the word entertain, instantly triggering the memory of gripping his head while he kneeled between my legs.

"I'll do whatever you want, spitfire." His thumb brushed along my lower lip, pulling it from where I'd unknowingly been biting on it. "All you have to do is ask."

Fuck.

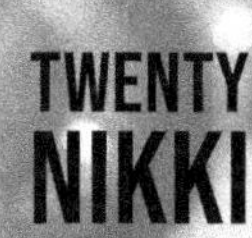

"WHY DOES EVERYONE KEEP ACTING LIKE THAT'S WEIRD?"

I'D KICKED Dex out after agreeing to his little proposal for the night. If I was really going to relax, I didn't want to do it in lingerie and Crystal's "murderous wife" robe—Dex's name for it, not mine. Groups of people milled about, their conversations acting like white noise to the music playing over the club speakers.

Ryan and I had carefully planned out Lotería's entertainment. Different themes and events occurred on different nights, and they switched fairly often—our way of enticing people to return. If tonight had been one of our choreographed nights, Dex wouldn't have been able to convince me to play hooky. But we'd pulled back on those ever since the incident with Mario. Ryan had said she didn't want to overwhelm me.

The sardonic laugh I let out caused the woman closest to me to turn her head, and I gave her a reassuring smile so she'd know it wasn't aimed at her. If only she could hear my inner monologue of kidnapping attempts and murderous ex-husbands. Actually, I didn't know if Yuri wanted to kill me or just reacquire what he'd lost. I hadn't exactly reached out with a survey of his thoughts and opinions.

I pushed my way through the bodies, choosing the path

that would take the longest to get to the bar. My nerves felt like pinpricks of electricity all over my body, and I couldn't put my finger on what was causing the reaction.

Then again, maybe it was *everything* causing that reaction.

Did I even know what it felt like to relax? Sure, I played the part of letting loose all the time. People saw me up on stage, shaking my ass for everyone to see—literally—but I was never truly relaxed. In the back of my mind, I was always aware that my past was haunting me.

Waiting for me to fuck up.

"There she is," Dex called out from one of the end barstools. The playful glint in his eyes turned dark as he dragged his eyes over my body, taking in the short black dress I changed into. My heart kicked up in my chest when his tongue popped out, swiping along his bottom lip. I was accustomed to being looked at, but this…his perusal of my body made my body explode in tingles.

The closer I came, the bigger his smile grew. It was bigger than the margarita in front of him. The thing even had those crazy straws with all the loops and shit—oh, and four umbrellas. I just *knew* he'd asked for that many, too, because it didn't come with that many usually.

Robert sat beside him, making wild gestures with his hands to Cassandra, our head bartender. She had her hands on her hips with a look that said she thought Robert was full of shit. The whole sight had me battling mixed emotions. On one hand, it looked like a group of friends having a fun night out. It felt…normal.

But my life wasn't normal, and I meant what I'd said when I told Ryan that not loving anyone was how I avoided being heartbroken. I'd broken that rule with her, and now I was dealing with the consequences.

Did I want to risk those feelings sneaking in again? But my feet had a mind of their own, not getting the memo that we shouldn't go make friends, and they picked up the pace.

"Nikki," Robert called out, his eyes wide as he turned to

face me. "Please tell Cassy here that I *absolutely* know what I am doing behind the bar."

"Did you make that monstrosity?" I asked, coming to a stop by Dex's side. There wasn't anywhere else to stand. Where they were seated was at the far side of the bar, the section on the end that only spanned about four feet.

Rob had taken the stool at the corner, while Dex took the one next to the wall, sitting at an angle so his back was to the solid surface. It was strategic, giving him a view of all the entrances and exits.

Andrei had taught me that. Then Ryan had hammered it home.

"Tasha, you never want your back to an entry point. You want to see your enemy approach."

Did everyone in the criminal world think this way?

Suddenly, Robert let out this dramatic gasp, clutching at his shirt like he'd just been shot. *"Pendeja.* You *never* take my side," he said as Cassandra called out a *"See?"*

I was doing my best to focus on anything but the tingling heat of Dex's hand on my waist. He smoothly maneuvered me to stand between his legs, making sure I wasn't hanging out in the hallway that led back toward the bathrooms. The touch was respectful, but after the look he'd given me... the contact set off a swarm of butterflies in my lower stomach.

"Just try it before you make a decision," he said, grabbing the glass and pulling it so one of the swirly straws was in front of me.

"I didn't even know we had these," I admitted with a playful smile as I wrapped my lips around the neon green straw and took a tentative sip.

"We don't." Cassandra pointed at Robert and Dex. "Dumb and Dumber brought them in a few weeks ago and demanded I put them in their drinks." She walked away to attend to another customer, telling me she'd be right back with a *real* drink for me.

The admission—and the gallon of tequila Robert had put in the mixed drink—caused me to cough so hard that Dex started patting me on the back. The giant didn't realize his own strength because I had to brace myself on the bar top so he didn't send me flying over it.

"Wait, you two brought your own straws?" I wasn't sure why I even asked for confirmation. Of course they had. For as long as I'd known Robert, he'd always laid back, and usually quiet and respectful. At least to me—I'd heard rumors of the trail of broken hearts he'd left in his wake.

But when he was around Dex?

I swore the two were living out their dreams of being fraternity brothers. One time, when we were preparing for the reopening, they ran around the empty club with Nerf guns, having an all-out war. Dex broke a table when he attempted to slide across the top like he was in a fucking action movie.

Ryan said if they didn't cut their shit out, she would join in—with her actual gun.

Robert's tan skin managed to disappear with the threat. I'd never seen him look so white. Then there was Dex, who told her he'd been shot before, and it wasn't that bad.

"Why does everyone keep acting like that's weird?" Dex asked, frowning like he really was confused. "We brought our own snacks too, since Ryan refuses to sell food here."

I chuckled at how he put out he sounded. "It's a complete bitch to get the permits to sell food here," I explained, taking another sip of paint stripper moonlighting as a margarita.

Dex looked around, searching for what ears could overhear what he was about to say next. "She fucking runs guns. Illegally. You're telling me she can't figure out how to get some tacos in here?" he whispered.

"*Punto*," Robert said in agreement, the two bumping fists over the top of my head.

Cassandra made her way back over, cutting off any conversation about illegal activities. Most of the employees at Lotería weren't involved with the cartel at all, and we did our best to keep them from knowing any of the grittier details of what else happened in the part of the club they didn't have access to.

"It's shit, right?" she asked, nodding her chin toward the drink as she pulled out four shot glasses. "Here, you need to cleanse your palate before you drink one of my drinks." She poured clear liquid into each of them before looking at us expectantly.

The delicious smokiness of mezcal traveled down my throat, the flavor lingering on my tongue before settling in my stomach, warming me from the inside out. Despite what most probably assumed, I didn't drink often, so between the shot and the monstrosity that Robert had made, I was already feeling light and fuzzy. The sensation amplified the excitement swirling in my gut whenever Dex brushed against me.

"How you feeling, spitfire, because your shoulders just dropped from out of your neck." His finger trailed along the tops of them. "Which is where they always seem to sit, lately," he said in my ear so I could hear him over the noise, his facial hair tickling my bare shoulder.

A giggle I couldn't control slipped out, along with a tidbit about my past that I hadn't meant to share. "Katya would beat me if she knew that." My body tensed, waiting for the question I knew he was about to ask, but it never came because Cassandra pushed another shot our way.

"One more, bitches. I have to serve a fuckin' bachelorette party tonight, and I need to be tipsy to deal with a bunch of screaming white women. Ryan's got people with dicks dancing tonight for them, too," she said with annoyance.

Another giggle slipped out from me at the way Cassandra wrinkled her nose. I wasn't sure if it was the bridal party or the thought of dicks that caused that reaction. She and Crystal had been a couple for as long as I could remember, and how they looked at one another *almost* made me wish I had someone like they did. Almost.

But that meant I'd have to be willing to let someone in to my fucked-up life.

Robert rubbed his hands together. "Fuck yes. I love some horny bridesmaids."

Dex barked out a laugh, shaking his head at Robert's

antics, but I couldn't stop the pang of—something— as I thought about whether I would be a wingwoman for these two all night. And why did that thought make me feel sick?

"*Que fueo, Beto. Fueo. Vamos.*" Cassandra lifted the shot glass. "*Pa' arriba, pa' abajo, pa' centro, pa' dentro.*"

All four of us let out collective groans.

"I'm too fucking old for this," Dex said. I looked up at him so I could remind him he hadn't even hit thirty yet, but I forgot how to speak when I caught him doing a weird thing with his tongue and the salt along the rim that was far too distracting. He winked when he caught me looking at his mouth, and I could feel the heat racing up my face. I turned away, hoping it would stop all the inappropriate thoughts I was having about my *friend.*

A friend you want to play tonsil hockey with.

Cassandra looked between the two of us. The expression on her face made me nervous. "So," she started in, "why have you been around so much lately, Dex?" Her words sounded casual, but her eyes were still bouncing between the two of us. "Seen you a lot in the last few weeks. And Crys says you went in their dressing room and pulled this one out before she beat someone's ass…" she said, signaling to me with a sly smile.

"Um." Dex locked eyes with me.

I hoped when he looked at my face, what he saw in my expression was me saying, "*I fucking told you we needed to know what to tell people. Mr. No One Ever Asks Me Shit.*"

"Oh, they're dating," Robert said matter-of-factly. Our heads whipped to the left, where Robert was weaving a story like he was a damn playwright. "Yeah. They wanted to give Brujita y *su güerito* some time together before they decided to bump uglies, too. You know?"

A choking noise came from Dex. "Bump uglies? *I* don't even say weird shit like that."

"The fuck you don't, Dex. Where the fuck do you think I got that from?" Robert asked, looking offended and completely unfazed that he'd just announced Dex and I were a thing.

Because something I knew for fucking sure, the rumor was already making its rounds. That's how it worked at this club.

I could see Cassandra texting behind the bar as Dex and Robert argued. Which meant Crystal now knew, and so did *all of* the girls. There was no way for me to say it wasn't true because they would see us together all the time since he had to watch over me, and the truth wasn't an option because we knew there was still a rat or two somewhere.

"So, y'all are a thing then?" Cassandra asked, bringing the conversation back to a subject I really would have liked us to move past. Dex's hands snaked around my midsection, lifting me in the air and setting me on one of his splayed thighs. The position left me no choice but to lean back into him. He kept one arm around my body to keep me from falling off to the side, but that meant his massive hand came to rest on top of my thigh.

My very bare thigh.

"Yup. It's fairly new and shit." There was a ruffling of my hair, and I swore he kissed the top of my head, but it was so brief I couldn't be sure. Dex's next words were said in my ear for only me to hear.

"Spitfire, I'm going to you need to give me permission to touch you. We're going to have to sell this fucking story Robert just started. Too many questions if we don't."

I knew he was right. It would've been nice to have a heads-up before Beto opened his big ass mouth, but really, it was the perfect cover. I interlaced our fingers and gave him two firm squeezes before turning my head to look at him.

For being a total goofball, he was intense when he wanted to be.

I pressed a kiss to his cheek. "Yes, you can touch me," I whispered just loud enough for him to hear.

"Y'all are fucking cute. Always knew you'd end up

together. Broken people find one another and fill in the cracks, ya know?" she said before walking away.

Robert stood and gave a shit-eating smile. "Alright, mom and dad, let's go find me a horny bridesmaid for our double date."

This was an awful idea. The threadbare strings holding up my walls weren't going to survive being Dex's "girlfriend".

TWENTY-ONE
DEX

THERE'S A "BELT LOOP GRAB" TO "PUSSY FLUTTER" PIPELINE. IT'S SCIENCE

HOW IRONIC THAT my first girlfriend wasn't even real.

Well, she was *real*. There was no doubt I was gripping onto her very real hips right now as she tried to send me into an early grave with the way she was grinding against me.

When Lotería had renovated, they'd added an area for patrons to dance, and Nikki had dragged me out onto it claiming she'd never gotten the chance to break it in.

Ugh. Please stop.

That wasn't what I really wanted, but it was really fucking hard to be respectful when the sexiest woman around was moving against me in the way she was.

Thirty minutes prior, I'd had to start force-feeding her water and some of the snacks she'd made fun of me and Robert for bringing in. The woman was a lightweight when it came to booze apparently, a fact I hadn't expected since she worked at a club. Tomorrow was going to be a bitch for her.

I should make her breakfast.

Where the hell had that thought come from?

A tug on my hair drew my attention down toward where she was plastered to my front, despite the space I was trying to force between her ass cheeks and my cock. The thin layer of her dress and my jeans was *not* enough.

I let out another groan, chiding myself for thinking about

her ass cheeks and my dick in the same sentence because now I had some very *unfriendly* thoughts playing in my mind.

She wrapped her arms up around my neck, and my stomach did a weird fucking flip. "Thank you," Nikki shouted over the music, playing with the ends of my hair.

"For what?" I leaned down so it would be easier for her to hear me, but I hadn't anticipated her turning around. Our faces were inches apart, close enough that I could see the specks of glitter in the lip gloss she was wearing.

"For forcing me to come have some fun. It's been a long fucking time since I've done that." She looked off into the crowd, but I could tell she wasn't actually *seeing* anyone out there. Her mind had drifted off somewhere. As quickly as it happened, it was over, and her blue eyes were back on mine with a glint of mischief that had me smiling. "Wanna do something else fun?"

Nerves bubbled up under my skin, a feeling which was completely foreign to me.

"Naked fun?" I asked, my voice hitching. "Because if that's what you're thinking, it's going to be a hard pass, spitfire." The frown she gave me had me rushing out an explanation. "I think you would cut off my balls in the morning and lecture me about how we are supposed to be friends and not fuck buddies."

The crease between her brows softened, and the rock on my chest lightened.

"That's a weirdly sweet thing to say. But also, aren't we a *couple* now? " she said. My cock didn't get the memo that she was messing around. "It doesn't have to be in a bed, either."

I groaned and let my forehead fall forward against hers.

"Don't say those things, Niks. I am not a good man. My self-restraint against fucking you is abysmal."

Something wet and warm traced the shell of my ear, and I nearly came.

"It could be right here. Or in the bathroom if you're shy," she teased, dropping back down off the balls of her feet. She did not realize how fucking close I was to bending her over and letting everyone watch.

I threaded my hand in her hair, yanking it back so she was forced to look up at me, her eyes sparkling with excitement. "That what you want, Nikki? Want me to take care of that greedy fucking cunt of yours right here?" I asked against her lips, shoving my thigh between her legs and pressing it against her clit. "Your panties are soaked, spitfire. I can feel it through my jeans. Did grinding your ass on your *boyfriend's* cock make you wet?"

She nodded her head, her lips slightly parted, pupils blown.

This was going too far, and I was reaching the point of no return. I closed my eyes, releasing the hold I had on her hair. "Niks, you gotta help me out here," I said in a pained groan. "I won't be able to say no. Tell me to back off, spitfire."

"You're right." Disappointment mixed with relief when she slowly extracted herself from my grip, adding space between us. "What I was *going* to say was, wanna learn how to pole dance?"

There was so much eagerness and hope in her voice I couldn't tell her no, even if I'd wanted to.

I smiled at her, tucking a stray hair behind her ear, my fingers brushing across her cheek. "Fuck, yes, I want to get on a stripper pole. Can I take my clothes off, too?" She frowned at the question, making me chuckle. "Come on? Just my shirt, then."

"Fine." She looped a finger into the front of my jeans, pulling me behind her from the hold, which was hot for reasons my brain couldn't comprehend.

I readjusted myself as I trailed behind her because I was hard as a fucking rock, and now I had to endure watching her dance on a pole.

Thank god I tucked up to the other side, or she'd see exactly what her touches were doing.

"Mom. Dad," Robert called out as we approached the larger corner booth where the bachelorette party was at. Of course, he'd inserted himself there—I would have, too, under normal circumstances. The weirdest part of this whole situation was I *knew* I was going to bed with blue balls. Well, not really, because I'd take care of it, but the job wasn't going to be done by a woman, and I was strangely okay with that.

"I am *not* qualified to be a mom." Nikki looked over at me as I plopped down in a chair away from the hungry vultures disguised as a bachelorette party. The way she was looking at me made me realize how guarded she normally kept her expression. "He'd be a good dad. Dex is observant as hell. And he's nice to me," she said matter-of-factly, the alcohol making her more open than usual.

Her words hit me in the solar plexus, and I was glad I'd sat down because they probably would have caused me to stagger. Robert arched an eyebrow at me, but all I could respond with was a shrug of my shoulder.

I truly didn't know where that comment came from.

"She's tipsy," I called out, miming drinking with my hand in case Robert couldn't hear me over the woman plastered to his side, who was either whispering in his ear or shoving her tongue into it.

A flash of blonde obstructed my view as Nikki popped into my line of sight. She clearly was not overthinking her statement the way I was. Seeing her so relaxed had the corners of my mouth tipping upward until I saw what she had in her hand.

"Woah there, spitfire." I yanked the drink out of her hand, chuckling at the look of irritation she gave me as she protested. "Where did you even get this, huh? I didn't get it for you. You need water." I made sure to enunciate the last word.

It wasn't just the fact that she did *not* need more alcohol, but she had people after her. I wanted to watch every fucking drink she had been made and be the one to deliver them to her. She wasn't going to be roofied on my watch.

"I thought you were going to teach me how to strip on a pole," I said, desperate to get her to smile again. My assumption was dead on because her face lit up, and so did the other women when they saw Nikki dragging me onto the stage in the center of the circular booth.

As if on cue, a new song started, and she grabbed onto the pole, doing a few full body rolls, ending it with the whipping around of her hair and a smile so sinful the devil wouldn't have been able to do a better job.

"Okay, sexy Dexy, it's your turn. Think you can manage to copy that? Or do I need to start even slower for you?" she asked, curling a finger and motioning me to come closer.

I reached up and yanked out the black band holding my hair up in a bun. If she wanted a show, I'd give her a damn show. I nearly popped out a hip with how I dramatically walked toward the pole, but it was worth the laugh she was trying to hide behind her hand.

The cool metal felt good against my hands, which had been clammy since the moment Nikki had dragged me out of my seat, pulling me onto the dance floor. I tried to figure out how not to pop a boner again from the feel of her skin against mine.

I leaned over, determined to win the challenge Nikki had thrown down. I was a competitive fucker, something people didn't usually anticipate. It was part of why I was so good at getting information. It felt like a game to see who would break first: my moral code or the person's hold on the information. Sometimes, the third option won out, and their body broke before the other two.

"How about a wager for every move of yours I can do?" I asked.

She arched a manicured brow. "What do you want?" she asked, her tone thick with suspicion.

I pushed away the images of her spread out on her bed, or even the one of her plump lips pressed to mine, because anything physical was out of the question.

Not after what just happened on the dance floor, which had only proven how poor my self-control was with her.

The crowd of people was the only reason I'd even paused,

and I didn't have any issues with public play, so the next time a situation like that occurred, I probably wouldn't be able to stop myself if she didn't.

Luckily, there was something else I really wanted.

I motioned her closer with my finger, the same way she had moments before. Her steps were hesitant, but there was something in her eyes. The way they glinted under the red lights told me she was excited to know what I had to say.

"When I win—"

"If."

Ignoring her, I continued laying out my terms. "I want to know something about your past. Something you keep locked away in here." The tip of my finger trailed up her torso, coming to rest above her heart, and I gave it two taps. Fear replaced the look of excitement, and I knew I needed to reel her back in.

"But, hey, maybe you don't want to take that bet because you know I really am talented," I provoked, twirling around the pole once, being sure to look ungraceful.

"You're on."

I tucked away my look of triumph before facing her again. The poor girl had no clue what she'd just agreed to.

"Now, how did that first one go again? Oh, that's right."

The space filled with the sound of horny women hollering as I did a full body roll while holding the poll, flipping my hair back the way I'd seen Nikki do countless times. I knew I didn't look nearly as good as she did while doing it, but our little audience seemed pretty damn pleased. Nikki, on the other hand, had her hands propped on her hips, rolling her eyes when I held out a single finger.

One point, Dex.

"That's literally the easiest move ever." She strode over, hip-checking me out her way. "Don't get cocky over a little body roll."

"There was a hair flip in there, too, which I think gets me two questions," I said.

"I think not."

There was something so sexy about seeing her slightly pissed off.

There was probably something trauma-related to why I liked angry women, but I had no interest in exploring the reasons. I was happy to reap the benefits of this particular quirk.

All thoughts stopped, and my mind blanked when Nikki took a running leap, gripping high up on the pole and letting the momentum swing her in a circle before she wrapped a creamy leg around and transitioned to twirling by the crook of her leg and a single arm.

The wink she sent me went straight to my dick. This competition was going to make everything that much harder —literally.

"Okay, *honey*. You're up." She came to stand at my side, a smug look on her heart-shaped face. But it dropped when I yanked off my shirt and took off into a run. The smooth metal rubbed against my callouses, ripping some of the hardened skin. It was asking a lot for my hands and the pole to support my two hundred and thirty pounds.

I was sure it wasn't as graceful as hers, but the way Nikki's mouth hung open told me she hadn't anticipated me being able to execute the move. The stage shook a bit when I dropped back down.

She stood still, just blinking her big blue eyes at me. I might have broken the woman.

"You're fucking playing me, aren't you?" she asked when I stopped in front of her. "This isn't your first time on a pole."

My cheeks hurt with how wide my smile was. "Never said it was. I only said I wanted an answer for every move I performed. Shall we keep going?"

Nikki stumbled, letting out a clearly drunk giggle.

"Sorry, spitfire. Looks like our little game is over," I said with a smile, lifting her up and throwing her over my shoulder. "Falling while standing still is a party foul and earns you a first-class trip to soberville."

Contentment wasn't a normal emotion for me, but that was the only way to describe what I was experiencing when Nikki's bedroom door clicked closed.

It wasn't an emotion I'd thought I still had access to.

She'd hate it if I told her she snored like a little cat. It was fucking adorable.

I'd led us to the back exit of Lotería and loaded her into Beto's ride. She'd looked at me like I'd lost my damn mind when I'd climbed into the driver's seat while Robert took my Harley, but hadn't asked.

For reasons I *really* didn't want to explore, the thought of having another man drive her home didn't sit well with me. Thank fuck, Robert hadn't given me shit for it, either. He'd just wordlessly exchanged keys and followed behind us on my bike.

Putting her in the car had been a good call, because two minutes into the ride, she'd passed the fuck out. That was how I'd learned she purred in her sleep.

"Quiet, asshole. Nikki's sleeping and the woman is going to need it with the way she was putting away drinks tonight," I said, sinking into the cushion next to Robert and poking a finger at his chest. "Oh, and what the fuck were you thinking announcing that Nikki and I are a damn couple?"

He let out a roar of laughter that I smothered with a pillow to his face to keep him from waking up the dead. Asshole *would* think it was hilarious to put the two relationship-averse people together.

"Yo." He swiped at rogue tears. "You should have seen y'alls' faces." Another round of laughter tumbled out when I flipped him off. "Listen, there were already rumors happening about the way you went in there and saved that chick from Nikki beating her ass, and then apparently, you did some romantic shit of getting her dressed and offering to take her out. So, I just helped y'all out with your problem of trying to explain away why you are about to be around all the fucking time."

Points were being made, but I wasn't going to let him off the hook that easily.

"Yeah, but my *girlfriend*, Beto?" I wished I had something in my hands to distract me from my mind, which was asking questions like, *did Nikki think me helping her get dressed was romantic too?*

He shrugged a shoulder, clearly not as worried about this whole situation as I was. Fuck, what was Nikki's reaction going to be tomorrow? She'd gone along with it in the moment, but she'd also been who knows how many shots deep.

"Listen, I see the way you look at her. She's clearly fucking hot, which is your type."

My fist tightened at his flippant response, anger flaring at how he described her, which was an odd reaction because nothing he said was offensive. Hell, most women would even consider it complimentary, but it didn't feel like it was... enough.

Hot wasn't all that Nikki was.

Instead of saying any of that, I forced my body to relax.

Robert continued on, oblivious to my internal battle. "Plus, y'all know each other well enough and seem to like being around each other. You can pull that lie off."

"And what about the whole intimacy thing, huh? What are we supposed to do then?" I asked tightly.

The look Robert gave me said, *you're an idiot.* "Oh, I am sure it will be a complete hardship for you. You're practically a priest with your vows of celibacy," he mocked, dodging the pillow I threw at him.

"Fuck you," I said, giving him the bird, and settling into the couch, trying like hell to keep my mind on our conversation, and not on the woman sleeping in the next room.

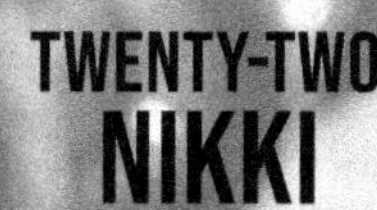

I'D RATHER LICK SATAN'S ASSHOLE THAN EVER SHOOT TEQUILA AGAIN

A GROAN BROKE through the silence.

It was so fucking loud— surely whoever it belonged to was dying.

"Fuck," I cried out when I tried to open my eyes. The light streaming in through the window blinded me, setting off the worst fucking headache of my life. This time when the groan went off, I was awake enough to realize *I* was the source of the noise.

Nausea rolled through my stomach so viciously I had to physically clamp my hand over my mouth and leap out of the bed to avoid yacking all over the sheets. Thankfully, it ended the moment I was vertical.

My clothing caught my attention because I was in Dex's black shirt that he'd given me the night all the shit had gone down with Jardani. My shoes and socks had been removed, and it felt like I'd been run over by a train and then shoved in a box before being kicked down a flight of stairs. Repeatedly.

How the fuck did I get home?

The night flashed in my mind, but it all felt like a jumbled mess. My cheeks heated when I reached the memories of how I'd looped my arms around the back of Dex's neck as I ground against him like I was trying to fuck him on the dance floor.

They heated even more when I remembered taunting him, and the way he'd pulled my hair, whispering to me about my wet pussy. My ass sunk into the mattress, my head dropping into my hands. God, how was I going to face him again?

Nikki, his head has been between your legs.

For some reason, that wasn't as embarrassing as what had happened the night before. And I knew exactly the reason for that: I hadn't wanted him to like me the first time. We hadn't known each other at all then, and he was nothing more than another one-night stand, like all the others.

His opinion of me hadn't mattered because I wouldn't ever see him again. All I'd wanted was my orgasm, and then we were supposed to ride off into the sunset in separate directions.

But now— fuck, now it mattered to me how he saw me, how he felt about me.

Another wave of nausea rushed through me, this time for a very different reason.

I reached for my phone to see what time it was—hell, what day it was—but was stopped in my tracks by the sight of the nightstand. There were three bottles of Gatorade, Tylenol, an envelope, and a note. My fingers shook a bit as I grabbed the stationery. Notes and I didn't have a good track record, and the dehydration didn't help either.

Thick, sure writing with a crooked heart was scrawled across the paper.

> *Morning, spitfire,*
> *Despite me forcing water down your throat and pulling drinks from your hands, I'm guessing you're feeling like you'd rather lick Satan's asshole than shoot tequila like that again.*

The laugh that line pulled from me sent another pang

shooting through my eye socket. Fuck him for being funny, and fuck tequila.

> *I wasn't sure what flavor you liked, so I left you options. Take two Tylenol when you wake up and drink one of them. Not too fast, though. Throwing up Gatorade is a total bitch, especially the red one. I don't make the rules, but those are the facts. I had to run out, but I'll be back shortly. So, if you wake up and I'm not here, don't freak. Oh, and sorry I only put you in my shirt. I tried to get shorts on you, but you were blitzed. Lightweight.*
>
> *P.S. Let me know if I owe you more.*

An emotion I refused to give a name to crawled up my throat from my heart as I pulled out a stack of bills from the envelope labeled "Sugar Daddy". Water collected along my bottom lash line, and I angrily swiped at the moisture, chastising myself for how ridiculous it was to cry over something so small.

But that was kind of the whole point.

I'd never gotten the small gestures from anyone.

"God, you're pathetic, Nikki," I whispered, following Dex's instructions. I'd never admit it aloud, but I chose the red one after several long seconds of wondering if it was Dex's favorite, and that was why he knew what it felt like to throw it up. And would it still be his favorite if it had made him sick?

The door creaked open, and the scent of bacon and eggs wafted through the opening, causing my stomach to growl like I hadn't eaten in weeks. I wasn't sure how two seconds prior I'd thought I was going to lose all the contents of my stomach, but now I was starving.

It wasn't just the heavenly aroma of breakfast food that had me moving toward the kitchen. It was the need to go yell at the person singing—very badly—that under *no* circumstances was I going to accept that money. I was joking when I'd told Dex he could pay me for my time.

I rounded the corner, stopping dead in my tracks. All good intentions evaporated.

Replaced by horny thoughts over a half-naked man.

Dex's heavily tattooed back was to me, a towel slung over one shoulder as he bent over to check something in the oven. There was no doubt in my mind that drool had to be pooling at my feet. The sight of his muscled physique covered in tattoos while he wore nothing more than a pair of gra y sweatpants slung low on his hips was already a deadly combination. Throw in him doing something as domestic as cooking…

Drool wasn't the only liquid pooling.

"The only thing better than this would be if you were, like, building me some furniture or some shit." The words were out before I could think better of them. The man didn't even flinch. Instead, he looked over his shoulder and yelled out the next line of lyrics while winking and throwing his head back, sending his hair flying everywhere.

"I'm glad you're up. It's so hard not listening to this song on full blast." He pressed the side of his phone, making the room flood with music. "Let me educate you on one of the best bands, The Story So Far," he shouted while air drumming like a damn pro. I couldn't help but smile at the way he yelled every word with passion.

Does he actually know how to play the drums?

Why the fuck did I even want to know anything about him? First, it was the drink flavor. Now, it was whether his impersonation of the not-so-little drummer boy was him making shit up, or carefully- practiced skills.

I forgot how to breathe when he turned and fully faced

me. Thank god he was so into the concert he was putting on — he didn't notice the way I eye-fucked him from head to toe.

I am no better than a man.

His front was as heavily inked as his back, and the silver bars running through both nipples had me shifting where I was propped against the breakfast bar. I was going to need to change my underwear ASAP. He pushed his damp hair back with one of his massive hands, and the smile he sent my way nearly sent me into cardiac arrest, it was so blinding and unguarded.

The music dipped to a level that allowed us to hold a conversation without needing to be inches apart and shouting. Part of me wanted him to keep going so I could just bask in the happiness he radiated when he was bouncing around like he was at an actual show.

"Sorry. Music helps me process shit. Without it, I'd probably be in a grave somewhere," he said with a laugh, but I heard the truth in his words.

"'Only If For A Night.'"[1] The words tumbled out before I could stop them, and instantly, blood pounded in my ears.

His brows pinched. "If only for what night?" he asked, confused.

I moved around into the kitchen, hopping up on the faux granite counter and staring down at my cuticles as if they owed me money or something. "'Only If For A Night.' That's the song I play on full blast while I sit on the floor of my shower, wondering if anyone's ever drowned under that stream," I said, trailing off, unsure of why I was even sharing this with him.

It was the first vulnerable thing I'd shared with anyone in years.

The last time I did vulnerability by choice was with Andrei, and that shit ended horribly. Who the fuck knew why I was doing it again now. But it seemed that now I'd started, there was no stuffing it back in the bottle. "And then 'Shake It Out' would play next to remind me that maybe I didn't want to drown," I whispered.

Warmth radiated against my shins as he stepped closer, tilting my chin with his finger until I met his hazel eyes. They were more brown than green today.

"In the pitch black?" he asked.

My breath caught in my throat at his question. In truth, it was more of a statement, but how had he known that? Words failed to form on my tongue, and all I could give him was the slight nodding of my head.

"Alexa, play ' What the Water Gave Me'[1] by Florence + The Machine," he called out, never breaking the contact of his gaze or his body. Melodic tones filled the kitchen, and my eyes fluttered shut.

I felt like a live wire.

Too sensitive to all that was around me.

"You can dance if you'd like." His hot breath brushed across my face from where he still stood. Like a boulder in a raging river, his presence anchored me as every emotion I kept locked up tight burst free.

My feet carried me to the living room as if I were being controlled by someone else—something else. I let the hauntingly beautiful lyrics flow through me as my body painted the picture of my grief, my insanity, my joy, my dreams.

A manifestation of my soul.

I danced barefoot in an apartment that wasn't mine with a man who didn't know my god-given name, but who seemed to see more of me than anyone ever had.

I didn't know where he was, but I could feel the heat of his attention on me as I moved into an arabesque. The only thing that would make this better would be if I had a pair of pointe shoes and a pole.

Time seemed to go on forever while simultaneously feeling like the blink of an eye. When I finally stopped moving, my chest was heaving, sweat pouring off me, and my muscles ached in a delicious way that was familiar but forgotten.

"That was the most beautiful thing I've ever seen," Dex's deep voice startled me, and a small grin played on his lips when I looked over my shoulder at him. "You forgot I was here," he said, sounding pleased, maybe because I'd felt comfortable enough to let go the way I had.

"Thought alcohol was supposed to cause you to let your barriers down. Not the hangover," I mumbled, hugging myself in an attempt not to feel so *exposed.* I needed to rebuild some of my walls. I'd shared more with that dance than I had with anyone since moving to the United States.

Ryan and the girls assumed I was good at dancing by sheer talent. None of them had witnessed what I'd just done for Dex, or knew that I had classical training. Of course, Katya would have called what I'd just performed a bastardization of ballet.

The thought had me laughing while wrestling with the mourning of the woman I'd never gotten to become.

For the second time since waking up, tears pooled in my lash line— this time, I wasn't fast enough to catch them. In two steps, Dex closed the distance between us, cocooning me in his arms.

His chest rumbled when he spoke.

"You know you can tell me shit, right?" He pushed me back far enough that our eyes connected, while keeping me close.

The way he searched my face made me nervous, like he was attempting to look past the camouflage I'd placed around my past. "I mean, we both know I can keep a secret. I didn't tell any of my brothers about the shit with Gunner being in the FBI. And those guys are family."

I still had so many questions surrounding that whole situation, but asking them now felt like I'd be opening up the floor for some form of Q&A time, and that was the exact *opposite* of what I wanted to do right now. So, I did what I always did.

Deflect.

"I know I can tell you shit. I'm just emotional because I'm tired and hormonal," I told him, pulling away from his hold. It felt too comforting and safe in his arms.

Too tempting to actually open up to him.

What looked like irritation or suspicion moved across his face, but it quickly disappeared behind a goofy grin. "Well, roomie, eat up," he said, moving back into the kitchen and piling enough eggs and bacon to feed a family onto a plate.

He pushed the mountain of food my way, and another annoying twinge of giddiness fluttered in my stomach—more like in my ovaries. I was chalking the reaction up to some biological phenomenon that had us recognizing when another human was capable of taking care of us.

That was it. The only reason I was reacting was because of biology.

Not because I actually *liked* Dex.

I moaned around the mouthful of fluffy eggs, distracted. Ryan and I were shit at cooking and rarely had anything homemade, so this was divine. Maybe I could convince Dex to let me come over for his food even after we weren't roommates.

"Woman." Dex's irritated tone knocked me out of my musing. "It is *extremely* hard to think of you in a friendly manner when you moan with a mouthful like that."

His genuine irritation had me covering my laugh with my hand as he flipped me off.

"New roommate rule: no sex noises," he said, pulling out a pad and pen and writing it in all capital letters before taping it to the fridge.

"Is this rule for, like, when I'm eating? I'm just wondering what I'm supposed to do when I'm getting off. Do I need to be quiet during my self-care routine?" I teased, not thinking through the consequences of my actions. One moment, Dex was beginning to make his way down the hall, and the next, I found myself trapped between the counter and his body.

It took all my control not to lean back into his chest. The way I wanted to fuck this man was at complete odds with the fact that I also did not want to fuck things *up* with this man. Which was new territory for the girl who made no attachments.

Yet here I was doing exactly that with Dex.

"You know, this brings up something important we need to discuss." His face was right next to mine, but I refused to look at him, pretending his proximity wasn't affecting me in the least bit. Thank god his shirt was oversized, because my nipples would have been a dead giveaway to how much of an effect he was having on me.

"You want to discuss what my favorite vibrator is?" I asked, hoping being so blunt would put us on a more even footing. He currently had me feeling too out of sorts.

"No. Although, I am a vibrator connoisseur." He spun the counter stool I was sitting on until our legs brushed against one another as he leaned over me.

Why do I always end up looking at him through my lashes like a lovesick woman?

"That's not what we need to discuss. We need to talk about the fact that you and I are now a romantic item," he said, a wicked look on his beautiful face.

"We are?" I squeaked, my throat suddenly dry as my brain tried to pull up vague memories of the conversation that happened last night at the club.

The smile he gave me was so sensual I wanted to melt. "Yes, Nikki, we are. And from now on, we are going to have to keep that little ruse up. What I need from you," he tilted my chin up so I was staring into his eyes rather than at his pierced nipples.

I wanted the ground to open up and swallow me whole when he gave me a knowing smirk, because I most *definitely* had been drooling over them. "Is for you to give me permission to touch you as if I really were your boyfriend."

All of the teasing fell away, and his face turned serious. I didn't think he had any idea how incredibly hot it was that consent was so important to him.

It was also depressing that something that should be a standard wasn't, and that I found it attractive when I found someone who respected the concept in the way he did.

I'd assume Dex would say as much if I brought it up.

His rough fingers held me in place so I couldn't look away even if I wanted to. Clearing my throat, I answered him honestly.

"Yes."

"Yes, what, Nikki?" The command in his tone had moisture pooling between my legs. I would do anything he wanted if he spoke to me in that confident tone while holding my chin the way he currently was.

"Yes, you can touch me the way you would your actual girlfriend."

Panty-melting. That was the only way to describe how he looked when one corner of his mouth curled up, and how he cupped my face, running his thumb along my bottom lip. But in the next instant he was gone, walking away from me toward the bathroom door.

"What the hell, Dex. I don't even get a *good girl* or some shit?"

He stilled. "That's not what you want, Nikki. You're not looking to be a good girl." He glanced over his shoulder as he yanked the door open. "I have a feeling you got tired of being called that a long time ago."

1 Put on Only If For A Night by Florence + The Machine and grab some fucking tissues. Cheers to a good sobbing session. Especially if you're an Aquarius since we don't do this often...

TWENTY-THREE

NIKKI

ALL MEN CEASE TO MATURE PAST MIDDLE SCHOOL. ANOTHER SCIENTIFIC FACT

INCESSANT POUNDING on my door was today's alarm clock. I groaned and tried to ignore it.

A rough voice called out, sounding sexy until his words actually registered in my sleep-deprived brain. "Nikki, if you don't get your ass out of bed, I will come in there and get you," Dex hollered from the other side.

"Go away," I yelled back, throwing a pillow and the blankets over my head to block out his bitching about us having shit to do. I'd spent all of yesterday laying around, chugging Gatorade, and eating every greasy hangover food Dex brought me. He was a real mother hen, and I wasn't sure if he was like that with everyone or…

Don't go down that line of thinking.

"Nikki, let's go," he called out in a sing-song voice that was far too cheery.

What the hell could we possibly have to do?

Ryan had given me time off, deciding it was better if I kept a low profile. The new rumor about Dex and I was the perfect cover-up. Everyone assumed I wasn't at work because I was busy fucking my brains out with my new boyfriend.

Instead, I was over here letting him see parts of me I didn't show anyone. My stomach flipped, thinking about our moment in the kitchen.

Fucking kicker was I'd *wanted* to share more with him. I wanted to tell him who I was, and who was after me. I wanted us to be like Ryan and Gunner, facing problems together. They made it through a hidden identity.

Why couldn't we?

Oh, I don't know. Because you have an evil ex-or-possibly-current-husband hunting you down...

Thudding footsteps filled the small room, cutting off my musings. Dex's heavy body landed on top of me, sending the air whooshing from my lungs.

"Get. Off. Me." He was an immovable mass, and I tried to ignore how much I liked the feel of his weight on me as I pushed on what I assumed was his chest. A deep chuckle sounded in my ear, his hot breath penetrating the thin white blanket.

"Make me."

Why were all men essentially middle school boys? His yelp made me smile from ear to ear.

"How did you find my nipple so easily?" he asked, ripping the blanket off my head, causing my hair to tangle in my face.

"My bad," he mumbled, brushing it back and tucking a strand behind my ear. The rough pads of his fingertips had my stomach flip-flopping in excitement. It didn't help that when my view was cleared, what I was left looking at was a shirtless Dex, straddling me. Any moisture in my mouth evaporated and traveled down south.

Shit. I'm not wearing clothes.

I gripped the edge of the blanket, holding it up under my chin. "What are you doing in my room, Dexter?" Bikers usually didn't go by anything other than their road names once they were patched in, but I found myself curious as to what Dex's full legal name was. I opened my mouth to ask, but the words lodged in my throat.

Was I going to share the same shit about myself with him? Because that is where broaching this conversation would lead.

The problem with wanting to know more about someone was it required letting them get to know you in turn, and I found myself not wanting to share all my usual lies with Dex. I *wanted* to tell him about me, Natasha. That was dangerous fucking territory, and yet, I found myself getting closer to it with every passing minute in this man's company.

Dex flopped over to the side, propping his head up to look at me, oblivious to my internal turmoil. "Come on. Get dressed."

"Why?"

"Because if you go in that sheer red set," he said, plucking the strap of my bra, the sting of the snap going straight to my clit, "you'll cause accidents. And since I'm letting you drive when you don't even have a license, that would be a fuckin' problem."

Dex loved to just say shit to me without giving any further context, and then I was left lying there looking like an idiot as I tried to decipher what he was going on about.

"What the hell are you talking about, Dex? I don't know *how* to drive." The statement was bitter in my mouth. I hated not being able to do basic things. They were reminders of why it was that I couldn't.

Like running from my home country and being here illegally.

"I'm fully aware you don't know how to, Nikki. That's the whole point of what we are doing this evening. Duh. Now, go cover your ass cheeks and meet me outside," he said, kissing me on my forehead before launching out of the bed and disappearing into the hall.

He was going to teach me how to drive? All I could do was stare after him, thinking about how no one had ever bothered to take the time to notice things about me the way he did, and I didn't know what to do with that realization. So I said, "Fuck it," got up, and got ready.

My sleep schedule had been fucked for years, and *morning* was more like six p.m. Hues of pink and orange painted the sky. I wasn't entirely sure if it was the Arizona heat or the nerves of learning to drive that had beads of sweat popping up around my hairline. Our apartment was on the ground floor, steps away from the parking lot.

My heart nearly stopped when I rounded the corner to find Dex leaning against a blacked-out SUV. His arms were crossed, his muscles pushing the limits of his white T-shirt. Always the same outfit of black dickies, slightly oversized graphic T-shirt, and white Air Forces. The man knew what worked for him, that was for sure. His hair was up in a bun at the top of his head, and the sun highlighted the golden tones interwoven with the brown.

He was painfully attractive, and it wasn't a wonder so many women fell over themselves to get into his pants.

"Why are you frowning like that? We haven't even started yet. You can't already decide you hate driving," he called out, tucking away his phone.

I flipped him off, letting him think he was correct in his assumption. Thank god he couldn't read minds, or he'd know that the face was because I didn't like the idea of him with other women. Which was preposterous since *I* wasn't with him either…not really.

He moved over to the passenger side and opened the door, motioning for me to get in.

"I thought I was driving," I said, climbing into the massive vehicle. "Shouldn't I learn in something…smaller?" I asked as he shut the door, jogging around to the other side and sliding in.

The engine roared to life. "First of all, most of my time is spent on a bike, so I don't exactly have a garage full of options for you," he said, adjusting things.

He was right. Where had this one even come from?

I didn't have to wonder for long.

"I took Robert's ride. He's not going to need it for a while since he's over in Santa Ana." He gripped the steering wheel with his left hand, throwing the other arm over the back of our seats and turning to look out the rear windshield.

"What's he doing there?" I asked after clearing my throat. Why was watching a man's hand glide over the wheel as he backed up so hot?

"Dunno." He shrugged a shoulder, his attention back in front as he drove us out of the parking lot and off to who knew where. "Los Muertos shit is my guess. We don't really talk particulars of our organizations. He knew about you and me because Ryan told him. Now, back to your other questions. Aside from this being the only vehicle available, it's also bulletproofed, in case anything goes south," he said, trailing off at the end.

Silence hung between us for a few moments, and I pulled my legs up onto the leather seats, hugging them to my chest. He rubbed at the back of his neck like he felt bad for mentioning that I was a target.

"Um. Anyway, you are going to drive. But I need to assess what the hell you actually know before I let you get on the road with other cars." He shot me a grin, clearly excited about the whole adventure he was taking me on. With that view, there was no stopping one from forming on my lips. "Have you ever driven at all?" he asked, pulling us into an abandoned lot of some warehouses.

"No, never really got the chance," I said vaguely, avoiding looking at him.

"Alright, so we will start with the basics," he said, without even a hint of him mocking me, or thinking I was an idiot for being my age and not knowing how to drive. I felt my shoulders relax and my jaw loosen. "Climb on over, spitfire," he said, turning off the car and stepping out.

I moved over the center console, placing both hands on the wheel just like he had.

"Okay, so these things here are your blinkers, your ignition." He reached down and gripped my ankle, placing my foot on one of the pedals. "Gas, brake ."

Did I only interact with assholes, or what?

Because there I was, swooning over him placing my foot on a pedal.

When he pulled his hand away his fingers brushed the back of my calves, and I wanted to skip the driving lesson so we could do something else in the car.

Dex went over how I wasn't to drive with both feet or yank on the e-brake to drift. I told him he was speaking a foreign language.

Finally, he let me drive. Kind of. We drove around the giant asphalt area, and he made me perform various maneuvers. Unsurprisingly, at least to me, he was a great teacher.

I constantly worked to hide myself from people so I could spot all the little things people tried to downplay from a mile away. I'd known since the first time I met him that Dex used his humor and goofiness to disarm people, letting them think he was aloof.

But at his core, he was so much more.

Sherlock Holmes had already deduced that I never looked in the rear view mirror, and shouldn't attempt to parallel park unless I wanted to pay to replace someone's bumper.

"Okay, ease out here now." His eyes bounced from left to right, searching the empty road. "Make sure you look—"

"Both ways." I finished for him, pulling out, a thrill shooting through me. I was actually driving on a road. My cheeks began to ache with how hard I was smiling.

"I'm doing it. I'm driving, Dex," I practically shrieked.

"Yeah, you are, babe," he said. My breath caught on the term. Something about it just did it for me, like when he called me spitfire.

He looked at me with such pride that my heart actually palpitated. He was legitimately excited for me, and not disappointed that I hadn't figured out how to do this years ago. I wasn't even sure what he was supposed to be doing right now. He had to have shit to do other than teaching me how to drive.

Why did he have to be so fucking kind to me? To actually see *me*.

His voice broke through my thoughts, humor in his tone. "Nikki, why don't we focus on the road instead of you looking at me like I shit sparkles," he suggested, smiling.

I whipped my head back, accidentally sending us into the other lane a smidge. A car horn blared at us.

"Oh, shit. Sorry," I yelled as if the other driver would hear us, but whoever it was proceeded to lay on the horn and tail my ass. "Fuck, it was an accident."

"Slow down," Dex said, an edge to his voice. My gut clenched at the idea of letting him down, but his attention wasn't on me. It was on the side mirror as he rolled the window down. I did as he asked, and the vehicle I'd pissed off came up beside us, rolling theirs down as well.

"Watch where you're going, bitch," the guy yelled, his face turned up in a snarl.

I was about to apologize when Dex pulled out a gun and pointed it at the other driver. "Say it again, asshole. Call my girlfriend a bitch." All the color in the man's face drained, causing Dex to sneer. "That's what I thought, *bitch*. Watch your fucking road rage, got it? Because you never know when you're going to be a dick to a fucker who's shot people for less. Now, apologize for being a dickwad," he demanded, looking dangerously close to getting out of the car and beating the dude's ass.

It took every ounce of my restraint not to laugh as the guy apologized, his voice shaking so badly that it was gibberish. I also ignored the nagging voice pointing out that Dex had called me his girlfriend in front of someone we didn't need to put on the show for. The level of overthinking I was doing in trying to decipher his reasoning was absurd. Meanwhile, Dex probably didn't even realize he'd said it.

Men.

"Good. Now, get the fuck out of here." The words were

barely out of Dex's mouth, and the small electric car was gone. "Damn, I was going to tell you to give him a little ram to the ass, too. Fuckin' electric cars are fast on the takeoff," he said, looking over at me. "You okay, Niks?"

"Yeah, I'm good," I answered, keeping my focus solely on the road. His attention and sincere concern were too much—I couldn't look at him.

Why couldn't he have been like a fuckboy. I mean, he kind of was a fuckboy, but a sweet one who made me breakfast and watched me dance in the living room.

One who brought me three different types of Gatorade since he didn't know which was my favorite color.

"Turn left up here—don't forget your turn signal. I think we need milkshakes," he said.

One who fucking teaches you how to drive and then buys you a milkshake after pulling a gun on someone who called you a bitch.

Romance wasn't dead…but I wasn't supposed to be looking for romance.

TWENTY-FOUR

DEX

LET US LIVE SINCE WE ARE DESTINED TO DIE

"YOU'RE LYING. You let his *wife* enter the private dance room instead of you?" I asked, sucking down the last of my milkshake. We'd pulled off the main road and parked out in the desert to finish our drinks, and I was doing everything in my power to stop thinking about how it felt dangerously close to a date.

Nikki's laugh bounced around the parked SUV. "Of course I let her in. That asshole was stepping out on his wife."

"Aren't most of the dudes in there doing that?" I didn't condone cheating. It was why I made it so abundantly clear to women that we weren't a thing. My eyes landed on Nikki, the setting sun washing her in warm light.

She made me rethink my stance on relationships. I had no clue why that was, but being around her made me feel like I was alive—bathed in her sunlight and warmth—and I never wanted to leave.

She pinned me with a look. "She was eight months pregnant," Nikki said flatly. "And if I know they are in a relationship, I won't take the dance. When she came in earlier in the night asking about the asshole, I instantly knew I was going to help her." She looked down into her cup, smirking. "Ryan threatened to beat him up."

"She could do it, too. Fucked up Torque. I still don't let him live that shit down."

We both broke out in a fit of laughter that faded into a comfortable silence.

"Hey," she said, her voice small and unsure, the opposite of the verbal jabs she'd been delivering only moments before. Without thinking it through, I brushed a strand of blonde that had managed to break free, tucking it behind her cute ear.

Fuck. When did you start noticing ears? And why are you not imagining the sounds you could pull from her if you sucked on that sensitive part of her lobe…okay, now you are.

She broke the daydream. Piercing blue eyes held mine, a mixture of uncertainty and determination in her gaze. It was a look that made my heart race.

"Remember the other day when we were in the kitchen?" she asked.

The memory of that day had left an indelible mark on me, etching itself into the corners of my mind. Of course I remembered. I'd never witnessed someone move as beautifully as she had in that moment, when she seemed to pour out her soul, barefoot, in the dingey apartment we were hiding out in.

But I didn't say any of that.

"We're in the kitchen together a lot, Nikki," I said casually, turning my body in the seat so I could watch her facial expressions.

She seemed to grow frustrated with my response, her nose scrunching up in a telltale sign of annoyance. I watched her closely, determined to unwind her tangle of thoughts and feelings.

Force her to share, no matter how stubborn she might be.

And if that meant playing the part of a dumbass to get her to spell out what she wanted, then I would do it every fucking time.

As she clenched her fists in her lap, I could see the storm of emotions swirling beneath her composed exterior. She turned fully in her seat. Her unwavering stare told me she was on a mission. It was a silent challenge, a dare, and I was more than willing to accept it.

"How did you know?" Her determination was so fucking cute that it eclipsed the worry in my gut with what she was asking.

Truthfully, we'd both been raw with our emotions that day. Even though we hadn't discussed them, we'd allowed one another to witness something private.

"What do you mean?" I asked, leaning back and trying to hide how my heartbeat had kicked up in my chest, my palms growing damp.

"How did you know I would sit in the shower in the dark?" she asked, so quietly I almost didn't hear her.

The question was a punch to the gut.

"I, uh…" I scratched at the back of my head, stalling. At the time, my heart had decided to speak before my mind could intervene, revealing a secret I hadn't intended to share.

Silence stretched between us, unspoken truth handing heavy in the air.

It wasn't an easy answer to tell.

I knew I had a choice to make. I could lie, brush it off as a lucky guess, and protect the fortress around my emotions—but I knew that would set us back. All the small morsels of herself that she gave me would stop dead in their tracks.

In that moment, I realized that getting to know Nikki and letting her in mattered more than locking up my own demons.

She didn't push me when I let another long stretch of silence grow between us. Instead, she reached her hand over and interlaced it with mine. Her unmarred skin was a stark contrast to my inked fingers, and I liked the sight of our joined hands more than I should have.

"I don't know when I last held hands with a woman," I said, turning our hands over and inspecting them. I liked the feel of her fingers intertwined with mine.

"Yeah. I don't think I've ever held hands with a man. Not unless he was dragging me behind him." The last part was so quiet I would have missed it if we'd been anywhere besides a parked car out in the middle of the desert. I wanted to know exactly what she meant by that—dragging her willingly? Unwillingly? Either answer had me wanting to hang someone by their ankles and flay them.

I wanted to know more about her. I needed to. And to do that, I'd have to open up.

There was no way I could look her in the eye while I shared the worst parts of myself. So, I stared out the windshield, watching the stars as they seemed to shift in the night sky. "How much has Gunner or Ryan shared with you about my past?" I asked, briefly stealing a glance.

"Nothing, really. I don't know much past you and Gunner knew each other before you joined Skeletons." She shrugged a shoulder. "Heard a few mentions of him making a deal to save you from jail time, and that you were both in the Marines, but that's pretty much it. I don't even know your real name…"

I didn't know hers either.

My head nodded, almost of its own accord, as I mulled over where to start. I didn't know if I was relieved or disappointed that that was all she knew. It would have been easier if she'd known more, and I wasn't the one to peel off the layers of scabs over my battered heart to relive what'd happened to Kell.

I took a deep breath, steadying my nerves. "Well, first of all, it's Derek Kelley, but I don't ever go by that. And that's true, we were both scout snipers in the Marine Corps. Long-range shots are a specialty of mine, despite Gunner getting the road name that reflects that skill. Grew up with a deadbeat dad who bolted when I was young enough that I can't even pull a face from my memories. My mom was young when she had me, and afterward, she hopped onto the dick of the first man who smiled at her."

There was no hiding the bitterness in my tone, and I spurred on before I could really lay into the woman. "Anyway, she got pregnant again, even though she could barely care for herself, let alone me. Nine months later, Kelly was born." I smiled, and Nikki squeezed my hand as if sensing that I needed the support to continue. "We were Irish twins and fucking thick as thieves." My little spitfire was observant as fuck and tensed at the use of *were*. "When we got older, I became both parents for her, even though we were essentially the same age. We saw our mom less and less, because she'd just disappear for weeks at a time."

An ache radiated from my jaw as I clenched to keep me from punching something. Dana was a real piece of fucking work.

Nikki spoke quietly as if sensing how I was teetering on the precipice of exploding. I stroked my thumb across the top of her hand, needing her to know I'd never lose my shit on her. Not in anger, anyway. Maybe in fear.

"I didn't grow up here, so I don't know, but they will just let you raise your siblings like that?" she asked.

Here, as in the United States?

That must have been what she'd meant, because anyone from here would know it was definitely *not* something you were supposed to do, not without applying for emancipation. I tucked away another piece of her puzzle, but answered her question.

"No. They won't let you do that. But Kell and I kept everything quiet, telling school staff and any other adult who'd ask that our mom worked nights or some shit like that."

It ha d worked until it didn't.

I cleared my throat, shifting in my seat. Sure, our childhood wasn't ideal, but what I'd just shared with Nikki was actually all of my *good* memories. It was the next part that haunted me. "I joined the Marines when I turned eighteen." I ran my free hand through my hair again. "I was young and stupid. We'd been on our own so long, I figured Kell would be fine while I was away."

I laughed, remembering the pact I'd made with Gunner when we were going through scout sniper training together.

"What is it?" she prodded gently, smiling.

"One night, I made Gunner swear he would ask Kelly to marry him." Her small gasp only made my smile grow wider, and I finally looked at her so I could explain.

Fuck. She was beautiful. The last streaks of sunlight shone off her blonde waves, making it look like she wore a halo. She'd hate it if I told her that—piety wasn't her goal in life.

"It wasn't a romantic thing," I said with a shrug. "If he'd married her, it would've made him eligible for housing and shit. We were all just going to move in together. I'd still have a dorm, but my time would be spent at their place. One big happy family…" My words trailed off, a barrage of memories battering against the walls I'd put up.

"But that never happened," Nikki whispered.

All I could do was shake my head and repeat my mantra.

In for four. Out for four.

In for four. Out for four.

"No. That never happened," I finally responded, my voice hollow and flat.

It was as if it were a completely different man informing Nikki how I got a call while I was on deployment from Kelly, and all I could make out were her pained screams as she begged me to help her. Like I was listening in on someone else, relaying how I'd failed the most important person in my life. I never should have left her alone.

The weight of those memories and the pain they carried had cast a heavy shadow over my soul. A piece of me had been left behind in that distant, harrowing moment. It wasn't just my beautiful baby sister who'd died that day.

The man I was had died, too. I'd built my walls as a feeble attempt to shield myself from the guilt and anguish that threatened to engulf me, wanting to believe that I had never heard those screams, that I had never failed Kelly.

And if I never let anyone close, I wouldn't experience that grief again.

Numbness flowed through me.

Nikki's warmth enveloped me, taking me by surprise. Her

body pressed against mine like she was attempting to thaw me out. Her head tucked beneath my chin as she sat curled up in my lap, her arms firmly wrapped around my middle. She was a lifeline in the sea of grief that threatened to drown me. I clung to her, desperate to feel her skin against mine.

"That's how you knew." Her voice was barely above a whisper, spoken directly against my heart.

I stroked my calloused hands up and down her arms. The touch made her nestle in closer, and I didn't know how I'd be able to go back to not holding her like this. My eyes shuttered closed. How ironic that I was describing the very event that made me renounce love to the girl who'd clawed her way into my damaged soul.

"What happened to her?" she asked, her voice quiet in the night.

I kept my eyes closed, tears welling up in the corners. "Our mom decided to make an appearance again after being gone for a fucking year plus." The memories came rushing back. Gunner had found out the details when he was in the feds, and told me once he felt I was stable enough to hear them. "She apparently owed some people money, some Russians money." She stiffened in my arms, but didn't pull away. "And they didn't want her usual form of alternate payment. So, she gave them something better." I spat out the last part, years of rage that still felt fresh. "Kelly was always more forgiving than I was. Probably because I didn't tell her half the shit our mom did. When our mom asked to see her, Kell went."

Nikki shook her head against my chest, anger in her voice. "She trusted her. Parents are supposed to take care of you. You're supposed to be able to trust them to keep you safe. To have your best interests at heart," she said, her voice hitching at the end.

Something about the way she said it made me hold her tighter, as if I could keep the hurt at bay. It took me a moment to realize she couldn't see me nod my head in agreement.

"Yeah, babe. Family should protect you."

Was that why she was so opposed to letting people in? Were the ones who should have protected her, the ones who'd hurt her? Fuck.

"How did you make it through?" she asked, cutting through my revelation about her. "You always seem so...full of life."

I smile at her question, because being happy while grieving was a mindfuck.

Sometimes, I wondered if I was truly insane.

"It started as a mask. To get people to stop asking. Stop looking at me as if I had a loaded gun and a twitchy finger. And then, one day, I realized I was tired of slowly dying. I decided to live. Make my mask permanent. Some days, it feels like there's a barrel to my temple whispering about the beauty of oblivion, but for the most part, I feel like...why not live since we are destined to die? Death will stick her claws in me eventually, but I'm going to have a fucking great time while I wait," I answered honestly, pulling up my shirt to reveal the letters resting over my chest. "It became my mantra. "Let us live since we are destined to die."

Nikki pushed back so her gaze met mine before reaching up and running a knuckle under my eye, capturing the stray tear. The act was so pure that my heart almost hurt.

That's when I noticed the damp spot on my shirt from where her face had been, and emotion welled in my chest thinking about her mourning Kell, someone she hadn't even known.

"She would have liked you," I whispered, cupping her face in my hand. I meant it, too. Kelly would have kicked my ass for not tying Nikki down already. That thought brought a small smile to my face.

Nikki's eyes widened at the comment, and there was a flicker of surprise and vulnerability, but she didn't shy away like usual. Instead, she took a deep breath and began to unravel a part of her own past, her voice soft and steady.

"When I showed up in Tucson, Ryan was completely different than anyone I'd ever met. No one else had ever cared about *me*. All they cared about was what I could do for them, but not about me as a person." She paused, canting her head as if surprised by her own thoughts. "Well, that's not entirely true—my ballet teacher seemed to care. Woman was a tyrant in the dance studio, but she...she was the mother figure in my life."

"You still talk to her?"

Nikki's blue eyes darkened, and she pulled her bottom lip between her teeth in thought before she went on. "No. I wasn't supposed to end up in Tucson, but the first chance I had to run...I took it. It's what Katya would have told me to do." She let out a laugh. "I was a damn mess. Up until that point, everything in my life was controlled for me. I didn't know how to do shit."

"Like driving?" I teased.

Her hand hit my chest, a faux scowl on her beautiful face before transforming into a breathtaking smile. "You should see me try to cook. I've set more than one towel on fire."

Her confession had me smiling back. "More than once is concerning, spitfire," I said, running my thumb across her bottom lip. "So how did you end up friends with an arms dealer?" I prompted, hungry for more about her.

"Oh, fucking hardass pulled me off the floor one night when I was piss-drunk and told me it was time to grow up and pull my head out of my ass." She smiled, nuzzling into the hand I'd yet to pull away. "She was great with words of affirmation like that," she added.

I laughed, the action jolting Nikki backward, the movement rocking her against the crotch of my jeans and reminding me that she'd climbed across the center console and was now snuggled up on my thighs. Up until this moment, not a single sexual thought had crossed my mind.

But now...

Nothing said sexy like dead sisters and deadbeat parents.

As if she sensed the shift, too, she hurried to keep talking.

"Have you ever met someone, and you just knew their soul was worth loving? That you didn't need to know anything more than what you saw before you? Nothing else would change how you were connected, because they'd already made a place in your heart?" she asked, her words coming out in a rush of emotion. I reached for her wrist, feeling the way her pulse had quickened.

My gaze locked onto hers, and I allowed my feelings for her to slip through. A silent confession. She had no clue she was describing how I felt for her, and I was jealous that Ryan was the one who'd earned Nikki's love. I wanted her to feel that way for me.

Even if it was only fleeting.

"Yeah, Niks, I do know what it's like to fall for someone when you know nothing about them—yet somehow know all of the important parts."

TWENTY-FIVE

NIKKI

FLIPPING A BITCH: APPARENTLY ONLY A WEST COAST TERM MEANING TO TURN THE DAMN CAR AROUND

HIS STARE MADE me feel raw. Those hazel eyes stripped me of every brick I'd placed in my walls, revealing the scared and damaged soul it surrounded—protected. And I wanted so badly to let him in, to trust him.

His words reverberated in my mind.

He's talking about you.

I wanted to scoff at my inner thoughts, spouting wishful bullshit. There was no way he could mean me…and when had my words shifted from sharing about Ryan to revealing how I felt about Dex?

My chest ached like all of the oxygen was being stolen from my lungs and the only way I would be able to breathe was if I let him in, sharing a piece of myself the way he had. Suffocating was the less terrifying option. Letting him in was a guarantee to heartache.

He's already in.

When had that happened? When had I let this man through my boundaries? He'd slipped in, filling in my cracks and making me whole—but I didn't tell him any of that.

I never got the chance.

A barrage of bullets hit the driver's side of the SUV, pulling a scream from my mouth.

"Fuck," Dex yelled, wrapping his arms around me and

tucking our bodies down near the floorboard. Another round went off, pinging off the glass but not piercing it. "Baby, I need you to stay down here, okay?" he asked, smoothing his hands over my hair, searching my face.

"Yeah." I swallowed down my initial shock, tucking away any fear. He needed me to be strong, not a fucking weeping mess. Luckily for both of us, this wasn't my first time being in shit like this.

"Got an extra gun?" I asked.

He untangled his massive body from mine, maneuvering into the driver's seat with surprising ease, "Spitfire, you don't need a gun. You've got me to take care of you," he said, throwing the car into drive and peeling out.

"That's fucking cute, but I've managed to survive for twenty-seven years without you, Dex. I'm not sitting on my ass while we're being shot at."

He chuckled, but the smile quickly fell. "Shit," he hissed.

Dread flooded me at the tone in his voice.

"Get in your seat, Nikki. Now. And buckle the fuck up." The car took a sharp turn that sent my head into the door. I scrambled up off the floor and buckled up, pulling my phone out and shooting off a message. It was dark out now, and the headlights of the car following us were so bright I couldn't tell the make or model.

"What's the pla—" I didn't get a chance to finish my question.

Glass shattered, the rear window exploding, sending shards of glass everywhere.

"Fucking hell, they have bullet piercing," Dex shouted, yanking the steering wheel to the side and directing us between a set of boulders as we moved farther out into the desert. Without a second thought, I started digging through the glove box.

"Come one, Robert, I know you've got to have." My hand wrapped the familiar grip of a gun. "Bingo," I said, unbuckling my seatbelt and crawling into the back.

Dex's hand grabbed my ankle, briefly taking his eyes off

where we were going to look me in the eye. "What the hell are you doing?" he asked, his voice thick with concern.

"You gonna throw a fit about it, or will you let me help?"

He shook his head, but released his hold, and I moved all the way to the ruined rear windshield. It was still in place, but there was a giant hole, and the entire thing was splintered, looking like a spiderweb.

"Well, this isn't going to work," I muttered, shoving the heel of my foot into the damaged glass, kicking out the window.

"Nikki, what the *fuck* are you doing," Dex yelled out, competing with the increased volume now coming in.

"Listen, I have good aim, but not that fucking good. I needed a bigger hole."

Whatever curse words he yelled at me got carried away in the desert air, now whipping through the vehicle. I braced my back against the side near the wheel well. Our speed climbed higher and higher, but our pursuer matched us. The empty stretch of desert didn't help—there was nothing to lose them in, not side streets or oncoming traffic.

Another barrage of bullets popped off, and I shielded myself with my arms. As soon as there was a break, I popped up, getting off a few rounds. They pinged off the car's front windshield.

"Bulletproof," I shouted, ducking back down.

"Fuck. We need backup."

I moved back into position, this time aiming for the front tires, something you couldn't bulletproof, but our angle was shit. "Already done," I yelled out, cursing under my breath when one of my shots barely missed my mark. "Sent Ryan an SOS and my location."

"I could fucking kiss you, Nikki," Dex yelled, yanking the SUV to the side. "Get back up here."

"What?"

Carefully, I maneuvered back into the passenger seat.

He didn't look at me, too focused on trying to outrun the

lighter car trailing us. "Climb onto my lap, baby. We need a better angle. If you flip a bitch—"

"You want me to flip the car?" My voice went up in volume. I knew he was wild but what good would flipping the car do?

I could hear the laughter in his voice. "No, it means make a U-turn. I want you to make it so they're on my side. I'm going to try and shoot their tires."

I was quiet for a few moments, trying to process the batshit idea, but then a bullet whizzed between us, making up my mind.

I climbed into his lap, placing my hands on the steering wheel with his. "I don't know if it's a good idea that they let us be together. You're just as reckless as I am," he said. Adrenaline pounded through my veins, and I couldn't tell if it was reality or a final wish that I felt Dex's lips on the back of my head. He rolled our window down. "Fucking hold on, babe."

He cranked the wheel, the harsh move sending us up on two tires for a moment before bouncing back down. "Okay, hold tight. And if I say duck, fucking *duck*," he yelled.

I didn't think, just acted, gripping the wheel and holding it steady as I pushed the gas pedal into the floor. Dex leaned out the window and popped off several rounds. He was a fucking great shot, hitting the gunman hanging out of the window. When they all took cover behind the bulletproofing, Dex aimed for the tire. His shot connected.

"Hell, yeah. That's my girl," Dex yelled as we zoomed past.

Now we had to make it back to the road in one piece and hope Ryan and backup were close, because a bullet in the tire wasn't as dramatic as in movies. They were still pursuing us, but the hole would make driving at high speeds unpredictable, and I was hoping it would be enough to give us an edge.

"There," I shouted, pointing to headlights in the distance headed our way.

"You sure they're friends and not foes?" he asked, a clear

edge of concern. His arm wrapped around my waist, acting like my seatbelt since we'd never strapped me in. As if he realized the same thing, he unbuckled, rebuckling the belt around both of us.

"It probably won't do shit, but I'm not fucking risking it."

I nodded in agreement, breathing out a sigh of relief when the headlights illuminated a pissed-off cartel boss.

"Thank fuck," Dex said.

We flew past them, and Dex pumped on the brakes as soon as we passed the line of SUVs and motorcycles, positioning at an angle like the others.

He scooped me up, unfolding us both out of the car and running in a crouch toward one of the Range Rovers parked farthest away.

Shouts and more gunfire went off from where our pursuer was finally reaching the line of Los Muertos and Skeletons. Dex ran his hands over my face and body, inspecting me for any injuries, nodding his head when he was confident I was okay. I returned the favor, batting his hand away when he complained.

"I knew spitfire fit you," he said, his mouth pulling up in a crooked grin before falling away. "I'm glad you're okay. It was a little touch and go there for a second."

I couldn't handle the look on his face and needed to add some levity back into the moment. I didn't do well thinking about how much he worried about me. Or worse, how much I worried about him.

"Do I get to learn how to parallel park in the next lesson?" I asked.

TWENTY-SIX
DEX

A FIRM SQUEEZE, MAYBE SOME LIGHT SUCKING

GETTING RID of a body would be far easier if we were in the funeral business.

"Imma buy a crematory," I announced, wiping the beads of sweat threatening to run into my eyes. They were already stinging like bitch from all the sand we'd managed to kick up.

I winced at the thought of getting on my girl in this condition, but unless a shower randomly appeared out in the middle of bum-fuck nowhere, my bike would have to endure my crusty ass. Without a doubt, I'd need to burn these clothes after tonight. It was too bad I hadn't brought extra—I could've added these to the roaring inferno we presently had going.

Going home in my birthday suit was a no-go. I knew from experience that my ball sack did *not* like being out on the open road. He was more into being cradled and caressed.

Maybe a firm squeeze every now and again…some light sucking.

"You're the only mother fucker I know who will randomly start talking out loud about their junk as if it were another person. You name 'em something stupid too, like Goliath?" Torque called out, busting up when I looked at him in confusion.

Fuck, I was tired. I hadn't realized I'd said all that out loud.

I'd sent Nikki home with Ryan after our attack. The woman was constantly surprising me. I could see the fear in her eyes when we'd been shot at, but she'd swallowed it down and taken action. If only I could get her to lower her guard enough to let me in. We'd made some progress when she'd given me a glimpse into her past, but she still guarded herself like Fort Knox.

Needing to pull my mind off my "roomie," I turned my thoughts back to what Torque had asked. He was right, my dick did have a name. It'd started as a weird joke that was created in a sleep-deprived haze during sniper training. I smirked, knowing they would lose their shit when I told them what I'd landed on.

"Big Poppa, aka Biggie Balls," I said.

The moment the words were out, Murphy's wheezing echoed through the quiet desert.

"When the fuck did a herd of geese show up?" I teased, my cheeks hurting from how wide my smile was. Fucker had one of those laughs that made you concerned he might go into cardiac arrest or something. Torque wasn't much better, rolling on the ground, slapping it like it'd disrespected his mom.

The assholes who'd attacked us were Reapers, which wasn't a surprise—I knew they'd continue their search for Nikki eventually. We got lucky there was only one car with the two men. It could have been way worse, like when Ryan, Gunner, and I had gotten pinned down with the box truck.

My gut was telling me shit was going to get messy soon.

Boe walked over, his pudgy face pinched in a scowl at the sight of us. "I finished getting the last of the accelerant on the burn pile. Let's get them on before the smoke calls too much attention," he said.

I could feel his eyes on me with that last part, but I ignored him. Boe and I didn't exactly get along, but that was nothing new. He *thought* I was an idiot, and I *knew* he was one.

Torque let out a gag from beside me. "How the fuck can

you do that without—" *gag*— "without throwing up?" he asked, referring to my task of removing the Reapers' chompers and other potentially identifying body parts. One body was already burning.

A squelching noise emitted from the dead asshole's mouth as I pulled the final molar. "Easy. I just remind myself there's no way I'm leaving that shit out here and chancing a murder charge," I said with a shrug, peeling off my latex gloves and tossing them into the biohazard bag along with homeboy's phalanges and teeth.

I left out that this was one of the least fucked up things I'd done. At least this guy wasn't feeling any of this shit—but that was only because it was hard to understand someone with a mouth of bloody gums.

This was all precautionary. I didn't want any charges coming back to the club or my brothers. I'd used my one get-out-of-jail-free card. Gunner was a full outlaw now, so there wasn't anyone to save our asses this time.

Heavy footfalls sounded from behind me. "Please, making sure the evidence is gone is the *least* Dex can do. He's already brought enough fuckin' heat down on the club." Everyone stilled at Boe's remark.

Boe and I patched in together. He'd never been all that thrilled that I'd been voted in as enforcer, which meant I had Pres's ear when he didn't. Guy had a real complex about wanting to be in charge. Truth be told, I'd always thought the fucker was pining after the President patch.

"Don't you agree, *Dexy boy*?" he asked, cocking his head to the side, the question laced with taunting sarcasm. "What's this, the second time you've fucked up over pussy?"

How had I never gotten in the ring on a fight night and beat his fucking face in?

Torque stepped between us, blocking my line of sight. His muscled arms spread placatingly like he was breaking up a schoolyard dispute. It always made me chuckle how diplomatic Torque was. Probably easy to have decorum when you could kick anyone's ass—anyone's except Ryan's. I'd never let him live down that he got choked out by a five-foot-two Latina.

The woman *was* terrifying, though.

"Okay, let's just cool it so we can finish up and get out of here." Torque's gaze bounced between us.

I shrugged a shoulder, crossing my arms over my chest to hide my white-knuckled fist. "It's okay, Torque. Boe seems to have some grievances he wants to air out, ones that can't wait for church," I responded coolly, moving around him to step closer. The last part was a clear dig.

This shit was meant for church. You had issues with someone? Bring it up with everyone present.

Bitch move to do this out in the middle of fuckin' nowhere.

"So, tell me, *brother*, what's on your mind?" I asked, my tone chilling. Boe shifted uncomfortably under the weight of my attention.

"Dex…" Torque called out, sensing the shift in my demeanor.

I lifted my palms in the air, hoping the placating motion would ease Torque's concerns. "Don't worry, I'm just asking so I can become a better man, Torque. Go on, Boe," I encouraged with a curt nod. Maybe I'd finally learn what the fucker's problem with me was.

"Can you even fucking do your job correctly with your anger issues? Did you get any information out of this one before you killed him?" He used the toe of his boot to nudge the body right where the bullet hole in his chest was. "We're getting into this fucking war because of you." His tone was smug, and he puffed out his barreled chest, trying to stretch his five-foot-eight frame. "Beat a man over a bitch, and then they had to send in your friend Greyson, excuse me, Gunner, to keep your ass in line. Like a fuckin' dog with a handler. Now some other bitch is costing the club problems."

Ice filled my veins as the puzzle pieces clicked together. Torque caught it, too, and moved back between us, his eyes never leaving me, like I was a wild animal about to attack. He wasn't that far off.

"Hey, Boe. Let's drop it, alright. None of this shit is on Dex, the Reapers have been stirring up trouble for a hot minute. And we all put it to a vote, we aren't turning Nikki over."

He scoffed at Torque's suggestion. Dumbass mistook my silence for admission and kept working his fucking mouth.

"Your owner in the room with you when you did this?" he taunted, moving around toward the feet of the dead Reaper. "What did these two tell you, Dex? Huh? They give you any information, or did you kill them before they could answer?" he went on, his tone bordering on almost desperate.

Fucking dumbass didn't even know that these two died after the car chase.

Burning rage bubbled in my gut, threatening to spill over, but on the surface, I was collected…calculated.

I cleared my throat, tucking my anger away. Boe didn't know a damn thing about my anger and ability to control it. "You're right, Boe. I'm probably not the right man for the job. When we get back, I'll let Pres know you have thoughts you'd like to share with the class."

He flinched when I flashed him a smile.

I knew how it looked—unhinged. I gave my subjects the same one when I tied them up in my mirrored room. Nothing fucked with the brain more than watching yourself get tortured.

"Now, let's get this fucker on the fire, yeah?" I asked, bending down to grab the upper half of the body.

Torque's questioning gaze itched at my skin, but I didn't pay him any mind. Murph was a smart fucker and had scurried off toward the bikes when Boe started spouting off.

"On three," Boe said, eyeing me cautiously. Clearly wary of how easily I'd dismissed the insults.

"You got it, man."

The rigid corpse flew through the air at the end of his count, and the instant it was out of my hands, I rushed forward, kicking out the back of Boe's legs. His knees slammed into the desert sand. A pained yell echoed in the night as I wrenched his hands behind his back, gripping the hair at the base of his skull. The light of the flames bounced off his face as I thrust it close to them.

Heat licked at my skin like a lover's caress, inviting me to fall further into chaos, but I reined in the impulse to add Boe's body to the pile. The killing of a brother was forbidden unless voted on by the club. Hell, this would have consequences as it stood, but I'd take the fucking punishment.

My lips brushed his ear, relishing the erratic pulse pounding in his throat and his pained cries. "Boe, maybe you should do some better research before you mouth off to someone so much bigger than you," I taunted as he flailed in my grasp, calling out for help from the other two.

Neither moved to his aid.

"That *bitch* that I beat the fucker's head in for, that was my sister. The one he'd sold to the Russians. So, you're damn right I'm not going to turn in another woman in my life to them." The snarl that slipped from my lips sounded more monster than human. He stilled at the admission, his shouts turning into whimpers. "And if you ever call Nikki a bitch again, brother or not, I'll beat your fucking head in with a bat. Got it? Now, admit you're a piece of shit who runs his fucking mouth too much."

He hesitated, attempting once more to free himself from my hold. All it did was piss me off further and rip free some of his greasy locks. I pushed his face closer to the flames, and he blubbered like a baby within seconds.

"I'm a piece of shit who runs his mouth too fucking much. I'm sorry, I didn't know."

I didn't believe him.

The whole fucking club knew why I'd done it—there was no way he didn't. But I was tired of this whole game and wanted to get back to Nikki before we had to make an appearance at the clubhouse tonight.

"You're lucky I'm not in the mood tonight, Boe, or I'd

have made sure you needed skin grafts," I said, my words laced with malice as I pulled him away, dropping him in a pile at my feet. The left side of his face was an angry red with blisters bubbling under the skin. The sheen glistened under the moonlight. It would hurt like a mother fucker when the wind hit them on the ride back.

Singed hair and flesh wafted between us, making my stomach turn. No matter how many times I'd smelled that, it never got easier to stomach. "Do you need another demonstration on whether I'm good at my job, *brother*?"

He shook his head, tears rolling down his cheeks, leaving streaks of dirt in their wake.

I turned on my heel and strode away. "Good, now fucking stay out here until the body's gone. Call when you need a ride."

Torque jogged to catch up. "He's got his bike here, Dex. He won't need a ride."

The click of my switchblade brought a smile to my face. "He will now," I said, jamming the knife into the tire of his hog. The low hissing sound of air escaping was music to my ears.

Murphy's brow shot up, but he was smart enough not to say shit. Messing with a brother's ride was as bad as fucking their old lady.

Sacrilegious.

Damnit, I needed a vacation. Or at least for the shit not to hit the fan for a while.

"Let's go, I've got my woman I need to check on."

Shit. Why had I called her mine?

TWENTY-SEVEN
DEX

REMEMBER, FRIENDS DON'T SUCK ON EACH OTHER'S TONGUES

"WHERE THE FUCK HAVE YOU BEEN?" I called out the moment Nikki walked into the apartment. There was probably steam coming out the top of my head, I was so pissed at her. I'd fully expected her to be home when I'd come home.

"Huh?" she asked, kicking off a pair of beat-up Vans.

"Where. Did. You. Go?" I bit out, pinching the bridge of my nose and counting down from twenty. She was not supposed to have been out tromping around god knows where after a fucking shoot-out.

When she answered, her tone was thick with attitude. "I was with Ryan, Dex. Remember, you sent me away after the car chase, telling me you needed me somewhere safe?"

Right.

I opened my eyes and moved closer, caging her between me and the front door with my arms. "There's a fucking bounty on your perky little ass. There was no way in hell I was going to keep you out in the open," I growled. The brat had the nerve to laugh instead of feeling ashamed. "At least act like you're sorry for giving me fucking gray hairs when I came back, and you were gone." I cupped her face, needing to feel her soft skin.

I really had freaked the fuck out when I came home to an

empty apartment. She'd had thirty more seconds before I went out and hunted her down. And I would have torn apart the fucking town to find her.

"Were you worried about me, Dexy?" she asked, her voice huskier than normal, challenging me.

Her cheek was soft and warm under my thumb, and I couldn't resist stroking it. Her breath hitched, drawing attention to her glossy lips. God, I'd wondered what they would feel like against mine.

I hadn't kissed a woman on the mouth in who knew how long. I never wanted to. It was too intimate and gave my hookups false hope that we might become something more. But now, staring at her pouty lips, I wondered if she'd be soft and gentle or fight me for dominance.

"We should probably practice before tonight," she whispered, her chest rising and falling a bit faster than it had been. Her tongue poked out, swiping along her bottom lip. It took a moment for my brain to register what she meant, but the moment I did, I slammed my mouth against hers.

My free hand came up and tangled in her hair, holding her in place as our mouths meshed.

Fuck, she was delicious.

I went deeper, pushing her up against the door as my tongue explored hers. Her fingers twisted in my shirt, drawing me in, but there was nowhere else to go unless I was inside her. A groan escaped me at the thought. My dick ached with how hard it was.

All over a fucking kiss.

Pulling away, I rested my forehead against hers, taking time to collect myself because if I tried to speak, it would come out either as nonsense or *let's fuck*. We weren't even supposed to be doing this right now, but all brain function ceased the moment I touched her.

"It's a good thing we practiced, because you're a shit kisser." Nikki's words came out breathy. What did she sound like after she got fucked?

Unable to resist, I nuzzled the side of her throat with my

nose, nipping at the delicate skin as I spoke. "Oh yeah? Maybe we should practice some more," I suggested, my hands finding her hips and pinning her to the door.

"That's probably a good idea," she moaned, grabbing my face and directing me back toward her lips.

Now I *knew* why people kissed. There was something so damn delicious about feeling their tongue slide against yours. I nearly came when Nikki sucked on the tip of mine.

I gripped her ass, hoisting her up and giving her no choice but to wrap her legs around my waist. Her giggle was like fucking sunshine, and the way her fingers went straight for my hair had me ready to get on my damn knees for her. Walking her over to the counter in the kitchen, I set her down next to the sink, neither of us wanting to let go.

"Now I see why people have friends of the opposite sex," she said between kisses, and I barked out a laugh.

"I don't think friends do this shit," I said, still pressed against her mouth.

She pulled back. "What the fuck is the point of having a friend then?" she asked, sincerely confused.

I shrugged a shoulder, watching the way she shuddered when I rubbed up and down her bare side, savoring how soft and smooth her skin was. "How the fuck would I know. I don't have any girls that I'm only friends with."

Something like guilt or discontent bubbled up. I'd never been ashamed about sleeping around, and Nikki wasn't the type of woman to turn her nose up at that, either. Yet, still, I wanted her to know I wasn't thinking about anyone else when I was with her, regardless of the authenticity of our relationship.

Fuck, if I was being honest, she'd invaded my mind for months now. No one else was able to break the hold she'd had on me.

"You're the only one, you know that? And you're mine tonight, you understand?" I practically growled out the command to her, gripping her at the nape of her neck, loving the way she sucked in a breath. Golden locks slipped between my fingers as I fisted them, pulling her head back. I was learning I had a thing for eye contact with her.

Her blue eyes practically glowed, cheeks flushed as she stared up at me. "Yeah, I understand." Her fingers tangled in my shirt, yanking me closer. "And you're mine." The growl in her own voice nearly sending me into cardiac arrest.

God, she had no clue what she'd unleashed by saying that.

"Careful," I warned, my voice husky and thick. "You start talking like that and I'll forget we're supposed to be friends."

She inhaled sharply, tongue running across her bottom lip.

I needed to change the subject. "Have you ever been to a one-percenter party?" I asked, needing to prepare her for what she was in for.

She shook her head as best she could with my hold. Her hands moved down to my shoulders, and she ran a single finger across my white T-shirt. I didn't think she even knew she was doing it.

"I've danced for plenty of bikers at clubs." My fist tightened in her hair, noting how her back arched slightly. "But I've never been to one of their parties. The other night with you was my first time in a clubhouse," she said.

I pushed down the flair of jealousy.

I'd ignore that emotion along with the others trying to surge forward from my no-go zone list.

It was a long fucking list.

"Well, they are all a bunch of rowdy assholes who will fuck anything with tits. For some of them, they don't even require that. So, you..." I pulled her even closer, but my dumb ass hadn't considered that her legs were still wrapped around my waist. The warm heat of her pussy was poised *right* where my tip was tucked. It took every ounce of restraint to continue talking, and it still came out sounding strained and choked.

"...Are mine tonight. Right next to me, every fucking moment of the night. Understand?" I asked, tamping down my lust so I could get my point across. Because if she didn't understand, she could end up in another brother's lap, and I really didn't want to fuck anyone's face up tonight.

"Right. Stay right by your side and sell the whole *fake dating* thing because friends don't suck on each other's tongues," Nikki responded, throwing in a salute.

"Fucking smartass," I said, pulling her hair again and tilting her face up toward me.

Her mouth was parted ever so slightly, like it was pleading for me to spit in it. *Fuck.* She was in the perfect position for it, too. Instead, I buried my nose in the crook of her neck again. The scent of coconut and *her* was just as tempting. What I needed to do was push away from her, but the thought of that was almost painful.

You're just practicing getting used to each other's touch for tonight. So it's believable. Look at you, you overachiever.

Even in my own damn head, I was a fucking liar.

We were teetering on a tightrope, playing with fucking fire, and I should've been concerned for the degree of the burn I'd suffer.

Because I would get burned with her.

"I'm serious, Nikki. I've *never* had an exclusive girl. All the girls I've fucked, my brothers have fucked too. This whole thing," I extracted myself from where I was still inhaling her scent so I could point between us, "is all fucking new, and all their horny asses will try and get in your panties. Don't make me fight off my own brothers, spitfire. Because not one of them gets to touch you," I said, my tone low and fierce.

Again, with the fucking growling?

Now I understood why Gunner had dressed Ryan in his shirt. I'd made fun of him and suggested he just pee on her instead if he was going to be that territorial. I owed the asshole a beer and an apology.

I lowered my head so that when I spoke, my lips brushed against hers. "Tell me, Nikki, that you understand my directions."

Her legs tightened around my waist, her breath quickening. We both could have come from the tension alone. When she wet her lips with her tongue, our proximity made it so it also brushed mine, and I moaned, snaking my tongue out to run across her lips, too.

I'd done all sorts of shit with all sorts of women, but *nothing* had ever been hotter than this moment. Us in this kitchen, as I stood between her legs, her head pulled back and my hand tangled in her hair.

Fucking utter perfection—and we were fully clothed.

"Ask me nicely," she said with a smirk. Our breaths intermingled as she parroted my words.

My brain malfunctioned.

God damn.

I might like a woman who followed directions, but I liked one who made me work for her obedience even more. So, I did what any man would do when a woman became so intoxicating and tempting that he wanted to keep her for his own…

I sprayed her with the hose function of the sink faucet.

She shrieked, her hands coming up to shield her from the onslaught of water. "Dex. What the fuck?"

She'd released her legs in her panic, and I'd untangled my grip on her hair. I stood a few feet away, pointing a finger at her.

"Stop trying to seduce me when we're not in public."

Her eyes narrowed. "You sprayed me because I was *seducing* you?" she asked in disbelief.

No. I sprayed you because you thaw the constant numbness that flows through my veins, keeping the emotions at bay.

"Yup." I popped the p, shrugging a shoulder. "Don't people spray cats when they're misbehaving?"

Nikki hopped down and shoved a finger at my chest hard. "I'm not a fucking cat, Dex. And *you* were trying to seduce *me* with that fucking growl in your tone and getting all caveman with me." Her nostrils flared. "And I am *so* flirting with your club brothers now," she said, storming off to her room.

Someone should probably study the way my brain worked, because why was I smiling from ear to ear?

I didn't make a move to follow her. It wasn't safe to be around her and horizontal surfaces—I'd find a way to fall into her pussy with my face, or my fingers, or my cock. All three, preferably.

We needed space to let the lust die down so we could remember we were trying to be just friends.

And friends don't suck on each other's tongues.

TWENTY-EIGHT
DEX

COMMITTING CREDIT CARD FRAUD IS ACCEPTABLE IF THE GUY YOU STEAL FROM IS AN ASS (THIS IS NOT LEGAL ADVICE)

WHO WAS in charge of the length standards of women's shorts? Because I didn't know if I wanted to kiss them or kick their asses.

"Did your butt cheeks stick to the seat of my bike? Because it's taking you a while to get off that thing," I asked, holding back my laugh when Nikki sent a scathing look my way as she hopped off. Her ass had literally played peek-a-boo with me as I'd trailed behind her to my bike, and then I had to ride with a half-chub all the way to the club.

"Your brothers are going to love them." She flipped her hair over her shoulder, giving me her middle finger in the process.

I'd let her get away with saying that shit back at the apartment because I *had* sprayed her with the faucet, but that shit wasn't going to fly now that we'd entered compound grounds. Laughter and the roar of engines were reminders of how many men, both ones I knew and ones I didn't, would be here tonight.

My finger hooked in the back belt loop of her shorts, hauling her backward until her back hit my chest. I loved the way her pulse quickened under the palm I wrapped around her throat.

"I don't give two fucks if they look, Nikki. You deserve

their attention. You're gorgeous, but they are *not* to fucking touch you," I whispered in her ear, tightening ever so slightly on her throat because I couldn't resist drawing out more of her little gasps. "This is my favorite handhold, spitfire. Maybe I'll just walk around all night like this."

She moaned, and I didn't know if it was because I'd drawn her lobe in my mouth or because I'd suggested collaring her with my hand. Not even a sheet of paper could have been slipped between us at that moment, and when she shifted her weight from one foot to another, the damn shorts she'd worn rubbed against my cock. Making me moan. The snicker she let out told me she knew *exactly* what she was doing.

"This what you meant by only seducing you in public, Dex?" She squeezed my crotch, palming my growing hard-on. "Because everyone is about to know how good I am at that." There was a bite to her tone, but I didn't get a chance to explore what had caused it.

"Dex, get your ass over here," Pres yelled out, looking the part of a pissed-off dad. My hold on her dropped, but I kept my finger hooked in her loop in case she thought she could run off. "We've got church, fuckhead," he added before turning and storming into the clubhouse.

Fuck.

I ushered her forward, trying to come up with a plan of what to do with her. Stashing her in my room was always an option—if I knocked her out, of course, because there was no way in hell she'd willingly let me put her in there again.

I'd forgotten that tonight was going to start with church. So even though I'd bitched to Nikki about plastering her pussy to me, I was the one leaving her with the damn wolves. While the patched members were all in church, everyone left out here were the hang-arounds and club bunnies. Damn, now I wished I paid better attention to the prospects, because I couldn't even assign one of them to her.

Not one I trusted.

"Go," she said as we passed through the threshold, slipping her hand under my cut and patting my chest. "I'll be fine. Believe me, this place is not as intimidating as other places I've been." Her eyes bounced around the room, and I could tell she was clocking all the exits.

That was something about Nikki that I'd picked up on early on. For whatever reason, no one else seemed to notice the way she watched her surroundings. To their credit, she did a damn good job of coming across as if she was trusting and naive to the uglier parts of the world.

But I saw it.

Right there in those big blue eyes of hers.

She was a wolf in sheep's clothing. There might not be a weapon in her hand, but I had no doubt she knew how to deliver a killing blow—even if it was by directing the hand of another.

Why did I want to be at her beck and call?

When her attention came back to me, she flashed me a smile that melted my cold fucking heart.

That was why.

Not even god himself could have kept me from slamming my lips onto hers in that moment. I wanted her damn panties soaked from this kiss. Our tongues fought for dominance as they intertwined. My hand found its way down to her ass, massaging the cheek in my hand before ending in a smack that caused her to yelp.

"Dammit, Dex. Get your horny ass in here," Pres's bitching cut through the mewling from Nikki.

Not horny, Pres. I might be enchanted, though.

Okay, I was horny too.

My lips landed on hers once more. This kiss was soft, sweet, and somehow made my blood stir even more than the others. "Anyone fucks with you, tell them I'll remove a body part for every word they say," I said, cupping her face.

Her giggle fell silent when she realized I wasn't laughing along with her. "Wait, you're serious?"

"As a fucking heart attack, spitfire." I kissed the tip of her nose and then jogged over toward Pres, who was busy glowering at me.

"Fuck. First Gunner, and now you? Am I going to lose all my best men to pussy?" he muttered, closing the door behind him.

I needed an entire keg after that church.

We were going to war with the Reapers. It had been a long time coming really, but the attack on Nikki and I changed everything. Who knew if the Reapers were aware there was a member of the Skeletons in the car or not, but that detail didn't matter to Pres.

The attack was a clear first aggression against us, purposeful or not. The whole club had voted to move forward with an attack of our own. All but one member, who was still voting to turn Nikki over. Votes were anonymous, but I didn't have any doubt who the fucker was.

Boe.

Pussy also put on a whole sob story in church about how I'd attacked him. I'd already made my peace about dealing with whatever punishment the club voted on—it had been worth it and I'd fucking do it again. But then Torque piped up, giving some extra context to how it all went down.

Boe had left out one particular part, the detail about how he'd decided to taunt me about my sister. That caused Pres's eye to twitch, his only tell when he was pissed.

Well, Boe, play stupid games, win stupid prizes.

I could tell by the glare Pres shot me that he wasn't happy I hadn't spoken up, but I was a glutton for punishment.

The party was in full swing when I exited church. My heart sped up when I didn't spot Nikki. I hadn't expected her to run up to me like an eager puppy, but I thought she'd at least be sitting at the bar so I would see her as soon as I came out.

A rock settled on my chest. What if something had happened to her? Or someone caught her attention. I wrinkled my nose at that second thought. A woman selecting someone else had never bothered me in the past, but with Nikki…

"Pay up, bitch."

I spun on my heel at the familiar bark of attitude. I'd been on the receiving end of Nikki's tone plenty of times.

"What the fuck did you call me?" someone else said.

Nikki was over by one of the pool tables, cue in one hand while she held her other out to some dude with a shaved head. His back was to me, so I couldn't tell if I knew who he was or not. More than likely I didn't, because I never bothered getting to know the hang-arounds. They were a bunch of bitch ass men who only wanted to *look* like they were in an MC, but didn't have the actual balls to get in. Same pieces of shit who'd call the cops instead of settling shit the real way- with a fight.

Nikki pulled her hand away, placing it on her hip. He was in for it now because, she was staring at him with her, *"I'm not the fucking one,"* look.

"I said. Pay. The. Fuck. Up. Bitch," she said, enunciating each word like he was an idiot. Which, clearly, the shoe fit. But I didn't like the way the asshole tightened his fist as if he was going to swing at her. He wouldn't even be able to flinch without me being on his ass.

On silent feet, I moved in closer.

"Fuck you. You played me, you whore." He practically spit out the last word, and I saw fucking red, plowing through people to get to her. But before I could even get there, Nikki was up in his face.

Every cuss word I knew spilled from my mouth.

She was too damn brave.

"Call me whatever the fuck you want. Unlike you, that shit doesn't faze me. But you owe me money. It's not my fault you're a shit player and bet too much." She flicked her eyes to me for the briefest of moments.

She knew where I was.

I moved behind him. My stomach did a stupid flip when her shoulders dropped ever so slightly. No one else would've noticed, but I did. She knew she was safe when I was around, and fuck, if that didn't have me standing taller.

"You must be new around here because all you are is a hole for us to stick our cocks in. In fact…" He began unzipping his jeans.

"I wouldn't do that if I were you," Nikki said, looking at her nails as if she was talking about the weather. If I weren't so entertained by her, I'd have shot the fucker thirty seconds prior. The sick part of my brain liked that she was toying with our victim, and I had a brief vision of her in the interrogation room with me.

Her weapon to wield.

I shoved away the thoughts, focusing on her.

The asshole wasn't too bright, and opened his mouth again even though she'd warned him. "And what the fuck are you going to do about it, whore? I can take you whether you want it or not," he spat.

Rage like I'd never felt flowed through me like, and in the next instant, his face hit the felt of the pool table—repeatedly. His yelps of protest were so pathetic that they only fueled my anger.

I wanted a fucking fight, to revel in the adrenaline of swinging fists and taking punches. Because the only thing that would tamp down the bloodlust that had taken route was either killing him or fucking someone.

A pool of blood appeared under where his face was landing, seeping into the felt and transforming the green into a deep crimson. Somewhere in the haze, I remembered that Nikki was standing nearby, and the burn of fury flipped to something I hadn't felt since Kelly's death.

Fear.

Fear that she wouldn't be around after seeing me lose my shit like this.

I wasn't ashamed of my violent nature. Take it or fucking leave it, but fuck, I didn't want her to leave *me*.

My lids fluttered shut, and I blocked out all the noise besides my inhales and exhales.

In for four, out for four.

Never in a million years would I have guessed what I'd see when I opened my eyes again. I thought for sure Nikki would have been long gone, probably calling Ryan to get her the fuck out of here and under the care of someone more sane.

Someone who could take better care of her.

Instead, Nikki was crouched on top of the pool table right next to where I was holding the asshole's face into the blood-soaked puddle.

"One, two, three. That's it. He's out." She swiped her arm across her body like an ump. "Damn, got your ass handed to you twice tonight. Should've just paid up, Chad," she said to the barely conscious man while delivering condescending pats to his head. "My boyfriend told me he was removing body parts of people who touched me, so you should be happy you're only walking away with a concussion and a fucked-up face." Reaching into the back of his pants, she slipped out his wallet, thumbing through his cards and pocketing them and the cash he had.

I let go of the piece of shit, holding my arms out so Nikki could hop into them. The moment my hands sunk into the soft skin around her middle, I never wanted to let her go.

I was going to carry her all fucking night long now, needing the peace that only she seemed to bring me. "Legs around my waist, babe," I whispered into her ear, adding enough bark that she knew this wasn't a negotiation.

She obeyed without hesitation, and I peppered kisses along her throat while carrying her to the bar.

"I'm keeping you in my arms the rest of the night, got it?" I bit the sensitive section of skin where her neck met her shoulder.

"Have anything you need to order?" she asked,

completely unfazed by my need to feel her as close as possible. She was like my personal drug, and I needed a hit to take the edge off.

I pulled my head away, confused by her random question. "What the fuck are you talking about?"

She laughed, holding up three of the dick's cards. "What do you think I took his wallet for? I'm going to spend that asshole's money." She said with a shrug like it was obvious. "I may not be able to beat someone's ass in quite as sexy a manner as you, but I do my own damage."

The laugh I let out had people turning their heads.

Somehow, she'd surprised me while not surprising me at all.

SOMEONE NEEDED to direct me to the nearest patch of grass so I could go roll in that shit because there was no way I was okay.

I'd literally said *aw* in my head when Dex had slammed that man's face into the pool table. There had to be a rule somewhere about how violence wasn't supposed to be considered sweet...so why did I feel like the man had just performed a grand romantic gesture for me?

Beating in his fucking face was as good as him telling me he loved me.

I froze at the use of the 'L ' word in my mind, studying Dex.

The man in question plucked one of the cards from my fingers as he positioned both of us on the barstool next to Torque, adjusting my body so I was sitting sidesaddle across his muscular thighs.

"This isn't your first time taking someone's wallet, is it?" he asked, a thread of humor running through the question.

It was a stark contrast to how he'd sounded when he was threatening the asshole a minute ago. It was deliciously scary the way he'd calmly slammed his head into the hard surface of the pool table. The sound of the guy's skull smacking the wood, mixed with his screams, wasn't something I'd easily forget.

Concerningly though, that wasn't because it bothered me. The opposite, actually. I liked the thought of those who wronged me experiencing the consequences of that, even if it wasn't my physical hand doling out the punishment.

"Hell no," I answered, forcing myself back into the conversation. "All my lingerie is gifted to me by men."

Dex stiffened under me, and not in a sexy way. I smirked at his reaction, enjoying his jealousy. For a woman who didn't want to be tied down, I sure was enjoying things I'd swore I never would.

"They didn't know they were giving me a gift until the fraudulent charges showed up on their statement," I finished with a wide smile, noting the way he relaxed.

Torque shook his head, throwing back a shot of something amber in color. "You two are the same type of chaos. We should all be *very* worried," he said.

Dex signaled for a beer while scoffing. "Please. Nikki and I are upstanding citizens," he threw back.

The look Torque shot him spoke volumes. These two were adorable together. They reminded me a bit of…

"Hey." Looking around the clubhouse, I searched for someone in particular. "Where's Gunner? Shouldn't he be here too?"

Torque was the one to respond. "Pres told him to go talk to Ryan about what we voted on."

"Torque," Dex said, a warning in his voice.

"It's not like she's not gonna know, Dex." The look Torque gave me had ice taking root at the base of my spine, crawling up at an achingly slow pace, so I had to endure the pain of unease. "We need Los Muertos to partner with us in our war with the Reapers."

"War? You guys are going to attack?" The words were barely above a whisper since I didn't know if everyone was supposed to hear this shit.

"We're retaliating, spitfire. For what they did to us in the car. They fucking shot at you." Dex slammed his hand down on the bar top. The bang echoed through the bar and cut through the noise. His chest was heaving against my side, and I placed a hand on him.

He lowered his voice, his arm tightening around me. "We're going to take care of it, okay? You're going to be safe soon." His pupils ate away at his irises, leaving nothing but black pits that swirled with fury. He was teetering on a knife's edge, and the next person to make a misstep might end up dead.

He needed a release.

Pain radiated from my lip as I bit down on it hard, a coppery tang filling my mouth.

"Ouch, dammit." I prodded the damaged flesh with my finger, noting the blood when I pulled the digit away. Dex's hand wrapped around my wrist, his hold like a damn vice grip.

"I told you biting on your lip is a bad habit," he said, daring me to look away as he slowly brought my finger to his mouth, sucking the blood off the tip. His warm tongue swirled around, and he hollowed his cheeks before pulling off with a pop.

"God damn it, Dex. I'm fighting tonight, and now I have to go beat off or think of kicking puppies or something," Torque grumbled from beside us.

Ignoring him, I focused all my attention on Dex. "You need to release all this pent-up energy," I said, licking my lips.

He hiked up a brow. "What makes you think that?"

Because despite all my best efforts not to get close, I know you, Dex.

I didn't share those sentiments aloud. "Lucky guess. What do you normally do to fix this?" I asked, gesturing up and down his body with my free hand since he still held my other one near his mouth.

There was a beat of silence as he studied my face, as if he wasn't sure he wanted to tell me. His throat cleared, and I expected him to break the eye contact we'd been locked in, but he didn't.

"I have to either fuck, fight, or torture someone," he answered truthfully, watching for my reaction.

Something in my gut told me how I responded was important.

I leaned in as close as I could without breaking our eye contact. "And which one do you want to do, baby? Because it sounds like there are going to be fights tonight, but you also have a *girlfriend* who is willing to help you with fucking out the frustration."

There was no mistaking the hardening of his cock under my legs, and I wanted nothing more than to straddle his lap and grind down on him while tasting his delicious mouth again. But this was all dangerous fucking territory because initiating sex with Dex felt like I'd open a door to something unknown.

Should I have even offered to help him find release through sex? Maybe I could help him without us having sex?

A lightbulb went off. I could definitely do that—I did that shit every day at work as it was. The thought left a sour taste in my mouth. Why did I want to give something different to Dex than I gave anyone else?

"Hey, where did you go?" He asked, his hand cupping the back of my neck and pulling me in so our foreheads rested together.

He had a thing for holding my face, and every time, I wanted to melt because it had me feeling like a treasure. How pathetic that so little meant so much.

"You don't need to do anything for me, okay?" he said, probably mistaking my silence as hesitation.

We were drawn in together, our faces only inches apart, making clear the conversation was for no one else's ears. For a man who'd never had a girlfriend, he was sweet. I gave a small nod.

The moment became too much. I wasn't sure how to react to Dex's pull on me. I could no longer tell if the logical move was to push him away or pull him closer. The switch was sudden, one moment I was all warm and fuzzy. The next…

Suffocating.

Like emotions were clawing up my throat all at once, damning my airway so I was choking. Scrambling out of his lap, I practically ran to the bathroom I'd found earlier, calling over my shoulder that I had to pee, and I'd be back.

In for four, out for four.

I'd hear Dex murmur the mantra a few times when he'd been overwhelmed, and it seemed to work for him. The bathroom door slammed into the tile wall, and I pushed past a group of women, gaining myself some scowls and *fuck you*'s.

The cold porcelain against the back of my legs grounded me. A curtain of blonde added another layer of coverage as I hung my head in my hands, working overtime at blanking out my mind.

You can't get attached. What if you get him hurt…killed?

A voice I hadn't heard in over a year echoed in my mind, dredging up memories I'd tried hard to bury.

"Tasha, you're a child, incapable of handling your emotions like a grown woman."

Andrei's words stung even more as memories, because now I saw the truth. I didn't have enough time to throw a pity party for myself, because what I needed to do now was slap on a smile, walk out there, and pretend I wasn't falling apart.

Pushing off my knees, I marched back out of the bathroom like nothing had happened, but I was stopped short when someone grabbed my bicep.

"What's a pretty thing like you doing with an idiot like Dex?"

His voice felt wrong, instantly raising my alarm. The man had a Skeletons of Society cut on, and that made it all the worse that he was talking shit about Dex.

I'd learned early on that men would tell you more shit if you played dumb—there was too much misogyny in that for me to unpack, but I used the tactic, nonetheless.

"I'm sorry, I don't know what you mean…Boe," I said,

batting my lashes at him, trying to hide my panic at how his fingers dug deeper into my skin.

We were standing at the opening that led from the main room into the small hallway he'd been lurking in, so I leaned against the frame, latching my free arm onto the wall in case the asshole thought he would drag me with him somewhere. It'd at least give me a few moments to make enough noise for Dex to hear.

Hopefully.

"Dex. The guy you just ran from?" He flashed what I'm sure he thought to be a charming smile, but it looked predatory, especially since he had a large bandage plastered across half of his face.

Being a dancer, you develop a sixth sense for men, picking up from a mile away the ones that took pleasure in trampling over your boundaries.

Boe was one of those men.

"Come with me. I could show you a good time." He sent a seething gaze over toward where Dex was sitting. "Someone really needs to take him out." He whispered the last part, probably not intending for me to hear that.

Or maybe he didn't give a shit if I did.

I stiffened, the fear I'd felt moments ago tipping into anger. Anger that this Boe person would say something like that about his brother.

His beady eyes locked back on me. "Let me buy you a drink."

Of course, my smart mouth didn't have an off filter or a self-preservation mode. "Aren't all the drinks here free? Who's that line working on?"

My arm ached where he was gripping. "That was a bitchy thing to say, Nikki."

Now my mind sounded like a damn chapel with every warning bell going off simultaneously. My plan for holding on to the wall failed because he rounded the corner *into* the main room, hauling me behind him like a naughty child.

Dex's eyes met mine, and he began to rise, sitting as soon

as I gave a slight shake of my head. I didn't want to cause a problem between these two, and if I could get more information on why one of Dex's brothers seemingly had it out for him, all the better.

I'd let the jerk get me a drink and then politely, for me, tell him to fuck off.

The look of hurt that flashed across Dex's ruggedly handsome face stung. But he didn't make another move to intervene.

"She'll have a Long Island," Boe ordered, drawing my attention back to him.

"No, I'll have a beer. Canned and still closed, please."

Boe's fists tightened where he had them resting on the bar top. "Oh, come on. You've got to at least take a shot with me. Don't be like that," he said, rubbing a finger down the side of my arm.

"Don't be like that." The only other phrase a man could say that pissed me off more was, *"You should smile more."*

It took everything in me not to throw up on him. Or throat-punch him. The only reason I refrained was because I was on his home turf, and he was a patched member.

All I was here was Dex's fake girlfriend.

Truthfully, I wasn't too worried about what would happen to me. How much worse could my life get? I already had a crazy Russian ex-husband possibly putting bounties on my head. I didn't damage Boe's larynx because I didn't want to make a mess for Dex.

"Why don't you come home with me tonight, huh? Get away from wherever Dex's got you stashed away at," he asked, oblivious to my violent thoughts towards him.

I plastered on a sweet smile, needing to move this whole conversation along so I could get back to Dex and ask how much his brothers knew about our protection detail.

"What do you mean stashed away?" I asked, adding a giggle to sell the airhead act.

His mouth opened and shut a few times before he finally answered. "Oh, I just mean I haven't seen you around, is all, and that can't be because you *want* to be around that idiot." He laughed. "I mean, who would want to be with him? He's an asshole who thinks he is so great at everything, but really, he's a dick with anger problems." He leaned in closer, his rancid breath flooding my senses. "A good girl like you doesn't want to be with someone like that, right?"

Good girl. Dex was right. I hated that fucking term.

I needed something stronger than beer. "Hey, I'll take a tequila, please," I called to the kid behind the bar. He had on a leather cut, but there weren't any rockers on it, only a patch that said prospect.

"She'll have whiskey," Boe corrected, shooting me a wink as if it was cute to blatantly disregard what I'd ordered.

"No. I'll have tequila. And make it a double, actually." The poor kid didn't know what to do. He was probably supposed to follow patched member's orders to a T. "Tell him, Boe. If you want to order for me, have at it, but I will drink what I want," I demanded, crossing my arms over my chest, making sure to push my boobs down rather than prop them up.

I didn't need his creepy eyes exploring any more of me than they already were.

Part of me expected him to yell at me, but the only tell of the anger burning inside was the flare of his nostrils and the narrowing of his eyes. He looked at me the way my father used to when we were in public—the look that told me when we got home, I'd suffer the consequences for my insolence.

He had never beaten me.

The man learned to manipulate me with his love. Toying with me by dangling the promise of his affection and pride like a carrot—and I'd fallen for it, all the way up to the altar. Even as I'd stood there in front of Yuri, I'd thought maybe my father would rush up and object to the union and admit he was wrong to give me away like cattle.

A pang of…something erupted in my heart.

My dad fucking gave me away as a bride without my consent, and I *still* had nights where I thought about him. Wondered if he'd felt bad about it. Like maybe it'd been a mistake, and if I hadn't killed him that day, he would have been out looking for me.

Stupid. Fuck him.

"Fine. Get her a double of tequila." Boe practically spat out the words, reminding me I was still dealing with this bitch of a man.

The glass appeared in front of me, and I snatched it up before Boe could touch it. He was shady as fuck, and I didn't want him touching *anything* I drank tonight.

The smile he'd slapped back on slipped, but he quickly replaced it, raising his shot to me. "Cheers," he sneered, throwing the liquid back.

He was about to be sorely disappointed.

"Thanks for the drink that you didn't actually buy me," I said, slipping off the stool and out of reach, walking as fast as I could toward Dex while ignoring Boe's shouts.

Dex's scowl turned into a look of concern as I barreled toward him.

"You good?" he asked, looking over my shoulder toward where I'd come from as he reached for me.

I scrambled into his lap, straddling him. Thank god my job had taught me how to do all sorts of things while holding drinks. My nerves settled the moment my body touched him. His hands felt like brands where he'd placed them on my hips.

"Your *brother*," I said the word as if it were a curse, "is shady as fuck."

Dex's face darkened, and the menace in his tone sent a chill down my spine. "What the hell did he do?" If his grip got any tighter I'd have bruises. What did it say about me that I liked the idea of being marked by him?

Friends, bitch. You two are friends...

"I'll tell you later. Right now, I'm going to show him exactly what I think about being with you," I said.

His brows furrowed in confusion as I lifted onto my knees, high enough so I was looking down at him. I cupped his strong jaw—his stubble was rough on my palm, and I desperately wanted to feel it on my thighs again.

He was beautiful, with his full lips and a nose that was slightly cooked. It was so him to have it pierced, too. My thumb pulled at his bottom lip, and he obliged.

Leaning down, I whispered against his lips, loving the way they curled up at the corners.

"Good boy."

The excitement shining in his eyes as he waited with his head tipped back and mouth open had me so turned on my underwear was soaked. I threw back the shot, loving the burn as I swallowed down some of the contents before leaning over and spitting the second half into Dex's waiting mouth.

His patience had run out, because there was a bite of pain at the back of my head where he'd threaded his fingers, slamming our lips together.

The hand that had been on my hip moved to my ass, and I yelped when he smacked it. He took advantage of the reaction. Tequila and mint overwhelmed me as his tongue invaded my mouth, sliding across my own.

"Need more," he groaned between kisses, pushing me down on his cock.

Fuck pants and their cock blocking ways—literally.

I was vaguely aware of the fact that we were in public, but it didn't stop me from grinding down on him.

"Dammit, Dex. You're so fucking delicious," I said between kisses.

Fuck, now I was so drunk on lust that I was saying my thoughts out loud.

The clearing of a throat broke us apart. Sort of—I was still plastered to his front, arms draped around the tops of his shoulders as Dex ground my pussy on his crotch.

Torque's cheeks were flushed, and I didn't know if it was drool or beer running down his chin. "So, um, you guys going to come to the fights or go fuck?" he asked, pointing his thumb toward where I assumed they held the fights.

"Fight," I said. At the same time, Dex responded with a

very different answer. I laughed at the full-on pout he had going on, but it died quickly. "Always with the cupping of my face," I said, attempting to diffuse how many emotions were swirling around.

He just leaned in, trailing the tip of his tongue along the shell of my ear. "I'm fucking you tonight, Niks," he said, thrusting up into where I still straddled him. My breath hitched with how hard he was beneath me. "I can feel how wet your pussy is for me, even through our clothes. I'm filling that greedy fucking cunt, with my fingers, with my tongue, and with my cock. Tonight," he said with confidence.

The mouth on this fucking man was so god damned *filthy,* and I loved every fucking second of it.

"Friends don't fuck, Dex," I whispered back, my voice sounding more like a moan.

He pulled away, looking me dead in my eyes.

"I'm not your fucking friend, Nikki."

THIRTY
DEX

HORNY

"FAKE" dating her had lasted all of two fucking seconds.

Why had I thought I could pretend with her and then step back into the role of a *friend*? The fact that I'd had my tongue shoved in her cunt and *then* became her friend was amazing. There was no way I could do that shit twice.

The problem was, I needed to convince Nikki that what was simmering between us—no, boiling—was worth exploring.

"Bye, Torque. Good luck," I said, standing up, Nikki's ass cheeks firmly in each of my hands.

Who knew what he said back, I was too busy listening to her squeal of delight. It was so fucking wholesome, yet it made me want to do some very bad things to her. There was no way I could make it back to the apartment, and I had never been more thankful for living at the clubhouse than I was at that moment.

Her hot mouth was licking and biting up and down my neck. I moaned when she latched on, sucking and pulling at the tender skin.

"Are you giving me a fucking hickey?" I asked, slamming her against the wall of the abandoned hallway, my mouth finding her flesh as well.

Everyone was making their way out to the fights, and this corner of the clubhouse was free of people.

"Too many other women looking at you," she said.

Her speech slowed like she was having difficulty concentrating on words as I rolled her pert nipple between my thumb and forefinger, using the wall and my hips to pin her in place.

The statement made me realize I hadn't noticed a single fucking woman when she was around. If anyone was trying to get my attention, it went completely unnoticed, because the only one I saw was her.

A damn moth to a flame.

"Is that so, Niks? You don't like others looking at me? I thought I was your *friend*. You don't want your friend to get laid?" I taunted, leaning forward and sucking on one of her nipples through her shirt. Her moan echoed off the walls as I pulled off one, moving to the next, making sure they received equal attention.

Her pupils were blown, and I loved how her lids closed to half-mast. There was no way I could resist being inside of her much longer. She squealed as I gripped her ass again and full-on sprinted to my room. Her laughter was like a balm to my broken soul—I wanted to listen to her laugh every day until I died.

Fuck. *When had that happened?*

When did she burrow herself into my soul, latching on so tightly that if she were ever to leave, my heart would be shredded?

My cock jumped at the sound of the door closing behind us, and I set her down so my hands would be free for everything I wanted to do to her.

The toe of my boot hit her shoes. "Spread them, baby," I commanded, smiling when she complied without any hesitation. My hand found her chin, tilting her head so she looked at me as I towered over her. "Look at how well you listen to directions, Nikki."

Her eyes lit with the praise, and I rewarded her with my

fingers on her clit, rubbing over the jean shorts I had a love-hate relationship with.

Good girl wasn't Nikki, but she liked to be told what a good job she was doing. Bet she'd like being told what a pretty little cum slut she was. I wanted to record all her little noises and make it my fucking ringtone.

Could you even still set a ringtone?

"I'm not fucking you yet, Nikki." She whimpered in protest. The sound had me smiling, knowing she wanted my cock as badly as I wanted to give it to her. "I'm going to take my time with you. But look how worked up you've got me." I took her hand in mine and shoved it against my crotch, showing her how much of an effect she was having on my body.

"Last time we found ourselves in this predicament, I ate that pretty pussy of yours, and you ran away from me." I stroked her cheek with my fingers before shoving them in her mouth. "Show me how well you know how to use your mouth, spitfire," I said, working the digits in and out.

The moan she let out shot straight to my cock.

Her hot tongue slid between the two digits, wrapping around one of them and hollowing her cheeks, giving a hard suck before pushing her head down and taking them in further, her spit running down the corners of her mouth.

Fuck.

The vixen knew exactly what she was doing as she peered up at me through her thick lashes. A siren, luring me to my demise, and I didn't give a fuck.

"You're going to get me to come without even sucking on my cock," I said, pulling them out and dragging my saliva-coated fingers down the length of her torso, slipping below the waistband of her shorts. She gave a sharp inhale when I swirled around her clit over the lace of her thong.

"Time for the real thing, Nikki, baby," I smirked. She licked her lips like she was about to have her favorite fucking meal, and damn, if I didn't hope it became just that. "I'm going to coat your throat with my cum. You going to swallow it down, baby?" I asked, running my fingers through her slick pussy.

She bit her lip, nodding her head. "Every fucking drop, Dex. Don't disappoint me," she taunted, biting my lip until she broke the skin, sucking on the wound.

I moaned so loud they probably heard all the way outside. It was rare to find a woman who had a mouth as filthy as me, and I wanted to know what else she would tell me before the night was over.

Without warning, I plunged my fingers inside her, loving the way her head fell forward against my chest, her breathing heavy. She was so fucking ready, it made my chest rumble with pride.

"Look how fucking wet you are for me."

I was dying to taste her on my tongue again, but I wasn't a total simp for her, so I settled for a compromise.

"Eyes on me, Nikki," I said, smirking at her protests when I pulled out of her pussy.

She watched me with rapt fascination as I cleaned her mess off my fingers with my mouth, biting her lip and rubbing her thighs together in an attempt to find some relief.

"You don't get to have all the fun, Dex," she said, dropping to the ground and pulling at my zipper. "I look good on my knees."

My cock sprang free, and I moaned loud enough to wake the dead when she languidly pumped my length, scooping up the bead of precum with her mouth.

I knocked her hand away, replacing it with mine.

"You look good all the time, Nikki," I breathed out. "But when you're on your knees with my cock in your mouth… you're fucking breathtaking."

I rubbed cock along the seam of her lips, her tongue poking out to meet my head, but I pulled just out of reach, relishing in the way she whimpered.

Nikki hissed as I gripped her chin, her desire clear as I angled her face to look at me. Cheeks flushed, eyes glassy, her lips swollen from our kisses…the image of how she looked right then would stay with me forever.

"Ask me nicely."

She blinked at me in disbelief before her open mouth curved up into a smile, and she leaned forward on all fours. Her lips peppered my thighs with kisses and bites as she stared up at me through her lashes before dragging her tongue up my inner thigh.

Fuck.

"Dex," she said in a husky tone, dripping in pleasure and sass. "Pretty please, will you fuck my mouth with your cock before you empty your balls down my fucking throat?"

I groaned, letting my head fall back so I was looking at my ceiling, asking god to save my fucking soul because I was about to commit some very sinful acts.

I didn't even give a shit that she was laying the dirty talk on thick to be an ass. My cock didn't give a shit that the words were dripping in sarcasm.

They were *exactly* what I wanted to hear.

Without warning, I shoved into her warm mouth, my vision going white. It felt like a fucking religious experience, and I hadn't even been inside her pussy yet.

She hummed around my cock, wet sucking sounds filling the room.

"Just like that, spitfire," I groaned, my hand sinking into her hair, guiding her mouth down my cock. "Look at what a pretty fucking cock-sucker you are. Taking every inch of my dick while spit drips down your throat." I thrusted, hitting the back of her throat, groaning when she choked on me. The sensation was divine, and the way she was peering at me told me she was loving this as much as I was.

Her hand snaked down her torso, disappearing out of my sight, but I knew exactly where it was headed when her lids fluttered close. I wanted to touch her so fucking bad, to shove my cock into her.

The temptation was too much, and I pulled out, moaning

as I watched a string of saliva stretch from her lips to my throbbing cock.

"I was enjoying that," she said, her brow quirking. Nikki's hand was still going to work on her clit, and the growl that erupted from me was more animal than man.

My fingers clamp onto her wrist, ceasing her movements. "Your orgasms are *mine.* You'll be coming on my cock, not your fingers. Now, go stand over by the bed, Nikki."

She glared, defiance dancing in her eyes, but did as she was told. Her obedience had my cock jumping.

"Strip before you bend over the bed and spread those fucking legs. Let me see how your pussy weeps for me."

"I swear I hate you, Dex," Nikki panted, moving into position, shimmying out of her shorts and underwear, and tossing her shirt.

Fuck me.

"You don't."

I let the sight of her bent over the bed, her slick cunt on display, soak in. The picture was perfect, her long hair cascading down between her shoulder blades, settling in that sexy curve of her back.

On silent feet, I moved toward where she waited. My hand connected with her ass and she yelped at the pain, before moaning as I rubbed the sting away with my palm.

"You've been wet this whole night, spitfire?" Another smack landed on her reddening ass.

"Yes."

Her response came out as a breathy cross between a moan and a whimper.

The sound made my dick twitch in my hand as I positioned myself behind her, propping her knee up on the rail of the bed frame and admiring how perfectly spread she was for me.

"Nikki, are you on birth control?" I asked, dragging my knuckle up and down her drenched slit, my fingers dipping into the first knuckle. A nod was all she could manage.

"Good, because I'm going to fill you with my cum, and I don't think either of us is looking for fornication trophies."

The laughter she barked out faded to moans as I grabbed two handfuls of her ass, driving my cock deep inside her. I was immediately lost in how fucking tight her pussy squeezed around me, slamming through every clench of her walls.

I knew she'd have bruises with how tightly I was gripping her hips and pounding into her, but the thought only fueled me, my hips pumping in and out of her even faster.

"Fuck. Dex," she cried out, her hand tangling in my sheets.

"Does that feel good, baby?" I rasped. "Cause I'm in fucking heaven."

Each thrust had my abs connecting with Nikki's tight ass, and I couldn't resist smacking it.

It was unreal. Pleasure like I'd never felt before.

I'd dreamt of having every part of her body in my possession. But every fantasy fell short of the reality of having her pussy stretched around me as she met me thrust for fucking thrust.

I just goddamn stood there in awe as she rode my cock.

"Fuck me," I hissed, thrusting my hands in my hair.

"I am," she sassed, looking over her shoulder at me and biting her lip. She fucking impaled herself on my cock, covering it from root to tip with her sopping wetness.

"You gotta be fucking kidding me with that pussy." I stood there, hypnotized by her bouncing ass. "Turn around," I growled when I felt myself getting close.

I'd barely slid my cock out before she turned and I was slamming back in. "Wrap your legs around me, baby."

Then I was grinding deep inside her, hitting her clit with my pelvis. I felt her nails on my back, her eyes widening as my name fell from her lips like a plea.

"Go on. Come for me, baby," I breathed out. Her pussy began to spasm, and I reached out and pinched her clit. I knew the second she came, she'd take me with her.

"Dex, fuck. Right there. Fuck right there," she yelled out, her heels digging into my ass as she held me against her, coating me in her wetness as she ground her clit on me, giving herself the stimulation she needed.

My mind went vacant, knowing nothing but fucking utopia as her walls shuddered around cock and I erupted in my own orgasm, filling her with my cum.

I was like a man possessed, thrusting inside her, still fucking her senseless as we soared and fell together.

"Mine. You're fucking mine."

There was no way I'd be able to walk away from her. She'd captured my heart, and I only hoped she'd allow me to do the same to hers.

EMOTIONAL TRAUMA IS WHY WE CAN'T HAVE NICE THINGS

"THAT WAS...FUCK," she whispered against my chest. We were naked in my bed, our legs tangled up.

I'd never cuddled with a woman after sex before, yet here I was, curled up with her, fucking entranced with the way her blonde hair was splayed out across my arms and chest.

Goosebumps pebbled up along her skin as I drew lazy circles with my fingers.

I could get used to this. I *wanted* to get used to this.

"You know, you still owe me three answers from our little pole dance bet," I drawled lazily, looking down at her.

She stiffened for a brief moment before burrowing closer. "I guess I do," she said with a shy smile on her glowing face. "But it's only two—the hairflip doesn't count as a separate move. What do you want to know?"

I thought about arguing but didn't want to push my luck. "Why do you hold back?"

The smile dipped, her eyes darting away. The pause was long enough that I wondered if she'd refuse to answer again, but then she spoke.

"You know how your mom was never there? Mine wasn't either. It was just me and my dad and he was… a lot. I never wanted for anything, but I didn't realize until it was too late that all the stuff he gave me was to keep me from noticing the golden cage I'd grown up in."

I trailed my fingers across her bare skin, taking in what she was saying, and what she wasn't.

"He did give me dance though," she said, a smile evident in her tone. "I thought I was going to be a professional ballerina ."

"Why didn't you? I saw you dance in our living room, Nikki. You were breathtaking." I rubbed at my chest, where it suddenly ached. She was breathtaking no matter what she was doing.

She turned and looked at me, her eyes dipping to my lips more than once, but I didn't close the distance, wanting her to continue letting me in.

"Have you ever talked about this with Ryan?" I asked, with a sick desire for her to say no. I wanted to be the one she finally spilled her secrets to.

There was another pause before she responded. "No, I've never talked about this with anyone."

Unable to help myself, I pressed my lips to hers, needing to taste her, needing to express with my actions all the things I couldn't say with words. She had no clue she was taking a fucking battering ram to the carefully constructed coffin around my heart with every smile, every secret shared, and every show of kindness. Why would she?

Nikki wasn't looking to make someone fall in love with her. Yet here I was falling, and I wasn't sure there was a damn thing I could do to stop it.

Or if I even wanted to.

She cupped my face, stroking my cheek, but there was something in her gaze that had me tensing. "But to answer your question, circumstances changed. My father didn't have dancing in his plan for my future. It wasn't an option he would give me. And I had no money of my own to continue."

"Why even let you start then?"

The laugh she let out was bitter, laced with anger and pain. "Because he'd know exactly where I was every day. It was nothing more than another cage. I actually wouldn't want to do it anymore now, even if I could. All I would think of was how it had been used to shackle me."

Her fingers began moving across my skin again, almost subconsciously. "Don't get me wrong, I still love dancing, but there's freedom up on the pole. I have autonomy over my movements, my outfits…my body. The first night I danced on a pole, that was the first time I'd ever held cash I'd earned on my own. It was addicting, knowing I could do shit on my own without relying on anyone else."

I tilted her chin with my fingers, needing her to see the sincerity in what I was about to say. "There's a difference between letting people in and relying on them, and someone trying to control you."

Let me be there for you. Rely on me.

Those were the words I wanted to say, but they died on my tongue. Instead, I spouted off something else without thinking of how she'd react.

"Who are you running from? I mean, really running from, because it's not *just* the Russians, is it?" She stiffened against me.

"I already answered your two questions, Dex," she said, her voice small. "I know Ryan told you to watch me and all, but this is my issue to solve."

How could she still feel that way? Hadn't we gotten far enough for her to see she could let me in?

"That's bullshit, Nikki. You know we can help." I sat up so I could look at her face while we had this discussion. Her throat bobbed, eyes turned down as she played with a strand of her hair.

"This is *my* problem. *Alone.*" There wasn't the normal venom in her tone from when we'd previously broached the subject of her past. This time she sounded sad—resigned.

"That's the fucking point, Nikki, you're not alone anymore," I said, sliding out of the bed, needing to do something with my possessive energy. Because that's what I was feeling for her.

Possessive.

Her words had been like a punch to the gut, stripping me of oxygen. I gripped her face between my calloused palms. "Quit trying to run from me. What more do I have to tell you to get that I want *you?* All of you. Including the shit you're running from."

Unshed tears lined the rim of her eyes, and she studied my face, dragging the tips of her fingers everywhere her gaze lingered. The emotion in her expression gutted me because it looked like a mournful goodbye.

"That wasn't part of the deal, Dex." It came out as a whisper. "We fucked. Nothing more. I thought you, of all people, would understand. I've never offered anyone any part of me other than my body."

What she said sounded hollow—rehearsed—but that didn't matter to me at the moment, my emotions were too frayed, and I lashed out.

Anger bubbled up inside me, working its way up to erupt at her, since I had nowhere else to put it. I dropped my hold as if she'd physically burned me, blanking my face. Every bit of warmth leeched from my body, leaving nothing but a cold shell.

"Fine, Nikki. That's what you want? A single fuck to get me out of your system?" I bit out the words.

The thought of only having her once was like a knife to the heart, but I couldn't give her more of me if she didn't want it.

A sob fell from her lips, her body curling in on itself like she was seeking protection and comfort. I wanted so badly to wrap her up in my arms and tell her it would be okay.

"It doesn't have to be the one time, Dex. Why can't we fuck and be friends or whatever this is that we have." She motioned between us.

I flinched away from her hand when it came too close to my bare chest, and she dropped it away, crestfallen. I couldn't handle her touching me, or my resolve to give her what she asked for would break.

I'd end up stealing her away, locking her up like Rapunzel in a tower, but that wasn't what either of us deserved.

"No. Choose, Nikki," I said in a pained voice, backing away from her, each step like a knife to my heart. "If you want to work through this alone and not let the people who care about you in, fine. That's your choice, and I don't ever want to take away your choices. But it's not only your wants and needs in this. I have to make a choice too, if you're not going to let me choose you. Because life is too short and too precious to be led around by the dick. If you don't want the man attached to it, that's fine, but this won't be a repeat, spitfire."

My lungs seized as I reached for the knob, pulling the door open before leaving without a backward glance.

How ironic, I got what I usually wanted—one fuck, and then they'd leave. But this time I wanted the woman to stay.

Because this time, I loved her. And I was pretty sure she loved me too—she just wasn't ready to admit that.

The slam of the door was like a gunshot—right to the heart.

THIRTY-TWO

NIKKI

BOE, YOU'RE A BITCH

THE NUMBERS on my screen read a little past one in the morning.

I hadn't seen Dex since he'd stormed out.

"Fuck," I muttered when the waterworks appeared for the fifth time. "It's better this way. You were getting too close. I mean, look at you, crying over a man. We said we'd never do that again…"

I let the words trail off. My lids fluttered shut but quickly opened again—every time they closed, all I saw was the look of hurt before Dex blanked his features completely. That empty look was so chilling, the room might have dropped in temperature.

He'd texted me, telling me he wouldn't be back tonight, and that Torque would take me home after his fight. But there was no fucking way I was going to ride home looking like the mess I was with one of Dex's club brothers. My phone vibrated, letting me know that my driver was here to pick me up outside the club gates.

"Where you going, Nikki?"

I nearly jumped out of my skin at the voice. Boe walked out of the shadows near the gatehouse, looking menacing in the low lighting. The hair on the back of my neck stood on end and I willed my body to keep walking backward toward the car.

"Just going home."

My fingers wrapped around the door handle. Boe hadn't made any sign of moving toward me, but that did nothing to calm my nerves. I didn't trust the guy—there was something off about him. Question was whether he was just a creepy fucker, or an actual threat.

"I'll follow you home. Make sure you make it back safe," he said, his smile making my heartbeat tick up.

"No need. I can manage on my own." I pulled the door open, moving around it to slide into the seat.

The corners of his mouth only pulled up higher. "I insist. Dex will have my balls if I don't make sure you made it back. Lead the way." He walked a few feet over toward where his bike was parked, not waiting for my response.

I chewed on my lip. Had Dex asked Boe to follow me? He said he'd asked Torque to take me home. Then again, he probably knew I wouldn't listen to him. Maybe Boe was the backup if I decided to do my own thing?

Part of me wanted to text him and ask, but I'd tried calling earlier, and it went straight to voicemail. Clearly, he didn't want to hear from me, since he'd turned it off.

"Where to, miss?"

Something still didn't feel right, but I wasn't entirely sure *what* was wrong. Trusting my gut, I spouted off an address near my house before shooting off a text to someone else I wasn't entirely sure would answer. Then I sat rigid in the seat, hoping I was overreacting, and dreading if I wasn't.

The bright lights of Val's corner store came into view, and my shoulders relaxed just a bit. Boe's motorcycle sped up when he saw where we'd pulled in.

I could have gone to Lotería, but I wasn't sure who would be there tonight. Robert had already left for California, and Ryan had left earlier, too—something about a meeting.

The car hadn't even pulled to a complete stop before I was

leaping out and running into the store, the rumble of the bike growing louder.

"What the hell, Nikki?" Val called as I barreled through the door, causing the bell to go crazy.

"Pretty sure this is another attempted kidnapping," I answered, slipping into one of the rows of alcohol, crouching down, and watching the mirror up in the corner, being mindful of staying out of the reflection.

If I weren't so focused on getting out of this situation, I would have laughed at how ridiculous it was that this was happening to me again.

"What the hell do you mean, *another,* girl?" Val shouted, reaching for the weapon stored under the counter.

The bell erupted into a new round of furious ringing, announcing Boe's arrival. His chest rose and fell as he stomped over to Val. I had to bite back another panicked laugh at how she peered at him over her gossip magazine, staring him down like he was shit on her boot. Boe flinched when she spoke.

"What the fuck do you want?"

"Where'd the girl who ran in here go?" he asked, piss-poor attitude back in full force.

"Why the hell would I tell you where a girl *running* from you went?" she asked pointedly, arching a brow.

A slam echoed through the store, Boe's hands hitting the formica top. "Listen here, old bitch. I'm taking the girl. Either you help or," he pulled out a gun, pointing the barrel to her temple, and I slapped my hands over my mouth, "I blow another hole in your fucking head."

There was no way I was letting Val get hurt because of me. "Hey, asshole. What the hell is your problem? I told you I could get home on my own," I yelled, stepping out into the aisle, praying that Val was smart enough to get the fuck out of there.

Boe turned, and I found myself staring down a barrel at fifteen feet away.

"You're not as dumb as you look," he said, licking his lips, eyes crazed.

"Thanks for the glowing compliment. That in reference to my ability to make it home, or knowing you are shady as fuck and not getting on the back of your bike?" I stepped toward the back, hoping to draw him away from Val.

"You must have a magical pussy, because Dex refused to turn you over to the Russians," he said, taking the bait and moving closer. "Dumbass doesn't want to get the weapons and manpower they're promising. He's willing to sacrifice his brothers over one fucking piece of snatch."

Boe's words did more damage than the gun could have ever done. Guilt over what my past had brought to Dex's doorstep threatened to overtake me, but I tried to hide my panic.

"My snatch is great, but ever think if everyone else isn't in agreement with you, maybe you're just wrong?" I asked, grabbing for a bottle heavy enough to do damage.

"You're not even a fucking Old Lady," he yelled, spit flying. "Pres *never* should have let this go. I'll do what the rest of them don't have the balls to do." He took another step, closing the distance faster than I could come up with a plan.

"Fuckface, no weapons in my store," called Val from behind Boe.

I was about to yell at her to get out of there when a shot rang out, and I ducked out of the way. A pained groan fell from Boe's lips as he lay on the floor in a puddle of red wine and blood. My brain was struggling to decipher what the hell had just happened.

"Oh, good, you had enough sense to jump out of the way," Val said, completely unfazed.

"You shot at me," I heard myself say, still in shock.

Her frail shoulders shrugged, not an ounce of remorse. "Call us even now."

My mouth fell open, searching for a retort, then I shrugged, too. "Honestly, fair. Is he dead?" I asked, toeing him with my boot.

"Nah. Not a real good idea to kill outlaw MC members. Most find themselves in a shallow grave for that."

Fuck. What's going to happen to her?

"Val, you've saved my ass twice now. You can't take the blame for this," I said, remembering all the help she'd given me when I first rolled into town.

She batted a hand my way. "Ah. Don't worry about it. I'll collect on it eventually. And I'll be fine, his president owes me a favor. Now, get the fuck out of here, girl. May I suggest, out of town, *mija*?" She jutted her chin toward Boe. "Since it looks like you've got two motorcycle clubs after you."

I wrapped my arms around myself, suddenly cold. "He said that Pres agreed not to trade me." The words felt weak. Val's scoff confirmed my thoughts.

"Baby, if what he said was true and you're not an Old Lady, then you don't mean shit to the club. Their president probably extended a *favor* to whoever your boy is. But after this…" Her eyes slid to Boe's cut, the club rocker standing out like a beacon.

A taunt.

She was right. Boe was a member of the Skeletons of Society—a brother. It would be his word against mine. Val's, too, but I wasn't sure how much her testament would mean to his president.

I wasn't worried about what would happen to me.

I was worried about what this would do for Dex. The club was his family, the thing that gave him hope after Kelly. Me being here was fucking up the thing he loved most, the thing he needed most.

Fuck, and Ryan.

How would I live with myself knowing I'd brought more devastation to her doorstep? That I was the catalyst for the people she loved and cared for being subject to more blood-shed? Okay, I got that they were in the cartel and bloodshed was par for the course, but this fight wasn't one they'd asked for.

A chuckle bordering on a sob slipped through. She'd be

pissed I was making these decisions for her—they both would. But neither of them would look at this objectively.

Tears rolled down my face, and I didn't move to wipe them away. I'd allow myself to mourn, if only for a little while. Another life I never got to live, lost, and more dreams I would never get to accomplish. This time, though, there was also love I'd never get to explore.

This city had been both our salvations.

And I would leave it in a heartbeat if it meant Dex could stay where he'd made a family.

"Val, can you take me to an airport?" I choked out, as salty drops fell to the floor.

THIRTY-THREE
DEX

"ARIANA, WHAT ARE YOU DOING HERE"<
—DEX AND GUNNER WHEN SCAR POPS
UP RANDOMLY

THE RIDE WAS SUPPOSED to help release the fucking rock that was sitting on my chest and slowly suffocating me. I 'd tried to lock away Nikki's rejection and fall into the feel of the road under my tires, but those fucking words kept banging against the barrier, wearing it down.

I'd finally decided I wanted to attempt the whole relationship thing, so of course I'd fallen in love with the one woman who didn't want anything to do with anyone. Hell, I didn't even know her real name. Not that I gave a shit—I loved her anyway. I'd take her past if she wanted to give it to me, but all I cared about was her present, and her future.

But that wasn't enough for her.

Or, more accurately, that was too much.

I jumped at Gunner's voice coming from behind where I still sat on my ride. "Hey, you okay?" he asked, looking at me with concern.

"Yeah. I'm cool. Just fucking tired, you know?" I took the bottled beer he'd brought me. "Didn't think you'd be back for a while. How'd it go?"

Gunner had pretty much burned every bridge he'd had with the FBI, but there were a few informants who liked him more now that the government wasn't paying him.

One of those dudes ran odd jobs for some of the smaller

organizations around Tucson. Bastard was a wealth of knowl-edge—for the right price.

"From the looks of it, the Reapers are lying low. My guy says the club is split, some of them wanna make a move whether they have the Russians' backing or not. The smarter half knows they will be obliterated if they go against us *and* the cartel."

The cool liquid from the beer did little to help shake off the heavy feeling of the night air. Something was off, and it had me worried.

"You know when we'd go out on missions," I asked, staring off toward the desert that surrounded our compound, catching Gunner nodding his head in my peripherals. "That gut feeling we'd get when something was about to pop off. Some instinctual warning system that told us the energy was shifting and something was coming…"

Our eyes locked, his body stiffening. He knew *exactly* what I was talking about.

"It going off?" he asked, taking a tentative sip of his beer. Cutting the connection between us, I stared forward once again, only answering with a nod of my head.

"You fell for her," Gunner said. It wasn't a question. "I had a feeling you would. You two are like twin flames."

I rubbed at my chest as another pang went off because, of course, heartbreak was fuckin' physical too. "That's not what I was talking about."

"Call it a change of subject then, since we can't do shit about something popping off until it does."

He was quiet, waiting for me. After draining the rest of my drink, I sighed. "Yeah, well, it doesn't matter how I feel. Nikki made it fucking clear that all she wants is a fuck," I growled, shifting on my ride.

"She tell you that, or you assuming?"

A humorless chuff left my lips. "She made it very clear. Shoulda taken the hint the first time she ran out on me. And then when she threw a shoe at me." I turned toward Gunner, shooting him a smile that probably looked like I was in pain. "Third time's a charm, right?"

He opened his mouth to respond, but was interrupted by Pres walking up. The way he held his body had me sitting up.

"Is a carrier pigeon the only way to reach you mother fuckers or what? Your fucking phone is off, Dex." He was clearly pissed.

"Sorry, Pres. What's up?" I asked, not bothering to give him my sad reasonings for why it was off.

I'd turned my phone off after telling Nikki that Torque would take her home. There was no way I'd be able to resist contacting her, begging her to reconsider, and tonight wasn't the time to do that. Not when we were both emotional, our judgment clouded. If she didn't want to be in a relationship with me, I'd respect that. But that didn't mean I didn't need time to process and try and wrangle my emotions into submission. Regretfully, I'd asked Torque to take over watching her.

It'd be too painful to sleep under the same roof as her and know we didn't feel the same way. At least, not right away.

"Boe's been shot," he said, staring me down.

"I didn't fucking do it."

Pres crossed his arms over his chest, rolling his eyes at me. He was well informed of our feelings toward one another. "Didn't say you did, asshole."

"He okay?" Gunner asked, but there wasn't any real concern in his voice. He didn't like Boe either, but the asshole was a brother so there wasn't shit we could do other than avoid him.

"Yeah, he's good. He was shot somewhere non-vital, but here's the problem. Your girl is involved, Dex."

The words hit like a goddamn freight train. "What the fuck do you mean she's involved?" I leaped off my ride, tearing my phone from my pocket and powering it up. "What did he do to her? Where is she?"

"I told you your brother is shot, and you wanna know what *he* did to her?" Pres asked.

A large hand landed on my chest as I barreled forward, and looking down I recognized Gunner's tattooed arm. "Easy, brother, let's keep cool heads and find out what the fuck is happening, yeah?" He spoke to me as if he were taming a wild animal.

Pres looked unfazed, drinking in my reaction.

"Sorry, Pres," I said, running my hand through my hair. The phone seemed to take eons to power up to the unlock screen.

"That your way of telling me she wouldn't have shot him unless he did some shit?"

Three missed calls from Nikki, but all of them were from right after I'd stormed out and then told her Torque was taking her home. The oily tendrils of guilt seeped their way into my body, infecting every cell. I'd left her *alone,* knowing there were people after her.

Like you did with Kell, you thought she'd be fine on her own. This was your fault.

Shards of glass went flying everywhere as my bottle shattered where I slammed it. "Fuck," I yelled so loud I thought I might break the mirrors on my ride.

"Where is she?" I asked, the words coming out as growls, my chest heaving. My lids fluttered shut when Pres looked down, tongue running along his bottom lip. He didn't know.

In for four. Out for four.

"She wasn't there when we got there," he responded.

Gunner gripped my face, forcing my attention on him. His green eyes were lit with fire, nostrils flaring as he spoke. "Brother, this isn't your fault. I know that look, Dex. I pulled you out of a self-dug grave last time you looked like that. You're no good to her if you fall back there," he said, refusing to let go until I nodded.

"Where's Boe?" I bit out, furling and unfurling my hands, Gunner's grip on my shoulder offering some grounding reassurance as he stood by my side.

"You know why they voted me in as President, Dex? Because my bullshit radar is never wrong. I pride myself on being able to see shit three steps ahead, and when someone is trying to pull some shit on me…I know it."

"I'm no—"

He held up a tatted hand, stopping me. "I'm not saying that in reference to you. We voted not to turn your girl over to the Russians. Seems Boe didn't want to go with that plan. He's in the shed."

The words were barely out of his mouth and I was storming off toward my playground, ignoring Gunner's shouts behind me. All I could hear was the blood pounding in my ears, the demon locked inside shedding his constraints and coming to the forefront.

My body moved on autopilot.

One second, I was outside, the next, I was looming over where Boe lay on a medical bed, my hand wrapped around his throat. The pounding of his pulse under my palm was addictive. Every kick and flail only fanned the flames of my thirst for violence.

"Where the fuck is she?" I asked, my voice nearly robotic. There was not a singe drop of empathy running through my blood at this moment. Boe was about to meet the worst version of the club enforcer.

Nothing came out as he tried to speak. He drew blood in his attempt to peel away my fingers from his throat.

"He's not going to be able to answer if you crush his windpipe, Dex," Gunner said from behind me.

I gave one more squeeze before loosening the hold. "Answer. Now." Boe's eyes were wild as he searched the room for someone to save him. I leaned closer, spit landing on his face as I growled out, "There are only devils here, Boe. No salvation, only damnation. I'm your executioner, mother fucker."

"She's not even an Old Lady. This is fucking ridiculous. We're going to risk brothers' lives for some pus—" The sentence was cut off with a scream. Warmth from his blood coated my hand as I dug into his wound, ripping the stitches as I forced my thumb into the bullet hole.

"You don't even know who she really is," he panted, dry heaving from the pain.

"She's mine. That's who the fuck she is, you piece of shit," I roared, the statement bouncing off the walls in an echo overshadowing his whimpers. "You *dared* to try and take what is mine, Boe. That comes with consequences. I really thought you were smarter than you look. You *know* I nearly killed a man—in fact, you taunted me over it not all that long ago. I should have held you in that fucking bonfire, watched your flesh peel off your bones as you burned alive."

Vaguely, I was aware of Gunner wincing at my words. He rarely saw me at this level of bloodthirst.

"Gunner." Without hesitation, my friend was at the bed holding the screaming man down as I gripped Boe's dominant hand. The cries for mercy grew louder when I reached down and grabbed the meat cleaver I'd somehow retrieved in my hypnotic state.

"It'll be hard to touch what's not yours if you're missing your hand," I said, pinning the appendage to the bedside table.

"You're fucking unhinged. I didn't even touch her," he screamed, renewing his efforts to break free, but he was no match for Gunner's massive frame on a good day. There was no way he'd shake him loose while injured.

"Tell me where she is," I demanded.

"I don't know. Told her you told me to follow her home."

My body stopped cold. Fuck, what if she believed I was in on this? That I'd betrayed her? My heart was threatening to break right through the skin with how hard it was beating. Boe was unaware of my internal turmoil and continued to spill what had gone down.

"She went to some corner store. Then the old bitch shot me instead of minding her own fucking business. I don't know where your girl went after that. I never fucking touched her," he spat at me, breath labored. Piss coated the front of his jeans, the scent competing with the copper tang of his blood pouring from the ripped stitches.

The blood-curdling screech that fell from Boe's mouth. The crunching of his bones had the corner of my lips pulling up into a sneer. "No, but you were going to. If you had, I'd have taken both hands," I said, tossing the bloodied cleaver aside while Boe turned, the contents of his stomach landing on the floor. He likely hadn't heard a word, the pain causing him to pass out shortly after.

"Ryan's tried calling Nikki. She's not answering," Gunner said, his green eyes tracking my every movement. Before I could reply, my phone began ringing.

The screen displayed an unknown number, so I pocketed the device, but it rang again. And again. On the fifth ring, I answered. "Who the fuck is this, and what do you want?" I barked out.

"I'm guessing you don't know your girl is on her way to my city," said a feminine voice.

Traitorous hope that no one had taken Nikki filled my blackened heart, but I kept it in check since I had no clue who was on the other line.

"Who the fuck is this?" I asked again, waving a hand at Gunner to be quiet when he asked me what was going on. Waiting for the unknown caller to answer my question.

"Watch your fucking tone," someone else said. The statement sounded like it came from someone farther away from the phone though. "Kenji, down boy," the female voice said with a chuckle. "This is Scarletta. I'm friends with Ryan. We've spoken once before, Dex. Sort of."

As soon as she said her name I pressed speaker so Gunner could hear as well, and she instantly said hello to him. "Now that you're done being paranoid, you can listen. Nikki is on her way to New York."

Dread filled my body. My hand vibrated as a text came in with a picture of Nikki in the same wig she'd worn the night she'd gone to the Reapers' club. The second photo was a security cam shot of her sitting at an airport terminal.

"Why's she going to New York? She going to see you?" I asked, staring at the side of Nikki's heart-shaped face.

"I don't know yet, but I doubt she's on her way to me. If she is, she's dropping in unannounced, because I haven't heard a peep from her."

"Well, find out," I bit out, still studying Nikki's face. The picture was too grainy to tell if she was injured, or what her emotional state was.

Scar said something else to someone in the background. It sounded a lot like *Let him be.* Then she was back in my ear. "I've got connections everywhere, but I'm not god. There's some shit not even I know. That was from about thirty minutes ago. Plane's already taken off, and I won't know more until she lands here."

I moved toward the door, yanking it open, Gunner following close behind. "You're going to go pick her up, right? I want her ass somewhere safe as soon as that fucking plane lands."

"What do you know about her?" She asked, ignoring my demands. Gunner cut in when it was clear that I was too upset to answer.

A large hand landed on my shoulder, and Gunner pressed the mute button. Which probably wouldn't work on Scar, but I didn't voice that.

"Hey, whatever the fuck you're telling yourself in your head about her, don't. As someone who had to lie about who they were to the person they loved, sometimes we have our reasons, and it's only because of shitty timing that we aren't the ones to break the news. Ryan still *knew* me, even if she didn't know my legal name," he said, his eyes pleading with me.

"He's right," Scar added.

A sigh left my lips as I rubbed the bridge of my nose. "How did I know that muting wouldn't do shit for you. Okay, clearly you know more than we do about Nikki, so just lay it on me." Even to my ears, I sounded tired.

"Nikki Adams is actually one Natasha Petrov, born and raised in St. Petersburg. Her daddy was a high-ranking member in the St. Petersburg Bratva." Gunner and I exchanged looks. "Yup, the same Bratva led by one Yuri Sokolov. Here's where it gets particularly interesting: Natasha, aka Nikki, was gifted to Yuri as a bride in exchange for power for her father, and then she went missing."

The puzzle pieces began to click into place. I'd always knew she couldn't *only* be another woman, but his fiancée? That one hit like a sucker punch.

"Her father *gave her away*?" I bit out, barely containing my anger at the idea of her being traded like a fucking piece of meat.

"Yup, and before you ask, he's deceased," Scarletta commented.

A million and one questions swirled in my mind. Luckily, Gunner was more level-headed as he furiously sent off a text. I assumed to Ryan.

"How the fuck do you know all of this?" I asked.

"I told her," answered someone with a deep voice. "Imagine my surprise when I spotted the infamous missing Bratva bride dancing at Lotería."

Scarletta cut back in. "Niko saw her when we visited Lotería a few weeks ago. Thought she looked familiar, so he started looking into her. Nearly beat his ass, thinking they'd slept together. Turned out he knew her because he'd been at their wedding-turned-massacre. So I dug up more information on her, since it didn't seem like Ryan knew she was harboring a missing person. Too many coincidences for my liking, with us killing Maxim, and then Ryan taking out Mario due to his new dealings with the Russians, then Nikki *happens* to be in the middle of this? Ironically, though, it is a coincidence. Nikki picked the wrong place to hide out—Yuri was looking to expand his skin trade with my uncle in New York. Mario wanted in on the action, and the dumbfucker fell into some luck when he discovered Nikki had a husband looking for her."

"Offered her back to Yuri in exchange for power," I said, filling in the missing pieces. "That's why they want her so bad."

Gunner piped up from beside me. "Her past is catching up to her." His eyes met mine. "The Russians want her, and the Reapers saw an opportunity like Mario had," he said.

"And like Boe did." My fist hit the cinderblock, knuckles splitting. I needed the physical pain to distract my mind from the emotional pain. "She probably thinks the Skeletons are taking advantage of her, too. I left her alone, Gunner. I was supposed to protect her, and I turned my fucking phone off and left her. Boe fucking told her I said for him to follow her. What if she thinks—" I couldn't even voice the possibility that she thought I'd sold her out.

Gunner grabbed my arm when I raised it to land another punch. "Or, Nikki probably doesn't see any other way to end this than to run. Figures if she's out of the picture, then the Reapers lose their meal ticket. Skeletons and Los Muertos are safe," he said. "Ryan did the same thing. These women are fiercely independent and love with their whole fucking chest. Even if they don't realize that's exactly what they are doing. She's not stupid, or even reckless Dex, but she's used to surviving."

We stood in the hallway of the shed, locked in a stare-down that felt like déjà vu. I gave my friend a weak smile. "Gunner, for a cocky asshole, you sure do have a warm and gooey center."

"Please don't use the words *warm* and *gooey* in the same sentence as my name ever again."

His jab did the trick, allowing my mind to relax enough to act objectively.

Scar cleared her throat. "Well, now that we have all of that taken care of, we can talk about the load of shit we are all in. Since the Reapers royally fucked up on getting Nikki, I killed Yuri's right-hand man when I offed Maxim, and apparently, he had another employee named Jardani go missing in your area—it was too much for him to ignore. The Boogeyman is on his way here."

Gunner and I exchanged looks.

"You three need to get your asses on a plane and get to

New York so we can nip this shit in the bud. Because we're about to experience the joy of becoming the focus of Yuri's full attention."

"And how do you know we'll all just hop on a plane to New York?" I knew we all would, but Scarletta was making a lot of leaps for someone Nikki barely knew.

The laugh she let out was sarcastic. "Well, one, there's no way in hell Ryan is going to let Nikki deal with this alone. The chick fucking Lara Crofted her way into an enemy compound not four months ago." Gunner grunted from beside me, still pissed she hadn't taken him with her.

"And you are in love with the woman Yuri is fucking obsessed with."

"I am no—"

A deep voice cut me off. "You totally are my man. It happens to the best of us. One day, you're pulling all the hoes," there was a yelp of pain on the other end of the line, before the guy continued, "the next moment, you're fucking running into burning buildings that she decided to go into so she could save the other man she's in love with. Why did we choose the independent unhinged ones?"

I wasn't fully sure if the question was rhetorical or not, but damn did I relate.

"Anyway, " Scar's voice was back. "That's why we have to address this, because we all know there's no way in hell you're letting Nikki run away to face this alone."

Fuck. She was right.

"Ryan's already on her way to my plane. I sent the coordinates to your phones." With that, she hung up.

THIRTY-FOUR
NIKKI

DUN, DUN, DUN DRAMA

TRUE DELUSION WAS BELIEVING that if you pretended your problems didn't exist, they'd go away on their own. That the monsters living under your bed wouldn't get tired of waiting for you to crawl into the dark with them.

But they always did.

And then they dragged you under, snuffing out the prettied-up fantasies you'd foolishly created.

I'd foolishly created.

A heavy sigh left my lips as the cab pulled down a dilapidated street. The sight had my nerves ratcheting higher, and I used the fabric seats to wipe off my clammy palms.

Corrugated walls of metal buildings lined this part of the city for as far as the eye could see, only broken up by smashed-in windows and darkened street poles.

I'd considered renting a car, but that would have required a license, and Dex's one lesson might not have been sufficient enough for me to try my hand at New York traffic.

The thought of Dex had my heart tightening, but I pushed the emotions away, locking them in a box so I could focus on what needed to be done.

The car rolled to a stop in front of a burnt dumpster and one of the only working lights. "You sure you want me to drop you off here?" he asked, leaning close to the windshield to peer at our surroundings before looking over his shoulder at me, clearly wondering what a five-six blonde woman would be doing here. He'd probably caught me wiping the sweat off, too.

It was a fair question, but not one I'd be answering.

"Yeah, I'm sure." I pulled out a small stack of bills, placing them on his center console before exiting my door. At the last second, I poked my head back in the cab. "Listen, if anyone stops you, tell them Andrei gave you a pass. And for the love of all things unholy, do *not* freak out. It makes you look suspicious," I told him, watching the color drain from his face. I wasn't sure if his reaction was because he was familiar with Andrei's name or because this was so far out of his comfort zone. Maybe both.

"Here," I said, pulling out a few more bills because he looked fucking petrified. I rolled my eyes when shaky fingers wrapped around the money, careful not to touch me. Like contact with me would taint him. "Maybe next time ask where they want to go before taking the fare," I added, throwing the door closed before he answered.

He peeled out seconds after it latched, filling the air with the scent of burning rubber. I shook my head.

He's for sure getting stopped now.

I didn't bother moving from my spot on the sidewalk. This whole area would be carefully monitored—Andrei knew I was here the moment I'd crossed into his territory back at the railroad tracks. The piercing whistle of a train horn sounded as if on cue.

My eyelids fluttered shut as I pulled in a deep breath, holding the polluted air in my lungs for as long as possible in an attempt to steady my heartbeat.

Even with all the noise, I heard the slamming of car doors. The echo joined the cacophony of clanging metal in the background. Metal wheels scraping along tracks really were the perfect camouflage for the sounds of an angle grinder. Not that Andrei really needed to hide his operation. The law wouldn't come this way—not if they wanted their families to stay alive. While I'd never actually made it over here, I knew enough about how it worked. Andrei talked about it often enough when discussing my exit plan from St. Petersburg.

I willed my body to stay loose. Unfazed. "Boys," I said in a lazy drawl, letting the accent I'd worked so hard to hide while in Tucson slip back in like an old friend.

The one closest to me caught my attention. His shaved head practically gleamed under the amber light, and he had a massive gothic cross surrounded by Cyrillic lettering adorning his upper arm.

Death before betrayal. God, it'd been forever since I'd read in my native tongue.

His hand moved toward his waistband, coming to rest on the gun tucked there.

I flicked my eyes back to his face, rolling my eyes at his attempt at intimidation. If only this man had seen the men I worked with at Lotería. Not to mention, I'd had a number of barrels pointed at me lately. Was this how Ryan and Scar felt? Bored?

A memory of Ryan showing me a gun popped into my mind.

Her look of surprise and pride when I shot that one Los Muertos asshole dead center between the eyes was on replay in my mind. *"Babe, that was great and all, but don't ever do that again when I'm standing in front of you."*

I forced myself to focus on the current situation. "We both know Andrei told you not to harm a hair on my head." I gestured to my blonde hair—I'd pulled off the ratty wig and contacts the minute I'd landed at J F K. "So, open the fucking door for me like a gentleman and take me to your boss." I moved toward the seat behind the driver's side.

A grunt was his only response as he climbed back into the blacked-out Mercedes . A young guy held the door open for me, looking me up and down. He couldn't have been older than nineteen, so he wouldn't have a clue who I was. Two and a half years was a long time to be away.

Especially for the Ruska Roma.

No one spoke during the short ride, but I could feel all three sets of eyes on me as I stared out my window. Their curiosity about who I was and what I was doing here was palpable.

Gra y eyes glared back at me in the rearview mirror. "Katya always calls ahead before she sends one of her girls."

I cocked my head to the side, holding his stare. "What makes you think I'm one of Katya's?" My voice was neutral, careful not to reveal anything.

A scoff filled the car. "I'm not stupid, girl," he growled. "You hold yourself like one of her dancers. Only the ones she beats sit and stand with such posture."

I smiled at the truth of his words. It was a trait I'd never be able to rid myself of since it had literally been whacked into me, usually in the form of a pointe shoe to the back of the head. Ryan always joked that I could be blackout drunk and I'd still have perfect posture. I always laughed and played it off as her being dramatic, because it hit too close to the truth.

"Well, Katya didn't call because she didn't send me," I responded, avoiding answering whether I was one of her girls or not because, truthfully, I didn't know what the hell I was nowadays.

We pulled up to a metal door. A few moments passed before it began to rise, revealing a busy chop shop. Sparks were flying, and men with cigarettes hanging from their lips ran around, tearing apart stolen cars for parts. Not everything got disassembled. The luxury ones would go straight onto the train after their VINs were changed, then get delivered to the port before making their way to Belarus.

At least, that's the way Andrei used to do it.

"OSHA would have a field day with this operation," I mumbled as the roll-up door closed behind us after we were tucked inside the building.

"Out," the driver barked as my door was wrenched open. Another young, unfamiliar face filled the doorway and hauled me out of the vehicle.

"Get the fuck off me," I spat, pulling my arm from his

tatted fingers. The back of his hand sailed toward my face as he called me a bitch in Polish.

My movements were choppy, but still, I had enough sense to duck. His arm passed overhead and I ran at him, wrapping around his lanky midsection and sending my knee flying toward his balls.

Once. Twice. Just like Ryan showed me. Well, in my mind, it looked like what Ryan had showed me, but it probably wasn't as badass as I imagined.

Yelps of pain spilled from his mouth. His body dropped, and I was forced to rush to the side to avoid being pulled down by his weight. All the noise in the garage ceased.

"Damn, that worked," I said, impressed. My eyes darted around the space, taking in the group of men now staring me down.

Fuck, that wasn't a smart move.

I dropped down to a crouch, not entirely sure what that would do, but it felt right. There was no way that move would work on *all* these men, especially since I knew driver-boy had a gun. No doubt others did, as well—at the very least, a crowbar.

Slow claps came from my right. Everyone turned toward Andrei, who was descending from what I assumed was his office at the top of a metal staircase. Maybe I was an idiot, but I relaxed at the sight of him. I didn't trust him, but one thing I knew about him—if he wanted me dead, he'd kill me himself.

"Tasha," his voice boomed. "The dead do come back to life, eh?" There was a sinister smile on his face as he stared down at me, an underlying tone of irritation in his words.

Walking away from Ruska Roma was unheard of—death before betrayal.

Showing up here meant I'd have to pay the toll.

SAY HELLO, AGAIN, TO ANDREI. HE'S CUNTY BUT I LIKE HIM

ANDREI HADN'T CHANGED in the years since I'd seen him.

Still the same handsome, smug bastard I'd crushed on. Back then, I'd thought I was in love. Now, I was sure that was never the case. He'd just been decent to me, and had given me a say in what I wanted to do next, two things that had been sorely lacking in my prior experience.

He leaned back in his leather chair eyeing me like a king did his subjects, one corner of his mouth pulled up in a smug grin. The man always looked more like a rockstar than a mobster with his lean, athletic body covered in tattoos.

He wore his hair shorn short into a bleached buzz cut. The style seemed to accentuate the sharp lines of his jaw and cheekbones. His blue eyes lightly lined with black.

I felt like I was being picked apart with every passing moment we sat in the silence of his office. He steepled his fingers on his desk, finally speaking. "Years later and you show up here unannounced? I'm guessing this isn't a social call, is it, Tasha?"

The guy I'd hit glared at me from the corner, waiting for the command that would allow him to retaliate.

I flipped him off. "You ice your balls yet?" The smart comment earned me a chuckle from Andrei.

"Still as feisty as ever. No clue how Yuri ever thought he'd be able to tame you."

The drop of his name reminded me why I'd come all this way and stepped back into my past. My irritation toward the guy drained, replaced by an icy fear.

"He knows I'm alive," I said, picking off an imaginary piece of lint before locking eyes with Andrei. "What do you know about it?" There was a shift in his features, but it only lasted a moment before he schooled them into a cocky mask.

"So you're here for my help? Who is it that you ran from this time?" he asked.

The truth in his words cut deep, but I pushed them aside and channeled my anger at him instead, dredging up the old wounds he'd inflicted on my battered heart before I'd shut it off to everyone.

"Fuck you, Andrei. What choice did you give me last time? You told me in no uncertain terms to get the fuck away from you."

He stood, moving around his massive glass and metal desk to close the distance between us. Lording over my seat, he caged me in with his muscled arms, his cocky smirk growing wider when I glared at him. This would have been what my naive dreams were made of a few years ago. Now I wanted to knee the asshole in the balls like I had his man and watch him writhe in pain on the floor.

"Let's set the record straight, shall we, *zaika*," he said with a sneer. "You latched on to me, and I did my best to dissuade your little infatuation. What kind of man would I be if I allowed you to attach yourself to me? A woman who was gifted to a man she wanted nothing to do with by her father. You didn't have feelings for me—you were simply looking for even an ounce of affection from anyone. For someone to let you make your own decisions."

He leaned in even closer so our faces were barely an inch apart, the scent of marijuana and cologne floating between us. "I didn't lead you on, Tasha. I pitied you and was *nice*. You'd never experienced that from a man." He pulled away shaking his head in irritation. "Stupid girl, I was *barely* kind to you. Your bar was on the fucking floor. I'm not a good man. No woman like yourself should ever want to be with someone like me," he hissed.

Any fight in me drained. What Andrei said rang true. Hadn't I just thought it myself?

He had never shown even a hint of affection toward me.

He'd just never treated me like fucking trash like the other men in my life had.

I took a deep breath and raised a brow, smiling. "You're right, Andrei. Anyone who likes you does have their standards on the damn floor. That why you're spending your evening in a chop shop filled with sweaty dudes who reek? No one wants you in their bed?" There was no real anger behind my words, I just needed to release some of the tension building between us. Especially if I was going to ask him for his help.

He laughed, sitting back in his seat across from me, resting his elbows on the edge of his desk. "I don't need a bed to fuck. Now, who is it that you left behind now, Tasha? Think long and hard before you decide if you really want to leave them, to re-enter this life. You've been gone for years now."

Was that what I wanted? To leave Ryan? Dex?

My voice lacked its usual confidence. "No. I don't want to leave them, but Yuri will come after them if I stay."

He shrugged his shoulder, rolling his eyes. "So kill him," he said in a matter-of-fact tone.

I scoffed at the suggestion. "Oh, yes, Andrei, because it's so easy to kill the head of not only the Russian Bratva, but the Circle, as well." I crossed my arms over my chest. "Or do you not remember that we've tried that once before. Look where it got us."

His smile sent a chill down my spine, like the fucking cat that ate the canary. "Oh, but Tasha, we have the perfect bait, do we not?" His icy eye flicked behind me, and he gave a slight lift of his chin before focusing again on me. "And speak for yourself. I am doing just fine."

"Then you won't care if I leave," I said, calling his bluff. There was something in this for him too. Not that he would ever share that with me, but I could tell he needed me.

His jaw stiffened at my call out. "From what I gather, Tasha, you have some very powerful friends you've aligned yourself with," he said, ignoring my words.

The cold surface of his desk met my palms as I slapped them down, shooting out of my chair. The action caused the other men in the room to move toward me, but Andrei waved them away, never letting his gaze drift from me.

"You leave them the fuck out of it, Andrei. They didn't sign up for this. That's the whole fucking reason I left them behind, so I wouldn't drag them down with me if all of this goes to hell." There was no way I would drag them into anything involving Yuri. For fuck's sake, I'd never even given them my actual name.

Now he wanted me to ask them to kill my ex-husband?

My facial expressions must not have been as blank as I'd intended because Andrei responded to my internal questions as if I'd voiced them aloud.

"You never told them about your situation," he stated, his eyes narrowing in a fashion that concerned me. He was cunning and couldn't be trusted as far as you could throw him, traits I'd decided to ignore when I was swept up in my infatuation with him.

"Your father really fucked you up, didn't he?" There was a hint of pity in the way he looked at me, and it caused my anger to spike.

"Oh, you're one to talk," I spat back, sliding back into the chair as a wave of exhaustion swept over me. Andrei was as much of a mystery to me as I was to my friends. He'd never revealed too much to me about his past, but there'd been one night when vodka made our lips loose, and we'd both shared more than we'd meant to. Trouble was, I didn't remember much from that night either.

"Do you care about them?"

The sincerity of his question took me by surprise. All I

could manage was a slight nod—uttering the words felt as if I were casting a curse.

The guarantee of a broken heart.

But wasn't I already experiencing that by walking away?

"Then you need to kill Yuri, because the bastard is on his way to the United States." Andrei wagged a tattooed finger at me while I fought off falling into a panic at the bombshell he'd just dropped. "I'd wondered why he was bothering to leave his secure palace atop the hill. Sure, Maxim was killed, and the cartel heir he was potentially going into business with was also. But people die all the time in this line of work. Men in his station don't drop everything and leave to do menial tasks themselves."

My stomach dropped to my feet, sensing the point he was making.

"But he's not coming here for a menial task, is he, Tasha? No. He's coming to collect his bride." He cocked his head to the side, a hard edge to his stare. "What do you think he'll do when he doesn't find you in Tucson, *Nikki*?"

I took a sharp inhale at the dropping of where I'd been living. The name. H e'd known. He was the one who'd selected it, for god's sake, but where I was living…

"What are you suggesting, Andrei?" I asked, proud that I'd kept most of the shake out of my voice.

He might have been kind to me when I'd showed up at his door looking to broker a deal. I'd give them information and access to Yuri if they'd help me flee. But that wasn't how it worked in the Ruska Roma, and I'd been required to join. Only reason I didn't have a tattoo marking my allegiance was because we hadn't wanted to risk Yuri discovering the ink before the ambush at the wedding.

But I'd never made it back to them after the attack. They held no allegiance to me.

Andrei may have been the one who'd told me to leave, and never to come back, but I had no clue what he'd told the others. As soon as I'd landed in the States, I'd booked a second flight to Dallas, and then eventually found myself in Arizona.

The door opened behind me, and Andrei's man rattled something off in Polish that I didn't quite catch. It apparently had something to do with me, though, based on the look Andrei gave me.

"What size are you? I need to get you something to wear to my club tonight." He pulled out a joint and lit it. When he leaned back, some of his tattooed skin peeking out from his unbuttoned shirt. Andrei was the epitome of the edgy bad boy. It pissed me off because it was utterly unfair that a man got to wake up looking that hot with zero effort.

His demand irritated me—I hated being kept in the dark. "Fuck you, Andrei. I did this little dance once and was nearly shot at the front of a cathedral." I leaned forward. "The little girl who took shit at face value with no questions asked? She died that day. Natasha? I buried that bitch."

The corner of his lips tipped up. It wasn't amusement on his face but something more akin to pride. "Looks like you did some growing up since I saw you last."

I gave a curt nod, unsure how I felt about his approval. "Tell me why the fuck you need me to come to your club instead of us hashing this out right now and coming up with a plan."

This time, it was amusement on his face. "Because we're going to need your friends to help us in the killing of Yu—"

"Absolutely not."

His smile grew wider, and my heart fluttered like a caged bird because arrogance shone in his eyes. "Well, you probably should've given them the memo, because they've already arrived in New York, and if I don't let them see that not a single hair on that pretty little head has been harmed, and soon, Scarletta Callahan will make her presence known in my little area of her city. Those boys of hers might think they are in charge, but it's pretty clear she's got them all by the dick and leads them around with those convenient little handles," he said.

My mind was busy processing what he'd revealed and was therefore unavailable for filtering the inappropriate thoughts that should stay in my mind. "I doubt they're little," I mumbled before I could stop the thought from popping out.

A bark of laughter echoed off the brick of the office walls. "Oh, Nikki. Your dad might have fucked you up, but I think you turned out pretty good."

I arched an eyebrow at that assessment. "I shake my ass for money, and my best friend runs firearms for the cartel." *And I fell for a tattooed biker who tortures men for me without question and fucks like a god.*

That time I managed to keep the thoughts to myself. "Wait —back up. What do you mean *they* arrived in New York? " I asked, my attention back where it needed to be.

He took another puff before answering. He might not treat me like shit, but he was still an asshole and would make me wait for his answer if I pushed too hard. Fucker.

"Exactly as it sounds, Tasha. Ryan Hernandez and two men landed. Oh…" he made a show of looking at the massive wristwatch. "Five minutes ago."

Fuck.

"Your ex-husband isn't the only one who doesn't want to let you go, it seems." He stood and moved toward a small cabinet with liquor bottles on the top. "Now, you're going to text Ms. Hernandez and let her know where to meet us tonight, so I don't have them attacking my operation."

He glanced over his shoulder at me before returning his attention to his ministrations. I wanted to flip him off, but I played nice for now because he was right. If Yuri was on his way to retrieve me himself, he'd start his search with Ryan.

"And you are going to tell them they are invited to my club tonight for a *business meeting*," he tacked on, handing me a crystal lowball with clear liquid.

This day hadn't gone anything like how I'd envisioned. All I'd wanted was to know if Andrei had an idea of what Yuri was doing, and where, because then I was going to head in the opposite direction. If he'd been feeling charitable, I would have asked for new documents.

Humorless laughter bubbled up, spilling over, right along with the few tears that had managed to escape. How ironic, two different sets of people I'd run from without a second glance were now coming together.

I should have felt dread, but there was nothing but relief. Andrei's hard eyes softened a touch at my complete breakdown.

"He did fuck me up, huh?" I said, referring to Andrei's earlier comment, clinking my glass to his outstretched one.

Andrei let out a grunt as he downed the vodka, wiping his mouth with the back of his hand. "I always knew you'd run," he said quietly. My brows furrowed in confusion.

"How could you possibly have known that? I didn't know I was running until I stood at the ticket counter."

"Because, Nikki, you didn't love me or the Ruska Roma. You needed a chance at freedom to figure out who you are. Why do you think I let you do it? Why do you think that no one ever came after you to demand payment? You know what the price of turning your back on the family is. I'm just sorry you placed yourself in a cell by not allowing anyone close," he said, his words cutting deep, and I had to break our eye contact.

The entire plane ride here, I'd sobbed in the bathroom, cussing out a few people when they'd tried to get me to come out. What the hell was first-class good for if I couldn't drown my sorrows in peace before I had to shove all the emotions away and fucking survive.

I'd wondered why I never let them see me.

Why I never gave *myself* a chance to know me. Like, fuck, what did I even like to do? Or my dreams? What would I have wanted to do as a career?

What was I going to tell them?

"Why would they even want to help?" I whispered into my hands, where I'd dropped my head.

"People don't get on a plane for hours to follow you if they don't care, Nikki."

RANDOM MURDER IS FROWNED UPON

"WHAT THE *FUCK* do you mean she said to meet her at a goddamn *club* tonight?" I growled out the question, clenching my fists to avoid sending them into the nearest wall. I was losing the fight to keep my anger in check. The problem was, when I spiraled, severed limbs tended to turn up.

And random murder was frowned upon.

Ryan looked up from where she sat at the giant island. We'd barely stepped off the plane and were on our way to Scarletta's place when the text came in to Ryan about meeting at some club. I ignored the twinge of pain at the fact she hadn't texted me.

"Andrei owns that place," said the big fucker leaning against one of the exposed metal I-beams in the swank apartment. Ryan had explained that Scarletta was married to the leader of The Syndicate, Caleb Callahan, but she was also fucking his best friends.

Which—good for her.

Good for them, too. Having someone to pass your girl over to when they were driving you fucking mad? The dream, because women were fucking headaches.

Like when you have the best sex of your fucking life after months of tension and falling for them, only to have them run across the country from you and send a fucking text invite to meet them at a club.

A hand clamped onto my shoulder. I grabbed it and twisted out of habit.

"Hey, dude, calm down. I was going to point out that all your inside thoughts were making their way to the outside," the guy who wore a katana said.

Kenji, I thought his name was. I'd decided I liked him the moment I saw him with the weapon strapped to his back and *fuck you* on his knuckles.

"Sorry," I muttered, releasing the hold. I'd been tense from the moment Scar's voice had filtered through the other end of the line.

"Don't worry about it. Better than cutting off my hand. That's what tends to happen to me," he said.

I stared at him for a beat, seeing if he was fucking with me. But the blank look he gave me indicated he was dead serious.

I smiled from ear to ear.

"Do you have an extra one of those for me to use tonight?" I asked, ignoring how Gunner shook his head next to me, muttering his objections.

"Dumb and dumber," shouted the third guy in the quadruple, the one with the Irish accent. He was Scar's actual husband, from my understanding—Caleb. "Let's focus. And neither of you is bringing one of those tonight. Pissing off Andrei isn't going to help us. I think that fucker is about as unhinged as you two are. Maybe even more." He mumbled the last part and the hair on the back of my neck stood on end.

That was who Nikki chose to run to? An unhinged mother fucker in New York? The realization was another blow to my heart.

Unaware of my internal heartbreak, Kenji rolled his eyes before mouthing to me that he had one for me too.

Maybe tonight wouldn't completely blow after all. I could cheer myself up with violence.

"Okay, so you're already all caught up on who Nikki Adams really is. Natasha Petrov, daughter of Aleksandr Petrov. This," Scar passed out a glossy photo of a man who appeared to be about ten years my senior, "is her ex-husband. Or current husband? Really, who knows, since the whole thing was a Bratva sham. Criminals have a weird thing about taking wives without their permission." She shot a look at Caleb, who only looked back with heated eyes.

I had a feeling that if we weren't in the room, he'd be fucking her.

Ryan took over as the two continued to eye-fuck one another. "I'd always known she was on the run from something, but I let people's shit be their shit. So, I never asked for specifics, but she did tell me about him when we were captured together." Gunner pulled her into his side, kissing the top of her head as a silent show of support. "When we were being held, she said she'd found a note, and that's what had led to Mario grabbing her. She made me swear not to mention anything. Said it was all probably nothing."

"But then another note showed up," I chimed in, revealing what Nikki had shared with me the night I'd tied her to my bed.

"What did it say?" Scar asked.

"Her birth name," Ryan said, which was news to me. Good to know Nikki had at least told Ryan that much. She'd trusted each of us with different pieces of herself, so hopefully now, we could put them together and get to the bottom of how the fuck to help her—and to get her back.

"She received the note while dancing at Lotería. It's why she went after Jardani. Yuri's been fucking with her. Of course, I didn't know any of that since she wasn't disclosing *who* was after her," I said. My mind was whirling about how this all connected. "Now it makes sense why the Reapers would risk a war. They figured they'd have a big bad Boogeyman backing them if they delivered his wife," I said with a sardonic laugh.

"Okay, great, we know all this shit. But why is she in New

York now, and with this Andrei fucker?" Gunner said, asking the million-dollar question.

Ryan's eyes flicked nervously to Scar, her information specialist. Scarletta's face was perfectly blank, a skill she'd probably honed for years.

"Andrei is high up in the Ruska Roma. They are rivals of the St. Petersburg Bratva," Niko answered for her as she passed another piece of what looked like a newspaper across the way. The article wasn't in English, but the photos told the story. "A few years ago, there was a Bratva wedding. It was a big deal. Everyone was to attend, which was how I ended up there. Yuri, the leader of the Bratva as a whole, was to be wed to his second-in-command's daughter, Natasha Petrov. Aleksandr Petrov would gain a sizable chunk of money and territory to control. As we told you when we called, shit went sideways at the wedding. The Ruska Roma has always opposed the Bratva. They are mortal enemies, essentially. Ruska Roma's men were also in attendance, hidden in the cathedral before the ceremony," Niko said as my eyes scanned the photos, my mind crafting images of Nikki there amongst the barrage of bullets.

"Did the Ruska Roma people kidnap her?" That would make sense—and then she'd somehow escaped them and hid out in the States. But then why the fuck would she run back to them?

Niko shrugged a massive shoulder. "Don't think so. She ran into me that day, and I let her go." All eyes were on him when he mentioned that bit of information. "I didn't think she spoke English since she didn't actually say anything to me, but she had this look of fear on her face and reminded me of…" his voice trailed off as he made eye contact with Caleb over Scar's head. "I knew how women get treated in criminal organizations and assumed she may not have actually wanted the marriage." He shrugged a massive shoulder. "But no one knows what happened to her. Or how they gained access. The location wasn't disclosed. Cars were sent to pick up attendees, and all of our phones, watches, essentially anything electronic, were taken from us before getting into the vehicles."

Frustration flowed through me. Did this Andrei fucker find her too? Maybe he'd threatened her, and that's why she was here.

"If I happen to impale someone at his club, what kind of trouble are we talking?" I asked.

"You're not impaling anyone," Caleb bit out. I wondered if the grumpy fucker was always like that.

"Decapitation is a bitch. Impalement is basically the same as punching someone. Harmless fun, really," Kenji said with a shrug. I studied his profile, waiting for him to break character, but he never did. He was being serious.

When Caleb reverted his attention back to whatever Scar was going on about, I held out my fist for my new friend to bump.

"Some don't understand," I whispered.

"We're all pretty fucking crazy, but Caleb likes to pretend he's got a better handle on the bloodlust. I like to wear mine on the outside." The smile Kenji flashed me was chilling.

Yup, I like this fucker.

Someone cleared their throat, and Kenji and I looked up to find an irritated Scar staring at us, her hand propped on her hip, a manicured brow arched. "If you two are done jerking each other off, pay fucking attention. We only have a few short hours to figure out as much shit as possible, so we don't show up looking dumb as fuck. We don't know the circumstances surrounding why she went to see him, only that several hours ago, Nikki landed in New York in disguise and then *chose* to go to Andrei's section of the city before texting Ryan about meeting at his club. All of us," she said, eyeing Kenji with what looked like irritation and lust.

Both Niko's and Caleb's hands were hidden from sight, and I couldn't help but wonder if they were both touching her at that moment.

"Yes, ma'am," Kenji responded, throwing her a mock

solute that made her roll her eyes, but I caught the way the corner of her mouth turned up.

I grunted as Kenji rammed an elbow into my ribs. "Ever meet a woman you wanna let step on your fucking throat while you thank her? Because that's her for me," he said, infatuation coating his words.

The psycho was definitely in love.

A ball of emotion tightened painfully, lodging itself in my throat, my teeth aching under the pressure of my clench. "Yeah. I know what that's like, but she stepped on my fuckin' heart instead," I responded, looking forward, trying to breathe through the turmoil running through my veins. "And now, I'm going to walk into a fucking club owned by the man she ran off to."

"Well, fuck," he whispered.

Well, fuck was right.

THIRTY-SEVEN

DEX

GUNNER IS NOW A RELATIONSHIP GURU,
AND WE LOVE THAT

"OF COURSE THE fucker's place looks like this," I mumbled as we pushed through the solid steel door of a building that looked like it was once a theater.

Andrei's club was a cross between a rock concert and an avant-garde runway show. The dark walls were covered in concert posters and graffiti murals, while gilded chandeliers cast dim lighting over the space. The old concessions area had been converted into a bar that was covered in stickers, with rows of colorful bottles on mirrored shelves. On the stage was a band performing as people leaped off it, crowd surfing.

"Does he have fucking pyrotechnics going off?" I asked, pissed off that I thought the place was cool.

"Europunk," Niko whispered in my ear. "That's what this style is called. Andrei loves all the post-Soviet Union anarchy aesthetics. Hence the name." He pointed out a giant neon light that had the name *Anarchy* illuminated in blue. The whole club was swathed in blue and green lights, and everyone who worked there looked more like rock stars than bartenders.

The woman leading us up the stairs to the VIP had on leather pants and a tank top that barely covered the bottom of her tits—in fact, I was pretty sure the underboob was the goal. Two sparkly 'X ' pasties peeked out every time she moved her arms, and her hair was bright green, placed up in two buns on top of her head.

I'd have thought I would stick out like a sore thumb with my white shirt and Air Force Ones. Turned out Europunk was more about the *fuck you* attitude.

If I didn't already hate the guy, I might have liked the club.

"Please, sit. Andrei will be with you shortly," the girl said before moving behind a bar that was tucked into the corner.

The VIP section was up in the private balconies. This one looked out over the concert. The rows of seating had all been removed and replaced with tables and velvet booths that looked more like beds, with pillows and fur pelts strewn across them.

Kenji plopped down on one of them, stretching his arm across the back. He looked right at home with his mesh tank top and black Dickies. Everyone had dressed to blend in, actually. Caleb stuck out the most in his suit, but he'd forgone a tie, and his tattooed hands and scowl helped. The fucker was downright dangerous- looking, so he was sticking out regardless—that and the fact that up until recently, he'd been a pretty sought-after bachelor in New York.

"Why the fuck did we think we'd blend in?" I asked, taking a spot next to Kenji, careful to keep my back to the balcony so I could watch the only entrance. "We're an intimi-dating bunch of fuckers."

"And hot," Kenji added, getting exasperated headshakes from Niko and Caleb. "Fine, fuckers. I'm hot," he corrected, leaning forward and snatching Scar's arm.

He hauled her into his lap and buried his face into the crook of her neck, causing her to let out a little squeal. She was different around him, and it was clear that each of these men fulfilled a different part of her.

"So is this fine piece of ass," he said, capturing her mouth.

I glanced over to see how the other two reacted.

It wasn't jealousy in their eyes. It was carnal hunger.

"Should we leave so y'all can fuck?" I asked, standing to grab a drink because god knew I needed one. Or five. Horniness mixed with anger and self-loathing? Yeah, vodka needed to be thrown into the mix too.

"Do you think Nikki is going to be with Andrei?" Gunner asked from where he'd followed beside me.

My jaw clenched. I had no clue, and worse, I didn't know what I'd do if she were.

"I don't know." I wiped a hand over my face. "Fuck, can I get a vodka Redbull, doll?" I asked the woman before turning to talk to Gunner. "I don't know what the fuck she's doing here, or why she asked us to come. I mean, how the fuck did she even know we were in New York? When she sent that text to Ryan, we'd *barely* landed."

"I think you do. I think you know Nikki better than she knows herself," he said. "Piece of advice, don't let her run because she's scared. Show her love is worth it."

"Is it, though?" I bit out, looking up at him. "She fucking ran. Obviously, I am not worth her time. She made it clear I was good for fucking her and calling when she needed shit. That's where the *relationship* ended."

Gunner shook his head. "I'm telling you man, it's worth it. You've already fallen for her, Dex. Fuck, we both know she *ran* because she cares. She thinks she's saving you."

A shot appeared in front of me.

"You sound like you could use this because if you're talking about the girl that showed up today with Andrei, she looks fucking hot tonight. So good luck convincing yourself to stay away," she said with a chuckle before going to prep more drinks.

"Fucking great," I mumbled before throwing back the liquid, savoring the burn as it slid down my throat, then asking for another.

"Listen, you and I both know life is fucking short. If you want to be with her, then tell her. What is that thing you always say? The thing you decided after Kell?" Gunner asked, his words causing me to stiffen.

I repeated the mantra that saved me once before. The one I believed in enough to tattoo on my body. "Let us live since we are destined to die."

Gunner slapped my shoulder. "So, fucking live, brother. Because we both know she makes you feel alive," he said before walking toward Ryan where she was sitting next to Scar and Kenji.

Fuck. He was right.

Nikki ran as soon as she thought she might be letting someone in. Did she believe that being alone was less painful than loving someone and having them leave? Hell, I'd been the mother fucker leading that choir, until I got to know Nikki.

She showed me that life was going to tick by regardless, and if I could get even a moment with her, I'd take it.

As if my thoughts summoned her, the door to the VIP balcony opened, and in walked the most beautiful woman I'd ever laid eyes on. Long, creamy legs were bare until they disappeared under a green satin dress that hit higher than mid-thigh, her arms covered up to her elbows in matching satin gloves.

Fuck me.

It looked more like she was out in a negligée than actual clothes, with the black lace corset top. Who the hell knew? Maybe that's exactly what it was. Regardless, I was a fan, and the crotch of my pants instantly felt too tight.

The room disappeared when her cornflower eyes met mine. Something like regret flashed through them before she pulled her gaze away, greeting everyone in the space. Trailing behind her was a man who looked like an honest-to-god rockstar. His hair was buzzed short and bleached so white it was practically silver. He wore an unbuttoned suit jacket, but had forgone a shirt, allowing all of his muscles and tattoos to be on display. I couldn't make out what half of them said since they appeared to be in Cyrillic, but the one on his chest read,

"Death before betrayal." Leather pants hung low on his narrow hips with a Glock tucked in the front, clearly not giving a fuck about who saw. He wasn't big like Gunner and I, shaped closer to Kenji with a tall athletic build. I'd put money on him being a fighter, though—his nose was slightly crooked and there was a scar running through his eyebrow, reminding me of the one Torque had from when it had gotten split open from a head kick.

Like his club, it pissed me off that he looked so cool. I probably would have liked the fucker under other circumstances.

He gripped Nikki by the elbow, leaning in to whisper something in her ear.

I hated the way she looked up at him. Too much of a reminder of how she'd looked at me.

A sharp pain radiated from my hand when a shard of broken glass sliced my palm, my curse coming out in a hiss. The vodka provided a cleansing burn.

"Oh, no," the bartender said, coming to the other side with a towel. She gripped my hand, turning it over to see the damaged flash. The sight of the cut made her tisk. "I should have served you in a plastic cup, it seems. Now I've got broken glass and blood all over my bar."

"Sorry," I muttered, my mind still stuck on the way Nikki and Andrei looked together.

She smiled up at me. The twinkle in her eye made it clear that she wasn't all that upset with me. "Let me grab the first aid kit."

The injury was nothing compared to what I'd experienced in the past and I almost told her not to worry about it, but then I looked over to where I felt daggers being sent my way. Nikki stared me down. The regret I'd spotted moments ago was gone, replaced by anger and a look of challenge. She pressed in close to Andrei, answering something Ryan asked all while never breaking eye contact with me.

Soft hands drew my attention away for a brief second. "I'll wrap this for you," the girl said, already at work. When I looked back at Nikki, her nostrils were flared, and I swore she was envisioning five different ways to castrate me.

Looks like you're not so "unfeeling" after all.

I ticked a brow at her.

If she wanted to play games, we could play, and she'd be my god damned prize.

THIRTY-EIGHT
NIKKI

YOU KNOW, SOMETIMES, YOU JUST NEED TO BE A BITCH

I KNEW I was being a bitch, and that this was all my fault, but that didn't mean I was capable of behaving rationally. Yes, I ran away like a total coward, but why the fuck was there a woman touching him tenderly with a stupid fucking smile on her face.

I never claimed to be a bigger person. Naturally, the only appropriate response to my jealousy was to creep closer to Andrei. He didn't seem to notice me, too busy barking out orders to his men as we all took a seat for this meeting from hell.

I bit the inside of my cheek, torn between where to sit. Maybe I'd stand in the background and hope everyone forgot I was here.

Yeah right. You're the whole fucking reason they had to come here.

Tingles ran up my spine, my nipples tightening behind the lace at the top of my dress. I didn't need to look to know who it was that now stood beside me. I bit my inner cheek as he leaned down to whisper in my ear.

"You're sitting next to me, spitfire. Right where I can keep an eye on you since you clearly can't be trusted." Regret turned in my gut at his word choice, but he didn't give me long to dwell on them as he pulled me down onto the bench.

Smack dab in the middle between him and Andrei.

I wanted to ask God what I'd done to deserve this, but there was likely a long fucking list to answer that question. Goosebumps popped up along my legs, a stark contrast to the burn of Dex's leg pressed to mine. Any closer and I'd be in his lap. I attempted to scooch over, but his hand clamped down on my bare thigh, his pinky brushing the edge of where my dress had ridden up.

The blood pumping in my ears drowned out the small talk that was going on amongst the group as everyone pretended we weren't waiting on pins and needles to hash out what the fuck was going on. The music was muted up in the balcony thanks to the thick bulletproof windows. Sound was pumped in through speakers, allowing Andrei to control the volume during his meetings.

"Well, why don't we get to the fucking point, shall we?" Dex called out, cutting through the chatter at the table, his hand still gripped onto my thigh. There was a beat of silence before Andrei barked out a laugh, leaning forward to look over at Dex. I'd never wanted to be swallowed up by an inanimate object like I did at that moment—if only the bench could've opened up and allowed me to crawl away.

"I like you," Andrei said.

Dex grunted. "Yeah, well, I don't like you."

Andrei's grin only grew wider at the retort, his blue eyes sparkling. Scarletta thankfully stepped in before the moment could escalate.

"Let's cut the bullshit and you can tell us why we're here," she demanded, not a hint of fear in her tone.

Andrei raised a brow, but otherwise didn't react to the command, asking for a drink in Russian before speaking. Bastard always did like doing things his way. "Yuri Sokolov is making his way to New York, and we need to kill him," he said bluntly.

Scarletta glanced at Caleb, having a silent conversation between them. They probably hadn't anticipated Andrei being so open. Or admitting that he wanted to murder the current Bratva leader.

Andrei leaned forward, drumming on the top of the table. "Listen, I don't really want to waste time with bullshit smoke and mirrors. Here's how it is. I've been trying to kill the bastard for a long time. I tried once before, but it was unfortunately *unsuccessful.*" I felt his eyes on me, but I didn't return the glance, too distracted by the way Dex's hand was creeping farther and farther toward the center of my thighs, drawing torturous circles along my skin.

"Yeah, let's start there, actually," Dex said. "How the hell did the Ruska Roma infiltrate a wedding that didn't even disclose the location? " His attention shifted to me. "And how did you wind up missing? Did they kidnap you?" he asked, his eyes searching.

Andrei let out a low whistle. "Damn, Tasha, you really didn't tell anyone a damn thing about you." He pulled the joint tucked behind his ears and lit it, gesturing to me with his hand. "Well, I think it's time for you to have a come to Jesus moment, not that I believe in the fucker, but the saying works well, no?"

My lids fluttered closed as I took a centering breath. There was no more running. No more secrets.

"No one kidnapped me that day," I said, opening my eyes back up and staring up at Dex, pleading with him to understand. I'd have to go back to the beginning.

"I never had a mother, not in the maternal sense. My father hired a surrogate to birth him a child. While most might have wanted a son, my father was a selfish bastard, and he wanted the power for himself. Not an heir. His goal was to have a bargaining chip—" I'd never said any of this aloud before, and the admission was like a knife to the heart all over again. Dex's hand stilled before he gave a comforting squeeze.

"A girl," he said, finishing the sentence for me.

I nodded before continuing on. "I was raised with the sole intention of being gifted to whichever Bratva leader was in charge when the time came. As I got older, I was naive enough to think that if I could make him proud enough of *me*, he would decide I was worthy enough to keep around. That his pride in me would mean more than more power." Angry tears welled up in my lash line, threatening to fall.

Dex cursed under his breath, clearly sensing where the story was going and pulling me under the crook of his arm. It was like coming home—warm, comforting. Something that felt like his lips brushed the top of my head.

Niko piped up from across the table. "You leaked the location of the wedding."

"That she did. Showed up on the doorsteps of the Ruska Roma when she was told she would be married off to Yuri, who has a reputation for *breaking* the women he's with. In exchange for help getting out of the country, she promised to join our efforts and get us into the wedding cathedral," Andrei said, sounding impressed.

"What happened?" Ryan asked. I looked over, expecting to see anger in her coffee-colored eyes, but it was the opposite of what greeted me. "I'm so sorry I never asked about you or your past, Niks. I figured you'd tell me if you wanted me to know, but I would have helped you murder this fucker a long time ago if I'd known."

A tearful laugh bubbled up. Of course that was how she would look at this.

"Scarletta probably would have helped too. She's always in for a good murder," Andrei said, glancing over at her.

There was a silent exchange before Scar let out a resigned sigh, clapping her hands together and looking around the table. The permanent scowl on Caleb's face grew deeper while Niko's expression remained blank. Kenji was the polar opposite of his chosen brothers, smiling from ear to ear.

"Since this is the one and only time we will have some fucked up, what did you call it, Andrei? A 'come to Jesus moment?' I happen—"

"Are you an assassin?" Ryan called out, her eyes going wide. "Because I knew there was no way you just did tech shit. You're far too calculating." She was practically giddy as she waited for an answer.

"This fine ass woman isn't *just* an assassin. She's fucking Cain," Kenji said, pride shinning in his face. Hell, all three boys were looking at Scar like she hung the damn moon.

The name meant nothing to me, but Ryan's and Gunner's eyes grew to the size of dinner plates.

"I fucking *knew* you were into more than whatever your uncle had you doing," Ryan said, but her response was drowned out by Gunner's booming voice.

"Cain, as in one of the world's most infamous assassins, Cain?" Gunner asked, his arms spread out across the table as he looked at her in disbelief. "Do you know how many three-letter agencies are looking for you?"

She smirked. "Of course I do. I'm backdoored into all of them." She cut Kenji a glare when he snickered. "Kenji, not the time to be thinking about my ass," she said, flipping him off.

"Whatever you say, my backdoor princess," he responded, making her cheeks grow red.

If I weren't scared of the woman, I would have laughed. I wasn't sure how Kenji wasn't scared of her.

Scar's mask of indifference slipped back into place, and she eyed Andrei. "How did you already know that? These three didn't even know before I told them," she said, pointing to the three men she was in a relationship with. There was a deadly edge to her tone.

Everyone's attention shifted toward him.

The hint of black that rimmed his eyes only made him look deadlier, the blue somehow icier. Cruel.

"Scarletta, if anyone should know what it's like to *allow* people to underestimate them, it's you. You're not the only one to amass power under people's noses. Now, back to the current problem at hand. We have a Bratva leader on his way here, and we need to band together to kill him."

"What do you get out of it?" Dex asked, his arm tightening around me when Andrei looked our way. He'd been relatively quiet during the entire exchange, but his hold on me was unrelenting, and I took that as a good sign. He wasn't done with me. At least not yet.

Andrei's eyes slid over us, lingering on where Dex was holding me.

"You're the one she was running from," he stated without preamble.

"The fuck does that mean," Dex spat.

"Andrei," I admonished, but he ignored me, continuing on.

"Natasha here tends to run instead of facing her feelings. When she showed up on my doorstep, I knew she was running from someone she'd managed to make a connection with and was avoiding. I assumed it was the arms dealer-turned- best friend." He took a drag of his joint. "But she ran because she is in love with you," he stated, pointing at Dex.

Dex's gaze burned into the side of my face, but I refused to turn and look at him. The noise in the room was eclipsed by the blood pounding in my ears. Thankfully, Andrei continued on, the conversation turning serious enough that we couldn't linger on the fact that my profession of love for Dex came via an asshole mafia man.

"Anyway, it doesn't matter what I am getting from this, because the rest of you don't really have a choice. It's either kill Yuri, or he kills you. What do you say?" he asked, his arms spread wide before glancing at the watch on his wrist. "I'd decide quickly because we probably have, I don't know, forty-eight hours before he lands."

Caleb let out a curse under his breath.

Shame swirled in my gut. "You guys should go home now," I said, drawing their attention. "You're in this mess because of me and my failed attempt at killing Yuri," I said, staring at my hands.

Warm fingers lifted my chin. "This isn't your fault," Dex said, but Andrei cut him off.

"It kind of is, actually. She was supposed to stab the

bastard that day," he said as I turned to glare at him. "What? You were."

Dex stood, shoving his finger into Andrei's chest. "Shut your fucking mouth, first of all. And second, you were going to make *her* kill the fucker?"

Andrei leaned back, spreading his arms across the booth, completely unfazed. "Surely you know your little bunny is actually a wolf." His blue eyes cut to me, holding my stare as he spilled the final secret. "The day wasn't a complete failure, she man—"

"I killed my father. Stabbed him in the stomach and twisted the blade," I cut in, needing to be the one to tell this truth myself.

Andrei smirked. Asshole. He'd wanted that to happen, forced my hand so I would have to reveal the final piece of the puzzle until I sat there stripped bare for all to see—to determine if they wanted to stick by me. He was like a fucked- up Cupid.

I was so busy staring him down that I didn't notice Dex until it was too late. I yelped when I was suddenly lifted into the air and thrown over his shoulder, his arm clamped over the back of my thighs, a hand holding down my dress so my ass wasn't on display.

"You fuckers figure out a plan, and then let us know what we've got to do," he called over his shoulder, heading toward the door that led back out into the main portion of the club.

"Have fun fucking," Andrei yelled out. I couldn't see his face, but I knew he had a smug look on it.

THIRTY-NINE

DEX

IF YOU'RE HORNY, THIS IS THE CHAPTER
FOR YOU. IF YOU'RE NOT, YOU WILL BE...

WE BARELY MADE it out of the room before I slammed her against the wall, her breath whooshing out of her as I let her body slide down until her feet were on the floor. Fuck, she was beautiful. My dick twitched—it'd been painfully hard since she walked into the room, settling briefly as her past was unraveled.

But when she revealed that she was the one to deliver the killing blow to her asshole of a father, fuck, I was rock hard once more. She sucked in a breath as I lowered my mouth to her ear, sucking on the tender flesh for a moment.

"If you hadn't killed that fucker, I would have hunted him down and dismembered him limb by limb for you," I said, running my nose along her neck, nipping at her flesh. I wanted to mark every part of her body.

Of her soul.

I didn't know if she'd find my words romantic or not, but they were the truth.

She turned her face into mine, our lips brushing as she spoke. "Is it wrong that now I'm turned on?" she asked.

Her response made me growl, pressing myself further against her and running my hands up her bare thighs until they hooked onto her underwear.

"What are you doing, Dex?" she asked, her voice husky

and excited. I leaned forward, unable to stop myself, and captured her mouth, the world melting away as her tongue intertwined with mine. Kissing Nikki was like breathing again.

The fresh air after a rainstorm.

She fisted my shirt, pulling me closer. My heart beat so fast, it felt like I'd leapt off a cliff. Loving her was an adrenaline hit. She filled the void inside my chest, illuminating the dark cave with her sunshine. The ache I'd grown used to ceased to exist when she was around.

Uncertainty crept in. I felt this way about her, but I still didn't know where she stood on the matter. She'd run from me more than once. Maybe I just needed to get the fucking hint and let her go.

I growled at the idea.

"Panties off, Nikki."

"What? No. Why the hell do you need those?" she asked, pulling her face away.

My hand snaked up, grasping her throat. "Because if you run off again, I want something to wrap around my cock as I beat off to the memories of fucking your tight cunt," I said, punctuating my words by yanking down her underwear.

Her inhale was more of a moan, and I drove my fingers into her now uncovered pussy.

"You're fucking soaked, spitfire." I pulled my fingers out, bringing them to my lips and licking them clean. "This for me? Your cunt dripping for me, baby?" I asked.

Her head nodded against my hand, her heart rate beating at a delicious pace under my palm.

I kissed her hard, shoving my tongue inside her warm mouth, letting her taste herself before filling her with my fingers again, pumping them faster and faster.

"Dex," she moaned. "We're in a fucking hall."

"And? If you want to run from me, then I'm going to fuck you in public so everyone knows you're mine. Stake my claim so no one dares try." I moved my mouth up to her ear so I could whisper the next part. "I'm going to paint you with my cum and make you walk through this fucking club as my little masterpiece. You understand? My cum is going to drip from your greedy cunt for the rest of the night."

She shivered against me, her pussy gripping my fingers. "Mmm. Seems your pussy is a fan of that idea, baby."

I dropped to my knees, pushing her legs apart, ignoring her protests about being in public as I lifted her legs, one at a time, pulling her thong the rest of the way off and pocketing it before diving under her dress and lapping up her pussy. The protests morphed into cries of pleasure as I sucked on her clit, adding a third finger. She fisted my hair, pulling on the strands harder and harder the closer she drew to release.

I wanted to watch her fall apart, but my head was full-on *under* her dress. I'd fuck her in public, but I didn't want anyone to be able to see what was mine. The thought had me moaning into her pussy.

Mine. That was exactly what she was. I began jerking off, needing to relieve some of the pressure before I came. Fuck, I wasn't even inside of her.

"God, I love watching you fist your cock while you eat me out," she panted, her words barely audible above the music. I pumped harder, humming in pleasure against her pussy at the praise. She was so fucking close—I could sense it. The desire to push her over the edge was so strong. I removed my fingers, replacing them with my tongue as they snaked back to her ass, my pointer finger pushing in up to the knuckle. She cried out my name as she came, her inner walls spasming around my tongue in a way that made my cock jealous.

I stood when she was spent, flipping her around and securing her wrists at the base of her spine, leaning in to whisper in her ear.

"I'm going to fuck you now, spitfire," I said, pulling my jeans down just enough to put it in her but not have my ass fully on display.

That was the only warning she received before I drove my cock inside her. I'd never wanted a woman the way I wanted Nikki, and I didn't want her for a single fuck.

"Middle name," I demanded between thrusts.

"What?" she asked, the word coming out in a rush of air.

"I need your middle name," I said, swirling her clit with my finger. "Now." I smacked the globe of her ass when she took too long to answer, caught up in the lust of the moment.

"Anya."

I pulled out, flipping her around and holding her leg up near my side so I could look into her eyes as I sank back in. "Natasha Anya Petrov, I want you for as long as I continue to breathe," I said, punctuating with a thrust as I cupped her face. "I don't give a shit if this is the least romantic way to tell you I love you. I can't wait any longer. Being without you isn't an option, and I am tired of letting you run from me," I said against her lips, kissing her. "I will hunt you down wherever you go, woman." She stilled in my arms, but I couldn't stop, needing her to hear all that was on my heart. "Life isn't worth living without you in it, spitfire. Fuck your past. All I need is your present and our future."

My words came out as a plea. I'd done the one thing I'd never thought I'd do again: pull my heart out of where I'd hidden it away, and risk it being broken.

But she was worth it.

I'd endure the pain every fucking time, if only for another moment with her.

She cupped my face, her eyes searching mine. A single tear escaped, rolling down her beautiful face, and I leaned forward, lapping it up with my tongue. "Let me in, spitfire. Let me love you," I whispered.

"I'm scared."

I held her, chuckling at the fact that I was nuzzling her neck with my cock buried inside her. Robert was right when he told me I didn't know what the fuck I was doing when it came to romancing a woman.

"Nikki, I don't know shit about being romantic or being a Prince Charming. But I will stick by your side and help slay all your demons. I'll cheer you on and hold you when you crumble." I captured another escaped tear. "I'll let you fucking fly and be at the bottom to catch you if you happen to fall."

She let out a hiccup, tears freely flowing now. My heart seized because I didn't know what they meant. My heart pounding with anticipation, I leaned in. Her salty lips met mine, and in that moment, time stood still. The kiss was a tender dance, a passionate expression of my feelings. I wanted her to feel all my promises in her soul.

"Forever and always, spitfire," I said against her mouth. "Even if you don't want me, I will be there for you."

A sob fell from her lips, causing my heart to clench. To break.

This wasn't what she wanted. She wasn't ready, and I didn't know if she'd ever be, but I would wait until that day came or until the reaper collected my soul.

I cupped her face once more, kissing the tip of her nose. "Just a warning, though, every man who comes near you will end up in a grave," I said, pulling out of her.

HE WAS LIKE A BATTERING RAM, determined to break down all my walls until I stood there unprotected and raw. The heat of his body started to disappear as he pulled away, removing the feeling of being complete.

"Where are you going?" I asked, gripping his shoulders and stopping him from pulling all the way out.

Confusion flashed in his eyes. "What do you mean? You're not ready, and that's okay, Nikki. You never promised me anything." He pressed a sweet kiss to my lips, keeping it brief.

I snaked my hands into his hair, biting at his lower lip and then shoving my tongue inside his mouth. He growled, melding his mouth to mine before ripping his face away and meeting my gaze with an angry glare.

"Cold turkey, Niks. I have to stop you cold turkey. I'm too in love to play this game—" His voice cracked as he looked away, his arms hanging loose by his side.

I hit his chest, drawing his attention back to me. "You are the biggest idiot, Dex. Stop talking for two fucking seconds so I can tell you I am in love with you," I said, raising my voice so he could hear me over whatever else he was saying.

He stopped mid-sentence, his lips parting as he blinked at me.

I curled my finger under his chin.

"Dex, I'm an Aquarius with daddy issues, so this profession of love isn't going to be sweet or poetic. I don't know how the hell to do any of that. But I've never been so scared or so sure I wanted to give my heart to someone. The heartbreak would kill me, but the life I lived while you loved me would be worth it. So, this scarred thing is yours, if you're sure you want it," I whispered.

The words were barely out and his lips were on mine, pressed so firmly it was like he was trying to crawl inside. Laughter bubbled up and I couldn't stop it from spilling over. Dex pulled back, looking at me like I'd lost my damn mind, which made me laugh even harder.

"We just," another round of laughter, and I struggled to get it under control enough to speak.

"Woman, what the fuck?"

"We just had this whole rollercoaster of emotions. Which we are already shit at, and we did it in a fucking hallway with your dick inside me," I said, struggling to get all the words out without falling back into a fit.

Dex looked down between us, where he was still firmly seated inside me, and I felt his cock twitch, hardening once more. Not that he'd ever gone soft, but it was a whole other level now.

"I don't know." He pushed forward, grinding his pelvis against my clit. "I think this works for us."

He wasn't wrong.

We worked because we were both fucked up, and we embraced that, never trying to fix it. All we wanted was to fulfill one another, to seep into the cracks and make each other whole.

"Fuck me, Dex. Mark me as yours."

His hand wrapped around my throat, and he thrust so hard that I thought he might send us through the wall behind us. His fingers squeezed slightly on the sides of my throat, giving me a euphoric rush. His hand dropped, lifting me up from behind my thighs and forcing me to wrap my legs around his waist as he drove into me.

"Your cock is my favorite thing," I said as I bit at his ear.

Dex moaned, kissing and sucking at my neck hard enough that I knew there would be marks. I was so full, his size making me feel complete again. His mouth found mine, swallowing my moans and whimpers as he pistoned his hips harder and faster.

He moved at a dizzying pace.

My pussy throbbed, and he slammed into me deeper than I thought possible. I dug my fingers into his back. He'd probably have permanent nail marks.

"Fuck, you're so fucking tight. I'm fucking you every day for the rest of my life, Nikki. Hell, I'm tying you to our bed so you can never leave," he growled.

I writhed against him as his fingers gripped my ass—pain and pleasure.

"So. Close," I bit out, my head swimming in sensation.

His finger found my clit and I fell apart, calling out his name loud enough I was sure the whole club knew what we were doing.

"Fucking beautiful," he said against my lips when I'd come down again, before dropping his hold on me and pushing me to my knees. My mind was still reeling from my orgasm, and I couldn't keep up with what was happening. Dex pumped his slick cock, threading his hand in my hair and yanking my head back before shoving his cock into my waiting mouth, hitting the back of my throat.

"Just like that baby. Show me how well you take my cock in your mouth."

I hummed around him, loving the way he used me. His head tipped back, the hold on my hair loosening as he got lost in the lust. I cupped his balls, rolling them in my hand, smiling as he let out a string of curse words.

Without warning, he pulled out, coming on the front of my chest. His hot release dripped between my cleavage. I knew he'd said he was going to mark me with his cum and let me walk out of here dripping— this wasn't what I'd pictured, yet somehow I found it hotter.

What the fuck is wrong with me...

Dex reached a hand down, rubbing his release into my chest and over the front of my dress.

"You said Andrei got you this dress?" he asked, a growl still in his tone. "Well, fuck him. It's my cum on it." He pulled me up to my feet, slamming his lips against mine, not carrying that he was getting cum on the front of his shirt, too. "Now, I'm going to get you to a hotel and fill you with my cum, too. Send him a picture of it leaking down your leg."

The promise had me shivering, ready for him to take me again.

Before I could respond, a slow clap came from off to the side. "No need, I got the message," Andrei said, leaning against the wall from about ten feet away, a cocky smirk on his face. Dex shifted to cover me with his body and tucked himself back in. "Also, no need to worry. There was never anything between us. Natasha is all yours. Wonderful girl, that one, but I tend to have a thing for women who are a little more...bloodthirsty," Andrei went on, his face taking a far-off look, as if he might be thinking about someone specific.

"How long have you been standing there?" Dex asked in a deadly calm tone.

Andrei only smiled as if the threat of violence excited him. Now I could see what he meant by his preferences. He probably wanted a woman who held a knife to his throat while she rode him.

"Not long. Don't worry." Andrei smirked. "Your friends are wrapping up. So, unless you want to show them the additions you two made to your dress, I suggest you get out of here."

Dex pushed me down the hall, blocking Andrei's view of me as he led us away, his hand burning on my hip. A shiver racked through me as the air hit the mess on my chest, but the reaction wasn't because I was cold.

"You like walking around coated in my cum, spitfire?" he whispered, licking the shell of my ear.

I opened my mouth to answer, but Andrei's cocky voice cut through the noise. "Oh, and I hope that you still know how to perform with clothes *on*, Tasha, because I don't think Katya will allow you on her stage in a thong." His words stopped me in my tracks, and not even Dex could stop me from storming back.

I ducked under his massive arm, moving out of reach as I stomped up to Andrei, stopping directly in front of him. His eyes looked over me lazily, lingering for a second on my chest, his lips curling into a smirk.

"Don't you look at her," Dex said threateningly.

Andrei lifted his arms up in mock surrender. "As you wish, but I might have to use that move sometime," he said, laughing when Dex lunged at him and then pulled back.

"What are you talking about, Andrei?" I asked, my stomach turning.

His light eyes that held so much darkness shifted to me, his smirk still firmly in place even as Dex loomed over my shoulder, hand on his Glock.

"You're going to be bait, Tasha."

Dex whipped out the gun, pressing it against Andrei's forehead. "The fuck she is. Find a fucking way that doesn't involve her," Dex demanded, finger barely hovering above the trigger.

Lightning fast, Andrei's hand whipped out from where he had it tucked in his pocket, gripping the barrel and pressing it harder into his forehead.

"Go ahead, shoot me, send her and your friends into an early grave with your stupidity," he spat.

Now I saw it, what made Andrei so dangerous—eagerness shone in his eyes. He wanted the fight, wanted the violence.

Anarchy.

Dex hesitated, his finger moving farther away from the trigger.

"That's what I thought," Andrei said, pushing the Glock

away and staring Dex down. "She is the only thing that fucker wants, the only bait enticing enough for him to come out of the hole he's burrowed into. If you don't think you can protect her without hiding her away, then you never deserved to have her to begin with."

I swallowed hard. The two men were locked into a battle of wills, but after a few tense moments, Dex gave a single nod.

"You're a fucking dick, and it pisses me off that I think you're cool," Dex grumbled out, holding his hand out for the other man to shake.

Andrei eyed the outstretched hand, grinning. "You're good for her, and I am happy she finally pulled her head out of her pussy to admit she was in love, but I'm not shaking your cum-covered hand, Dex." He turned on his heel and walked away, throwing one last instruction over his shoulder. "Get into the black town car out front. My driver will take you to a spare apartment I have, so you don't have to fuck again in the hallways of my club."

<h1 style="text-align:center">FORTY-ONE
NIKKI</h1>

DEATH BEFORE BETRAYAL

THE DELICIOUS ACHE between my thighs and in the back of my throat wasn't enough to eclipse the nerves coursing through me as I moved up the steps of the converted cathedral.

The irony wasn't lost on me that I'd come full circle and was back in a church, standing in front of the crucifixion with full intentions of being an accomplice to murder.

I'd like to think that even god hated Yuri and would be okay with it.

I'd awoken to a message from Andrei asking me to meet him here this morning. He wanted to go over the plan with me. I would've taken Dex with me, but I'd rolled over to find the bed empty, his side of the sheets already cold to the touch.

Dex had text me too, it read that he had something to take care of with the others.

A tinge of disappointment shot through me when I woke up alone, but it was quickly snuffed out by the reality that I had up and left him without a single word as to where I was going. So I could suck it up and be a big girl if he was going to go off and do shit. This was essentially a taste of my own medicine, and I needed to own it.

My heart hummed with happiness. He loved me, and damn, did I love him. There was no way I was going to give up my life a second time because of Yuri—whatever it took, he was going down.

I was done living in the shadows of my past.

Footfalls echoed off the stone, reminding me that I was not in the safety of the apartment. Candlelight flickered, the only source of light other than the sun streaming through the stained-glass windows that adorned the top portion of the walls. Noise filtered through two giant arched wooden doors in front of me, but I couldn't make out what was being said, or who was in there.

Andrei's text had been vague.

Unease crept into my bones, but I moved forward, pushing open the doors and stepping into the sanctuary. It was beautiful, bathed in amber lighting from giant candelabra chandeliers. Where the pulpit would have been was a giant stage where I could see a row of ballet dancers all performing an arabesque.

"Again," snapped a familiar voice that sent a flurry of emotions running wild through my body.

"Are you going to continue to stand back there, girl?" Katya asked, not bothering to look behind her.

I hadn't even realized I'd stopped walking. My back went rigid, my shoulders pressing back, chin steady. Even after all these years, her bark had my body responding. I wanted to laugh at the automatic response, but that would probably earn me a hit to the back of the head.

Katya didn't care for words, she wanted action, so I didn't bother responding. I just made my way toward where she sat in the front pew.

I didn't think I could ever quite classify Katya as a *mother* figure, but she'd made an impact on my life. She'd been the one who'd encouraged me to seek out the Ruska Roma. At the time, I hadn't even realized she worked for them, a plant embedded into the Bratva for years. An ear close to the enemy.

She'd risked everything to help me.

I paused at the edge of the pew, waiting for her instruction. It was so familiar that I smiled despite my nerves. Her silver hair was tied back in a severe bun at the nape of her neck. Blue eyes cut over to me for a brief moment before focusing on what was happening in front of us.

"Not one of you had acceptable back legs. Again," she yelled, folding her hands into her lap. "Why did you come back, Natasha? You were free." She turned her head, finally looking at me.

My heart seized in my chest, and I had the strangest urge to hug the rigid older woman.

There was a slight shake in my voice when I answered. "We both know that's not true, Katya. I will never be free, so long as Yuri is alive."

She searched over me with her eyes, for what exactly I wasn't sure, but when she was satisfied, she gave a single nod toward the space beside her and faced forward once more. I slid in next to her, mimicking her posture.

"You think you will be able to do it this time, girl?" she asked, no judgment in her tone.

When Andrei first suggested I try and kill the Bratva leader again, I thought it was stupid. Then I realized there was no freedom for me unless Yuri was gone. And I refused to sink back into hiding, merely existing rather than living.

Rather than loving.

"I should have done it the first time, Katya. There's no way I will let him live a second time."

"You might never have gotten the Roma branding, but you are a part of us. You have our protection. You know that, right?" she asked, turning toward me. The look in her eyes caused my skin to erupt in bumps. "No one faulted you for not killing Yuri that day. It was ridiculous that they even asked that of a young, barely trained girl who was facing the worst betrayal a woman could experience. To be given away by the one who was supposed to protect you." She let out a sound of disgust, her poised demeanor slipping. "The fact that you killed your father is a feat that we were all proud of you for."

"But I ran."

She held my stare. "That you did, Natasha. Perhaps the bravest of all your actions."

Andrei walked up at that moment, and she seemed to stiffen, tipping her head in greeting. His hands were tucked into leather pants that sat low on his hips. The white dress shirt he wore was only buttoned to right above his navel, sleeves rolled up on his forearms, leaving his tattoos on display.

"Wanna tell me why I'm here, Andrei?" I asked before tacking on, "Actually, I don't really give a damn if you want to or not. Tell me what's going on."

He smirked. "You're going to eat him alive. She ready?" he asked, ignoring my demand.

Katya shifted her gaze from the dancers over to Andrei, lingering on me for a second. "Not yet."

"Well, no time like the present, no?" He looked at me. "Hope you remember how to do something other than strip, Natasha, because you're going to be the lead in a performance," Andrei said, tilting his head to the side and looking down the length of my body. There was nothing sexual about his gaze, only calculating, and it made me uneasy.

"What is that supposed to mean?" I asked, analyzing their body language. Andrei looked relaxed, a cocky grin on his full lips, but Katya was tense.

"It means you need to go and change," he said.

I crossed my arms over my chest, "Now, Andrei, maybe you've taken one too many hits to the head or perhaps your English comprehension is lacking, but I want to know what's happening."

Katya piped up from beside me. "Peter and the Wolf, Natasha." She gripped my hands between her gnarled ones. "You remember the story, no?"

I nod my head. Something in her tone made me feel as if she was trying to tell me more than what the actual words meant.

"I remember. The boy traps the wolf that threatened his

friends and then parades him to the zoo, despite the hunters wanting to kill the wolf. A tale on the lesson of bravery… and mercy. All of us children were taught Prokofiev's tale."

She nodded, seemingly pleased with my answer, but I wasn't sure what recalling a Russian folktale had to do with anything. She turned back toward the stage, passing a duffle bag over before whispering to me.

"Change the ending, Nikki. Kill the wolf."

I'd forgotten how uncomfortable a leotard was, the way the elastic cut into the crease of your leg, threatening to slip out of place and expose half my labia. That was probably the reason we wore tights and sprayed hairspray on our ass cheeks in an attempt at keeping the piece of fabric in place. Twirling my fingers in my hand, I studied the movement outside the window.

"You going to share with the class how this works, Andrei? And not some cloak and dagger answer, either."

"You're going to go dance in a performance that Yuri is attending." He tapped his fingers on his crossed thigh, his body language giving nothing away. "I'm taking you to the practice so we can check out the venue and look for vantage points. Your friends will meet us there."

His answer matched the texts I'd gotten from both Ryan and Dex, saying that they would meet us at the rendezvous point. They were gathering whatever the fuck we needed for this plan, but something still ate at me. Probably the nerves of them being so close to Yuri.

"And the rest of the plan? You've yet to share that with me," I pushed, my bullshit meter going off.

Andrei's eyes slid to me from where they'd been staring out the window. I was once again stuck with how magnetic he was—it was no wonder I'd latched on to him like a love-drunk fool. But it was clear this man had his heart firmly locked away in a deep, deep pit.

"Well, someone decided to go into the hallway and have their tits painted instead of paying attention to the plan," he threw back, the memory making my cheeks heat, and I had to fight the urge to look away while he continued to speak. "I already told you, *zaika*, you're to be the bait. You are Yuri's greatest temptation, after all." He leaned forward, folding his hands together. "I'm not sure if he wants you so badly so he can kill you or fuck you. Either way, he'll take the bait," he said coolly.

The car suddenly felt claustrophobic, as if all the air was being stolen from my lungs, but still I managed to hide my fear with a quip. "I'd say I made the right choice. Getting fucked is far more enjoyable than listening to how I am going to be dangled like a piece of meat again," I said, my eyes narrowing.

Andrei smiled. It almost looked genuine, but I didn't think he knew how to do that.

"Oh, how your father must be rolling in his grave knowing that the blushing bride he promised Yuri was so properly deflowered."

What did it say about me that I was proud of the shame my father would feel if he knew how I liked to fuck?

That thought was quickly eclipsed by the reality of seeing Yuri again. Maybe it was delusional, but I hadn't considered what I would do if we crossed paths after the wedding. I'd always assumed I'd be able to outrun him, or that he would forget about me.

Yet here I was, *willingly* placing myself in his sights.

"Yuri is attending a gala with some influential men in town, which is where you'll be performing on stage for him." I stiffened at his words. "He'll see you up there, become obsessed, and go running after you. Then, *bam*, we get him," Andrei said, smiling, but the expression was anything but comforting.

That was the plan?

"Seems a bit like a shit plan."

"Oh?" he arched an eyebrow. "Are you now a criminal mastermind?" he asked, the sarcasm so thick you could wade through it. "You know what some of your friends and I have in common, Tasha?"

"Please enlighten me, because I can't think of a single thing they have in common with a cocky ass like you."

He laughed. "Please, they are all cocky assholes, they just like you, so you aren't on the receiving end."

I shrugged before breaking into a grin because he was right. "You may have a point there."

He cocked a brow in an *"I told you so"* manner before continuing. "It's that we are willing to do the *unsavory* for the greater good of the goal. We have the balls to get shit done when others are unwilling." He paused, his eyes searching over me once more. "Even if it means making more of a mess before ultimately cleaning it up."

"Is this some type of life lesson I am supposed to be learning?" I asked, folding my hands in my lap.

He let out a chuff. "Something like that, *zaika*. Something like that."

"Well, there's something you're forgetting, Andrei. The girl you once knew died at that wedding. The one who blindly followed orders and couldn't sense when someone was using her."

A shutter slid over his features at my callout. Where most made men carried a scowl, but Andrei's face transformed into a cocky smirk, arrogance wafting off him. The problem was that the asshole could back it up. He was scary because he genuinely didn't appear scared or intimidated by anything, and I wasn't sure how much was an act versus truth.

My door opened, a hand extending to help me out of the car and onto the sidewalk of wherever it was that we were. I eyed the building towering above us, the small pinpricks of nerves transforming into a full maelstrom of electric shocks. On instinct, I sent my location to Dex.

I jumped at the warm hand that landed on my lower back,

pushing me forward. Andrei leaned in to whisper in my ear. "Natasha, you are so much more than your father made you believe." I turned my head to meet his gaze, but he'd pulled away and continued to look forward as he spoke.

"Death before betrayal, *zaika*. Remember that." This time, his eyes connected to mine, and they were shockingly unguarded. "I will always choose death before betrayal. You understand?"

It was almost as if he were pleading with me, but before I could answer, the doorman was in front of us. I schooled my face, hiding my confusion at his words.

I kept my chin tucked as Andrei led us through the lobby of some swanky building. Each step sent adrenaline spiking through my body.

Death before betrayal of me? Or of the Ruska Roma?

There was next to no one around, and the hair on the back of my neck stood on end. Where the fuck was a performance supposed to happen in this place?

One of Andrei's men opened a nondescript door, and he pressed me forward with a hand dug into my shoulder. My legs threatened to collapse under me the moment I passed the threshold, even though I'd had an inkling this would happen.

My pride may have wanted to stare him down, unwavering, but my knees buckled like a newborn fawn. Andrei gripped my other side, the forceful support of the two men the only reason I remained standing.

"Well, if it isn't my bitch of a wife in the flesh," Yuri sneered, leaning back in a leather club chair. He'd barely aged in the years I'd been away. A few more frown lines and a peppering of gray around his hairline were the only real signs. Bastard was still handsome, and I still wanted to shove a knife in his back.

Blood pounded in my ears, the edges of my vision turning black, and I forced my lungs to keep working. But it felt as if there was a blockage clogging my throat, preventing the oxygen from entering.

"You know, Andrei, when you called and said that you

had my wife, I thought it was a bluff," Yuri said, blatantly leering at my body. "Figured if you didn't show up with her, I'd just kill you."

"I'm sure you would have loved that, Yuri," Andrei drawled. "Yet here she is, and we both know you'll be letting me walk out of here." He tilted his head, his mouth pulling up into a smile that could induce frostbite it was so chilling. Yuri's smile slipped, his eyes darkening under Andrei's attention.

Whatever he had on Yuri, it was keeping the asshole in line. Bastard didn't even say anything when Andrei winked at him. No one moved, the two factions staying on their sides of the invisible line.

How many times have these two talked in the past?

For a brief second I wondered if Andrei had sabotaged the attack at my wedding, but there was no chance of that. Everything had gone to plan *except* my portion. If only I could shoot everyone in the room with the Glock tucked into Andrei's trousers.

But my body was frozen in place.

"Did you bring what we agreed upon?" Andrei asked, an edge to his tone.

My brain finally kicked back online, and I began to thrash. "Get the fuck off of me," I yelled, kicking and punching, but Andrei just pulled me into his side, clamping down on my arms so I was unable to move.

Yuri smiled at my struggle. "You will be so fun when I break you. A shame you are no longer pure, but no matter, a cunt is a cunt regardless."

I swallowed down bile at his words.

"My men are excited to get to you," Yuri taunted.

Like a rabbit caught in a snare, my fear was replaced with anger, building like a pressure cooker low in my gut.

"This is fun and all, but where's my payment?" Andrei asked again, drawing Yuri's attention.

The Bratva leader rolled his eyes, tossing a USB drive onto the floor between us. "There, your *payment*," Yuri scoffed.

Andrei motioned with his head, and one of his men picked up the small drive before pulling out a laptop and plugging the device in, then giving a curt nod. I felt Andrei's body relax, but only slightly. He still held himself rigid, though to everyone else he looked relaxed.

"And the ten million," Andrei drawled.

Ten million. Fuck, that's what I was worth.

I almost understood why he'd turned me in.

Yuri's voice took on an irritated tone. "Yes. That has been sent as well," he bit out, standing and walking toward me.

As pissed off and hurt as I was by Andrei, I still burrowed into his side, my whole body shaking as Yuri approached. Andrei's hand slipped down, tapping on my hip. Warm air brushed past my ear, and he spoke so low I almost thought I'd imagined it.

"Kill the wolf."

The words were eclipsed by fear as Yuri gripped my chin, yanking it up. He turned my face from side to side, inspecting me as if I were some prime specimen—it was a pretty accurate description of what he thought of me.

"Welcome home, *wife.*"

SAME TIME ACROSS TOWN

"WHAT THE FUCK was so important that I needed to get out of a bed that held a naked woman ready to be fucked?" I yelled, storming into the apartment that Gunner and Ryan were staying in. A squeal sounded from somewhere to the left, and Gunner's voice boomed.

"Dex, what the fuck are you doing in here? I swear to god, if you saw *any* part of Ryan's body, I will carve your eyeballs out."

I smiled, my lids already squeezed firmly shut. I'd had a feeling he would react that way, just like I had a feeling they would be doing some freaky shit.

"No need, brother, walked in with them sealed tight. Can I fucking open them yet?" I asked, feeling around with outstretched hands so I wouldn't eat shit. Gunner mumbled insults under his voice, but I ignored whatever he was saying.

"Yeah, you're good," he grumbled. I snickered when I caught him adjusting himself.

"Oh, good, you have to suffer with blue balls the same way I do."

I'd woken up to a message from Gunner saying I needed to get over to his place right away for some club business. I'd left Nikki since it was something regarding Skeletons—no need to wake her. I was hoping I could get back before she woke up. Maybe I'd bring her something to eat.

"What the fuck are you doing here, Dex?" Gunner asked. The sincere confusion in his voice had my smile faltering and my blood chilling in my veins.

My words sounded hollow when I answered. A pang shot through my stomach as it clenched. "You texted me to meet you here," I said, already knowing what he was going to tell me.

Gunner's face sobered, and he gave the faintest shake of his head.

"Fuck!" I roared, picking up the nearest thing and throwing it against the wall. The vase shattered, sending shards raining down around the room. I yanked my phone out and dialed Nikki.

In the background, I heard Ryan asking what the hell was going on, but I was too engrossed in listening to Nikki's phone kick me straight to voicemail. Over and over.

If I didn't need the fucking thing, I would have thrown it, too.

"She won't answer. Her phone's been disabled," said a feminine voice from behind me.

Scar stood in the entryway, arms crossed over her chest as she stared me down, her three men all flanking her, looking ready for war in their tactical vests.

Something about the way she stood there, eyeing me, had my chest heaving. She knew something the rest of us didn't.

"What did you do?" I bit out, knowing she was involved.

Ryan started to speak, but Caleb's voice cut in. "I'd watch the way you speak to my wife. These three are the only people I truly like, and I have no problem putting a bullet in you if you prove to be a problem," he said matter-of-factly.

Kenji winced a bit at the statement, looking at me with an apologetic grimace. "It would probably only be like the thigh or shoulder, but yeah, he will shoot you." He gestured toward Scar with his arm. "I mean, we drugged Scar to kidnap her when we thought she wouldn't cooperate." He shrugged as if it were no big deal, and Scar rolled her eyes. "If it makes you feel better, he's lying about not liking you. He just doesn't like you *enough* not to shoot you," Kenji finished, patting Caleb on the shoulder as the Irishman continued to stare me down with a glare that almost made me want to break contact.

Niko had yet to say anything, but I doubted he'd step in as the voice of reason. His face was a blank slate, but his hulking mass was poised to strike quickly. Efficiently. These three were truly unhinged.

But I wasn't as nice of a guy as I presented myself to be.

"Been shot more than once. It's amazing what damage you can manage to inflict while adrenaline courses through you," I replied, my hand moving my cut out of the way to show the Glock on my hip. "So now that we've all proven we're ruthless fucks, tell me where the hell Nikki is."

A shot rang out that had us all ducking and reaching for our own weapons as we turned toward the noise. Ryan, who'd been trying to get in a word, was standing on the island, her pistol out and a pissed-off look on her face.

Scar chuckled, tucking one of her guns back into her thigh holster. "Shoot first, ask questions later. Your life motto, Brujita."

"Yeah, well, all you assholes were too busy comparing dick sizes to listen to me," she grumbled, hopping back down. Gunner was leaning against the island, completely unfazed. His reaction made me wonder if her meetings down in Sinaloa had been similar to this one.

"Wanna explain what the fuck is happening, Scar?" Ryan's tone held an edge to it, but if it bothered Scar, she didn't show it.

"That's what I was trying to do." She turned back toward me, staring me down as she spoke. "Try not to shoot me when I tell you this."

That comment had all my warning bells going off. I plucked my gun from my waistband, handing it over to Gunner. "My self-control isn't great," I bit out, stuffing my now empty hands into my front pockets. I knew I wasn't going to like whatever it was she had to say, but I'd been in the military long enough to know I couldn't go running in with my dick in my hand. Or in this case, my gun.

Whatever intel Scar had, I needed to know it.

"I disabled her phone this morning, just like I sent you the text that you needed to meet Gunner here." Her voice was cold. Calculated. I could suddenly see how it was that this woman was an accomplished killer.

"Why?" The word came out as a growl, more animal than man.

No one had moved. We were all rooted in place, making the tension spike even higher since it felt like a standoff. Too bad I'd given Gunner my Glock.

The deep breath Scar took was almost imperceptible, but I noticed it nonetheless and braced for the blow I knew was about to come because *that* was her sign of being nervous.

"Because she is meeting up with Andrei, who is taking her to Yuri," she said.

My body was moving before my mind could register the reaction. Shouts erupted from all over, creating a chaotic symphony, but Scar didn't falter, not even when I wrapped my hand around her throat and squeezed. It took a second for the haze of rage to lessen, and for me to notice the gleaming blade poised at my wrist. My eyes cut over to Kenji, who still wore a friendly smile.

Caleb and Niko were being blocked by Gunner and Ryan, who both had firearms shoved to their temples.

"My man, I'm letting this slide since I'd do the same if it were my girl, but if you don't remove your hand in point two seconds," his facial expression shifted, turning concerningly devoid of emotion, "I'll remove it for you and then shove it down your throat."

I loosened my grip, and Scar took a sharp inhale, but didn't bother rubbing at the red marks now marring her skin.

"I'll have to use that one," I muttered, my hands up in surrender. "Never thought about shoving their fist down their throat." I tipped my head at Scar. "Go ahead. Finish what you were going to say."

God, I'd thought that Ryan was scary, but Scar was another level, completely unfazed from me trying to *choke* her. Caleb shocked me by letting out a dark chuckle.

"She has that effect on people. When I tried to choke her, she pressed into my hand and told me I had a small cock," he said, then pointed to his face. "Your face was saying, *'What the fuck?'* Not too hard to figure out what you were thinking."

Scar ignored him, continuing on. "Andrei came to me after you all left the club with an alternate plan. Actually, it was probably the original plan, but he knew you three wouldn't go for it. We're not quite as...emotionally attached." She moved toward the island, placing her hands on the marble surface while the rest of us followed. "There was no way we were going to be able to get close to Yuri. The bastard is notoriously paranoid. Always has been, but you can imagine how that increased after his wedding. There was no way he'd ever come out into the public, so we needed to deliver Nikki to him," she said, locking eyes with me. "And she needed to have a believable reaction to being betrayed."

"She doesn't fucking know this is all a plan," I roared, slamming my fists down on the counter, splitting the skin on my knuckles. The pain helped keep my head clear.

Niko was the one to speak this time, his large hand landing on my shoulder.

For a big fucker, he sure was silent when he moved.

"It was the only way. I know Yuri well, my family reported to him. If he sensed at all that her reaction was disingenuous, he'd put a bullet in her brain right there." I opened my mouth to protest, but he ignored me and continued. "And there was no way we were going to get anywhere near him otherwise. The man has no moral code. He would have sent man after man to get her back, killed without discrimination. Your entire MC brotherhood would have been wiped out," he said, his face showing no sign of deceit.

In for four, out for four.

In for four, out for four.

Numbness slipped over me, my heart rate back under control. This was who Nikki needed, the collected killer who knew how to handle the stress of a dire situation. I wouldn't succumb to my emotions the way I had with Kell.

I'd save Nikki.

"Okay," I said, crossing my arms over my chest and widening my stance. "What's the plan?"

Gunner slid next to me, adopting the same stance, and warmth bloomed in my chest for the asshole. Brothers through and through—regardless of when we fought or fucked up, we'd always have each other's backs.

"Andrei is bringing her to Yuri under the guise of betraying her. He said he'd try his best to give her clues that this was all a plan, but he can't be too obvious and risk her not reacting. She's got a tracker on her, so we can see where Yuri takes her. From there, we ambush the place," Scar said.

My dislike for Andrei took on a new life. "What's he getting out of this?" I bit out. There was no way the plan was as simple as that, not that it really was simple. We'd have to pose an attack on enemy territory with very little planning and even less intel.

Scar shrugged a shoulder. "Who knows? He said he had something to ask of Yuri that was believable enough to make the Bratva leader think Andrei really was turning her in. Which he is—Yuri doesn't know about the double cross."

Gunner spoke this time, his voice curt. "You didn't ask him what he wanted from this?"

Caleb stepped forward, his usual pissed-off look even more prominent. "Listen, law enforcement," he spat. "Welcome to the big leagues. We don't give a shit what he's getting out of this as long as we get ours. That's how it works here. We stay out of people's shit."

Scar grinned like the cat that ate the canary. "Or you at least let them think you're staying out of their shit until you need to step in." The grin slipped slightly. "But as it turns out, Andrei has quite a bit more power than we knew about. In this case, it's better to be a friend than a foe." She looked at her wristwatch before pulling her phone out and typing something.

My phone vibrated, my heart doing a flip when a pin drop came through. "Nikki sent me her location," I said, laying my phone down on the counter.

"She sent it a while ago," Scar said offhandedly, her attention still on her phone. "I just unjammed her phone, so anything she tried to send is just now coming through."

"How the hell do you even have that kind of pull?" Gunner asked.

"I stopped asking a long time ago. She won't answer," Ryan commented, not sounding the least bit concerned about the situation.

Ryan's reaction actually helped me tamp down my anger toward Scar. If she was willing to trust these four, I would too. Truth was, Scar was probably the reason Nikki was going to live, because she was willing to act without emotions clouding her judgment.

"Nikki's on the move. Andrei has already made the trade." Scar looked up at us. "He says he left about five minutes ago. Niko."

The giant of a man placed a massive duffle bag I'd missed onto the counter, pulling out three ballistic vests and enough firearms to make me come.

"Close your mouth, Dex. You're drooling," Gunner joked weakly as he reached for a rifle.

"Put them on and pick your poison," Scar said.

Ryan smirked. "Well, well, well, don't these look familiar."

"I've got a good source. She can be a bitch, though."

Niko tossed a vest over to Ryan, who was flipping off Scar.

"I've narrowed down where they're going to two potential locations. Both are shit, but we'll make due," he said.

"Warehouse," Scar called out, focusing back on her phone. "They're making their way toward the warehouse."

"No running into a burning fucking building this time,

Scar, or I'll tie you to a chair again," Kenji said, cupping her face. She smiled, but her eyes drifted over to Niko, looking him up and down. "That goes for you too, big guy. Hard to fill her up if we're down a dick."

Gunner choked out a cough.

Scar winked, but moved straight back into business mode. "Okay, we've got rides parked outside. Ryan and Gunner, you're with Niko. He knows the place like the back of his hand since it's a Bratva building." She turned toward me. "You're with us, Romeo. Let me know right now if you can do this or not, because if you can't keep your shit together, I *will* have Kenji tie you to a chair."

"I've got the good rope, too."

There was no way in hell I was staying behind. Her weapon to wield, that was what I'd promised. I yanked the ballistic vest over my head, grabbing a handgun and tucking it into my waistband.

As much as I wanted to be up close and personal, my specialty was long-distance. There was a reason I was the one up on top of the shelving units waiting to take out Mario.

"Yeah, I'm sure I can do it," I said. "But I've got a few tactical suggestions. You got a sniper rifle somewhere?"

Kenji full-on beamed at me. "I fucking knew you were cool as shit. We should get best friend tattoos after we get your woman back."

FORTY-THREE
NIKKI

"I'M GOING TO KILL YOU."

Yuri's words burrowed themselves beneath my skin as he shoved a gag between my lips before pushing me into the trunk. Tears streaked my face, and it pissed me off because they were a result of my anger, *not* of my fear. I'd always known this was a potential outcome. The union my father had arranged for me was always destined to end in a funeral.

I'd hoped that it would be Yuri's, but knew it was more likely to be mine.

All I could hope for now was that my death would mean that my friends would be safe.

The next tear that fell wasn't fear, either. It was the heartache of knowing what my death was about to put Dex through again. My heart clenched.

I hoped he knew this wasn't his fault, that he wouldn't find solace in the oblivion. That he would live life for the both of us.

More tears ran down my face as I curled up in the trunk of the town car, thankful for the silence and my last few moments alone.

Fuck. What was I going to do?

We'd been in the car long enough for my hip to hurt from

lying on it, but I could tell by our speed that the wait was due to traffic as opposed to distance.

Would they come for me? How would they even know?

That thought caught my attention.

How the fuck had I gotten text messages from them this morning saying they were going to meet us at the rendezvous point if Andrei was planning on betra…

"Death before betrayal, zaika. Remember that."

Was this whole thing part of a plan? Katya's words came flooding back.

"Peter and the Wolf, Natasha. You remember the story, no? Change the ending, Nikki."

"Kill the wolf," I breathed out, a resurgence of hope filling my spirit.

I was going to kick Andrei's ass, and anyone else who was in on this fucking plan to leave me in the dark, but that would have to wait until after we murdered Yuri.

The car rolled to a stop, light blinding me as one of his men popped the trunk. "Time to get out, bitch. You're going back home."

My arms ached where they gripped my biceps, hauling me out of the car and carrying me between them into what looked like a warehouse. Doubt crept in as we neared Yuri. His lips were pulled back in a snarl, eyes gleaming with malice.

I wasn't sure who hated whom more.

"Natasha, look at all the fucking trouble you have caused me."

My head snapped to the side, the slap causing my ears to ring, drowning out the chuckles of his men. I prodded at my mouth, a coppery tang overwhelming my senses. Fucker had busted my lip.

"Plenty of other pussy to fuck, Yuri. You could have let me be," I said, turning my head back to face him.

"I'll have to break you of that fighting spirit, *wife*. Can't have you feeling hopeful that your life is going to be pleasant."

Fuck, it would have been nice to know what they were planning. Was I supposed to distract him? Get him to stay here? Get us to leave?

Whose bright fucking idea was it not to tell me a damn thing other than a coded message about a Russian children's musical and a criminal organization's motto? I'd have rolled my eyes, but it would probably earn me another case of whiplash via Yuri's hand.

"You never should have run, Natasha," he bit out before gesturing to his men. "Let's go. I want out of this fucking country."

Ice seeped into my veins, and I looked around for any sign that they were there.

My chest tightened when Yuri dragged his fingers down the side of my cheek, probing at the spot a bruise was beginning to form. He smiled when it caused me to wince. "You know, when Mario reached out to say he'd found my missing bride, I assumed the gnat was making another sorry attempt at getting into my good graces. But then he sent a picture of you acting like a whore up on stage," he said, pressing into the cut on my lip, but I didn't cry out.

Instead, I spat in his face.

"You fucking bitch!"

I didn't have great leverage since my hands were bound in front of me with zip ties, but I used the momentary distraction to drive my knee into his groin.

I braced for the retaliation, my eyes closing.

It would be worth it. I'd rather die than be used by him, and if the Grim Reaper was coming to collect, I was going to inflict as much pain as possible on my way out.

The shattering of glass and the pinging of bullets threw the warehouse into chaos. I dropped to my knees, the world seeming to shift into slow motion as people in black tactical gear converged into the room. Yuri's men fired back, two of them rushing to his aid. Like dé jà vu, I knew I needed to move while he was distracted.

I made my move to run, but a searing pain radiated from

my head as Yuri gripped my hair, yanking me backward. "Oh, no, you don't," he breathed into my ear, the barrel of a gun digging into my temple. "Get the fuck back. Unless you want me to blow her fucking brains out."

The warehouse went deathly silent at his threat.

In my peripherals, I caught Ryan, her face turned up in a murderous rage.

"Set your fucking guns down."

One by one, Ryan and the others did as they were told.

"It's not because they care about you, Natasha. They are surrendering because you're not worth the bloodshed. Look, that motorcycle member isn't even here. Fucked you and forgot you, it looks like," Yuri whispered. His words sent dread pooling in my gut, not because I believed him.

He was full of shit.

But he was right about Dex not being here. I looked at the bodies lying on the ground, hoping and praying none of them were him. Relief was short-lived when I didn't recognize any of them , though, because where the hell was he?

Ryan's voice drew my attention. "Let her go, and we let you live." Our eyes met, and she made the slightest move of her head.

I followed the movement, spotting what looked like an open window up near the roof. The black barrel sent my heart into overdrive as Yuri's arm banded tighter around me, pulling me close as he yelled at Ryan.

"Let me live? You're the ones who have put down your weapons. I am going to walk out of here with my prize, and then, in return, I will hunt and kill you all."

"How is that a deal?" I asked, unable to keep my smart mouth shut.

My question was met with another rough yank of my hair as he led us backward, using me as a human shield with the gun pressed to my temple. Tires screeched, echoing off the corrugated metal. Yuri's Range Rover pulled up behind us, a door thrown open.

Fuck. I knew if I got in there, I'd be gone forever, and the sick fuck would make sure I wasn't able to die before he was ready. The situation left me no choice.

I squeezed my eyes shut, my hands fisted by my side as I tried to relax as much as possible.

Planting my feet to prevent us from going any further, I yelled out at the top of my lungs, hoping he hadn't gone soft on me. Hoping he'd do what was needed.

"Pull the fucking trigger, Dex! "

Then the world exploded.

It felt as if I were underwater. All the sounds were muffled. I could tell by the look on her face that Ryan was yelling, but I couldn't hear what she was saying. Bodies moved, but my eyes couldn't track where they were going, and then, in the next instant, the world sped back up.

Noise hit me like a freight train.

The last thing I caught before the world went black was Ryan screaming.

"You fucking shot her?"

I smiled as I slipped into oblivion.

I knew my man could do it. I knew he would save me.

YOU SHOULD HAVE KNOWN BY NOW THAT SOMEONE WAS GETTING SHOT OR STABBED...

WE'D TAKEN off on motorcycles as soon as Scar knew the location they were headed in with Nikki.

Gunner was practically foaming at the mouth at the sight of Ryan on one, and I was ninety-nine percent sure that a bike was in her near future, even if the sole purpose was him fucking her on it.

Yuri was taking Nikki to an old warehouse that was sometimes used as a hangar for the Bratva. We assumed he had a plane waiting for him to take him out of the city before making their way back to St. Petersburg.

It was now or never.

Nikki was as good as gone if the plane took off. According to Andrei, there was no fucking way we'd get to her on Yuri's home turf. I wasn't entirely sure what Andrei's intentions were, but the fucker was geared up and armed to the teeth with a fierce look on his face.

I'd be watching him, but for now, I had too many other things to worry about.

While a Harley was my preferred ride, the Ducati Kenji put me on was fast as hell, and that was what we needed to make it to the place before Yuri. Earlier that morning, Caleb had sent Andrei's and the Syndicate's men to both potential locations, so we'd have people in place when the tracker sewed into Nikki's leotard tarted moving. I was fucking glad that those four were on our side because they really knew their shit, dotting every I and crossing every T they could.

When I asked how the fuck we were going to get there before Yuri, the smirk on Scar's face had been downright scary.

"Yuri thinks he's a god, but he's just another entitled man who's too cocky to see that a woman is about to carve out his heart. I'm going to make sure Nikki gets what she's owed," she said.

I gaped at her, trying to find something to say to that, but the only thing that came to mind was, "Well…when you put it like that, let's do the fucking thing."

Now I knew what Ryan had meant when she said that Scar had this dangerous air about her. The chick was steps ahead of her mark before they knew she was after them. Like the fact that she'd hacked into New York's street lights years ago in case she ever needed to manipulate traffic, which was the key factor in us making it to the warehouse and getting into place before Yuri and his entourage pulled up.

It was no wonder Cain was so sought after.

"Black car incoming at main gate," Kenji said over the comms. "Their driver is shit. If I were Yuri, I'd have shot him just for driving like we were on a cruise through the country-side and not trying to get our asses out of town."

"Kenji, we *want* him to drive like that, dumbass," Caleb quipped.

The banter between the two made me smile despite my tamped down rage.

"They remind me of us," Gunner said from beside me.

"Yeah, if you had a stick permanently shoved up your ass, making you constantly act like a dick."

We'd split off when we'd arrived, everyone taking up their posts. Gunner and I were up on the roof. "Like old times, brother. Sniper and spotter."

"Yeah, don't fuck it up," Gunner teased, knowing I needed some levity. Because this wasn't exactly like old times —I'd never had a woman I love mixed up in the middle. But

Gunner had, so if anyone was going to be able to help see me through this, it was him.

In for four, out for four.

I relaxed my shoulders and unclenched my jaw, sinking lower into my position. The mantra had been running on a loop since I'd laid out on top of the roof with my barrel peeking through a ventilation window. I'd never been more thankful for my ability to shut out my emotions in times of stress, because I fucking needed it now.

"Alright, Dex. Keep your cool here."

There was no need to ask what Gunner was referring to. Nikki was being carried between two men into the warehouse. Blood pounded in my ears when her head snapped to the side. The fucker had slapped her, hard.

"Breathe, brother. We can't move too soon," Gunner whispered, worry in his tone.

I was too engrossed in what was happening down on the warehouse floor to respond, but I kept my finger off the trigger. The two exchanged words, both of their faces growing angrier with each word. They were too far for me to hear what they were saying.

My heart ached when she seemed to look around, searching for a way out or someone to save her.

"Easy. You'll be down there with her soon, Dex."

Gunner seemed to have a mainline to my thoughts. His timing with words of encouragement was perfect. And thank fuck he didn't require a verbal response because I was vibrating with anger and hanging by a thread, relying on every calming technique I knew to stay in the pocket. At one point, Yuri ran a hand down Nikki's face, pressing at the spot he'd hit her. Pride swelled in my chest when my spitfire spat blood in the asshole's face.

"You fucking bitch," Yuri yelled loud enough for me to hear.

My finger moved from where it rested above the trigger right as Scar's voice sounded on the comms. "That's our cue, boys."

The warehouse exploded into chaos, glass shattering where our men broke through, bullets pinging off the corrugated metal. We were equipped with ballistic gear and mowed through Yuri's men with ease.

"Come on, baby, get out of there," I whispered, my eye pressed to the scope.

Relief flooded my veins when she ran, but everything came to a screeching halt the moment he wrapped his fingers in her hair, dragging her back—the barrel of a gun shoved to her temple.

"Set your fucking guns down," he yelled.

Gunner shifted beside me. "We planned for this."

"Yeah, but we didn't plan on him being fucking short," I growled. "Headshot's fucking blocked."

"Fuck."

Fuck was right. Yuri held Nikki directly in front of him, but they were nearly the same height, making the headshot a no-go. Yuri and Ryan were exchanging words, none of which I could quite catch, but whatever it was, it had Nikki looking directly up at me.

A surge of emotions swept through me. She knew I was here, but the moment was cut short. Screeching tires echoed through the space, a blacked-out Range Rover pulling up behind them.

"Guys, that thing is fully armored. We can stop them if they leave in it, but..." Niko paused. "But it's not going to be easy, and I can pretty much guarantee Nikki's going to get hurt, and I don't know how badly..."

Gunner answered for us. "Dammit. We may not have another option, the asshole is dragging her back to the car with her as a fucking shield. We'll get down there ASAP. Get the fucking ride ready."

Nikki's voice boomed, yelling at the top of her lungs. "Pull the fucking trigger, Dex! " Her voice was steady—sure. She was a fucking sight to be seen, like a damn golden goddess holding her chin high, determination in her face.

Time seemed to slow, the rest of the chaos falling away, leaving nothing but her and I.

Those blue eyes taunted me, seeing if I had the balls to pull the trigger. To trust her.

To give her a choice.

"There's no fucking way you're going to sho—"

I didn't give Gunner a chance to finish his sentence before I sent a round through the top of Nikki's shoulder, right into Yuri's chest.

For the second time, chaos erupted in the warehouse, our men back on the offense, taking out Yuri's guys as they attempted to make it to where both he and Nikki lay in a growing puddle of blood.

"You fucking shot her?" Ryan screamed, taking out everyone in her way.

But I was too busy getting into the firefight to think about what kind of shit I'd be in with her.

All that mattered was Nikki.

FORTY-FIVE
NIKKI

KILL THE WOLF

SOMETHING MOVED BELOW ME, shoving me off to the side. Pain seared through my shoulder, and stars danced behind my eyelids.

What the fuck?

The muddled noise grew to a roar. Shouts of pain mixed with gunshots, kicking my mind into high gear. My eyes popped open, everything rushing back to me. I was in the warehouse, and Dex had taken the shot straight through me, like I'd asked him to. Yuri's body had broken my fall, the round going through my left shoulder and into his chest, but the fucker was still clearly alive.

I scrambled to push myself to my feet before Yuri could grab me because there was no way I was going to take two fucking bullets. A scream ripped through my lips, my wound weeping blood with each movement.

How the fuck do Ryan and Scar do this? Getting shot hurts like a bitch.

"You bitch." He spat the words out at me, but his voice was weak. "You're going to pay for this," he said, reaching for his gun.

We realized it had landed a few feet away at the same time. My eyes zeroed in on the Glock, and every survival instinct kicked in. There was so much adrenaline flooding my system that I barely felt my shoulder as I ran for the gun, snatching it up between my bound hands, thankful they'd put them in front.

My heart beat so quickly that I thought it would break through my chest as I turned toward Yuri. He was a disheveled mess lying there on the cracked concrete floor. His perfectly quaffed hair was in disarray, his suit stained with dirt, and there was a growing dark splotch where he'd been shot.

Nothing else existed except him and me.

Each step forward filled me with a sick sense of glee. *Now* I understood why Ryan and Scar did what they did. To be under the thumb of a man and then exact your revenge on them…it was a sense of satisfaction nothing else could match. Yuri's body shook, a cry leaving him when he failed in his attempts to push himself up onto his forearms and move away from me.

"How does it feel, Yuri? To watch as your life comes to an end? To have someone else play god with your future?" I asked in a chilling tone. Even to my ears, I didn't sound like myself. I felt more akin to a vengeful spirit than the young girl he'd been given as an unwilling bride.

"I'll leave you be, Natasha. Give you whatever you want. We can part ways here and never see one another again," he pleaded.

I laughed at his proposal. "That's pathetic, I'd thought you'd have more balls than to beg like a pussy. Hell, I took a fucking bullet instead of giving up. And I'm not an idiot, Yuri. You'd never let that happen." I closed the distance, sneering down at him. "And I want revenge for the life you took from me."

He shook his head, eyes wild. "I never killed your father. That was the Romas."

My smile grew wider. "No, that was me." I dug the toe of my shoe into his wound, relishing in the way he screamed out in pain, trying again to get up on his elbows. He shoved himself away from me with his feet, but it was useless.

He called out for his men, but no one ran to his aid, all of them too busy being mowed down by my friends.

"Sucks to feel helpless, huh? For someone to use their body against you." I knew I didn't have much longer before the adrenaline wore out, already feeling unsteady, but I wanted this—needed this.

Warm hands wrapped around me, sending me into a panic for a split second before Dex's comforting voice whispered in my ears. "Easy, spitfire, just here to lend a helping hand." With a quick flick of his blade, he cut the zip tie, lowering my damaged arm with care. I hadn't realized how much tension I'd held in my body until I sank back into him, letting him hold me up.

He was home. Freedom.

"Alright, let's kill this fucker so we can get you to a hospital. Unless you want me to take him back to the shed and hack off parts of his body," Dex said, loud enough for Yuri to hear.

Whatever color had been left in his face drained, and he yelled insults in Russian.

There was no way that line should have made me smile, or made my stomach flip in excitement, but it did.

Note to self: have the doctor check for a concussion…

"As romantic as that sounds, I'm going to end his miserable life right here. Kill the wolf," I whispered the last part, but he must've heard, because I felt him hum in satisfaction against my back.

Dex's hand slid down my arm, offering stability and helping me aim. "Your weapon to yield, baby," he whispered. "Forever and always."

A shot rang out, and Yuri's head slammed back into the floor—a hole dead center between the eyes.

But I barely saw it before turning. All I wanted was to look into the eyes of the man I loved.

Dex took the gun from my hand, his hands cupping my face and kissing me with so much passion it stole my breath.

"You shot me," I said, smiling against his lips. Ryan was going to kick his ass for that.

"You were in the way, spitfire," he teased, his hazel eyes danced with happiness and relief before they turned serious. "And I trust you and your choices, Nikki."

I knew he was holding it together by a thread for my sake. He was basically holding me up at this point, and his gaze kept cutting to my shoulder. "You guys got a surgeon on retainer?" he asked the group.

Movement from beside us drew my attention. My crew of friends stood there looking downright terrifying in their tactical gear and blood splatter.

Caleb nodded. "Sent for him the moment your girl yelled out the command." His attention was locked onto Dex. "We all decided to fall in love with wild women, didn't we? " All of the men shared a good laugh in agreement, and Ryan and Scar flipped them off, shooting each other a wink because there was no denying the truth of his statement.

Dex's face pulled down into a glower as Andrei walked up, coming from who the fuck knew where. I rolled my eyes at his state—he had a gun in each hand and a bigger one strapped to his back, looking like he was getting ready to shoot a music video with his leather pants and tight black shirt under his vest. "Ballsy move having him shoot through your shoulder." He was practically beaming. "You got your Ruska Roma mark after all, Nat—Nikki. You ever need us, you know how to find me, but it's time for me to go."

"Wait," I called after him as he turned to leave. "What the fuck happens now? With the Bratva and The Circle? Didn't we create a bigger fucking problem here?" Dread settled in my gut. Fuck, I didn't want a war with a bunch of billionaires. My body sagged even more, and Dex lifted me into his arms bridal style, which was becoming a habit.

An SUV pulled into the hangar, a man throwing the door open and calling for Andrei. He signaled for them to give him a moment before turning back. "Don't worry about the Circle or the Bratva. I've got plans for them," he said, a sinister smile on his face, throwing us a wink before climbing in and driving away.

"We really going to trust that guy?" Gunner asked from where he stood with his arms wrapped around Ryan.

My throat hurt from all the yelling, but I still managed to speak loud enough for everyone to hear me. "Death before betrayal." There was confusion on all their faces, aside from Niko's and Scar's.

"It's the Ruska Roma's creed. They will die before they betray a fellow member," Niko answered, all my strength tapped. "And Nikki here has earned her mark. She may not have the traditional tattoo, but that scar on her shoulder guarantees their loyalty."

"And we don't have to trust him. Andrei knows I'll be watching," Scar added.

Dex looked down at me, leaving the others to their conversation and carrying me toward an awaiting car. "You're mine, Nikki. I love you with every breath in my body and every fiber in my being. Forever and always."

The last thing I remembered was the press of his lips to mine.

TWO-ISH MONTHS LATER

"OH, *FUCK*," I groaned, thrusting my hand into Dex's hair.

With a low growl, his mouth dropped between my legs, tongue delving between my slick folds. The sensation was so otherworldly I swore I could see sounds.

His tongue dragged up and down my slit, moving higher until it reached its destination. He turned me into putty under his mouth when his lips wrapped around my throbbing clit, humming against it.

"Fuck, me," I cried out, my body lifting from the bed.

The smug bastard smiled up at me, swirling the tip of his tongue around, teasing it until I was gasping and clawing at the bed sheets. "That's coming, Nikki. Just like you will be." He winked, loving the control he had over my body when I was spread out like this before him.

My retort died on my tongue, the words transforming into a moan when he shoved two thick fingers into me, continuing to suck on my clit until I was shaking, so fucking close to coming it felt like I would explode into a million pieces.

"Not yet, baby," he said with a chuckle, pulling away right when I was at the brink of bliss.

I yelled out in frustration, raising my head to shoot

daggers at him with my eye, but my mouth went dry at the sight of his tattooed hand wrapped around his thick cock, languidly stroking himself. The look of desire on his face caused my breath to hitch.

"Spread those beautiful thighs for me, spitfire. I'm going to fuck you so good the entire party will know why we're late."

Shit. We were going to be late.

But I couldn't seem to get myself to care as I followed his instructions, whimpering at the sensation of the head of his cock slipping between my slit, teasing my opening.

"Stop fucking around, Dex. If you don't fill me with your cock I'm going to use one of the dildos you broug—" He pushed into me, cutting off my bitching.

All I saw were stars, my eyes rolling back as he filled me with every thick inch of his cock, his mouth crushing against mine. Our tongues fought for dominance as they entangled with one another.

"Wrap your legs around me, baby," he ordered against my lips, and I locked my ankles behind his muscled back, digging my heels into his ass.

Suddenly, his heat was gone, and he stared down at me from above, a sly grin pulled at the corners of his lips. "There you go, so good at following directions," he praised.

I shuddered as his cock flexed deep inside of me, his hips pulling back before pistoning forward. "Look at you, spitfire. Look at how your greedy fucking pussy is so eager for my cock."

God damn, his dirty fucking mouth.

My eyes locked on to the spot where his slick cock plunged in and out of me.

He lifted my chin with his thick finger, our gaze locking. The intensity stole my breath—love, desire, and devotion swirled in his hazel eyes. Without a doubt, I knew they mirrored the emotions in mine.

"Forever and fucking always, Dex," I vowed, loud enough for him to hear over the slapping of our skin.

My words sent him into a frenzy, my eyes rolling back as pleasure snaked over every inch of my skin. "Eyes on me, Nikki. I want to see those beautiful blue eyes as you come." They fluttered open, taking in his smirk. "Forever and fucking always, spitfire. Not even the devil can pry me from your side."

Emotions surged through me. I'd never felt so loved—so cared for. And it had nothing to do with how he fucked me. It was how he *saw* me.

All of me, even when I'd fucking hid from him.

He rolled his hips against me, the pleasure stealing my attention. I was too engrossed with how his thumb worked my clit, like he was a fucking expert on my body. By this point, he was. For weeks after he'd shot me, Dex had shown me how sorry he was with his mouth, even though I was the one who'd ordered him to take the shot to begin with .

But there was no fucking way I'd turn away his offer to get me off.

The next thrust hit so deep I swore I saw god as I came apart beneath him, shouting his name.

Dex's groans echoed mine, dropping his head to the crook of my neck. "Fuck, you feel so good milking my cock," he growled in my ear as he fucked me into the mattress, moving faster. "Just like that, spitfire. Grip me with that greedy fucking pussy."

His hand clasped my chin, squeezing it slightly so my lips parted before spitting into my mouth.

Why was that hot?

His chuckle made me wonder if I'd asked that aloud, but I was too distracted by his next command to figure it out. "Ask me nicely for my cum, Nikki."

For the second time in my life, I thought I was going to have a heart attack, this time from being so turned on. My entire body began to clench, my vision going white.

"Please."

"That's not what I asked for, Nikki. You want me to

fucking come inside you? Beg." The possessiveness of his voice in my ear had me teetering on the edge.

I gripped Dex's face, not to be outdone. "I want to feel you fucking drip down my thighs. Please."

The growl he let out was like dropping a match on a pool of gasoline—I exploded. Pure ecstasy shattering through every nerve in my body. Dex found his release seconds after mine with a final thrust, holding himself inside me and spilling his hot cum.

I was vaguely aware of his whispers of love between the kisses he trailed up my chest and neck.

"That was a religious experience," I whispered, forcing my eyes to open, only to find Dex looking at me with a self-satisfied grin.

"Next time, yell out Skydaddy instead of Dex?"

He was so damn cocky and loved to make me laugh. It was like a high for him. Every time I resisted, not wanting to stroke his ego, but it never worked. I supposed it would make up for all the years I'd missed out on making smile lines. "Please, I didn't even call out your name this time," I said, rolling my eyes and biting my lip, still fighting back a laugh.

His lazy grin grew into a full-fledged smile. "Oh, baby, you call out my name like it's the only word you know," he said, rolling off my body and crouching by my feet, his cock bouncing with the movement. Now, I was biting my lip for other reasons.

"You keep looking at me like that and we will never make it to the party," he promised, taking my leg in his hand and pressing the flat of his tongue to my ankle before dragging it up, lapping his cum as he went.

"Can't we skip it and stay in bed and fuck?" I asked, moaning when he made it to the apex of my thighs, pushing his cum-coated tongue inside my pussy.

This man was...fuck.

There was no thinking straight around him. As quickly as he'd started, he stopped, pulling away and grinning at me.

"As much as I want to do that, we have to make an appearance." His eyes sparkled with mischief.

FORTY-SEVEN

DEX

CUE HAPPY TEARS

IT WAS nice to see the club really enjoy a party without the threat of the Reapers hanging over our fucking heads. The level of ease was evident in the number of beer cans Torque had taped together.

"Fucker, neither of your sticks is going to impress anyone," I called out, wincing when Nikki hit my shoulder.

"Leave him alone. He's celebrating his job well done."

I took a swig of my beer, kneading my girl's thigh. God, I couldn't get enough of her skin, her scent, her goddamn laughter.

"Please, they did half the work for him," I said to rile her up. My favorite pastime was pissing her off and then apologizing by burying my tongue inside her pussy. Sometimes, I thought she'd storm into our apartment to pick a fight with the sole purpose of getting me on my knees, and I fucking loved her angry woman energy.

"Be nice. Torque did your job hunting down the rest of the Reapers so you could play nurse for me," she said.

She wasn't wrong, and I was forever grateful to him for that. While we were away in New York, the boys back here decided to make their first move on the Reapers. But when they'd arrived at the compound, it'd been quiet as a cemetery.

Rats fled town in the middle of the night when they'd learned there wasn't any aid coming from the Russians.

Caleb's doctor had been waiting back at their apartment for us, happy with how the wound looked. The bullet had gone right through with no fragmentation. But it was still a gunshot to the shoulder, requiring Nikki's arm to be in a sling until a few weeks ago.

"Speaking of doing other people's jobs, I hear you're the new manager of Lotería, Nikki," Scar piped up from across the firepit where she was sprawled out across all three of her men, her ass in Caleb's lap, legs spread across Niko's and Kenji's.

I tugged on a blonde strand of Nikki's hair, loving when she got to brag about the shit she was doing. "Turns out, dancing on a pole is a bitch to do with one arm." She pointed the bottle of her beer at Ryan, who sat next to us, curled up in Gunner's arms. "Mother hen over there wouldn't even let me try."

"I'm not paying more in worker's comp because your stubborn ass decided to get up on a pole with a bum arm." She smiled wide at the finger Nikki gave her. "Besides, I can't be as involved in the club now that I've got a bunch of grown-ass men to babysit."

"Hear fucking hear ," Scar called out, raising her bottle in the air while her three men grumbled about not being that bad. The whole group burst into laughter.

Fuck, did my heart feel like it was on cloud nine. I looked around the compound, all of my brothers laughing and having a good time while I sat with the love of my life in my lap and my chosen family surrounding me.

My breath lodged in my throat.

There was no manual to grief. No guidebook to walk you through the moments two opposing emotions collided. When you were happy and content with all of the blessings raining down around you, only to feel the sucker punch of loss at the realization someone you loved wouldn't be there to enjoy those wins with you.

To witness big life moments.

Gunner's hand landing on my shoulder jolted me out of my daze. I'd completely missed him getting up and moving to stand beside me.

"She'd be proud of you, brother." He nodded to Nikki. "And Kell would have liked her," he said, before moving back to Ryan and dropping a kiss on her lips.

My sister really would have loved Nikki.

As if she could hear my thoughts, Nikki looked over her shoulder at me. She beamed, mouthing *I love you*, her smile like a wash of sunshine on my soul. Every day, I fell more in love with her, and it was bittersweet knowing the two most important women in my life would never meet.

Life was so fucking short. Death didn't care how many things you had left on your bucket list for life.

How many kisses you had left to give—how much love left to show.

Let us live since we are destined to die…

Without a second thought, I stood, lifting Nikki up in my arms so I could take her with me. She squealed in delight, and I hoped she'd keep that happy energy with what I was about to do. "Anyone in this bitch able to officiate a marriage?" I yelled out over the rowdy party.

"Dex, what the hell? What are yo—"

I silenced her with my lips, pushing as much of my emotion as I could at that moment. "Nikki Anya Petrov, I've already told you I want you for as long as I continue to breathe, but I don't just want you as my girl or an Old Lady. I want you as my wife." Her blue eyes widened, tears forming at the corners, her lips lifting into a quivering smile while I rambled on. "I know you've had shit luck with weddings and husbands…but, spitfire, if you give m—"

"Who can fucking officiate," she yelled out, her smile practically touching her ears. "I have the love of my life to marry."

"Us, too," Kenji called from behind us. "What? Where else

do you think we are going to be able to have a wedding with four fucking people?" he hissed at Caleb.

"Nowhere," boomed Pres. "Now, let's have us some fucking clubhouse weddings, everyone." A roar of cheers erupted, but the noise fell away when I looked into Nikki's eyes.

"Forever and fucking always, Nikki Anya Kelley."

"With every last breath, Dex."

HIGH STICKING THE HEART

ARIELLA CONTRERAS DOESN'T HAVE TIME FOR DISTRACTIONS.

She's fought hard for her independence, determined to break free from cultural tradition, family expectations, and anything that could derail her career. So when a tall, cowboy hat-wearing Texan with Wranglers tight enough to test the strongest will begs her to pose as his fake date to dodge an ex? She should've stuck to her first instinct and told him to get lost.

Because the man she was never supposed to see again? Turns out he's the star player for the hockey team she's just been hired to coach on… and the son of her new boss.

ARIELLA

I'M A STRONG, INDEPENDENT WOMAN WHO DOESN'T NEED ANYTHING FROM A MAN—EXCEPT FOR HIM NOT TO TALK TO ME

I'd never realized swamp-ass was a *literal* thing and not just a figure of speech.

"Why didn't you tell me you lived in the bowels of hell, Graciella?" I yelled into the open doorway, wildly throwing my head around in an attempt to redirect another droplet of sweat threatening to run into my eye.

It had been two weeks since I'd breathed freely, living in air-conditioned air so cold I was left with a choice between switching to thicker sports bras or heading out to endure hell's atmosphere.

"There is a *river* running between *mis nalgas* at the moment. This is not *a little* humidity. This is the end of times or something."

Sure, I knew logically that moving out of California meant leaving California weather, but I hadn't fully grasped what that would look like.

My new reality?

Every time I stepped outside I resembled a drowned rat with my hair plastered to my head thanks to perspiration, all while I sucked down breaths, hoping I'd finally inhale something other than hot, thick air.

I looked at my cousin's blunt bob, contemplating chopping mine, but since my wardrobe consisted solely of black leggings or shorts, my long hair and colored sports bras were the only fun, girly accessories I had.

Fine. I'd learn to endure the torture.

Gracie's voice cut through the inner bitching. "Foul, Ariella. That was foul. And don't let a Texan hear you speak poorly on their state."

I rolled my eyes at the warning. They had to know their weather sucked, right? Who was happy in these conditions?

"Well, you know what would have been nice to know before I decided to move out here with you? That there was enough humidity in the air to drown you," I said, carrying in the last of the boxes I'd shipped to my new residence.

In typical cousin fashion, Gracie only shrugged, ignoring my suffering. "You're the one who decided to move here at the end of August." She tugged at my shirt and wrinkled her nose. "Yeah, that shade of gray? Never wear it again. At least not in summer."

My groan echoed off the brick walls.

"I wish I could say you get used to it, but you don't," she added unhelpfully, reclaiming her spot on the worn green velvet couch so she could watch me play live-action Tetris with my boxes of shit.

There were only three of them, but Gracie's place—now *our* place—was the size of a rich housewife's walk-in closet. Not tiny, but we had to take turns walking in certain areas.

Nearly every corner had bits of her style—yellows and greens with dainty details. But now there were also bits of my bright oranges and hot pinks, as well.

Our personalities were as different as our favorite colors, yet somehow, we worked. Like the sun and the moon, we complemented each other.

She was sunshine and fun, always seeing the best in the day. I was fiery and fierce, and my mood was liable to shift on a dime.

"Thanks for helping me carry that, by the way," I bit out with faux irritation, shooting her a glare over my shoulder when the final box was precariously placed on top of the others.

She shrugged, unfazed by the attitude. "*¡Órale!* What was I supposed to do with these?" She gave a pitiful attempt at flexing her bicep. "You're the one who has a job showing men how to pick up heavy things. Mine requires me to keep up with what's trending."

"Strength and conditioning, Graciella," I explained for the hundredth time. "I'm a strength and conditioning coach. You should know this—you work in sports too."

She waved a manicured hand in the air dismissively. The stupid smirk on her face told me she hadn't forgotten what it was called.

"Correction, I work in sports *marketing*. It's not the same. I have to make sure my clients' brands look good and capture content for sports shit. *You* yell at men in the gym." She smirked. "It's honestly perfect for you. Anyway, the point is, you're the strong one. We both know if I need something carried, I'd delegate it to a man. You should try it sometime," she said, pointing at me over her screen.

I clucked my tongue at her awful idea.

"I'm a strong, independent woman who doesn't need anything from a man…except for him not to talk to me," I said, pulling off my sweat-soaked shirt, grimacing at the wet plopping noise of it hitting the concrete flooring.

She rolled her eyes. "Are you done yet? I'm ready to do something fun," she complained, tucking a stray hair behind her ear and setting her phone on the table, giving me her full attention now that she was bored.

Gracie's outlook on a fun night was very different from my own. To me, a *fun night* consisted of some cafecitos, no bra, and a murder show. Maybe throw in an overpriced FoodRun delivery.

Hers usually involved a margarita and a man.

I walked to the kitchen, taking my time to finish the heavenly cool water I'd poured myself so I could weigh my options on how to respond.

I'd put her off since getting to Dallas, and if I didn't agree to go out with her soon, I was afraid she'd hire someone to kidnap me and force me out of the house.

Probably one of the guys she matched with on an app because, apparently, that was how my cousin got everything she needed done.

Leaky sink? Get a Tinder match.

Need new tires? Get a Tinder match.

I wasn't sure if she was setting female empowerment back or shooting us forward…

Sighing at the thought, I finally asked, "When you say *fun*, what exactly are you talking about, Graciella Xochitl Barrera?" She opened her mouth to answer, but I cut her off, concerned by the twinkle in her eyes. "I do mean, *exactly* what are you talking about? Because I do not want you to tell me we are going to some kickback at your friend's with only a few people, and then I find myself crammed into the random room of a frat house off of 11th and San Antonio St. where a random dude is playing his DJ set while a bottle of UV Blue is being passed around. It's shocking we are even alive," I scolded, my hands on my hips to keep from flailing them around.

A habit that was hard to break, truthfully. I was pretty sure it was a trait ingrained in our cultural DNA to talk with our hands and add emphasis with sound effects.

As if to prove my point, Gracie made a clucking noise with her tongue, waving away the accusation. "Well, the first problem in that scenario is we aren't in San Jose, so there's no chance of that. Plus, how pathetic would it be if two twenty-five-year-old women showed up to frat parties to get drunk? I'm not *that* desperate for a man. You, on the other hand…"

She fell into a fit of laughter when I chucked my sandal at her, grazing the top of her head while I called her every insult I could think of.

"Okay, okay." She held her hands up in surrender, attempting to control herself. "No men. It will be a *primas* night. One of my clients knows of a sports bar's soft launch happening tonight. The guest list is all athletes, agents, and marketing people." She sat up on her knees, looking like an excited puppy. "It will be fun," she promised, wagging her eyebrows, trying to entice me.

There was definitely no way I was getting out of going somewhere with her tonight.

"So let me get this straight. You want to have a *primas*-only night at a bar crawling with hot athletes?" I asked, the cold stainless-steel biting into the exposed skin of my torso as I leaned against the countertop.

Her smile was so sickly sweet I was shocked she still had all her teeth. "*Nothing* says girls' night like free margaritas and staring at athletes' asses," she said.

"Oh, now the margaritas are free, too?"

"They are if you wear that black halter top that makes it look like your boobs are in your chin."

I shook my head at her logic. She wasn't wrong, but I wouldn't tell her that. It would go to her head.

Pointing my finger at her, I tried my best to sound stern, "*Mira*, we will go—" An ear-piercing cheer cut me off.

She'd been hoping for that answer for days, but I'd avoided going out until now, using that time to try and adjust to the new time zone, weather, and the fact I didn't live in my childhood home anymore.

There was a reason I'd applied for the job in Dallas. I'd needed a reprieve from my family's expectations, and there was no way in hell they'd be okay with me moving out of state by myself. Explaining that concept to my white friends was always a humiliating experience. It led to some variation of the same questions.

"What do you mean you can't make those decisions yourself?"

"But you're twenty-five…you're an adult."

Yeah, it wasn't that simple in my household. Cultural expectations and generational normatives loved to cockblock a woman's independence. What made my situation particularly difficult was that I loved my family.

It would be far easier to be the family's disappointment if I didn't care what they thought. Sometimes I wished they were shittier to me so I could justify cutting them off completely and living my life on my terms.

Ironically, thousands of miles didn't stop my dad and brother's onslaught of questions or attempts at control. They wanted to know what I was doing, where I was going, or the million-dollar question—who would I see?

I sighed, rubbing at my chest. I hoped that with more time apart, they'd start to see I was living my own life and that the weird sense of guilt sitting on my sternum for wanting to do my own thing would subside.

Gracie hopped off the couch, rushing to the mini bar she'd set up on a wall shelf. "This calls for a shot."

The declaration caught my attention. Tequila and Graciella had trouble written all over it.

If I was being honest, tequila and *me* had trouble written all over it.

"No trying to set me up while we're there, Gracie." She rolled her eyes at the warning, passing me a shot glass. The clear liquid balancing precariously at the top of the rim threatened to run down the side of my hand. "I'm being serious. I'm out here for my career, to show everyone I can do this…" The last part was barely above a whisper.

Her eyes softened, the corner of her pink lips pulling into a sad smile. If anyone understood the cultural pressures coming from home, it was Gracie.

She'd managed to break the hold when she left for college, but it came at a price. My *tío* still refused to speak to her. Despite the differences in opinions on how I should live my life, I had comfort in knowing my family would never cut me out the way my uncle had with her.

I shook my head, needing to clear the sour mood.

"*Vamos*," I said, raising my glass and waiting for Gracie to join. "To new opportunities, breaking generational machismo—"

"And amazing cousins who let you move in with them," she added.

I smiled at her, all of my earlier worries suspended for now.

"*¡Salud!*"

ALSO BY MARIE MARAVILLA

Skeletons of Society

Syndicate of Sins

City of Salvation

My sweeter side, Marie M.

High Sticking the Heart

HEY BOO

Writing a book was only supposed to be a bucket list thing to check off; now, here we are. I wrote my first book, Skeletons of Society, after struggling to find books in the mafia/romantic suspense genre with strong, morally grey women.

As it turns out, readers were looking for that, too, because it's one of the most praised aspects of my writing. That prompted the creation of Syndicate of Sins and then City of Salvation.

My author brand centers around writing unapologetic feminine rage with FMCs as badass as the boys who fall for them.

I currently live in Tenessee and try to survive the cycle of working, writing, mom-ing, and consuming questionable amounts of caffeine.

XOXO
Marie Maravilla

instagram.com/authormariemaravilla
tiktok.com/@authormariemaravilla

HEY BOO

Writing a book was only supposed to be a bucket list thing to check off; now, here we are. I wrote my first book, Skeletons of Society, after struggling to find books in the mafia/romantic suspense genre with strong, morally grey women.

As it turns out, readers were looking for that, too, because it's one of the most praised aspects of my writing. That prompted the creation of Syndicate of Sins and then City of Salvation.

My author brand centers around writing unapologetic feminine rage with FMCs as badass as the boys who fall for them.

I currently live in Tenessee and try to survive the cycle of working, writing, mom-ing, and consuming questionable amounts of caffeine.

XOXO
Marie Maravilla

instagram.com/authormariemaravilla
tiktok.com/@authormariemaravilla

COULDN'T HAVE DONE IT WITHOUT THESE GEMS

The first thanks goes to all of you because, oh boy, in early 2023, I truly had no clue how this book would get done. If it weren't for all the love all of you have for these characters and this series, I might have crawled into a hole and picked up a new hyper fixation.

I was in a burnout for about seven months and didn't write more than maybe a thousand words. None of them were on this project.

Then, my good friends Lex and Halle told me about the wonderful editing Goddess Kearstie with Between Chapters Creative Co. This was mid-August when I reached out to her and told her I needed to have this book ready by January 18th, and she was so f*cking cool, didn't even bat an eye.

So, thank you to Kearstie for being my cheerleader. Lex, for keeping me accountable pretty much every day with your check-ins and our random rants.

GoodGirls PR for EVERYTHING that you did and waiting on me since like last year to get my sh*t together. And thank you to Ashleigh, you lifesaver, you. You've literally been there from the beginning, and I am SO glad you are part of helping me grow and not lose my mind. Best PA ever.

Also, a shout-out to Rae with Booked with Rae for reading this early and sending me crying pictures of you. And to Isabella with Como La Flor author services for fitting me in with proofreading.